THE WOUNDED YANKEE

BOOKS BY GILBERT MORRIS

THE HOUSE OF WINSLOW SERIES

[1]with Lynn Morris   [2]with Aaron McCarver

05A

GILBERT MORRIS

the WOUNDED YANKEE

BETHANYHOUSE
Minneapolis, Minnesota

The Wounded Yankee
Copyright © 1991
Gilbert Morris

Cover illustration by Dan Thornberg
Cover design by Danielle White

Published by Bethany House Publishers
11400 Hampshire Avenue South
Bloomington, Minnesota 55438

Bethany House Publishers is a division of
Baker Publishing Group, Grand Rapids, Michigan.

Printed in the United States of America

Library of Congress Cataloging-in-Publication Data

Morris, Gilbert.
    The wounded Yankee / by Gilbert Morris.
        p.   cm. — (The house of Winslow ; 1862)
        Summary: "The story of one woman's courage and honesty overcoming the bitterness of a man's heart"—Provided by publisher.
        ISBN 0-7642-2954-0 (pbk.)
        1. United States—History—Civil War, 1861–1865—Fiction. 2. Winslow family (Fictitious characters)—Fiction. I. Title. II. Series: Morris, Gilbert. House of Winslow ; 1862.
    PS3563.O8742W6   · 2005
    813'.54—dc22
                                                                2004026017

To Mike Haley

If, once in his lifetime, a man has a boss who is also a brother, he is fortunate. If only once, a man has a friend he can trust, admire and respect, he is blessed. If once along the way, a man finds a confidant worthy of all trust, he is to be envied.

And I have found all three of these in Mike Haley—

Brother—Friend—Confidant

GILBERT MORRIS spent ten years as a pastor before becoming Professor of English at Ouachita Baptist University in Arkansas and earning a Ph.D. at the University of Arkansas. A prolific writer, he has had over 25 scholarly articles and 200 poems published in various periodicals, and over the past years has had more than 180 novels published. His family includes three grown children. He and his wife live in Gulf Shores, Alabama.

CONTENTS

PART FOUR
THE VIGILANTES

THE HOUSE OF WINSLOW

★ ★ ★ ★

THE
HOUSE OF WINSLOW

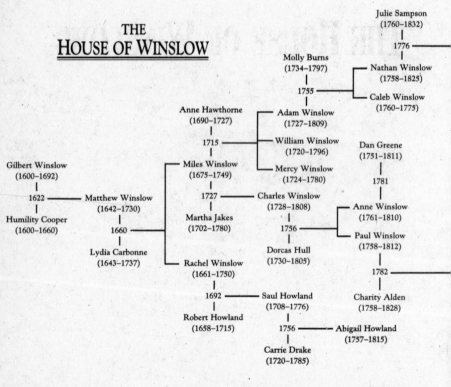

Gilbert Winslow
(1600–1692)
|
1622 —— Matthew Winslow
(1642–1730)
|
Humility Cooper
(1600–1660)
|
1660 ——
|
Lydia Carbonne
(1643–1737)

Anne Hawthorne
(1690–1727)
|
1715 ——
|
Miles Winslow
(1675–1749)
|
1727 ——
|
Martha Jakes
(1702–1780)

Rachel Winslow
(1661–1750)
|
1692 ——
|
Robert Howland
(1658–1715)

Adam Winslow
(1727–1809)

William Winslow
(1720–1796)

Mercy Winslow
(1724–1780)

Charles Winslow
(1728–1808)
|
1756 ——
|
Dorcas Hull
(1730–1805)

Saul Howland
(1708–1776)
|
1756 ——
|
Carrie Drake
(1720–1785)

Molly Burns
(1734–1797)
|
1755 ——

Dan Greene
(1751–1811)
|
1781
|
Anne Winslow
(1761–1810)
|
Paul Winslow
(1758–1812)
|
1782 ——

Abigail Howland
(1757–1815)

Charity Alden
(1758–1828)

Julie Sampson
(1760–1832)
|
1776 ——
|
Nathan Winslow
(1758–1825)

Caleb Winslow
(1760–1775)

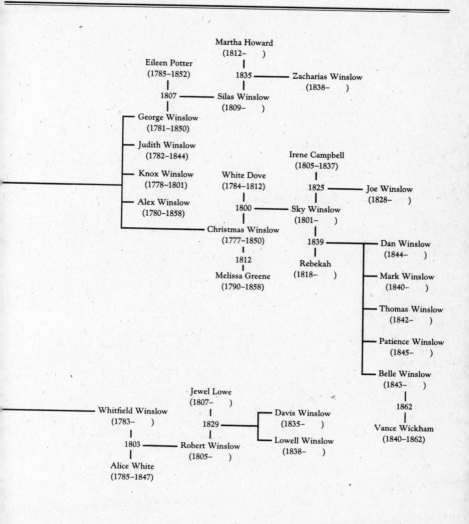

PART ONE

THE HERMIT

★ ★ ★ ★

CHAPTER ONE

A FAREWELL TO ARMS

★ ★ ★ ★

Zacharias Winslow said goodbye to the Army of the Potomac July 4, 1862, after serving one year. During that time he had risen to the rank of sergeant. He had fought at Bull Run, Shiloh, the Peninsula Campaign, and The Seven Days, and been wounded twice—first at Bull Run by a sharpshooter who severed the right middle finger, and then two days before his discharge by a shell fragment that penetrated his right buttock, leaving a deep track.

It wasn't the first but the second injury that bothered him. In the first, the loss of his finger, he had simply wrapped his bleeding hand with his handkerchief and continued fighting. Observing this, Captain Futrell ordered, "Winslow, Yates has been killed—take over as sergeant!" Despite Zacharias's inward protests, he complied.

The second wound, however, affected Winslow deeply—not physically but psychologically. The ribbing he endured from the men grated on his nerves. On the day of his discharge as he bent over to gather his personal belongings, a streak of pain shot through him. He grunted, straightened up carefully and twisted his head to see if any blood had soaked through the thick bandages the surgeon had applied. Seeing none, he tossed his razor and socks into a small carpetbag, turned and left the tent to join his squad for a late breakfast of bacon and bread. His discomfort did not go unnoticed.

"Hey, Sarge—sit down here and have some of this fresh bread," Nate French yelled, then snapped his fingers as if he had just remembered something. "Well, shoot, I forgot about your wound. Here, we saved *standin'* room for you, sure enough!"

Zack grimaced and took the food Jimmy Little handed him. Biting into it hungrily, he glanced sourly at him.

"Now, Zacharias," Little said, winking at French, "how you gonna show that girl of yours the scar when you git home? If she's nice, why, it'll be plumb embarrassin', won't it?"

"Don't think I'll mention it, Jimmy," Zack said, ignoring the men's laughter. "How about a cup of that stuff you call coffee?"

"But won't she think it's a little *unusual*?" French insisted. "I mean, you ain't gonna sit down, that doctor says, for maybe a month. How you gonna explain that to her?"

"Won't take her anyplace except dances where nobody sits," Zack answered. He let the men have their fun, for he had grown close to them the past few months, especially French, the young man from Michigan, who had been with him the entire year. The three-month volunteers had gone home after Bull Run, with new men replacing them.

After the meal was over and everyone had said goodbye, Nate French walked with him to the gunboat waiting to take the wounded to hospitals in Washington.

"Shore do hate to see you go, Zack," French said as they waited in line at the gangplank while the wounded were carried aboard. "Don't see why you can't sign on for another year." His long face and beak-like nose squirreled around to scrutinize the sergeant.

"What for, Nate?"

The cynicism in Winslow's answer reflected in his keen blue eyes, and French hesitated. He had known for sometime that his friend had been disillusioned with the war, but had hoped the officer would stay with the outfit. "Why, Zack," he said, "we all get fed up with the army from time to time. But we got to settle this slavery thing, don't we?"

"Not me," Winslow said adamantly, then asked, "Did I ever tell you how I happened to be in the army, Nate?"

"Don't recall as you did."

"Well, I was doing real well in the hardware business with a good friend named George Orr. We had one store in Cincinnati free and clear, and were getting ready to open another one when this blasted war came along."

Although Zack was three inches under six feet and looked almost fragile, there was a solid quality that was deceptive. He had heavy thighs and a thickness to his upper body, rather than breadth. The strength of his long smooth muscles constantly amazed the men.

Zack took off his forage cap, wiped his forehead with the back of his hand, then moved closer to the boat as the line of men crossed the gangplank.

The sun was hot, and his wound was beginning to itch, but Winslow gave no indication of his discomfort. A wry expression curled his lips upward as he continued his account. "I had it all, Nate—good health, money, and was engaged to a beautiful girl named Emma Lawson. Then Lincoln sent out a call for 50,000 men, and I was one of them."

Nate nodded, "So was I, Zack."

"But you didn't join up at the flip of a coin, Nate," Winslow countered. The old memory raked across him, and he spouted the next words out rapidly. "Emma got all patriotic, as most of us did. We thought we'd run down to Richmond, whip the Rebels, then come back home by fall. Both my partner and I wanted to go, but one of us had to run the business. So we flipped a coin—and I won."

"Move on down, will you, Sarge?"

The walking wounded had moved from in front of him, so he stepped back and let the private in charge pass. Zack stuck out his hand to French. "So long, Nate. I'm sick of it all. We ran away like rabbits at Bull Run. The Rebels pushed us all over the map at Shiloh. And now with 100,000 men in our army, Lee's slammed the door in our face—so we're headed back to Washington like whipped curs!"

"Why, everybody in our outfit knows you're the best fighter in the whole company!" French said, knowing all the officers had tried to persuade Winslow to stay. "We'll whip those Rebels yet!"

Winslow picked up his bag. "Not me. I'm going to get married, make a mint, and have ten kids. I'll never fight again. And if you're smart, you'll get out when your enlistment's up."

French watched in dismay as his friend limped across the gangplank and disappeared through the narrow door. "He shore was a fighting man when the show started," he mused. "But I guess he figures he's done enough for a lifetime." French turned and made his way across the camp, half wishing that he, too, could leave.

★ ★ ★ ★

The gunboat was crowded, and Zack stood most of the time. When he did lie on the straw ticking given him, he favored his right side. The men wanted to talk about the battle, what McClellan would do next, but Zack never joined in. They were interested in only one thing—war.

Zack looked down at the muddy waters of the James River, his thoughts on Emma, a petite brunette with sparkling black eyes and provocative lips. She had moved to Cincinnati only a few months before the war started, and Zack fell for her the first time he saw her—at the Fireman's Ball. Winslow had never been seriously interested in a girl until he saw Emma. There he instantly vowed, "I'm going to marry that girl!" Several other men contested, but he went at his courtship like everything else—single-mindedly and aggressively—and beat every suitor. His persistence finally won her.

His partner, George Orr, had been attracted to Emma, too, but realizing Zack's determination, he disqualified himself. When Emma finally agreed, Orr said, "Zack, you just didn't give that woman any choice—she either had to marry you or go crazy! When you want something, you put everything into getting it!"

The boat docked at Washington a few days later, and the wounded were taken to a small military hospital located on the edge of town. Since Zack's wound was not as serious as most of the others, he had to wait two days. During that time he took a lot of ribbing about his injury. He finally withdrew, keeping to himself and daydreaming about Emma.

The doctor eventually attended Zack's wound, his fat sausage-like fingers moving deftly over the area. He started to make a joke about its location, then changed his mind when he saw his patient's steady eyes fixed on him. "Guess you've taken some ribbing, eh, Sergeant?" he said.

"Just about all I'm going to, Doctor," Winslow nodded. "Nobody thinks a wound is funny—unless it's in the rump. Put that bandage on tight. It's going to have to last all the way to Cincinnati."

"Well, the wound is in good shape, but don't let a few jokes cause you an infection. Keep it clean; that's the main thing. And you're going to have trouble if you sit all the way to Ohio."

A week later he got his discharge marked "Wounded, Honorable Discharge," and took a train headed north that afternoon. Making the long trip without sitting for long periods had worried him, but he discovered a way. He found the conductor, a small man named Ezra Plunkett, and said, "Caught a fragment in my backside in the war, and I can't sit, but I'll pay extra for someplace to stretch out."

Plunkett's suspicious eyes bore into him. "What outfit?"

"Third Ohio."

Plunkett nodded, satisfied. "I got a boy in the First Michigan," he said, considering Winslow's request. "You can spread your bedroll in the crew car." Zack followed him to the last car, and the conductor motioned toward a lower bunk built into the side of the car. "Take mine," he said, pointing. "Won't use it much. Me and Johnson can sleep on the top one. Help yourself to that coffee, Sergeant," he added as he bustled off.

Zack became well acquainted with Ezra Plunkett and the brakeman, a muscular young fellow named Sid. Had it not been for Plunkett's kindness, Zack would have had to stand all the way in the crowded train. At noon when the train stopped to take on passengers, he stepped outside and bought three box lunches and some fresh fruit. As the train got under way, he called Plunkett and Sid to join him. They plunged into the food eagerly. "Boy," Sid said, "these peaches sure hit the spot!" After they finished, the two railroad men lit up pipes, leaned back and sipped the bitter black coffee they kept hot on the small stove in the car.

War was the topic of conversation. Sid, all fire and enthusiasm, was on the verge of enlisting. He waved his pipe wildly as he spoke of the battles that had taken place, and when he discovered that Zack had been in most of them, he latched on to him, pumping him for details.

Zack related his war experience to the news-hungry brakeman. Not wishing to encourage the man, yet trying not to show his own disillusionment with the war, he spoke in an impersonal manner.

When Sid left, Plunkett stared at Winslow shrewdly. "Not too happy with the war, are you, Winslow?"

"Well . . ." Zack hesitated, then shrugged his shoulders. "I'm glad to be out of it, Ezra."

"You think we'll lose?"

"No. I think we'll probably win. But it's going to be a long war, and lots of deaths—both sides." He leaned against the side of the car to ease his cramped legs, his eyes thoughtful. "When I signed up, the worst thing I could think of was that the war would be over before I saw action. Most of us did, I guess. But no more. Those fellows from the South mean *business*, Ezra! They're going to fight as long as they've got breath."

Plunkett nodded, his eyes sad, thinking of his son in the First Michigan. "Always felt it'd be that way." He got to his feet, replaced his cup, and regarded Zack thoughtfully. "Don't let it make you bitter. Nothing worse than a man who's gone sour." Then he moved away, saying, "Thanks for the lunch."

For the rest of the trip Plunkett's words kept returning to Winslow: *Nothing worse than a man gone sour.* He finally blocked them out by rationalizing that he had done his part of a dirty job. Now it was time to get on with living and let some other fellow take care of the war.

When they reached Cincinnati, he said to Plunkett, "Thanks a lot. You really took care of me."

"Take care of yourself, Zack. Marry that girl and have a family."

"Hope it'll go well with your boy," Zack replied, then limped along the car, easing himself carefully down the long step to the platform. It was early in the afternoon, time enough to go to the store before it closed. He walked through the nearly empty station, recalling his last time there. That was July, a year earlier, and the place had been packed. He and the other recruited privates had worn their new uniforms proudly. A picture flashed into his mind as he spotted the newsstand where he'd pulled Emma aside and kissed her.

"Oh, Zack! I can't bear it!"

"Don't take on so, Emma. We'll whip the Rebs and I'll be back in three months! Then we'll be married."

"How can I wait—I love you so much!"

He remembered the pressure of her firm lips on his, the urgency in her voice, and her arms around his neck as he had held her until the train had uttered a warning blast.

He picked up his pace, excited by the thought of seeing her again. He chose a cab and climbed in carefully, and leaned to one side, saying, "You know where the Cincinnati Hardware Company is?"

"Over on Washington? Sure, I do."

Cincinnati looked different to him, busier and with more of a purpose. There were almost no empty buildings, and people seemed more serious and intent as they plunged along the street. He had heard in one of his rare letters from George that the war had created such a demand that businesses were springing up all over town. That had been over three months ago, and he had heard nothing since. His letters from Emma had been frequent at first, but the past few weeks, during the hard campaign, mail had been difficult to get through, so he assumed hers were somewhere in a stack with the others.

"Here you are, soldier," the cabby said, adding, "Welcome home!" as Zack tipped him.

Zack turned toward the sign on the large building: *Cincinnati Hardware Company.* He recalled the day he and George had stood here looking up as the last paint was added to the sign. The two had worked hard and furiously to get the business started. It was now theirs! George had thrown his arms around Zack, tears in his eyes, as he cried excitedly, "We did it, Zack! We did it!"

Zack smiled as he remembered how they had celebrated by going to a carnival in town, where Zack had been pulled into a boxing and wrestling show with a promised reward of a hundred dollars if he stayed in the ring a certain number of hours. He had won!

Now, standing under the sign, he shook his head, thinking

of that wild night. Being in the army had at least taught him not to crawl into a ring and get his face smashed.

Laughing joyously, he pushed through the door. Three clerks worked busily along the counters, but he recognized only one—Alex Southerland. Business must have increased, requiring new help, he thought. Alex was weighing out nails for a customer, so Zack walked through the store, noting the new changes, with several added departments. *George sure has been busy,* he mused.

He opened the door leading to the office. That, too, had been enlarged and redecorated. It had been a combination office for him and George, where they did their bookwork and kept supplies. Now there were three large roll-top desks along the center of the room, filing cabinets neatly ranked along the back wall, and a series of charts and maps on the east wall.

At Zack's entrance a man looked up. He was tall and expensively attired. Turning to a younger man, obviously a clerk, he said, "We'll finish this later, Ray."

Smiling at Zack, he said, "May I help you, sir?"

Zack hesitated. "Why—I'm looking for George Orr."

A flicker touched the gray eyes, but he said easily, "I can give you his mailing address."

"Mailing address?" Zack frowned. "Isn't he here?"

"No. I'm Ralph Sawtell, the owner."

A tiny alarm rang in Zack's head. He settled back on his heels, studying Sawtell's face. Then he said carefully, "I'm Zack Winslow. The name mean anything to you?"

Sawtell shook his head. "No, I'm afraid not. Have you done business with us?"

"I own this place. My partner is George Orr."

The man nodded to the clerk. "Leave us alone, Ray." After the door closed, Sawtell said carefully, "You're in the army, I see."

"Just mustered out. Wounded and discharged." Impatience seized him and he said, "What's going on here?"

Sawtell nervously pulled a cigar out of his pocket, his hands unsteady as he lit it. After taking a few puffs, he jerked it out and snapped, "I bought this place from Orr two months ago. He never said anything about a partner!"

Zack froze. Finally he took a deep breath and exhaled slowly. "He didn't say anything to me."

"I think we'd better check into this, Sergeant," Sawtell suggested. "Do you have a lawyer?"

"Yes."

"Go see him—and then, unless I'm mistaken, you'd better go to the police."

"The police?"

"Yes. I went over this business very carefully before I bought it. There's always a chance that a lot of debts are not listed in the books, for example. I made sure the title was clear. According to my lawyer, George Orr was the legal owner."

"We did put it in his name when I went to the army because it would make it easier for George to handle the business."

Sawtell's eyes flickered. "Winslow, go see your lawyer, then come back. I'll do the same. But it looks like you've been taken."

"I don't think so," Zack replied.

"He's not living at his old address," Sawtell said. "I know that much. A month ago I needed to talk to him about something that came up. Sent a man around, but he returned, saying that Orr had moved—apparently right after he sold the store. I have the address he left with his landlady." He went to a file and pulled out a slip of paper. "Not much help, I'm afraid."

Zack stared at the note. "General Delivery, New York City."

"Sergeant, take the advice of an older man—go to the police at once. Your friend has sold you out."

"I'll be back." He whirled and stalked out.

Zack jumped into the first cab he saw. "241 East Walnut," he directed. As the cab rolled along, he chewed on the incredulous news. Perhaps that was why he hadn't heard from George in weeks. *Got to be a reason,* he finally decided.

When the cabby pulled up in front of a two-story brownstone, Zack paid his fare and hurried up the steps. He pulled the brass bell hard.

"Why, Mr. Winslow!" a middle-aged woman exclaimed as she opened the door. "Come in, sir!"

He entered quickly. "Is Emma here, Mrs. Johnson?"

Mrs. Johnson blinked and seemed disturbed by his question.

"Why, Mr. Winslow—Emma hasn't lived here for two months! Didn't you know?"

"No, I didn't." The warning bell in his head rang again. "Did she leave an address, Mrs. Johnson?"

"N-no. Is something wrong, Mr. Winslow?" she asked. "Is Emma in trouble?"

"I don't know," he answered.

Zack continued questioning but got little response. Though the landlady was sympathetic, the news was scanty. "Emma was mighty busy the weeks before she left," Mrs. Johnson said. "Then she came in one day, packed her things and took off. Paid her bill, she did, but wouldn't leave an address. Told me she'd write when she got settled—but never did. She's not in any—"

Zack ignored her question and left. He walked the streets, trying to unravel the mystery, a sense of foreboding dogging his steps. Finding himself downtown, he strode into the office of Bart Tyler, a young lawyer with a struggling practice who had become a good friend to both Orr and Winslow.

The minute he saw Zack, his cheerful smile vanished. He faltered, then stuck out his hand. "Hello, Zack."

"Where're George and Emma, Bart?" Zack demanded.

Tyler drew his shoulders back in surprise, then said, "Zack—they got married and left town two months ago. Right after he sold the business to Sawtell." He swallowed. "Emma said it was hard, writing you about her and George."

"She never wrote."

Tyler saw the smoldering anger in Winslow's eyes, and he asked quickly, "But you did get your half of the price of the store?"

"I got nothing, Bart—no girl, no friend, no business—except getting shot by the Rebels while my friends betrayed me!"

CHAPTER TWO

A NEW VOCATION

★   ★   ★   ★

"That young friend of yours sure got a rotten deal," Nolan Bryce said as he rocked in his chair, his eyes resting on Bart Tyler, the young lawyer. "But as I see it," he went on, "he let himself in for it. Must be a trusting sort of fellow—signing his business over to Orr like he did."

Bart Tyler had brought Winslow to see Nolan Bryce, the chief of police, two days before. Bryce had listened to Zack's account and then promised to look into the case but couldn't give him much hope.

"Well," Tyler said, "he was trusting. Don't know if he'll ever do it again."

"Giving someone the power of attorney—anyone—is dangerous business. Like I told him, he'll have trouble getting his money back," said Bryce.

"He thought Orr was his friend," Tyler said, remembering how Zack had unloaded to him. The lawyer knew there was no recourse for Winslow. So did Zack, but he had to check out every possibility.

Tyler and Bryce were at the police station, waiting for Zack, who was in the next room checking one final time with the detective. Tyler went on. "About all I could do was keep him out of trouble when he got drunk. He never was a drinking man."

"Guess he thinks he's got a good excuse," Bryce said. "Bad enough to get shot up in this war, but to come home and find your best friend's skipped out with your cash and your woman—that's tough!" He examined the amber liquid in his glass critically and took a sip. "He's got a pretty hard look in his eye—for which I don't blame him a bit."

"Zack's always been a happy-go-lucky sort, Chief. Smiling and full of fun. Maybe a little too trusting. But he's different now." His eyes filled with regret. "He won't talk about it much, even to me—hurt's too deep. But when he got drunk night before last, he said, 'They done me in, Bart—but they won't do it again!' I don't think he was talking just about Orr and Emma. He's not going to trust anybody for a long time."

The door opened, and Zack entered. "Get the deposition all made out?" Bryce asked.

"No." His eyes were like steel. "It's a waste of time, Chief. Thanks for listening."

The hard light in the man's eyes bothered Bryce. Though he was used to the underside of life, including these small tragedies, the look on Zack's face saddened Nolan. He put his glass down, and came over and put his hand on Zack's shoulder. "I'm sorry about this thing. Wish I could do something to help."

Zack gave him a careful look, and the Chief realized that this was no longer the cheerful man Tyler had described. From now on he would weigh everyone's actions. His round face was smooth and boyish, but his blue eyes were steady and reserved as he said, "Sure. One of those things, Chief." Then he turned to Bart. "Ready?"

"Let's go."

As they left, Bryce walked to his window and waited until the pair came out the front door. He shook his head. "That young fellow won't be easy to fool anymore."

The two men made their way down the crowded street. "Let's get something to eat," Bart suggested.

"You need to get back to your office," Zack said.

"I'm more hungry for food than work. There's a little place I like over on Hill Street." He led the way to a cafe with red-checked tablecloths draped over round tables. "Bring us two steaks, Anna," he said to the pretty waitress. "And some of that

German beer if you've got it." He noticed the girl giving Winslow a look, and after she left said, "Guess the girls all go for a uniform, Zack. She's a cute kid, too." But at Winslow's shrug, Tyler thought, *He won't pay much attention to women for a spell!*

While they waited for the food, Tyler kept up a steady flow of light talk, mostly about changes that had taken place in Cincinnati while Winslow had been gone. Then as they ate the steaks, he drew his friend out of his shell to some extent, so that by the time they were devouring the apple pie, Tyler felt free to ask, "What's next, Zack?"

"Don't know, Bart."

"Need some money?"

A brief grin touched Zack's wide mouth. "No—but thanks for the offer." He sipped his coffee, staring out the window. "I've got a grubstake, Bart. My mother had a house, and when she died I sold it and banked the money." His lip curled as he added, "George didn't know about it—or that would have gone into the business, too."

"Why, you could go back into business, Zack," Bart exclaimed. "Town is booming, and—"

"Nope. I'm pulling out."

Tyler stared at him, then nodded slowly. "Sort of figured you might. Hate to see you leave, Zack—but guess it's best to shake off a place that's got bad memories." He took a bite of pie, then asked thoughtfully, "Any ideas where you'll head for?"

"Some place so far in the backwoods the only company that'll come calling will be squirrels and timber wolves."

"Oh, come on, Zack! A hermit?"

"Why not?" Zack stared at his friend. "That's *exactly* what I'll be!" He shifted uncomfortably in his chair, and said with an air of determination, "Soon as I'm well enough to sit longer, I'm heading west."

Tyler saw the stubborn cast on Zack's face. He and Zack had been fairly close, and the lawyer was a sharp observer of men. With heavy heart he realized this was not the same happy young fellow he'd known before the war. The easy ways and careless manners were gone. Now he saw a man filled with cynicism. "Zack, you've had about as rough a bump as a man can get— but don't let it ruin your life. Sure, take a trip out west. Be good for you to wander around and see the country. But you'll be back."

"No. Once bit, twice shy. All I want is to be alone—and I'm going to find a place where I can do just that!"

"I don't think you'll do it, Zack. Don't think a man ought to bury himself." He leaned back in his chair, then sat upright. "But if you've got to try this hermit thing, I've got something that might interest you."

"What?"

"I defended a fellow just after you left, Zack. He was a small-time crook and guilty as sin. I got him off with a suspended sentence, but he had no money to pay me. He did have title to a piece of property, though. I knew it was probably worthless, but I had to take it."

"Far from here?"

"Just this side of the Rockies. Thirty miles to the closest town. He had gone out there to live, but said it was so lonesome it drove him nuts. Even got to talkin' to himself."

"Surprised he told you how bad it was."

"Probably wouldn't have if he hadn't been drunk," Tyler said. "But I can't see you living that far back in the woods. He said there're some Indians close by, and they've been known to raise a scalp." Tyler leaned back and thought about what his client had said. "Guess it's a pretty place, right enough. Snow caps on one side of the valley, and evergreens on the other. Cold in the winter, nice in the summer."

"How big a place?"

"Hundred acres, the deed says, but my client said it was too hilly for farming. He tried raising sheep."

"Now that's an idea!" Zack said, his eyes bright. "I sort of like it, Bart. No people—just sheep."

"But you don't know anything about sheep!"

"I know they don't steal from you and run off with your woman," Zack said bitterly. "What's to know? You feed 'em grass and sell the wool and the meat. How much you want for the place?"

Tyler studied Winslow carefully, reluctant to sell, yet anxious to help his friend. "My fee was two hundred dollars. Wilkins—

that was my client—claimed the place was worth three times that."

"I'll give you six hundred!"

"No! I don't even want two hundred, Zack." The lawyer shook his head. "I never expected to sell the place. Just take it. Get this hermit foolishness out of your head."

"Nope. I'm gonna buy the place, Bart, and that's final!"

The two argued briefly, but when Tyler saw that Winslow was dead serious, he reluctantly agreed to take two hundred. "If you're going to do this fool thing," he said, "you'll need cash to get started—there's no house on the place."

"I'll build one!" For the first time since Zack's return, Tyler saw excitement in his friend's eyes. "I'll build me a fine cabin, just big enough for me, and then I'll put up some corrals for the sheep—and just sit around and watch them get fat." He slapped Tyler on the shoulder. "Why, they'll be growing while I'm asleep, Bart—making me rich!"

"You'll go crazy in six months," Tyler predicted. "On the other hand, this may be a good thing for you, Zack. After all the fighting and—and the other things, it'll do you good to work at something different."

"Wish my rump was healed," Zack said ruefully. "I'd like to leave today!"

"You'll get sick of looking at those dumb sheep soon enough—and tired of eating mutton, too!" Tyler laughed. "Come on, we'll go get the title deed."

Three days later, they were standing at the train station. Zack had the deed to the land in his pocket, along with all his savings—a sheaf of banknotes totalling almost two thousand dollars. Now as the train gave a final warning blast, he gripped Tyler's hand. "Bart, I'm glad there's one good fellow left in the world!"

"Oh, there're lots of us, Zack," Tyler protested. "I wish you'd put this off for a couple of weeks. You're not able to sit for long rides yet."

"I got to get away, Bart," he said. "I've had enough of people to do me for a lifetime. When I get my ranch all set, come see me, okay? I was planning to make only one chair, but for you I'll make another."

Tyler shook his head, and as the train lurched forward and Zack stepped on board, Bart called out, "You'll be back in six months!"

"No, I won't!" Zack yelled. "I'll be the hermit of Alder Gulch the rest of my life!"

* * * *

After the rigid control of military life, Zack Winslow's trip from Cincinnati to Alder Gulch was a delight. The train rolled across Indiana and Illinois, then dropped south to Missouri. Zack changed trains four times, but managed to wrangle sleeping space with each crew. His uniform was almost as good as a pass, and he paid for his bed by repeating his war experiences. Most of the railroad men had relatives in the Union Army, and all were vitally interested in the battles he spoke of. For Zack, the war itself became dim as the trains moved him toward the west. He sensed the detachment, marveling at how time and distance had the power to remove such horror. Though he remembered the blood, the wounded, the mounds of dead soldiers, they were more like pictures from a book—except occasionally in dreams or at certain times of consciousness. Then the memories were vivid and poignant—but these came less often as time went on.

At St. Louis he bought passage on the *Polaris*. The trip up the Missouri was the most enjoyable journey he'd ever experienced. The *Polaris* was an old gilt-tarnished Mississippi riverboat, but Zack didn't mind. He paid for a private cabin, thinking with a streak of humor, *A real hermit wouldn't share a cabin with another man!* When he was not walking the decks or standing in the bow watching the brown waters break up into curling ripples around the boat, he would retire to his cubicle and read. The captain noted him standing alone for long periods in the bow, and asked him to supper. Winslow spent a pleasant evening with Captain Evans, telling once again of the war. Evans, too, had much to share, for he knew the country territory well.

"Trapped a couple years on the Yellowstone," he said as they sat at the table over coffee. "And the Bitterroot country, where you're headed, Winslow—know it well. Beautiful country! Love to get back there." He spoke of the cold mountain streams and the dark stands of timber, the abundance of game and fish. "You'll like it," he concluded. "Not many folks around, though."

"I've seen enough people for a spell, Captain," Zack said. He had not shared his misfortune, but his silence had made Captain Evans give him a quick glance. And when he had gotten off the *Polaris* for a smaller craft at the junction of the Yellowstone, Evans had shaken his hand, saying, "Good luck, Winslow. You better know God—because God and Indians—that's about all you'll see where you're going."

"God will be all right," Zack grinned. "The Indians can mind their own business. Thanks, Captain Evans."

He found a small trading craft headed farther up the Missouri. This one didn't even have a name, much less any gilt paint or fancy woodwork. He slept on a thin bedroll in a cramped cubbyhole over the wheelhouse—but it was a refreshing trip for Zack. He liked the bones of the country, beginning to stick up in austere ranges of rock, capped with snow so white it was hard to believe anything could be that pure. The air was cool after the sweltering days through the rolling country on the Missouri, and he felt an excitement as he got off the trading boat at Helena.

He spent the day buying a chestnut gelding and a packhorse. The owner of the trading post took him for a greenhorn, but Zack's time in business had made him an astute buyer, and he bargained until he got his outfit at a reasonable price. "If you're going down toward the Bitterroots," the trader mentioned as Zack was leaving, "there's a pack train going to Virginia City tomorrow. Fellow named Beidler is takin' 'em through." He added with a shrug, "Indians ain't been acting up lately—but a lone white man is pretty tempting for the devils. Beidler'd be glad to have you, I reckon. He's only got one other man. You can find him in the corral over by the river."

"Maybe I'd better talk to him. What's his first name?"

"Don't really know. He's just called Dutch. He ain't too big, but don't give him any trouble—he's about the toughest man in these parts."

Dutch Beidler turned out to be a cocky Dutchman with a bulldog face. He was eating corn dodgers from a paper sack when Zack rode up and dismounted and stated his business.

Beidler was wearing a peaked hat with a flat round rim. He

had a scraggly mustache and dark blue eyes that bored into Winslow, taking in the uniform. "Union Army?"

"Used to be. Mustered out now."

"Come along if you want. Won't hurt to have another gun along. Reckon you can shoot?"

"Yes."

"All right. We'll pull out at first light."

The chestnut was feisty when Zack mounted up the next day while it was still dark. He almost threw Zack to the ground, and for a time it was a question of whether he could stay on. He managed to hang on, and finally rode the animal, smiling as he said, "Guess you're ornery enough for a hermit like me. Matter of fact, that's not a bad name—Ornery."

Dutch Beidler and his man, an Indian named Three Dog, had the pack animals loaded as Winslow rode up, and Beidler grunted, "Let's make tracks." He carried a shotgun, which Zack learned was almost part of the man's body. That was the longest speech Beidler made that day, and Three Dog said less. It amused Zack, who murmured as he trailed the train of mules, "I guess it's a good thing I'm studying to be a hermit. These two sure won't bend my ear none."

That night squatting around the campfire eating beans and bacon, Beidler talked more freely. He cautiously sounded out Zack's views on the war, and when he stated that he was opposed to slavery but would take no more part in the war, the stubby rider seemed to relax. "I ain't got no dogs in that fight myself," he confided to Zack. "Ain't got but two cousins back in Tennessee, and they're so sorry the Yanks would be doin' everybody a favor to shoot 'em. Not much on slavery my ownself." He asked where Zack was headed, then nodded, "I know that country. 'Bout half way betwixt Virginia City and Bannack."

"Think sheep might do pretty good?" Zack asked.

"Don't see why not—if you can keep the Injuns from eatin' em." He grinned across the fire at the Indian who was observing them with obsidian eyes. "Hey, Three Dog, Injuns like sheep?"

"Mule more good," the Indian replied, looking at the pack animals grazing a short distance away.

"You heathen!" Beidler rapped out. "I catch you eatin' one of my mules I'll send you to the Happy Hunting Grounds!" He stuffed a piece of bacon in his mouth and added, "Ain't much market for sheep round here, Winslow. Most folks shoot what they eat—or raise a cow. You ain't likely to get rich."

"Don't aim to be rich," Zack said. The day in the saddle had been hard on his rump, and he limped over to get his bedroll. He unrolled it, put it down back from the fire, and lay down on his left side with a sigh of comfort. "Just want a place that isn't all cluttered up with people." He grinned at Dutch, adding, "I aim to be a hermit."

Dutch grinned at that and took a gulp of coffee from his tin cup. "You'll be that, all right, if you get back in the Bitterroot country. "Ain't no white people atall between Virginia City and Bannack. Reckon you'll have all the room you need."

They took a week on the trail, driving hard during the daylight hours, camping beside small streams at night. The climb over MacDonald Pass took the wind out of the animals, and they camped that night on the edge of a great timber range that rose up on the east. Three days later they rode into Virginia City, a small town of no more than five hundred people. Beidler said, "Soon as I deliver these goods we'll eat someplace."

"Guess I'll lay over at the hotel," Zack said, and went to get a room. His wound had been irritated by the constant hours in the saddle, and he got a room in the one hotel the town boasted. The barber shop had a tub in the back room, and the barber had a Chinese fill it with hot water. Zack eased himself into it, grimacing when the hot water hit the wound, but after soaking for an hour, he felt relaxed. The wound, he noted, was knitted together well, and needed no bandage. He put aside the uniform and donned the clothes he'd bought in Helena—light blue breeches with a broad leather belt, a soft tan shirt, a black vest, a comfortable pair of soft leather boots. The store had not had a hat to suit him, so he left the barber shop and wandered over to the dry goods store to find one.

He found Dutch Beidler inside buying shotgun shells. When the stocky Dutchman invited him to eat, he said, "Let me get a hat first."

He looked through the selection, finding none he liked particularly, and was about to buy one of the rather shapeless felt models, when the clerk said, "Got one here that we'll never sell."

He reached under the counter and came up with an English derby. "Don't know how it got mixed in with our stock," the clerk added. "We sure never order nothin' like this."

"Let me see." Zack took the hat, which was a bowler type very common in the East. It was expertly made of beaver, he saw, dyed a light fawn color, and when he slipped it on his head it was a perfect fit. He glanced in the mirror on the wall behind the clerk and smiled at the reflection. "Beautiful hat," he remarked. "But it'd be worth a man's reputation to wear a dude's hat out here."

Beidler's face split in a rare smile. "Thought you was determined to be a hermit, Winslow? Now, a real hermit don't give a continental what other people think about what he wears."

A rash streak of humor ran through Winslow, and he asked the clerk, "How much?"

When the two left and walked into the cafe across the street, people stared at the hat. Zack was half regretful that he'd succumbed to the impulse and said as much to Beidler as they sat down, but Dutch didn't agree. "Man ought to wear what he likes."

Zack looked up and read the sign on the wall: "If you don't like our grub, don't eat here." He smiled. "Not much of a cook myself, Dutch, but this might be the last good meal I'll have in a while."

"You serious about starting a sheep ranch?"

"Well, it's an idea. May not be a good one."

They talked about the possibilities, and when they were about to rise and leave the table, a well-dressed man with a round face and neat mustache walked in. He gave them a cursory glance and walked over. "Hello, Beidler. Didn't know you were in town."

Beidler nodded, "Brought in a pack train from Helena."

His words seemed dry and short, and he made no effort to introduce the two men. "My name's Henry Plummer. I'm sheriff of Bannack and Fairweather."

"Winslow," Zack said, and took the sheriff's quick grip.

"Just come in?" the sheriff asked idly.

"Yes. I came in with Dutch."

The sheriff waited for him to continue, but when Zack said

no more, he nodded, saying, "Let me know if I can help you with anything."

He sat down, and the pair left. When they were outside, Zack asked curiously, "Why were you so sharp with him, Dutch?"

Beidler shrugged his shoulders and said shortly, "Don't like him." He changed the subject, and they strolled along the main street of Virginia City. Beidler was well known, and several times they were stopped by men who wanted a word. Beidler introduced Zack to them, and they were cordial enough, but were met with a cool reticence from Winslow. This happened several times, and when they got to the saloon where Beidler was headed, he asked, "You don't take to folks much, do you, Zack?"

"Not too much."

Beidler had spent most of his life in the West, and was accustomed to this sort of reticence. He had formed a good opinion of Winslow, and studied him carefully, saying nothing but weighing him in his mind. "You're serious about this hermit business?"

"I've had it with people, Dutch. I just want to be alone."

Beidler gnawed his lip, then said as he turned to leave, "Well, if a man wants to be left alone, that's his right. Good luck."

Zack realized Beidler felt rebuffed, and for a moment he wavered. Then he hardened his jaw, turned and stalked away to his room. *Maybe I'm a fool, but a hermit I'll be.*

CHAPTER THREE

CHOIYA

★ ★ ★ ★

A cold wind swept down off the hills, numbing Zack's lips as he manhandled the last rafter of his cabin. He had raced the weather, working through the blistering heat of August and September, cutting and trimming logs, hauling them out of the timber to his site, notching them and moving them into place.

Raising the walls alone had been the hardest job, but he had done it single-handedly, a feat that gave him a touch of pride as he admired his handiwork—the neat fit of the notches and the narrow gaps between the logs. The first logs had been fairly easy, but as the walls rose, he had been forced to devise new methods. The usual way was to lean two poles against the top of the wall; then two or three men would roll them up until they were locked into the pre-cut notches by two men on the walls.

Zack had created a block-and-tackle system whereby he could fasten both ends of the log to ropes, then inch by inch skid them up the poles and slip them into place. It had taken a long time, but he had cut the notches carefully and the logs fit tighter than any log cabin he'd seen. It gave him a keen sense of accomplishment.

He could have had help. On his trips to Virginia City for supplies during the summer, he had met Parris Pfouts, owner of a supply store. Pfouts was a Christian, and was trying to start a church. He had often suggested recruiting some men for a cabin raising. "Zack," he had said, "don't be so stubborn. You've got your logs all cut—now let some of us give you a hand."

"I reckon not, Parris," Zack had said. And when Pfouts had pressed him, he said shortly, "I'll take care of myself. Don't need anybody."

"Why, that's wrong! We all need somebody. That's the way men are." The five-foot-five Pfouts was a frank, honest man of fifty, neat and smooth shaven. "You'll not survive with that attitude," he went on, his dark eyes filled with compassion.

Zack had refused his help—also Dutch Beidler's, who had moved to Virginia City. "Don't know anybody I'd rather have help me, Dutch," he had said when Beidler offered, "but I've made up my mind to do it alone."

"You've made up your mind to do more than that, Winslow," Beidler had said, studying him. "You've shut the whole world out."

Zack shook off the memory of Beidler and Pfouts' disapproval as he surveyed his work. The cabin perched on a rise that swelled up out of a small fold of hills, giving a view of the rolling hills that fell away toward the north. To the east the Tobacco Root mountains shouldered their way upward through the evergreens. Directly in front, Hollow Top Mountain, capped with glistening white snow, stood 10,500 feet high, and to the west the Pioneers completed the ring. When he picked this spot, he felt the mountains were citadels, giants that crowded their big shoulders together to form a wall between him and the world.

Virginia City was too close to his liking, but it was a tiny place, not likely to crowd him, and Bannack was seventy miles to the west. A few trappers roamed the hills for rough fur, and one fairly large Indian camp lay ten miles south of his place. He had run onto it almost by accident while hunting elk. The hair on the back of his neck raised up as several of the braves encountered him. One of them, a tall Indian named Fox, spoke some English. Zack had kept his rifle handy and shared some of his sugar and coffee. Fox had seemed pleased enough to invite him to meet the chief, Black Pigeon, a short, bulky man with a hatchet face. He was not overly hospitable, but Zack was careful to give him a gift—a Bowie knife he'd bought for his own use.

The gift had brought a light into Black Pigeon's eyes, and an invitation to visit the camp.

The solitude had been just what Zack had desired. The creek on the northern boundary of his land was clear and cold, even in summer's heat. Game abounded, and as he worked by day and soaked up the brooding silence of the woods and mountains by night, he felt the bitterness slip away.

That same sense of well-being flowed over him now as he rolled into his bunk after devouring a steak cooked over the campfire. In the distance he could hear the mournful sound of a timber wolf. Above, the stars glittered in the clear sky, piercing the velvet blackness. Part of a moon moved solemnly over the sharp peaks of Hollow Top colliding with a veil of clouds. Finally he drifted off to sleep, his last thought, *Got to go to town tomorrow.*

He was up at dawn, ate cold meat and hot coffee, and hitched the mules to the wagon. "Hate to leave the place." But he would be in town only part of the day. The thought that he might be able to finish the cabin in a week cheered him.

"Hello, Pfouts," Zack said as he entered the store.

"Well, the hermit himself! Glad to see you, Zack."

"Still working for the rich, I see."

"If the Lord so wills." Parris was a devout Calvinist, and his calm belief that nothing could come to a man except what God designed baffled Winslow. "We have a real preacher coming to church next Sunday. I'd like you to come."

Zack shifted uncomfortably, for he liked Pfouts, but the pressure from the storekeeper caused him to say, "Give up on me, will you? I'm just not religious, Parris."

"All men are religious. We all choose our gods—and all of them are weak except one."

Not wishing to argue, Zack said, "That's all right for you. But when I saw men at Shiloh killed like cattle in a slaughterhouse, I decided God didn't have anything to do with us." He gave Pfouts a curious look. "How could a merciful God allow war and sickness?"

"Those are not from God, Zack," Pfouts replied. "Every good gift comes from Him, but man made a wrong turn. Now it is through Jesus Christ we must be made into what God intended."

The dignity and simplicity shone out. Zack studied him. He

had heard little preaching, but no man had impressed him as Parris Pfouts did. Yet he felt only a desire to drop the subject.

"You have any lime, Parris?" he asked abruptly. "And I could use some cedar shakes for my roof."

"Ah, the lime we have—and Tod Cramer's got a little mill over on the Ruby River." He carried the sack of lime and a few other supplies out to Zack's wagon, then pointed. "Take the trail down to the crossing. There's a road that winds through the woods and leads right to the mill. Tell Tod I said to give you a good price."

"Thanks, Parris. Maybe next week I'll have you and Beidler out to christen my house."

"We will come, Zack."

He found the mill with no difficulty and bought the shakes and enough rough-sawn boards to floor his loft and the cabin. Cramer was an older man with bright blue eyes and a wrench-like grip. "Pfouts tell you about the preacher that's comin', Winslow?" he asked as Zack handed him the cash for the shakes. "Hear he's a real devil killer! Like to have you come to the service."

"Maybe sometime." Zack was noncommittal and drove away, anxious to get back to the job. By dark he had finished most of the roof. The next day he nailed the last shingle on, and spent the rest of the day working on the fireplace. He'd stopped by Alder Creek every time he'd crossed it, bringing back flat stones for the job. For the next four days he worked steadily, laying the stones carefully, and installing the large hooks that would support his pots. The outside stack was built of short lengths of small logs and lined with a mixture of mud and lime.

On Saturday he completed the job and let it cure for three days, using the time to cut the openings for two windows. He had bought windows with glass from Pfouts, wanting the place to be filled with light. Finally he fitted the door and installed the latch.

On Wednesday evening, he cooked beans in a black pot over his first fire, and fried an elk steak in a frying pan over the hot coals. He'd wrapped a potato in mud and let it cook in the hot ashes. There was no furniture, so he sat on the floor, never so content in his life. The steak sizzled in the skillet, the beans bubbled in the pot, and when he cut the potato open, the steamy white insides gave off a mouth-watering aroma. He ate slowly, washing the food down with draughts of black coffee, and finishing the meal with an apple.

After he washed his dish and fork, he rolled up in front of the fire, watching the sparks fly upward, and thinking drowsily, "Just make me a table, a chair, and a bed—and I'm set to get me a few sheep. Then just lie back and do nothing." But later after he went to sleep, he dreamed of Emma, of her laughing eyes and firm body. When he awakened, the fire had died to blackened ashes and the room seemed small and insignificant.

The next day he went hunting. He shot a doe, came home and dressed her, then started working on his furniture. There was no hurry, so he built it well, using some of the lumber he'd bought from Cramer for the table. He smoothed out the roughness carefully, and did the same with the floor. He had planned to make only one chair, just to make sure that his determination to be alone would be obvious to a visitor; however, when he finished his bed, he made two more chairs just for the pleasure of it.

As October came to an end, everything was done—except for firewood. "I completely forgot!" he said out loud.

The sound of his own voice startled him. It sounded raspy with disuse, and he smiled, speaking again as he went to hitch up the team. "Guess I better start talking to you two. You got more sense than most people, anyway."

He cut down several tall oaks, dragged them into the yard and spent three days bucksawing them into lengths and splitting them into chunks. He was stacking them against the side of the cabin where he could get them when the snow came, when a rider came out of the woods. Zack dropped the log and moved over quickly to where his rifle was leaning against the cabin wall.

It was Fox. The Indian rode up to the cabin, halted his pony, and raised his hand in a gesture of peace. "Winslow," he grunted, then waited.

"Hello, Fox," Zack said. "Get down and have something to eat."

Fox dismounted and the two went inside and ate cold venison. Fox ate a great deal of it, then went after Zack's biscuits

piled high with jam from Pfouts' store. He drank the coffee thirst-
ily and asked, "Whiskey?" and when Zack said, "Don't have
any," he belched loudly, and stood to his feet.

"You come," he said. "Woman in trouble."

"Woman?" Zack repeated. "What woman, Fox?"

"White squaw. She maybe dead now."

"A white woman?" Zack got to his feet, trying to figure out
what the Indian was saying. "What's wrong with her?"

"Plenty sick. You come."

"Why, I'm no doctor! You better go to Virginia City."

"No. You come. I promise woman I find white man. I go
now."

Zack hurried outside, his mind racing, but the more he asked,
the clearer it was that Fox had done all he intended. He latched
the door, threw the saddle on Ornery, and followed the Indian
out of the yard and down beside the creek. As they went along,
Fox opened up and told him more of the story.

"Woman drive wagon. Young men find her, come and tell
Black Pigeon. We go with them." Fox shook his head and there
was a flash of something in his dark eyes. "Man in wagon dead.
We bury him, take wagon to camp. Woman very sick—has baby."

"A baby?"

"New baby—maybe week." Fox shook his head and continued. "Medicine man say his medicine no good—white squaw
too sick now. She beg us go get white man. She dead now, I
think."

"Let's hurry!" Zack said, pushing Ornery to a fast gallop. In
two hours they pulled into the Arapaho camp.

Black Pigeon came out of a tepee. "Plenty quick! Woman gone
almost."

Zack ducked his head and entered the tepee. The darkness
blinded him, but as he became adjusted to the gloom, an Indian
woman spoke and guided him to the left. He could barely see a
figure on a raised platform. He leaned down and by the flickering
fire in the center of the tepee, he saw a woman. At first he
thought she was dead. Her eyes were closed, her face sunken
with illness, giving her a skull-like appearance. Beside her was
a bundle, and pulling the cover back, Zack saw a baby's face.

"Ma'am?" Zack whispered. "Ma'am, are you awake?"

The eyes opened slowly, and a flicker of life came into them as she made out his face. She moved her dry lips, but he couldn't make out her words. "Could you speak a little louder?" he asked, and leaned his head a few inches from her lips.

"Thank—God!" she whispered sibilantly. "Take—my baby!" He waited, and there was a rattle in her chest as she struggled to speak. "God sent—you—to save—my Samuel!"

She reached out a skeleton hand, and he took it. She gripped it and half rose up in a burst of strength. "Promise me—take care of my baby! Promise!"

Zack felt a touch of fear, but he nodded, saying, "Yes, ma'am, I'll see to your boy. I promise."

The dim eyes searched his face, and her head fell back. "Me and Pete—we got no people—to take him. Swear to God—you'll raise him right!"

"I—I'll do my best—"

"No! You got to make vow—to God!" The eyes begged and the lips trembled as she pleaded. "You're the only one—I can ask. Please—! Swear to God!"

Zack swallowed, trying to think of a way to assure the woman. Her eyes were pools of sorrow, and her hand plucked at his arm pitifully. He set his teeth and nodded. "I swear to God I'll see to the boy, ma'am!"

The eyes fluttered shut, and a tremor passed through the emaciated body. She lay there, a smile slowly touching her thin lips. She whispered so quietly he had to lean forward to catch her words. She said, "Thank you, Lord Jesus—for sending a man—to care for—my son!"

Then she expelled a long breath, and settled into the finality of death. The Indian woman spoke a word in her language, and he moved aside as she took his place.

The fire was gutting noisily in its bed of stones, and above the crackle rose the cry of the baby. The Indian woman picked up the child. She said something that Zack didn't understand, but he knew she was asking him what to do with the baby.

He shook his head and walked stiff-legged out of the tepee. Fox and several other men were there, along with Black Pigeon. "Squaw die?" Fox asked.

"Yes."

"Too bad," Fox nodded. He studied the face of Winslow, then offered, "Maybe we bury woman beside her man?"

Zack stared at him, unable to think clearly; then he nodded. "It would be kind. I'll bring a stone for the grave. The boy may want to come back."

Zack could see the snow lurking over the mountaintops, and he knew the woman must be buried right away. Three hours later Zack stood over the grave next to another mound. Fox and the other Indians who had come along to help with the digging stood back, watching him. He stared at the raw mound. What should he do? Pray? Finally he took off his hat. He had no faith, but the woman had, he knew, so he bowed his head. "God, this was a good woman, I reckon. She asked me to take care of her boy—so you take care of her, and I'll do my best to take care of her baby."

He clapped the derby on his head, and they rode back to the camp. On the way he said, "Fox, I need to talk to Black Pigeon."

Fox nodded and as soon as they returned, he led him to a tepee somewhat larger than the others and called for Black Pigeon. When he appeared, Zack said, "I have an offer for you, Chief."

Black Pigeon glanced at Fox, said something in his own language and went back inside. Zack and Fox followed. The chief sat down and began to puff on a pipe, listening as Fox interpreted for Zack.

"Chief, I promised the woman before she died that I'd take care of her baby. But I live alone. I'm a hermit, you see."

Black Pigeon shook his head and asked a question, which Fox translated. "Him say—what is 'hermit'?"

"Man that lives alone. Doesn't have anything to do with other people."

When Fox repeated this, both Indians stared at him, and then the chief nodded, so Zack continued. "Well, I can't take care of a baby. Don't know anything about babies—except that they've got to be nursed."

A smile touched the chief's lips, and he nodded and said through Fox, "You not be hermit now."

Zack was nettled at the words, and hurriedly said, "You've got to give me a hand. Don't you have a mother here who can feed the baby?"

46

"No," said Fox at once. "Have bad year for babies. Most die, and three squaws with babies go south—no like cold."

Despair began to grip him. Then he rose to his feet, remembering a comment Pfouts had made: "Someday we'll have lots of families around. Only a handful of women here now—except for dance-hall girls."

Fox broke into Zack's thoughts. "Chief say he maybe help."

"Help? How? Don't reckon he can nurse a young'un."

A glint of humor flashed in Fox's eyes, and the chief grinned when he understood the words. Black Pigeon spoke and Fox explained. "One woman here—Cheyenne squaw. We take in raid. She not true Cheyenne. Her father, he white. When we capture she soon have baby. We kill her man—bring her and she have baby."

"Why, she can take care of the baby, then!"

The muscles in Fox's face twitched. "No. She no stay with us. Too big trouble."

"What's wrong with her?"

Fox grimaced. "Too much white, too much Cheyenne—too much pretty woman." He lifted his chin in hostility. "We fight all time with Cheyennes. And we no want white blood. But"—he made a sour face—"young braves, they no care if she Cheyenne or white. They fight over her. One brave already killed. Woman laugh at them—they fight anyway."

"What do you mean?"

"You take woman. No more fights."

Zack blinked. "Why, that's crazy, Fox! I'm not taking any half-breed woman and her kid with me."

"Then you go now!" Fox snapped. With eyes fixed on Zack, he related the situation to Black Pigeon. The chief nodded, "You go now. Take woman or not."

They got me whipped! Zack thought. *These two heathen know I need the woman—and they're using me to fix their problem.* Feeling trapped, he sighed, "All right. I'll take her—but she's got to know it's a matter of business—with pay. She can stay until the baby is weaned. Then she'll have to go. I'll take her wherever she wants. That's the only deal I'll make. Tell her that."

"You tell," Fox said. "She talk your tongue. Come, we go see." He stopped at the flap of the tepee and looked back with a sly glance. "Her name—Choiya. In your tongue mean cactus."

They walked down a line of tepees and stopped at the end. Fox called, "Choiya!"

Startled at the tall, well-formed beauty appearing before him, Zack stared. She had full lips, wide and red with health, olive skin smooth as silk over high cheekbones. Her eyes were wide and well shaped, dark and mysterious. Her hair was black, but not coarse like that of most Indian women. She listened as Fox spoke to her rapidly, then fixed her eyes on the white man.

Zack had never felt so awkward, and for some reason took off his hat as he said, "Guess Fox told you what's going on. I have this baby to care for, you see, but I don't know how to do it—unless you'll help me." He waited for her to reply, but she continued to watch him, warily. He rushed on. "It's a job. I mean, I'll pay you for taking care of him until he's—until he's old enough to make it on his own. Then I'll take you anywhere you say." His face flushed, and he added quickly, "You don't have to be afraid that I'll bother you. Just a nursemaid is all I'm looking for."

He clamped his lips shut, feeling foolish as Fox grinned, but it was Choiya who studied him. Her attitude was different, he noted, for while most Indian woman were meek, she stood regarding him fearlessly. There was, he thought, deep anger reflected in her eyes, no doubt from the brutal tragedy she had faced.

Finally she spoke. "I have a baby."

"Bring him along," Zack said, relieved at her obvious consent.

When she disappeared into the tepee, he asked, "Can you lend me a horse, Fox?"

"Yes."

Fox put a halter on a little black pony. "I come get sometime," he said, then took Zack to the wagon that had been brought to the edge of camp. Inside, Zack found a Bible with some family names, several letters, and a diary written in a woman's hand. He put these in his bedroll, and turned to see the woman coming, carrying a baby in one arm. He walked to the tent to pick up his new little charge, and the Indian woman handed him the bundled-up baby.

With some awkwardness, he mounted Ornery, then settled

in the saddle. He stared at the Indians who had gathered in a crowd to watch their departure. "You did me in, didn't you, Fox?"

Fox nodded. "This time white man get bad deal—Indian good."

"You ready?" Zack turned to Choiya.

She didn't answer. Instead, she faced the crowd, said something in their language—then spit at them.

A rumble of anger erupted. Alarmed, Zack said, "Come on!" and they galloped away.

When they were well beyond the camp, he turned to Choiya. "What'd you say to them?"

She looked at him steadily. "I told them they were even more dung heaps than white men."

Zack swallowed, and stared at her. She returned his gaze— with vehement hatred.

CHAPTER FOUR

"He's Like All Other Men!"

★　★　★　★

Zack felt the first touch of snow on his cheeks before they reached the cabin, but by the time he turned Ornery into the yard the flakes were slanting lines, driven by a gusty north wind. He slipped out of the saddle, the baby cradled in his arm, and turned to help the woman. However, she was off as soon as he, and watched him with derision.

"Hold the baby while I tie the horses." He looped the reins around the trunk of a tall poplar, then stepped to the door. Throwing it open, she entered, carrying both infants. With his back to the door, he motioned to the bed, saying, "Guess you can put them there while I get a fire going."

The coals were still glowing, so he fed them with small wood, then larger, until soon the fire crackled, sending showers of sparks up the chimney. As he finished, he heard one of the babies crying, and turned to see the woman pick up the white child. "Anything wrong?" he asked.

"He is hungry."

Zack made for the door, saying quickly, "I'll put the horses in the shed." He fled the cabin, taking more time than usual with the animals. He had built a shed roof slanting down off the east side of the cabin to shelter the firewood, He tied both horses securely, grained them, and checked their water supply.

The snow was falling fast, leaving strips of white on the dead leaves. He had heard that snow could be four or five feet deep in a severe winter. But it was still late October, so it couldn't be that bad until later. He picked up a huge armload of wood, staggered around to the front, and stepped inside. Choiya was standing beside the fireplace, and he walked over and dropped the logs in a wood box in the corner.

"What's your baby's name?" he asked, brushing the bark off his coat sleeves.

"Hawk."

He nodded and smiled slightly. "Nice name." She stood with her back to the wall, her dark eyes expressionless, her lips pressed firmly together. She was wearing a fringed doeskin dress, soft leather moccasins that came up over her ankles, and a short, fringed jacket with white buttons. Her hair was pulled back from her forehead, braided and reaching almost to her waist.

He could see she had no intention of answering, so he said, "I'm going to bunk up in the loft. Don't have enough covers, but if you can make out with the babies tonight, I'll pick up more blankets tomorrow at Virginia City." He waited for her response, but she made none—just kept her eyes fixed on him. It made Zack nervous. "Guess you're getting hungry. I got a quarter of an elk hanging outside, some bread and a few beans. We'll have to make out till I get groceries."

She did not so much as nod, so he went outside to get the meat from a small cabinet he had built under the shed for storing food. "Snowing harder," he said, placing the meat on the table. He took out his knife and sliced off a large steak, then nodded toward the fire. "There's a frying pan."

"You hired me to take care of the baby, not to be your cook." Her voice was short and terse.

Zack looked up in astonishment at her good English. But her expression was filled with resentment, her eyes smoldering with anger. He wanted to force her to cook, but knew she would rebel. He knew as well she realized this. Slowly he cut another steak, then moved toward the fire. "That's right," he said, and put the frying pan on the grill tossing the steaks into it. As they began to sizzle, he spooned some coffee into the pot and set it over the fire, then put some bread on the table. There was only one cup, so he found a used jelly jar. That and two tin plates and a couple of forks was the extent of his supply.

He ignored the woman, squatted in front of the fire and poked the steaks with a fork from time to time, turning them twice. When they were done, he rose and put one steak on each plate, then tossed the skillet down on the hearth. Taking out his handkerchief, he wrapped it around the handle of the coffeepot, filled the cup and the jar, put the pot back, and sat down at the table.

Choiya watched, still keeping her distance. He took out his sheath knife, cut his steak into bite-sized portions, cut a few slices of bread, and tossed the knife on the table beside her plate. He began to eat hungrily, ignoring her completely. She did not move. When he finished, he rose, put his plate beside the frying pan, refilled his coffee cup and set it on the table. He reached into the saddlebags and drew out the things from the wagon.

Still ignoring Choiya, he began to examine each item by the light of the fire. The front page of the Bible stated that Peter Thomas Rogers, of Nashville, Tennessee, had been married to Emma Perkins, of Franklin, Tennessee, in Nashville on May 20, 1857. Under this in wavy spider-like lines were the words: "Born to Peter Rogers and his wife Emma, a son, Samuel Taylor Rogers—October 23, 1862." Another note, "May God bless you both," was signed Hannah Pierson Rogers, Memphis, Tennessee.

Zack scanned the pages. Sometimes a verse would be underlined. Often a star was placed beside a passage, and frequently a note written in a fine hand: "God has quickened this promise to me this day."

He put the Bible aside and got the kerosene lamp from the mantel. Choiya still watched him, her arms folded adamantly over her chest. He began reading the letters, two from Hannah Rogers, one from a man named Dixon, and the last simply signed "Kate." He didn't even look up when one of the children cried and Choiya walked over and sat on the bed. Zack read the letters quickly, searching for an address. He wanted to get the child to some of his people if possible. The woman had said, "Pete and me don't have any people," but surely someone would want the boy!

Hannah Rogers was Peter's mother, and from her letters he decided she must be a widow—and a poor one. Here he found an address. Dixon talked about people the Rogerses had known, but he seemed to be a friend rather than a relative. The letter signed Kate was postmarked Dallas, Texas, possibly written by Emma's sister. There was no address, but perhaps the postmaster would forward a letter. He would write Hannah and Kate.

He picked up the journal and began to scan it, resting his head on his hand. The first entry was August: "Well, we are off to Oregon next week! Praise the Lord, He will be with us."

The words saddened Zack, and he thought of the two graves ten miles away, hidden on one of the thousand folds of the mountains of Montana. *God wasn't with Pete and Emma after all,* he mused gloomily. As he continued to read, he felt the table move slightly; then there was a sound of munching as the woman began to eat. He didn't look up, but kept his head bent over the journal. It was a typical story, for people were moving west in large numbers. Pete and Emma had sold their farm, bought a wagon and set out for Oregon. Pete had been fearful to take a chance with a baby coming, but Emma was full of faith. "God will take care of us," she had written over and over again.

The journey had been exciting at first, but an entry dated September 29 read: "Pete is very sick tonight, but I have anointed him with oil and prayed for him." The next entry was October 10: "Pete is worse. Could not get up at all today. God willing, we will come to a town soon. My time is close!" Several entries described the tragedy briefly; always the husband was worse. Many times Emma recorded her prayer: "God, send a man to help us!" On October 23 she had written, "A son! I will call him Samuel, entrusting him to God as Hannah did her Samuel."

Then on October 25 the stark words: "My beloved husband, Peter Thomas Rogers, went to be with Jesus this morning at dawn. As the sun came up, he took my hand and whispered, 'I'll be waiting for you and Samuel, Emma . . .' Oh, I thank you, Lord Jesus, that he is past all suffering and resting with you."

There was only one more entry, dated October 27: "I must go to be with my husband. The Indian promised to find a white man. Lord God, you have never failed me—never! Even as I pass from this life, I praise your holy name, for you are my strength and my redeemer. You will answer my prayer—you will bring a man of God, and he will care for my Samuel! Even if I die before that man comes, he will come, and I praise you for your faithfulness!"

That was all. Zack stared at the last passage for a long time. Finally he looked up at the woman who had finished eating and was back beside the children who lay quietly on the bed. He rose to his feet, put the books and letters on the mantel, and then said, "Blow the light out when you go to bed." There was no ladder to the loft, so he leaped up, caught the lip of the opening, and with a surge of strength, pulled himself up chin high, and swung his legs up and over like an acrobat.

Choiya watched wide-eyed. She had been as tense as a spring ever since leaving the Indian camp, and now her shoulders slumped. She walked over to the water bucket and took a long drink of water. As she stood there, her eyes fell on the books the white man had been reading. Her head jerked up to the loft at the sound of stirring. When it was quiet again, she walked quickly to the mantel and grabbed the books. She leafed through the Bible, replaced it, and took the letters, opening to the first page of the journal. Reading it quickly, she returned that and the other letters to the mantel just as the white child began to cry. She picked him up and sat before the fire while she nursed. This child was so different from her own, the fine blond hair a sharp contrast to her dark-haired son.

The fire crackled as the logs shifted, and she watched the sparks fly upward. The wind moaned as it found the crevices between the logs, but the cabin was much warmer than the tepee where she would have been sleeping if Winslow had not come. Her eye fell on the skillet, and she pondered how he had cooked her food without a word. She could not understand it. For a long time after the baby was satisfied, she held him, thinking of what had happened to her—wondering how she and her baby would live in this new world with this strange white man.

One thing she knew. Every man she had known had brought her trouble. *This one will be no different,* she thought, and her heart hardened as she got up and put the baby down. *He's like all other men— he will come after me sooner or later—and when he does, I will put a knife in his heart!*

* * * *

"A baby? Where in the name of heaven did you get a baby, Zack?"

Two men looking at a rifle down the aisle of Parris Pfouts' store gazed quizzically at Zack standing in front of the storekeeper. One of them laughed and said something under his breath that made the other smile.

A heavy-set woman who had been fingering a piece of checked cloth moved closer, her eyes avid with interest.

Zack ignored the customers and said, "Let's go in the back, Parris." As soon as they were in the back room, he snapped, "Did you have to broadcast it all over town? This couple died at Black Pigeon's camp! The baby's at my cabin, but there's got to be some woman here who can take care of him!"

Parris stared at Zack, not certain whether to take him seriously. "You left a baby alone at your cabin in this snowstorm? He'll freeze to death!"

"Well—I got an Indian woman to come along with me. She has a baby of her own, see? But I need to find some white woman to take care of him."

Pfouts shook his head. "There's no woman around with a baby that age."

"Parris, you *have* to help me," he insisted. "There's got to be some way! I've written letters to some people back East—but it'll take months to hear from them."

"Zack," Pfouts said stolidly, "I'd help if I could, but your best bet is to stay with that Indian woman—and thank God you've got her!"

Winslow stood there helplessly. "By gravy," he muttered bitterly, "it's come to a pretty pass when a poor hermit has to start a nursery and his best friends won't even lend a hand!"

"Didn't say that, Zack," Pfouts countered. "I'll work on it. Maybe we can find somebody at Bannack—or even at Helena. But for now there's no choice, man!"

Zack bit his lip. Finally he reached out and slapped Pfouts on the shoulder, forcing a slight grin. "Sure—I was out of line, Parris." He handed a paper to the storekeeper. "See how much of this stuff you can come up with, will you? I've got to get back before the passes close."

Pfouts worked quickly, and soon they were loading Winslow's purchases onto the mule he had brought along behind Ornery. As Zack pulled the strings of the pack tight, Pfouts said, concern on his face at the falling snow, "Hate to see you start out in a storm like this—but you'll make it. I know you don't believe God is in all this, my friend, but He is."

Zack swung into the saddle. "Thanks. If you come up with an answer, Parris, send someone out to my place."

"I'll come myself," Pfouts called out as Zack rode Ornery down the street at a fast trot, the mule kicking in protest.

The trip back was hard, and both animals stumbled from time to time on the rough snow-covered trail. The gulches undulated softly at first, then broke up into more rugged country. By three o'clock the snow stopped, and the temperature dropped sharply. Zack's feet had gotten wet crossing Dancer Creek, and the freezing temperature sent chills through him. Soon it began to snow again, coming down like a thick curtain, clouding visibility to only a few feet ahead. He got down and led the animals, but by now he'd lost all feeling in both his hands and feet, so after a while he mounted the horse and rode the last mile, stopping often to check the trail. Finally he reached the cabin and guided Ornery under the shed, towing the mule, then forced his legs to move in order to dismount; as soon as they hit the ground, his legs collapsed. He beat his hands together, and got to his feet by holding on to the logs of the cabin. He stomped the ground until he could maneuver his feet enough to tie both animals and pull the pack off the mule and drag it to the wood pile.

With numb fingers he picked up the pack, staggered around to the front door, and almost fell inside as the door swung back. Choiya stepped back as he entered, watching as he dropped the pack on the floor, then stared at her almost drunkenly. His reflexes were slowed down by the cold, and he moved like an old man as he turned and went back outside. *Can't go into that warm room until I thaw out*, he thought. He broke the ice on the barrel he kept filled, watered the animals, and jumped up and down, stamping his feet and swinging his arms furiously. Finally, sheltered from the wind, the feeling began to return to his hands and feet, and prickles on his face tingled. He walked back inside, the warm air hitting him like a blast from a furnace.

He picked up the coffeepot carefully, noting that it was empty, and moved to the food cabinet to get coffee. His body seemed reluctant to respond to his mind. *Now I'm going to get some coffee out of the cabinet.* But his arms moved very slowly, and he found it difficult to open the jar with his numbed fingers. Eventually he got the coffee in the pot, set it on the fire, then slumped down in the chair. Fatigue hit him like a blow, and he closed his eyes. *Can't sit here very long,* he thought. *Got to get my boots and socks off.* It had been a close call, he realized, as he changed into dry socks. He could have lost both feet—if the cabin had been another couple of miles.

He almost dozed off, but snapped back when one of the babies cried. He struggled out of his chair, his hands beginning to tingle, and poured a cup of scalding coffee. He stared into the fire as he sipped the coffee. *Not much between us and a grave,* he thought. When his feet and hands began to throb with pain, he shoved a table under the loft to help hoist himself up mumbling as he sank into the warm space, "Most of the stuff I went for is in the pack."

Choiya examined the food. He had brought even more than she had said the babies would need. Slowly she looked at the items, pausing more than once to look upward where he lay. Finally she began putting the foodstuffs in the cabinet, and then noticed he had brought several thick blankets. She was certain there was none in the loft, so she picked up one and walked to the table. She stared at the opening and was about to climb up and toss the blanket to him. Then she stopped, hesitated, and stepped back, her lips in a firm line. She wrapped the babies and herself in warm blankets, put another log on the fire, and went to bed.

CHAPTER FIVE

A NIGHT VISITOR

★ ★ ★ ★

After the snowstorm, winter retreated in the face of a warm front from the south, and the ice on the creek melted. One morning in mid-November Zack rigged a line and went fishing. The sun soaked into his back as he searched for a good spot until he found a bed of plump red-eared perch. He threaded a cricket on the hook, swung the line gently over a deep place, and waited. It must have proven an irresistible sight to the fish, for suddenly the pole bent double and the line zigzagged wildly through the water.

Zack let out a wild yell. "You little darlin'!" he crooned as he removed the plump perch, "you and me have a date for supper tonight!" He slipped the fish into a cloth sack, secured the opening with string, then tied the sack to a sapling and tossed it out about two feet from the bank. The fish lived longer that way, he had found.

By three o'clock he made his way back to the cabin with his ample catch. He carried his rifle as usual, out of cautious habit. The Arapahos to the west had been on the warpath, and though he didn't expect them to hit this far away, his caution let him take every measure of safety.

When he got back to the cabin, Choiya was outside boiling clothes over a fire in a black washpot. As usual she said nothing but watched him as he came into the yard. For two weeks she had communicated only what was necessary.

The first few days Zack had tried to establish some sort of relationship—an armed truce, at least. But when he saw her deliberate silence, he gave up. It had been uncomfortable, but he had grown accustomed to it. Now he went about his business making no attempt to speak with her. He kept the larder filled with fresh game and when he got hungry he cooked something, always making enough for her as well. She never made a meal for him, and apparently ate when he was gone. She didn't do any cleaning in the cabin either, which irritated him, but he said nothing, doing what little was necessary.

As he started to clean the fish, he saw that she was washing some small blankets she had cut up out of one large one. Some of the cloths she used for swaddling clothes bobbed in the boiling water as well, and a red blouse she had worn once or twice. *Wouldn't kill her to wash out some of my things*, he thought.

He picked up a worktable he had made and moved it away from the house, got a large washpan, and pulled a fish from the sack. It took no more than a minute to clean and scale each fish. He was so engrossed in the task, he was startled when she spoke.

"Leave the heads on some of them."

He looked up and saw that she had come close to watch what he was doing. "Leave the heads on?"

"Yes. I like them."

He studied her carefully, wondering if she was coming out of her shell. "You like fish heads?"

"It's the best part of the fish," she said. The evening sun made her smooth skin glow with a ruddy color, and her hair was clean and fresh, so he knew she had washed it while he was fishing.

"Like this?" He inserted the tip of the knife into the fish's vent, ripped upward, then opened the slit and with deft movement removed the entrails. He turned the knife over and scaled it, then held it up.

"That is good," she said. "You are very fast." Suddenly aware that she was carrying on a conversation with him, her full lips turned up in disdain. "The men of my people do not clean fish. That is women's work."

He longed to say, *If you'd do a little work, I wouldn't have to clean fish*. Instead, he shrugged and picked up another fish. Choiya had expected him to say exactly that, but when he refused to argue, a puzzled light filled her eyes. She went back and removed the clothes from the pot, wringing them dry. As she worked, she watched him surreptitiously. His whole attention focused on the fish—and that was the thing about him she could not understand.

She had been the beauty of her tribe since early girlhood, and as was the way with her people, had been courted from the time she was thirteen. Many braves had wanted her, and she quickly learned she could have any man. When she had gone to be White Eagle's wife, she knew that men still watched her. After she had been captured and White Eagle killed, the men of Black Pigeon's tribe had been after her constantly.

But this man did not watch her in that way. For weeks she had expected him to touch her, but he did not even give her those sly looks she could discern so expertly. This had been a relief. Now, she began to wonder if she had become ugly. The small shaving mirror on the wall told her she had not, and her figure was as slim as before Hawk was born. Still he ignored her.

A streak of perversity rose in her. She took the wet clothing inside to hang it in front of the fire. She fed both babies, and soon after, Zack came in with pink fish in the pan, all washed and ready to cook.

As usual he moved to the fire, stirring up the coals, then set the big black skillet on the iron grill. He walked over to get the bacon fat he kept in a jar, and she moved in the same direction. He had not expected her to do so; and as they both reached out to open the cabinet, her body brushed against him.

He jerked back as if he had touched a hot stove, and looked at her, startled. She had a strange expression in her eyes, waiting for something. Her touch had stirred him, but he simply said, "Sorry—didn't see you."

She stood absolutely motionless, waiting. She knew any man she had known would have interpreted her action as an invitation, but Winslow had retreated instantly. His reaction increased her determination to make him notice her, and she smiled for the first time. "I will cook the fish."

"Why—that'd be handy," Zack said. He moved away, hiding

his confusion by saying, "We're low on water. I'll get a couple of buckets from the spring."

As he hurried down the path, she watched through the window. Her eyes narrowed, and she touched her cheek. Finally she nodded and turned to get the fat out of the cabinet.

Zack was gone a long time, and when he returned, the aroma of frying fish filled the cabin. "You like hush puppies?" he asked.

She shook her head. "I don't know."

"When the fish is done, put a little more fat in the skillet."

Zack walked to the larder and began to put items on the table. She watched as he mixed cornmeal, baking powder, salt, a chopped onion, and flour together, then added some canned milk. He rolled the mixture into balls about two inches in diameter, and when she was finished with the fish, he stepped to the fireplace and dropped the balls into the pan. He browned them well, then placed the cornmeal balls on a tin plate.

He put the hush puppies on the table, noting that the fish was already there, along with some bread. He sat down to eat, placing a piece of fish and several hush puppies on his plate. He picked up the fish, and carefully began to pull at the top dorsal fin. The entire top section of the skeleton came out, and he tossed it on the table. Then he bit into the hot, sweet flesh that fell off in chunks. As he chewed, he picked up a hush puppy, dipped it in the bowl of butter and bit off half.

"Is *that* good!" he breathed. He looked up at Choiya, who was standing back from the table watching him eat, and remarked, "Fish is going to get cold."

She hesitated, then with a decisive movement, sat down. He had no conception of her action, for she had never eaten with men. But she lifted her head proudly and put some fish and cornbread on her plate. She chose a fish with a head, and ate that first, nibbling delicately. When she saw him give an involuntary start, she smiled. "You waste the best part." She picked up the hush puppy, dipped it in the butter as she had seen him do, and bit into it. Her eyes opened with surprise.

"Good?" Zack asked.

"Yes—but why do you call them hush puppy?"

"My pa used to keep dogs, and they'd make a lot of racket sometimes. He'd toss them one of these and say, 'Hush, puppy'!"

Her face broke into a smile, making him uncomfortably aware of her rich beauty. His one firm determination was to have nothing to do with the woman. He dropped his head and continued eating. Choiya saw the change pass over him, and wondered.

When the meal was over, she rose and began to clean the dishes, including Zack's. He said nothing, just walked over to the babies and squatted down, staring at them carefully. Choiya watched him, curious. She knew he had taken the white baby against his will, that he had no real obligation. His actions seemed strange to her, for she sensed he was trying to get away from people. Fox had come back for his pony, and had spoken to her, telling her of the white man's desire to be a hermit—to have nothing to do with anyone. Among the men of her race, she knew of no one who would do such a thing. Nor would they have taken her and her baby, she reflected, not without expecting her to be their woman in every way.

She finished cleaning up, and walked over to where he was still studying the babies. Impulsively she reached down and picked up Samuel. "Hold him," she said, thrusting the child at him as he stood up.

Startled, he protested, "I might hurt him!" He saw the little fist wave in the air, and added, "He's so tiny!"

"He's tougher than you think," she said with humor in her eyes.

Zack held the baby awkwardly, looking into the blue eyes. The child hiccupped, then smiled. "Look at that!" Zack exclaimed. "He's *smiling* at me!"

Amused at his reaction, Choiya asked, "Haven't you ever held a baby?"

"No." Zack was examining the tiny hand. "Look at this—fingernails, Choiya—just like a real person's!"

Surprised at his use of her name for the first time, she realized he had not even noticed. "He *is* a real person," she said. "Like nobody else in this world."

He raised his head, saying thoughtfully, "Why—that's right, isn't it? We're all different." He looked at the child again. "Wonder what he'll be like when he grows up."

"Probably like you." His head jerked up and his jaw dropped. She added, "Many boys grow up to be like their fathers."

"I'm not his father!" Zack protested.

"I think you'll have to be," Choiya said quietly, considering him carefully. "Who else will be a father to him?"

He shook his head. "I'm trying to find his people. They'll want him."

"I talked with the white woman many times before she died," Choiya said. "She told me there was no one to take the boy. That was why she always prayed to her God to send a man—and at the end I think she believed you were sent by God to be Samuel's father."

Zack's face grew taut. He shook his head, and handed her the baby. "That can't be," he muttered. "I'll find somebody—I'm only a hermit."

Nothing more was said, but Choiya knew the thought troubled him. That night he read the journal again, as he had many times before, and then thumbed through the black Bible, seeking for an answer.

Finally he sighed, closed the Bible, and put it back. He was about to go up to the loft when Choiya said, "Somebody has been stealing." When he looked at her curiously, she added, "For the last two nights I have heard him. He waits until the middle of the night, then comes and takes food."

"Probably an animal sneaking around. A skunk maybe."

"Can a skunk open the catch of the meat cabinet?" she demanded. "I checked the food. One of the rabbits was gone yesterday—and last night he took two potatoes."

"Don't like the sound of that. I'll try to catch him tonight." He looked at her. "You think it could be an Indian?"

"No. He's too clumsy. If it were one of my people, I would have never heard a sound."

"All right. I'll wait until dark and slip out through the window." He took his pistol from a peg, checked the loads, then cleaned his knife and slipped it into the sheath. When it was fully dark, he let himself out into the blackness. He could hear the hobbled horses and mules moving around the house, stamping and blowing from time to time. He slid down behind several sacks of feed, and made himself as comfortable as possible. Two hours went by, and he grew stiff from the cold. Another half hour, and he was about ready to give it up when he heard a faint sound in the yard to his left.

He gathered his feet under him, drew the gun from his belt and waited. Someone was moving around the house and had turned into the shed. *Choiya was right,* he thought. *Whoever it is, he's too clumsy to be an Indian.* With bated breath, he waited. Suddenly a shadow fell between him and the night sky, cutting off the faint stars. It was a fairly tall person.

The prowler went straight to the meat locker. Zack waited until the door squeaked, then stood up quietly. Lifting the gun he said, "All right—hold it right there!"

A startled cry rang out, and the intruder wheeled and started to plunge away. Zack fired a warning shot and said, "I'll put the next one in your head." Then he called out, "Choiya! Bring a light!"

She must have been waiting, because immediately the lamp flickered on. She walked outside and came into the shed.

"Let's have a look at you," Zack said to the prowler. "Choiya, hold the light on him."

He peered at the figure and exclaimed, "Why, it's just a boy!"

He lowered the gun, and moved closer. "Son, what do you think you're doing?"

Choiya saw a thin white face, and knew there was no danger in this one. "Bring him inside," she said.

"Move along, boy," Zack commanded.

Inside, the boy turned to face them, and a streak of pity ran through Zack. He walked across the room, hung the pistol on the peg, then came back and studied the boy. "What's your name, son?" he asked quietly.

"Buck Smith." The boy was an inch or so taller than Zack, but thin as a rail. His arms, like broomsticks, stuck out of a ragged coat much too small for him. His tousled blond hair and large brown eyes protruding from a gaunt face evoked only sympathy. He was scared but trying not to show it.

"Why didn't you come and ask for something to eat instead of stealing it?"

The boy shrugged his thin shoulders. He blinked against the light, and Zack said, "Put that light down and let's have some hot food."

Smith's head jerked and he muttered, "I don't want nothin'. Just let me go."

Hawk woke up and started crying, and Zack said to Choiya, "Tend to Hawk and I'll fix some grub. Buck, you sit down there."

The boy had no choice. He sat down and watched his captors like a wild animal. The woman was sitting on the only bed in the room, with her back to him as she nursed the baby; and the man, he decided, was nobody to fool with. In a few minutes the coffee pot was simmering and the left-over fish had been re-heated. His stomach gave a sudden twist as the smell reached him.

"Eat that—and then we'll talk," Zack said, putting the food on the table. He poured himself a cup of coffee, and sat there watching as the boy ate. "I'm Zack Winslow, in case you want to know."

The boy shrugged. Even as the boy bolted the food down, his eyes wandered to the door, seeking an escape. When he stuffed the fish into his mouth, Zack said, "You're going to choke on those fish bones if you're not careful, Buck."

Finally the boy pushed the plate back and asked sullenly, "Can I go now?"

"No." Winslow's face was mild, but there was no give in his manner. "If I let you go, there's no place closer than Virginia City for you. Where'd you come from, anyway? You a runaway?"

Smith clamped his lips shut and stared at Zack defiantly. "I ain't done nothin'."

"You stole my food," Zack said. "I could have you jailed just for that."

"Go on and do it then! I don't care!"

Choiya rose from the bed and came to stand behind Zack. She held the baby and regarded the boy steadily. He looked back at her uncertainly, then dropped his head.

"How old are you?" she asked.

"Fifteen, I guess." He shrugged, and said, "I dunno." He took another drink of the hot coffee. "The law ain't after me—but a man named Richards is. He took me to raise from an orphanage, and I run off from him." His brown eyes flamed with anger. "I ain't no slave—and I ain't goin' back to that—!" He broke off, then loosed a rough curse and glared at the two across from him, daring them to challenge.

"You've got no people?" Zack asked. When the boy shook

his head, Winslow nodded. "Well, you can stay here tonight. Where've you been sleeping?"

"In the woods. I got a bedroll. Tried to make a lean-to, but it blew down."

"You were out there during the snow?"

"Yes."

"You don't have a gun?"

"No."

"Must have been pretty tough," Zack suggested.

"Not as bad as staying with ol' man Richards!"

Zack went over and got a blanket. "Come on up in the loft. We can talk about it tomorrow." He tossed the blanket up, then pulled himself into the loft with a single athletic leap.

The boy stared, then turned to Choiya. "Ma'am—I can't do that!"

"Here, push the table over under the hole." He did and she put a chair on it. "Now you can climb up."

He clumsily mounted the table, then the chair. Before jumping up, he said, "Ma'am. . . ?"

"Yes?"

"I—I'm sorry I took that grub." He didn't wait for an answer, but pulled himself into the loft.

"That's your blanket, Buck," Zack said, adding, "Don't worry. I'm not going to turn you over to the law."

The boy thought once of getting down, pulling the gun off the wall, and making his escape. But the good food, warmth, and weariness overtook him and he succumbed to sleep.

CHAPTER SIX

A TRIP TO TOWN

★　★　★　★

After breakfast, Zack hitched the team and drove out with Buck beside him. He called out to Choiya, "Be back by dark, I expect." He'd never done that. Why did he feel compelled to do so?—and why did she give him a grave nod and answer, "All right"?

Zack mused over the change in her as they left the yard. By now the sun had come up, warming the chilled earth, but winter was only playing possum. Zack made little attempt to talk to the boy, knowing it would only stiffen his resistance. At the creek they paused to water the horses, and Zack remarked idly, "This creek reminds me of the one we crossed at Shiloh—only that one was red by the time we were out of it."

"You fought in the war?" Buck asked.

"One year." Zack sat slackly in the seat, thinking back, and said softly, "There was a young fellow in our company, couldn't have been a day older than you, Buck. Name was Cotton Sykes. Fine boy, always ready to help with whatever needed doing."

Buck waited for him to go on, but finally saw that Winslow was finished. "What happened to him?"

A frown crossed Zack's face, and he shook his head. "He went down at Malvern Hill. We thought the fight was over, and we were cheering—and then one Reb took a shot. Caught Cotton in the belly." He thought back to that time, and said softly, "Took him almost two days to die."

"What you gonna do with me?" he asked.

"Try to find you a place. Got to be some farmer or somebody who needs a good hand."

Buck said bitterly, "If there's a place, then I sure ain't found it. I been put out with three families, and all three of 'em tried to work me to death. I ain't gonna stand for it no more, Mr. Winslow!"

"I guess you can call me Zack." The team picked up its pace as he slapped them with the lines, and he said, "Not all folks are mean, Buck."

The boy wasn't convinced. "Why don't you live in town then, if people are so nice? Why you livin' way out on the edge of no place?"

The boy's question stung, and Zack had no answer. He merely shook his head. "You're too young to be on your own. Couple of years and you can do as you please."

That ended the conversation, and when they got to Virginia City Zack drove straight to Pfouts' store. "I got to talk to a fellow, Buck. You come on in and let's get you some clothes."

Buck climbed out of the wagon slowly, reluctance in every line of his thin face, but he said nothing.

"Well, Zack—how are you?" Parris greeted as they entered.

"Fine." Zack turned and said, "This is Buck Smith. Needs some duds."

"Of course." Pfouts did not appear to notice the boy's rags. He led him to a stack of shirts and breeches, and soon had an outfit picked out, including boots and socks. "Go in the back room and try these on, son," the storekeeper said.

While the boy was gone, Zack quickly sketched the situation for Pfouts, and ended by saying, "I got no intentions of putting the boy into a bind, Parris—but he's too young to be on his own. It's a miracle he didn't die out in the mountains."

Pfouts nodded, his brow creased. "You're right, Zack—but aside from having him locked up for burglary, I don't think there's a lot you can do. He's too young to take care of himself, maybe, but he's too old to just do otherwise."

"He reminds me so much of a kid in my outfit." Zack paused.

"I tried to look out for him, but he took a minie ball. I still have bad dreams about him—thinking that somehow I should have done a better job of looking after him."

To Pfouts, this was an interesting side of Winslow. The young man was very hard, despite his youthful appearance and innocent face. But what he had just said let the merchant know that some of Zack's adamant proclamations were more on the surface than within. "We'll have a try, Zack. Let me look around this morning—see what I can turn up."

"It'll have to be real, Parris," Zack warned. "Buck's pretty well had it with people who want him just for what they can get in the way of work."

"I'll think of that."

Just then Buck emerged, and Zack exclaimed, "Now lookee here! Clothes do make the man, don't they, Parris?"

Buck's emaciated form was somewhat disguised by the new clothing. He looked less like a beggar—except for his hair. "Let's get a haircut," Zack suggested. "Then I have a few more errands. Meet you for lunch at The Rainbow, Parris."

"Right."

"What do I do with these old clothes?" Buck asked.

"Stuff them in the wagon. They'll do for fishing." As they went toward the barber shop, Zack rambled on about how good the fishing had been.

"Yes, sir?" the barber said, getting out of his chair at the sight of Zack. "A haircut?"

"Get in the chair, Buck. If this barber does a good job on you, I'll let him try his hand on me."

He sat down and read a two-month-old paper while the barber cut Buck's hair. The war news was not good. Lee and the Army of the Northern Virginia had invaded the North, meeting McClellan's Army of the Potomac in the bloodiest battle of the war. The paper said that out of 87,000 troops under McClellan, 12,400 were casualties. Once again, though heavily outnumbered, Lee had made a fool out of the Northern general. Zack put the paper down, wondering if French and the rest of his friends had made it. The bloody war depressed him, and the barber had to speak to him twice before he realized that Buck was out of the chair. He gave a start, saying, "Why, you look pretty good!" then got in the chair.

After his own haircut, Zack paid the barber, and left with the newly groomed boy. The two strolled down the streets. "I've got to find something to read," Zack said, stalling for time while Pfouts looked for a place for Buck. "Let's amble around and see if we can find somebody with books to sell." Books were not the hottest item in Virginia City, but they discovered a store that sold just about everything. A tall sad-faced Texan waited on them. "Yep, I got books. Schoolteacher got this far, then went broke. I bought all he had." He shook his head. "They didn't help him a whole lot, did they? He went broke in spite of all his education."

Zack had always been a reader, so he spent the next two hours browsing through the books. Finally he bought about twenty, all well bound. He'd never heard of most of them, but the nights were long at the cabin and he figured when he got rid of Choiya and the babies, he'd have time to read. Buck had been drawn to some cheap paperback novels about Indian fighters and gunmen of the West. "Probably all lies," Zack had grinned, but added, "Guess they'll do to pass the time." He paid for them, and put the package into the wagon.

"Let's see if Pfouts is at the Rainbow," Zack suggested.

Parris sat alone at a table, and waved them over. His face did not bear good tidings.

They finished their meal, and Zack sent Buck on an errand down the street in order to have a word alone with Pfouts. "You didn't have any luck, did you, Parris?"

"Not much," he admitted. "Manning needs a stable boy, but he's pretty much of a drunk. The mill's pretty dangerous work for a boy." He took a sip of his coffee. "I've only one idea left, Zack—a couple named Mize. They're pretty low-down. Emmet's a bum, but not vicious, just lazy. They got three kids, and I figure one more wouldn't hurt. I think Mize would take the boy—if I paid him a little on the side."

"I'll do the paying if it comes to that, Parris." Zack thought about it, and finally said, "I'll take the boy there and check it out."

"Don't expect much," Pfouts warned. "They're not the best, but can't blame the kids for that. Some of us try to help with clothes and things."

"Where do they live?"

"Over the Oriental Saloon—just about the worst spot you can think of. Emmet does some shilling for Clyde Foster who owns the place, I guess."

"Here comes Buck. I'll let you know what I decide."

"See you in church," Pfouts said as usual.

"You go to his church, Zack?" Buck asked.

"Well, no, but if I went to any, I'd choose his."

"What kind is it—Baptist?"

"Got no idea. Whatever kind it is, with a man like Pfouts running it, it's got to be good." He cleared his throat and said casually, "By the way, Pfouts told me about a place might be good for you."

Buck's face hardened. "What kind of place?"

"Oh, just a family you could stay with. Name is Mize. Let's check into it."

The Oriental wasn't difficult to find, and at the end of the street Zack saw a small boy and a girl even smaller playing in front of a building next to an alley. It looked like an old store with windows boarded up and smoke coming out of a smoke stack sticking out of the window on the alley side. Zack stopped and looked down at the boy in front of the saloon. "Your name Mize?"

"Uh huh." Dark eyes below a thatch of black hair peered up at Zack. The little girl had the same coloring. She shyly moved to stand against the building, sucking her thumb.

"Guess this is it." Zack knocked on the front door and waited.

Finally it swung open and a young girl, no more than fourteen or fifteen, stood framed in the doorway, looking at them suspiciously. She had the same black hair and dark eyes as the two children, but the thin dress she wore revealed her growing womanhood. Already she would have difficulty hiding her shapely form—if she wanted to. There was a boldness in her stare and provocative curve to her full lips as she examined them. Finally Zack said, "We're looking for the Mizes."

The girl shrugged and stepped back. "Come on in." She shut the door and walked to the door in the center of the back wall, calling out, "Ma! Somebody's here!" Then she returned, put her hands behind her back and stood watching them, never taking her eyes off the visitors.

The shabby room had been some kind of shop at one time. The walls were lined with old newspapers, peeling free. One table with four mismatched chairs, a black cookstove, some wooden boxes nailed to the wall with a few groceries inside, and a battered couch with springs punching through completed the furnishings. Large cockroaches darted from refuse in one corner. The smell of unwashed bodies and stale food permeated the place. Zack's heart sank.

When Mrs. Mize appeared, Zack was even more disappointed. The thin, sickly looking woman whined, "Yeah? What'cha want?"

"We'd like to see your husband," Zack said.

"He ain't here," she replied, scrutinizing them. "What'cha want with 'im?"

"Just a business matter," Zack said. "Know where we might find him?"

"Down to the Oriental Saloon, drunk I guess."

"I'll take you," the girl said, pulling a flimsy sweater from a nail. As she left, her mother yelled, "Lil, you try to git 'im to come on home, ya hear?"

Zack and Buck followed the girl, who made her way up the street. "Pa won't come home—not as long as he's got the price of a drink," she laughed shortly. When they reached the saloon, a man leaning against the wall saw her and grinned. "Hi, Lil."

She was instantly transformed, running a hand over her long curly hair and flashing him a bright smile. "Hello, Harry."

"Got that bracelet you admired," he said as they passed. "See you later."

"All right, Harry."

They entered the Oriental and the girl headed straight for a back table where a large man was playing cards. He looked up and cursed, "What'cha doin' in here, Lil? Didn't I tell you I'd take a strap to you if I caught you in here?"

The girl showed a trace of fear. "Somebody wants to see you, Pa."

Mize looked at Zack and Buck, then said to his daughter, "Git home, you hear me—and don't take no shortcuts."

"Yes, Pa," she said, hurrying out.

"My name's Winslow. Pfouts talk to you about taking this young fellow in for a spell?"

Mize spoke slowly, obviously trying to control his speech. "Yeah, I 'member he said something 'bout it." He looked at Buck, studying him. "Boy, I don't stand for no sass, you unnerstand?"

Buck just nodded, but his eyes were angry.

"An' you stay 'way from Lil or I'll bust you up," Mize ordered. He turned to the man across from him, "You hear 'bout how I busted Ad Cantrell up, Clyde?"

"I did." The man was short and squat, with hard eyes and a tight mouth. "That wasn't too smart, Emmet. Now you'll have to watch out for him. He'll backshoot you if he gets the chance."

"Naw, he ain't got the nerve," Mize spat out.

"Ought to keep the girl home if you don't want men chasing after her," the saloon owner said. "Not safe for a pretty one like that."

Mize didn't answer, but turned to Buck. "You do your work an' don't give me no sass, an' you can stay." He threw Winslow a look. "You the guy who lives way back in the hills—the hermit?"

"That's me, I guess," Winslow said, then nodded, "We'll let you know."

"Let me know?" Mize's brutal face flushed with anger, and he lurched to his feet. "You talk like we ain't good enough for this punk to stay with!"

"You're drunk, Mize," Zack said, and turned to go. He never saw the blow that caught him on the side of the head and drove him headlong to the floor. Catlike, he rolled over and sprang to his feet. Mize started after him, but stopped when Foster cried, "Cut it out, Emmet!"

All three stared at Zack, expecting him to take up the fight, but he had no inclination for a brawl with a drunk, so he said, "Let's go, Buck."

Back on the street, they saw no sign of the girl or the man named Harry. *Went to get her bracelet*, he thought sourly. He walked rapidly, getting control of his anger, for the blow had aroused him. Was I afraid of that man? he wondered, then dismissed the idea, realizing he was getting older. Mize was big, but slow, and very drunk. It would have been no victory to have fought. He could have cut the man to pieces.

He glanced at Buck, who was looking at him with a peculiar expression. *Expected me to fight*, Zack thought. *Probably thinks I'm a coward.* That bothered him, but he knew more about his courage than Buck, and had no desire to prove it.

By the time they got to the wagon, he had made up his mind. "Buck, you can't stay with Mize," he said, and noted that a swift flood of relief washed across the boy's face. "Tell you what, you come out to my place. I got lots of work to do. I can't pay you much, but you'll have a place to stay and you can bunk in the loft with me."

Buck was struggling with his feelings, and though he was desperately relieved that he didn't have to stay with Mize, he had been hurt too often to allow himself to show any feeling— or so he thought.

"Well—I got to work long enough to pay for these clothes," he said, trying to speak from deep in his chest. "Guess it'll be all right."

"Be a help to me," Zack said. He was not happy about taking in another stray, but thought that Pfouts would find something for Buck soon. "Let's get on back to the place."

He stopped to tell Pfouts what he'd done. "It's just for a little while," Zack said loudly. "You try to find him a place, Parris. I got to get rid of all these strays as soon as I can!"

Pfouts nodded, suppressing a smile. "I'll see what I can do."

When they got back to the cabin, Buck said, "I can unhitch the team." He took the lines from Zack, and struggled to say something, but nothing came.

Zack started toward the cabin just as Choiya opened the door, holding both babies. She saw Buck unhitching the team, and murmured, "You brought him back?"

The question, she saw, irritated Zack. He nodded shortly, then looked at her and the two babies, then toward Buck.

"He can stay until I find a place for him—and that's all!" He saw her soft lips curve upward at the corners in a knowing smile. Flustered, he took off his derby and turned it around in his hands, then with a sudden flash of disgust, threw it against the wall, and walked inside without a word.

Choiya knew Buck had watched the action. She looked down at the hat, the smile still on her face. Then she shifted Hawk from her left arm, and, holding both babies in her right, bent down in one graceful movement and picked up the hat. She looked at it carefully, and gave Buck a smile before she turned and entered the cabin.

PART TWO

THE MISSIONARY

★ ★ ★ ★

CHAPTER SEVEN

A COMMITTEE OF THREE

★ ★ ★ ★

Captain Nels Swenson carefully guided the *Harvest Moon* to the dock, raising his voice once to warn the Bos'n: "Careful there! Hard over!" He would have been more profane in his command, but just as he spoke he saw his only female passenger standing on the foredeck with a hand on the capstan's bar.

The captain had protested vociferously against bringing a woman on board. "It's a rough enough trip around the Horn," he'd warned the owner. "And a woman is bad luck on a ship— and she'll have the men all stirred up." But the owner of the *Harvest Moon* had been adamant. "This one will give you no trouble, Captain Swenson. She's *different!*"

Now six months out of Southampton, Swenson had to admit that the owner had been right. As he moved down the deck to where Bronwen Morgan stood looking at the outline of Portland, he thought of the first time he'd seen her. She'd come aboard the night before sailing, and he'd gone to her cabin to lay down some hard and fast rules. At his knock, she'd opened the door, and the sight of her hardened his resolve, for she was not a dried-up old maid as he'd hoped, but one of the most beautiful young women he'd ever seen.

He remembered standing in the middle of her tiny room, looking down at her. She was twenty-five, had fiery-red hair, and green eyes that examined him warmly while he blustered about having no nonsense. "I'll tell you straight, Miss Morgan," he had warned her as he noted the light dusting of freckles across her nose, uncomfortably aware of her deep-bodied, well-proportioned figure, "my men are a rough lot. They can't change their way of speaking to please you. If you want fine manners, I'd advise you to get a berth on a clipper ship." Her smile irritated him, and he'd added bluntly, "I don't have time to waste, so if any of the men make a remark to you, or try to romance you, don't come crying to me."

"I promise not to do that, Captain," she said.

Now as he took his place beside her at the rail, he thought how well she'd handled herself on the long cruise. *She's been no trouble at all. I wouldn't have believed a woman could have tamed this rough crew.*

"You'll be rid of me tomorrow, Captain," Bronwen said, turning to face him, a smile lighting her countenance. "You've been a very good host—and I've been a great trouble to you."

"That you haven't," Swenson protested, pulling at his droopy mustache. Then he grinned down at her. "Good thing we got here today, Miss Morgan. Another week at sea and you'd have turned the *Harvest Moon* into a floating Methodist church." He was referring to the services she had held on deck every Sunday morning since the ship sailed. At first she was totally alone, standing beside the rail, singing hymns, then reading from her Bible as though she had a congregation of a hundred. On the second Sunday, after a week at sea, she'd made two converts, Ernest Hill and Lars Johnson. The pair had joined her, in spite of the jeers from their shipmates. *Give in to a woman preacher? Never!* But the next week, the trio had swelled to seven; and on the previous day, the captain had stood there with practically every seaman not needed to sail the ship, singing with the rest, and listening as Bronwen balanced herself against the roll of the *Harvest Moon*, reading the scripture and preaching.

"I'm afraid some of your converts will backslide when you leave the ship," Swenson said. "Not to be impolite, Miss Morgan, but I'm afraid some of them came to services because they were fascinated by the sight of a beautiful lady preacher." His white teeth flashed under his mustache as he grinned. "That's why I joined you, I'm afraid."

"The Lord's Word will not return to Him void," she said, lifting her heart-shaped face to study the seaman. "You will find God, Captain. Jesus Christ is on your trail, and He'll capture you in the end."

Morgan's direct approach had fascinated both the captain and crew. Several of the men had spoken to her roughly to frighten her, but were unsuccessful. Swenson thought uncomfortably of his own indiscretion. He had found her alone on deck, and made advances. Instantly she had put him in his place. "You have a wife, Captain, and two children. What of your wedding vow?" Her words had cut deeply into Swenson's pride, but in the following days she had never indicated by word or attitude any recollection of the incident.

He nodded toward the streaky glow of Portland's waterfront lights. "Your young man is there, you say?"

"Yes." A smile played around the edges of her mouth, and she touched her cheek gently, her eyes shining with anticipation. "We'll be married this week."

"And then off to preach to the Indians," Swenson said, shaking his head in wonder. "That won't be easy."

"Jesus didn't save me for an easy life. He said, 'Take up your cross and follow me.' " Her lips firmed as she spoke.

"What's the young man's name? I forget."

"Owen Griffeth."

Many times they had talked on the long voyage about her plans. Now he said slowly, "I don't understand, Miss Morgan. I've gone to church off and on most of my life, but God never told me anything. How do you and Griffeth *know* you're supposed to preach to the Indians?" Skepticism surfaced as he went on. "Did you actually *hear* God's voice?"

"It came through the Spirit, Captain Swenson," Bronwen replied. "Owen and I were saved in the revival that swept across Wales two years ago. We began to read the Scriptures and to ask God to instruct us in His will for our lives."

"Don't they need preachers in Wales? Why not serve God there?"

"We did think of that, but soon we felt God wanted something else." She looked up, laughter dancing in her eyes. "Captain, don't you sometimes know a storm is coming before there's any sign of it?" He nodded and she continued. "If you tried to tell me how you *knew* that, you wouldn't be able to make me understand. You've spent your life at sea, watching it, thinking about it. You've learned there's something in the smell of the air, the shape of the clouds. But even if you couldn't explain that to a landlubber like me—you *know* in your spirit that it's going to storm."

"Why, that's so!"

She nodded. "That's what Owen and I did. We prayed and fasted and read the Word. We talked about the will of God—we sought for it! And it came. Not in one day," she added quickly. "It was just an idea, and I laughed. Me, going to the Indians in America! But it kept returning."

"What about Griffeth? Did you tell him?"

"No. He'd asked me to marry him, and I put him off." She grew pensive, looking out across the bay, and her voice grew softer. "But finally I knew I had to come to America, so I went to Griffeth and told him about my call. He said God had spoken to him as well. But I was afraid we wouldn't be called to the same place, so I said, 'Write down the name of the place God has called you to.' I did the same, and we stood holding the slips, afraid to look."

"And I take it, his slip said the same as yours—America?" he asked, his voice doubtful.

"You find that hard to believe, Captain Swenson?" She put her hand on his arm impulsively. "Why would it be difficult for God? He made this earth and all the universe. Couldn't He whisper into the hearts of two people?"

"I don't know about these things."

Bronwen's grip tightened on his arms. She said softly, "I have prayed about your son. God has told me he will be well by the time you get home."

"My Karl?" he whispered.

"Yes," she said, speaking with conviction.

Swenson had two sons. The older, Peter, was healthy, but the four-year-old had been sickly since birth—little strength in his legs and slow in other ways. Captain Swenson had lain awake many nights on the ship worrying about the child, for he had seemed worse just before the *Harvest Moon* had sailed.

"God has touched him, Captain," she went on. "When you get home you will find him as well as your other son." She examined his face carefully. "Do you believe that?"

Swenson had been at sea since he was fourteen, and life had hardened him. To him religion was for landsmen, and though he had gone to church to please his wife, he had never felt a need for God.

Now the image of his afflicted son came to him—twisted legs and pain-filled face. He struggled with his doubt as Bronwen waited. Astonishingly, another picture flashed before him—his son running across the green grassy yard, his legs straight and strong, his face filled with health and joy as he rushed to his returning father with outstretched arms, crying, "Papa—Papa!"

Swenson's eyes misted, his throat constricted, for he was not an emotional man. He swallowed and said thickly, "Yes!" and turned away lest she see, then wheeled and cried, "Yes—I *do* believe it!"

He spent a restless night, calling himself a fool many times—but the vision of his son did not fade. The next morning when he stood beside the gangplank to say goodbye, his face was pale but peaceful.

As the crew filed by, she called every man by his name and gave each a personal word: "Keep taking that medicine, Charles . . ." "I'll be praying for your wife, Little . . ." Even the most hardened, Swenson noted, were gloomy as they shook hands and said goodbye.

When the last farewell was said, the captain walked ashore with Bronwen. "Miss Morgan," he said, doffing his hat, "I'm not a Christian man. But," he paused, searching for words, "I believe what you said is true." He told her about his experience and the vision of his son healthy and strong. Taking her hand, he said, "I don't know much about prayer—but I will ask God to be with you. Goodbye and God bless you!"

"Thank you, Captain," she replied with a smile. "And I will pray for you." Then she laughed happily and shook her head, the morning sun catching the fiery red hair. "But Christians never say goodbye—for if we don't meet in this world, we're sure to meet on the other side!" She gripped his hand firmly, then disappeared around the corner.

At the last glimpse of his female passenger, Captain Swenson left the dock and returned to the ship, longing for the days to pass when the vision of his son would become reality. Even though Bronwen Morgan was not present, the certainty that Karl would run was as real as the ship on which the captain stood!

★　★　★　★

"Reverend Spenlow? I'm Bronwen Morgan."

David Spenlow was in the middle of preparing his Sunday morning sermon when a knock on the front door interrupted him. His wife usually answered the calls, but she was gone for the morning.

He grunted with annoyance, and tried to ignore the caller, thinking it was a household matter, but the knocking grew more insistent, so he finally slapped his hand on the table and walked to the door.

"Why—why, Miss Morgan!" he stuttered, and hesitated, for an enormous problem had leaped into his mind. "Come in," he said, stepping back. "My wife is gone for the morning, but I'll have our housekeeper fix some tea."

She smiled as she entered, asking as he led her to the parlor, "Is Owen here?"

"Ah—n-no, I'm afraid not," Spenlow said uncertainly. He indicated a horsehair chair beside a library table. "Please have a chair while I speak to Mrs. Lewis."

He found the housekeeper in the kitchen. "Mrs. Lewis, go at once to the church and ask my wife to come home!"

"You mean—leave the meeting?" Mrs. Lewis was a thin woman dressed in black. "She can't do that, sir!"

"Tell her I need her immediately!"

"Well, I'll tell her." Mrs. Lewis's voice was filled with doubt, but she obeyed.

Spenlow desperately wished he didn't have to face Bronwen Morgan, but he had no choice.

"I sent Mrs. Lewis for my wife, Miss Morgan," he informed her as he entered the parlor. "The church is just around the corner." Giving her no opportunity for questions, he asked, "Tell me about your voyage."

Bronwen began to sketch the details of her trip, noticing as she spoke how fidgety the minister was. The small man nervously licked his lips and blinked his weak-looking eyes, crossed and uncrossed his legs. Once she tried to interrupt her story to ask about Owen, but he insisted she continue. As she was ending the narrative, the front door opened and a short woman with brown hair and keen hazel eyes entered.

"Ah, my dear," the minister sighed with relief, "Miss Morgan has just arrived. This is my wife, Elsie, Miss Morgan."

"Miss Morgan." Mrs. Spenlow took Bronwen's hand. "I'm sorry I wasn't here when you arrived. I meet with the mission committee every Tuesday morning."

Bronwen smiled, "Of course. I was just telling Reverend Spenlow about my trip."

"Such a long way," Mrs. Spenlow murmured.

"Yes, and I was so anxious to get here. Has Owen been well?"

An ominous silence fell on the room, and Bronwen saw the couple's dismay. "What's the matter?" she cried. "Is Owen ill?"

"Sit down, my dear," Mrs. Spenlow said gently. "I'm—I'm afraid we have some distressing news."

Stricken, Bronwen waited with sinking heart. She should have known. Reverend Spenlow's nervousness, his reluctance to mention Owen—or even to let her mention him. She stared at them. "What happened?"

"You tell her, my dear," Spenlow said, licking his lips. "I'll be in the study."

When they were alone, Mrs. Spenlow said quietly, "Miss Morgan—there was no way to reach you. Three months ago an epidemic of cholera swept through Portland. It was dreadful! Almost every family lost someone. In some cases, entire families died within a few days." She paused, bit her lip, then brightened. "Mr. Griffeth was marvelous! He cared for the sick in the poor sections until he wore himself out—and then—"

"He got cholera?" Bronwen whispered.

"It happened so quickly!" Mrs. Spenlow exclaimed. "That's the way of that dread disease! One day he came home and seemed fine, except perhaps tired, but we all were. The next day he had a slight fever, but he insisted on caring for the sick." She paused for a moment, then said, "He came home late that evening, very ill. We got the doctor immediately—but it was hopeless. He died two days later, in this house."

Bronwen sat motionless, numbness seeping into the marrow of her bones. The voices were far away. She rose and walked across to the window. Fall had turned the leaves on the maple red and orange, but some were already brown and crisp. They had fallen on the ground, making a carpet on the brown grass. Now and then, a curling leaf would loose its hold and flutter to the earth.

Time ran on, and Mrs. Spenlow waited, her hands clenched, her eyes wet. She had been very fond of Owen Griffeth. He had often talked about his beautiful fiancee and their hopes for the future, anxiously waiting for her arrival. Now she was here, and he in a grave—all their dreams crushed, struck by cholera.

Finally Mrs. Spenlow said, "Let me take you to your room, Bronwen. Do you mind if I call you that? And you must call me Elsie."

"Thank you," Bronwen said. She knew she would weep later, but she stood there, dry-eyed. "Did you talk with him much before he died?"

"Oh yes! My husband and I were with him constantly. He was very dear to us!"

"What did he say?"

"Let's sit down, Bronwen, and I'll tell you."

They sat on the sofa, and for nearly an hour Elsie Spenlow spoke. Bronwen drank it in, her eyes fixed on the older woman's face. Her own face was very pale, but her voice was steady as she interrupted from time to time.

"He loved you so much, my dear—so very much!" Mrs. Spenlow paused. "Next to the Lord, he loved you most of all. That was the last thing he said."

"Tell me."

"We—we thought he had slipped away. He was so still! But then as I bent over and called his name, his eyes opened, and he said, 'Tell Bronwen I'm sorry we won't be going to the Indians together.' "

Bronwen's eyes flooded, and she bit her lower lip. "Did he say anything else?"

Mrs. Spenlow hesitated. She and her husband had decided it would be better not to pass along Griffeth's last words. But now she knew she had no right to withhold a dying man's last message to his beloved.

"He said one more thing before he died. 'Tell Bron not to be afraid to go alone. The Lord has told me that He will not let her suffer any harm.' " Mrs. Spenlow was weeping as she relived the moment. She bent over with her face in her handkerchief, then took a deep breath. "Of course, you can't go alone to that wild country, Bronwen."

"Not go?" The eyes that had been damp with tears suddenly flashed with fire. She lifted her head high. "I'll preach to the Indians though Satan himself and all his demons line up to fight me—and there it is!"

"But—my dear, you could be murdered!"

"And if I am, it doesn't matter!" She stood to her feet and looked out the window as if seeing beyond the hills that rose in the west. She turned and said evenly, "I am Bronwen Morgan—and the Lord God has told me to preach His gospel to those who sit in darkness."

"But—the mission committee will never sponsor you! Not a single woman going to such a dreadful place."

"I have a committee, Elsie—a committee of three."

"Why, I wasn't aware of that. Is it some mission board from Wales?"

"Much larger than that! My committee," Bronwen said, her face set like a flint, "is the Father, the Son, and the Holy Ghost!"

CHAPTER EIGHT

BRON AND BILLY

★ ★ ★ ★

Reverend David Spenlow called the Committee on Indian Missions for a special session, and for the first time in its five-year existence every member was present. The ecumenical group was composed of clergymen from several denominations—Baptist, Presbyterian, Methodist, Congregationalist, and one Episcopalian, the Reverend Isaiah Culpepper. The chairman of the committee was Bishop Jonathan Beecher—the largest, loudest, and most influential.

Bishop Beecher had called the meeting to deal with the Arapaho mission in Montana, and as usual had thoroughly investigated the issue beforehand. Though he listened to David Spenlow's report, Beecher had already made up his mind as to the proper course and had informed the committee of the decision they would be expected to render. As he rose to call the meeting to order, he was prepared to go through the formalities.

He called upon Reverend Joseph Wallace, a Baptist, to begin the meeting with prayer, and was fully satisfied with Wallace's theological position throughout the petition. He then asked Reverend William Clark, a Congregationalist, to give the minutes of the last meeting, followed by Reverend J. A. Hightower, a Presbyterian, with the financial report. After the important elements of the committee had been permitted a voice—he did not include the Reverend Isaiah Culpepper, the Episcopalian, in this group—he said, "Thank God for those reports. In His mercy God has permitted our work to prosper. We will now take up the first matter of business, which is—ah, the work with the Arapaho in Montana. Reverend Spenlow, will you give us your report?"

Spenlow got to his feet, dwarfed by the huge form of Bishop Beecher. He traced the work in Montana, but was cut short by the bishop, who urged him to move along. "Well, as you know, we had accepted a pair of volunteers from Wales—Reverend Owen Griffeth and Miss Bronwen Morgan. Reverend Griffeth came last year, and I believe all of you have heard of his tragic death three months ago."

"No. I hadn't heard," Reverend Culpepper said. He was a tall, thin man with sharp features and bright black eyes. "He was most promising."

"Indeed, he was," Spenlow replied. "My wife and I have been puzzled as to why the Lord would remove our young brother just when his ministry was about to begin."

"We must not question the ways of God, Brother Spenlow," Bishop Beecher said ponderously. "Now, I understand that the young woman—what is her name?"

"Miss Bronwen Morgan, sir—Reverend Griffeth's fiancee," Spenlow prompted.

"Yes, of course. She is waiting outside, I presume?"

"Yes, sir."

"Ask her to step inside, if you please." As Spenlow walked to the door, the bishop said, "Our hearts go out to the young woman, gentlemen. We must do all we can to comfort her." He rose to his feet as Spenlow escorted Bronwen into the room, saying, "Ah, Miss Morgan—I am Bishop Beecher." He named the other members of the committee, and invited her to be seated.

"Thank you, Bishop." As Bronwen sat down, the members of the committee were all mindful of the bishop's words: *A fine young woman, no doubt, but far too young for such responsibility— and in any case, we cannot send a single woman to the field.*

"Now, my dear Miss Morgan, let me serve as spokesman for our committee. We grieve with you over your loss—but it is not yours alone. We shall all miss our young brother."

"Thank you, gentlemen."

Her brief response caught the bishop off guard, and he lowered his eyes and shuffled his papers, grasping at the proper way of disposing the young woman. Finally he lifted his head and smiled pontifically. "Miss Morgan, we on the committee are at your service. It has been a long journey, and your grief has added to the burden. Before you return to Wales, I want to offer you the hospitality—"

"Return to Wales?" Bronwen's head shot up. "But I'm *not* going back home. Didn't you tell them my plan, Reverend Spenlow?"

"Ah—as a matter of fact, Miss Morgan, I didn't," Spenlow replied, embarrassed.

"But I thought I made it clear that I intend to go on with the mission to the Arapaho people!"

"Spenlow, you said nothing of this!" The bishop's stern gaze fell on the hapless minister, and Spenlow knew he was in for a difficult time.

"Sir," he said nervously, "I have made Miss Morgan familiar with the policies of our mission—that we do not send single women—but she is determined to pursue the matter."

Beecher settled down in his seat, the jovial expression replaced by a heavy scowl. "Why, there is no way we can violate our policy, Miss Morgan! No way at all."

"Then I'll go by myself," Bronwen rejoined.

A murmur swept through the room; then Reverend Hightower rose to his feet. "My dear Miss Morgan, I don't think you know what you are proposing. It's difficult enough for a couple to survive. We've had several who couldn't. Why, it's unthinkable. A young woman. Alone and unprotected."

Bronwen fixed her eyes on him for a moment. "But I'm not alone. Did Jesus not say, 'I will never leave you nor forsake you'? I'll not go unprotected. The Lord is my strength."

Bishop Beecher coughed loudly. "That's all very well, Miss Morgan, but we must be practical about this."

"Practical? If I'd been practical about it, I'd never have left my home at all, Bishop. And if I've read my Bible rightly, neither the Lord Jesus nor any of His disciples were very practical."

A flush spread across Beecher's full face as he said with a touch of harshness, "We'll not argue theology. I have a proposal I trust you'll accept. The board will pay your passage and all expenses back to Wales."

"God has called me to go to the Indians, Bishop," Bronwen said quietly.

"You'll get no support from this committee, young woman, and you'll not be permitted to use the facilities on the field!"

"This committee must do as God leads," she said.

"You refuse to accept passage back to Wales?"

"Yes, sir."

The bishop was unaccustomed to being crossed, and though he was not mean, resistance brought out the worst. "Very well, you may consider yourself a free agent. I trust you will not be stubborn enough to pursue this plan, but we are free from responsibility."

He half rose when Reverend Spenlow surprised him. "I do not agree with you, Bishop."

If Spenlow had announced that the sun had ceased to shine, Bishop Beecher could not have been more stunned. David Spenlow was a mild man, and never once had he questioned the bishop, but now he sat with a pale face and a stubborn look in his eyes.

"Did I hear you correctly, sir?" Beecher asked in astonishment.

"I feel that if Miss Morgan insists on going to the field, we are bound to help her any way we can."

"Yes! Yes!" Isaiah Culpepper slapped his leg and nodded vigorously. "If God has spoken to Miss Morgan, and we go against her decision, we are fighting against God. I move we stand behind her."

J. A. Hightower had long felt that Bishop Beecher was too domineering, and seeing that turn of the tide, he said, "I second the motion."

Beecher stared at him, his face growing redder by the second. "I would like to discuss the matter fully."

"Certainly, sir," Reverend Wallace nodded. "I will begin the discussion by stating that our Baptist people will do as much as we can to get the Word of God to the savages through Miss Morgan's ministry."

That left William Clark, and he was as delighted as his good friend Hightower to see the bishop thwarted. "We Congregationalists will not do less than our Presbyterian and Baptist brethren. I wish to commend you, Miss Morgan, for your dedication."

Beecher had not become a bishop by being a fool. He looked at his cards, and realized he was facing a stacked deck. Being an able politician, he soon shifted his position so adroitly that one coming late to the meeting would have thought he had been the supporter of Bronwen Morgan's mission endeavors, for he spoke to the other members of the committee, giving a glowing account of her journey.

But what he gave with one hand, he took away with the other. He held the purse strings, and with great regret told Bronwen that she could not expect as much support as had been planned for the man-and-wife team. "You are to use the facilities, of course," he concluded, "and we trust the finances here will soon improve that we may do more."

"Thank you, sir," Bronwen said with a gleam in her eye.

On their way home after the meeting, Bronwen said, "You surprised me, Reverend Spenlow. I didn't expect you to disagree with your bishop."

"Frankly, I surprised myself," Spenlow admitted. "He's not a man one desires to oppose."

"Will he make it difficult for you?"

Spenlow smiled unexpectedly. "You know, my dear, I don't think he will. He spoke to me just before he left, saying, 'Spenlow, I was somewhat shocked when you disagreed with my decision—but I'm glad to see you've got a backbone!' "

"Wonderful!" Bronwen laughed. "I must be telling your wife how well you managed the whole thing!"

True to her promise, Bronwen gave a full report. "Really, you should have been there, Elsie! Your husband took on the entire committee—and the bishop was quite impressed! He said as much to him after the meeting!"

A flush of pleasure and pride rose in Elsie's face. "It's about time you took a firm hand, David," she said, adding, "I'm so *proud* of you!"

Spenlow was pleased that the meeting had turned out so well but felt uncomfortable at the praise.

"Whatever I accomplish on the field, sir," Bronwen told him, "will be because you made it possible."

He shoved the adulation aside. "Oh, it wasn't all that much!"

"Brother Spenlow, I disagree. When a man stands for God in the face of opposition, it is a wonderful thing, indeed." She smiled. "Now, when can I leave?"

The Spenlows protested, but Bronwen had made up her mind. Truthfully, though, she was somewhat frightened of her decision. No matter how boldly she stood up to the missions committee, the thought of leaving the safety of civilization to plunge into the wilderness haunted her. She had lain awake at night, begging God to let her go home, but could not escape the sense that she had no choice but to go where He led.

"I will go as soon as possible," she said, impulsively embracing the pair, revealing that strong emotion women of Wales have, "God be thanked for the pair of you. Look how happy I am to have you as my brother and sister!"

Her gust of emotion surprised the pair, but they held her for a moment, loving her, yet fearful for the future. When she stepped back, Spenlow said, "I'll make the arrangements, Bronwen, but it'll be like losing one of our own."

Five days later, the Spenlows stood at the foot of Washington Street, waving farewell to the young missionary as the *Liberty Belle* began the journey to Lewiston. They watched until the ship was out of sight. "God be with her," David said.

"He will be, dear," Elsie nodded. She tried to smile and added, "God wouldn't be so cruel as to take both of them!"

Reverend Spenlow was not at all certain as to the theological truth of her thesis, but for once he followed his heart: "No. He wouldn't do a thing like that!"

★　★　★　★

The trip up river to Lewiston was exciting to Bronwen. She had a stateroom but spent most of her time on deck watching the dark forest flow by as the ship twisted and turned, following the Columbia River. Five hours out of Portland the boat nudged ashore, and she joined the other passengers in a carriage, getting aboard a smaller boat—the *Abraham Lincoln*. She stayed on the deck most of the afternoon, despite the cold breeze, going to the small restaurant for tea twice. At dusk the ship docked, and the purser told her, "It's The Dalles landing."

She got off the boat, and stood beside her luggage, not knowing which way to turn as passengers rushed by. The Dalles' principle street paralleled a river whose lava rock margins lay jagged and black.

"Are you lookin' for the hotel, Miss?"

She turned quickly to find a young man of about twenty-five watching her with keen brown eyes. He was just under six feet, slim, and well dressed. As he removed his hat, a large diamond flashed, and he had better manners than most of the men she'd met.

"Why, I suppose I am."

"If you're going up river, the boat won't leave until morning." He smiled easily. "You'll need a carriage for your luggage." He hailed one, assisted her in, and helped the driver lift her trunk into the rear. "Umatilla House," he directed.

As the carriage rumbled along, he said, "My name is Billy Page."

"And I'm Bronwen Morgan," she answered. "It's thanking you I am for your kindness."

He cocked his head and gave her a curious look. "Not from this country, I take it?"

"No. I come from Wales."

He studied her, trying to figure her out, but she wasn't the sort of woman he was accustomed to. "Wales? I guess that's England, isn't it?"

"The Welsh would fight you over that, now!" She laughed deep in her chest. "But that's close enough."

"I saw you get on at Portland," he continued. "You're going to Lewiston?"

"Oh, much farther than that," she nodded.

He was surprised, but asked no questions. When they arrived at the Umatilla House, he carried her small bags in, and the driver brought the trunk. When Page paid the man, she said, "I must pay half."

He had more tact than most, for though she expected him to

argue, he named half the fare and accepted it without comment. It was done easily and Bronwen knew he was a man with sensitivity.

"Will you join me for breakfast?" he asked. "We can make the trip to the boat together."

"I'd like that very much."

"The boat leaves at seven o'clock, so I'll meet you in the restaurant at six." He smiled and tipped his hat.

She arrived a little before six, but Page was already waiting to seat her. He entertained her with light talk, but said nothing about himself, nor did he ask about her directly. After breakfast they had just enough time to make the train, which ran fifteen miles around the unnavigable rapids to the landing at Celilo. There they boarded the upper riverboat *Oro Fino*. The boat sailed between the black walls of the Cascade Range, which gave way to the dun-colored grasslands; far ahead the silver surface of the river moved between the emptiness of a sagebrush plain.

Page saw Bronwen again at the noon meal, and at her invitation, joined her. Afterward they walked to the forward end of the cabin deck and watched the riverboat churn through shallow rapids. "You say you're going on from Lewiston?" he asked.

"Yes. I'm going to Montana," Bronwen answered.

"You are? I'm going there myself—to Helena," he said.

"Is that close to Virginia City?"

"North of it." He studied the river for a moment. "It's a rough trip after we leave the boat. No stage makes that run."

"How will you get there?"

"Buy a horse. It's about the only way, I guess." Page leaned his back against the rail, grinned, and said, "I guess I'll have to come out and ask you, Miss Morgan—why in the world are you going to a godforsaken place like Virginia City?" His boyish charm broke through and he bantered, "Tell me to stay out of your business."

"I don't mind telling you," she said, laughing. "I'm a missionary. I'm going to our mission station for the Arapaho near Virginia City."

Doubt furrowed his brow. He hardly knew how to take her, for she was different from any woman he'd met. "Well now," he said, "I've got to admire your courage. It's a rough place in general, and the Arapaho are a treacherous band."

She smiled and said with forthrightness, "They need God, Mr. Page—all of us do."

He dropped his eyes and studied the deck as though doing research. "I suppose that's so." He found an excuse to leave, and she didn't see him again until the boat docked at Lewiston.

It was a lusty town, she sensed as she made her way along the rambling main street lined mostly with saloons. She found a room at the Gold Dollar Hotel—unfortunately over the bar, so there was little rest from the continuous tinny piano and the shrieking laughter of women. The next day she went downstairs and asked the clerk, "How can I get to Virginia City?"

The clerk looked at her strangely. "Why, I don't think that'll be too easy, ma'am," he said. "No railroad, of course—and no stage either. It's overland all the way."

"Could I hire someone to take me there in a wagon?"

The clerk rubbed his head nervously. "Let me see if I can find somebody. I'll get my relief to watch the desk."

"That's kind you are!" she smiled.

He was dazzled by her smile, and left at once.

I guess breakfast is next, she mused and entered the restaurant. Billy Page was already eating, and when he saw her, he stood up and smiled, "Join me, Miss Bronwen. I'm tired of my own company."

She accepted, saying, "My friends call me Bron."

"Never knew a girl named Bron. Call me Billy." He ordered her breakfast, and spoke of the country between Lewiston and Virginia City, then posed his questions in a way that evoked a response from her. She talked about her happy homelife in Wales, the deep green countryside, and lifestyle of her people. As she relaxed, her face softened, and she realized how much she missed it.

When she looked up, the clerk was heading for her table. "Sorry to interrupt, ma'am, but I thought you'd need to know." He shifted uncomfortably. "Jeb Taylor's got a team and wagon he'd sell you, but the problem is gettin' a man to drive you there. Don't think you could handle that job."

"Will you ask around for a man who'd be willing to take me?—I don't have much money."

The clerk was skeptical, but said, "Well, I'll see what I can find—but men are scarce right now. Gone to the gold diggings."

He turned and left the restaurant, and Billy said, "Bron, don't even think about making that trip alone."

"I may have to."

Page was not a man who cared greatly about the problems of others, but he felt a strange compulsion to help this young woman. Without debating the matter, he offered, "I'll drive the wagon for you, Bron."

"Would you, Billy?" She was surprised by his offer and gave him a warm smile. "It's kind of you it would be!"

Page asked, curious, "How do you know you can trust me? How do you know I won't knock you in the head and steal all your money?"

"Don't be silly. You're not that kind of man!"

"You don't know anything about me."

"Yes, I know you're kind to a girl who needs help."

"Bron, the world will stop and roll over for a beautiful woman. You could get plenty of men to drive you to Virginia City—but they'd all want a price from you."

She sobered and leaned forward to study his face. It was, she saw, not a weak face, but one that took life as it came. His manners with her told her that he was accustomed to being with women, and she went right to the heart of the question.

"Will *you* want a price from me, Billy?"

He flushed at her direct question, and gave a short laugh. "I've been called a womanizer, Bron—with some reason, I guess." He sobered as he looked at her questioning face. "But you don't have to be afraid of me."

"And so I'm not," she said, laughing gleefully. "Isn't it good of the Lord to put us on the same boat together, and then let us make the rest of the trip together?"

Page marveled at her simple trust. "I'd better go dicker for the team and wagon," he said, avoiding any further theological references. "We'll need to buy some grub and some cooking gear—and some blankets. And we better get a couple of tarps."

"Let me go with you," she urged, and they hurried out to collect their supplies. They spent the morning purchasing the team and wagon and the things they'd need on the trip. She took a keen interest in all of it, and as they walked about, Bron holding on to Billy's arm, he was aware of the envious looks of other men. She was oblivious to her beauty, he thought, and totally unaware of the instant effect she had on men who had not seen a woman like her for months.

By noon they had everything put together in the wagon, and she suggested, "Why not leave now, Billy? No sense paying another hotel bill. I've told the clerk you offered to drive me."

"Why not?"

They pulled out of Lewiston an hour later and camped that night in an abandoned house. It was a picnic for her, and he watched with a smile as she prepared the food as if nothing had ever given her more pleasure. After the meal, he moved to go outside to sleep in the wagon, but she shook her head, saying, "It's cold outside. There's plenty of room here."

He rolled up in his blankets across the room from her, and watched as she silently read from her Bible. After twenty minutes, she put the Bible aside, went to her own blankets, knelt there for about five minutes, then lay down, saying sleepily, "Good night, Billy!"

"Good night, Bron," he said, and wondered again at her audacity in trusting herself with a man she hardly knew.

The next day they reached the junction of the Palouse and turned northeast along a route heavily marked by travel. Two days later they were at Spokane and swung east, curling around the Coeur d'Alene Lake.

After this they left the open rolling land, with plenty of shelter in toll-ferry houses or lone horse camps, and hit the rough timbered heights of the Bitterroots. They forded creeks and slipped through deep mud. Five days out from Lewiston, they arrived at the summit of the Bitterroots and reached the St. Regis River. It rained that night, and they made their beds inside the wagon, wrapped in the tarps they had bought.

They followed the St. Regis, passed Hellgate, and soon saw peaks showing white high above them. At Deer Lodge they swung south, and ten days from Lewiston the country fell into long rolls. "That's Virginia City over there," Billy said.

At daybreak they were on the trail, and camped that night on the Beaverhead. As they sat around the campfire, she asked,

"Billy, what are you looking for?"

He grinned, his teeth white against his tanned cheeks. "I guess I just want to be rich and famous," he joked. Sobering, he said, "I don't know, Bron. Never think about such things. I want to have enough money to do what I like. A good meal, some nice clothes—a fine horse." He sipped the strong coffee, and gave her a direct glance. "I guess you think I'm a pretty worthless character."

"No. You're not worthless." Bron hugged her knees to her breast, and her eyes were green as glass by the light of the fire. "Jesus died for you—so that makes you worth more than anything in the world."

He studied her in silence, for she spoke often of Jesus—something no other person he knew had done. The fire crackled and popped and he shook his head. "You're something, Bron! What about you? What do you want?"

"I want to bring the gospel to the Indians."

"But is that all? Don't you want a husband and a family?"

She sat very still, lifted her face to the sky, and spoke haltingly. "I—I don't know, Billy. I had a man. We were to have been married when I got to Portland. But he died."

He had not known this, and considered her with a new interest. "You loved him?"

"Yes." She nodded slowly, and then said, "Yes, I did love him. I don't think I'll find another man to take his place."

"Makes it hard on the rest of us," Billy said.

She shook her head. "Good night, Billy." She rolled into her blankets and soon heard his regular breathing, but she did not sleep. She thought of Owen—his smile, his ready laugh, and his deep faith. "Oh, Owen, my own!" she whispered. "How can I go on without you?" She tried to pray, but for some reason it was difficult, and finally she fell into a fitful sleep.

The next day Billy drove the wagon down the drab and lifeless main street of Virginia City. "Let's go see Parris Pfouts," Billy said. "He's always trying to get a church started—so he'll know about the Indian Mission."

He pulled up in front of a store, leaped down and tied up the team, then helped her down. They entered the store, and Billy said, "Parris, come here. Got someone for you to meet."

"Ah, Billy—you've come back." The man shook hands and then looked inquiringly at the young woman. "Did you bring a bride back from Portland, Billy?"

"No such luck! This is Miss Bronwen Morgan. Miss Morgan, meet Parris Pfouts."

"It's happy I am to know you, Mr. Pfouts," Bronwen smiled at the merchant.

"She's come to work in the Indian Mission," Billy informed Pfouts. "Got all kinds of supplies and is raring to go."

The smile fell from Pfouts' face, and he said, "I'm happy to meet you, Miss Morgan. I've been waiting a long time for the missions board to send some workers, but—"

He hesitated, and Bronwen asked, "Is there a problem?"

Pfouts bit his lip and nodded. "I'm afraid so. Two months ago there was a fire at the mission."

"I see," Bron said. She studied his face. "How much damage did it do?"

Pfouts coughed and shook his head regretfully. "Everything is gone—the buildings, the supplies—everything."

"How'd it happen?" Billy asked.

"Nobody really knows, but it could have been a band of wandering Cheyenne. They've been feuding with the Arapaho, and it's the sort of thing they might do." He shook his shoulders and a smile came to him. "But there's plenty to be done, Miss Morgan. It's been hard trying to get a church going here, but you'll be a great help."

"It's glad I'll be to do what I can for the church here, Brother Pfouts," Bron said. "But God called me to go to the Indians— and to the Indians I will go, God be praised!"

Billy laughed at the expression on Pfouts' face. "She'll do it too, Parris! Those poor Arapaho don't have a chance against this lady preacher—buildings or no buildings!"

"God is more than a building, Billy," Bron smiled.

Pfouts thought, *Watch out, Montana. You've never seen the likes!*

CHAPTER NINE

BRON'S DREAM

★ ★ ★ ★

Billy Page beat the heavy snows by only two days. Had he not acted on his whim, the passes would have been closed. He had racked in a big win in a poker game in Helena, and decided on the spur of the moment to visit Virginia City to see how the lady preacher was doing. Despite the warnings of the stablehand about the impending blizzard, Billy saddled up and set off. He often acted on impulse, for he was a restless man, never satisfied to stay long in one place.

He circled around Elkhorn, rode through Homestake Pass, then followed the trail that paralleled the Ruby River. The Tobacco Roots shouldered their way upward in an ominous fashion, outlined against the somber gray sky that gave birth to the blizzards which sometimes raced across the country killing every living thing. Once or twice he thought how foolish it was to travel in such weather, well aware that many men had died when caught in the open by a blizzard. But that knowledge had little effect on Billy, for he was a man who had little fear of danger—in fact, he cared little for most things. If death overtook him, it was his time to go, and life was too short for a man to waste it hiding in a hole, dreading things that might never happen.

When he rode his horse into the stable, he knew he had pushed his luck almost too far. Boone Helm, the burly owner of the stable, called out, "Where in blazes you ride in from, Billy?"

"Helena," he said, his lips so numb he could hardly frame the word. Page had difficulty getting out of the saddle. His legs refused to obey his command, and when he finally struggled to the ground, they bent like rubber.

"You're crazy," Helm said, taking the reins of Billy's horse. "If you'd got caught out there, you'd be dead meat."

"Didn't get caught," he answered with a faint smile. He turned to go, then asked, "That girl still here, Boone? The one I drove in from Lewiston?"

Helm nodded glumly. "You should have left her there."

"Why? What's wrong with her?"

Helm stripped the saddle off the horse, cursed, and gave Page an angry look. "Thinks she's too good for a man," he snarled. "Going around preaching in saloons and handing out Bibles!"

Billy scratched his head, but said nothing. He made his way down the street to the Silver Moon, a saloon owned by Ned Ray, a short, stocky man with a black patch over his left eye. Ray looked up as Billy entered. "Hello, Page. Didn't know you were in town." He was a hard man, a mark of his trade and from spending several years in prison. Without being told, he set out a bottle and glass. "On the house."

Billy drank the whiskey, then another, letting the warmth soak into his bones. The room was well filled for that time of day. One of the customers, a slim, fine-looking man, approached the bar, and Ned Ray said, "This is J.W. Dillingham. Plummer just made him our deputy. Meet Billy Page."

Dillingham's blue eyes, set in a hawk-like face, scrutinized Billy. He acknowledged Page, set his hat on his neatly combed yellow hair, and drawled in an old Virginia accent as he left, "See you around, Page."

"He's a cut above most of Plummer's men, Ray," Billy remarked. He swallowed one more drink, and left the saloon to get a room at the hotel. He was so exhausted he slept soundly for three hours. When he awakened, he dressed and made his way to the Rainbow Cafe where he was pleased to find Bron having supper with Parris Pfouts.

"Billy!" Bron cried with a flash of pleasure in her eyes. "When did you get in?"

"This afternoon," he said, taking the chair Pfouts pushed at him. "Got bored in Helena."

Pfouts grinned. "Any man who'd leave Helena to come to Virginia City in the middle of a blizzard because he's bored hasn't got enough to do."

Blackie Taylor, the owner of the Rainbow, came over at once. The red-faced man had lost all but a fringe of hair around the back of his skull, but it didn't hinder his cooking. "Hello, Billy," he smiled. "What'll it be?"

"Steak and potatoes—and whatever kind of pie you've got, Blackie." As Taylor left, Billy leaned back in his chair, a gleam of humor in his eyes. "I hear you've been trying to convert Boone Helm, Bron. Any luck?"

Pfouts interrupted, growling, "He's no good. He stopped Bronwen on the street just outside the Silver Moon." His mild face was set with anger as he spoke, which was unusual for the man. "He put his hands on her—tried to drag her into the saloon."

Page frowned. "Helm ought to know better—but he's a rough one. What'd you do, Bron?"

"Why, I went with him into the Silver Moon."

"You didn't!"

"Yes, she did," Parris nodded. "I heard about it later from Doc Steele. He nearly laughed his head off."

"Doesn't sound so funny to me," Billy remarked. "Boone needs a lesson in manners."

"Oh, he got his lesson," Pfouts nodded, and smiled. "The way Steele tells it, as soon as Helm got Bronwen inside, she started preaching to the whole bunch. Just pulled out a Bible and let it fly! Quite a sermon."

"What did Helm do?" Billy asked.

"Tried to shut her up—but Dillingham put a stopper on him," Parris answered. "He's a new deputy—and a decent one for a change. He just set Helm down and told the whole crowd if they didn't want to listen, they could leave."

Page laughed and cast an admiring glance at Bron. "Didn't Ned Ray act up? He's a pretty tough guy."

"Not as tough as Dillingham, I guess. He just stood there, Doc said, and listened with the rest."

"Pretty tough congregation, eh, Bron?" Page asked. "Anybody get converted?"

"No, not then. But two of the men began coming to church," Bron said. "We had over twenty last Sunday, didn't we, Parris?"

"It's going well. If we can get you and the hermit to come, we'll know the church is really prospering."

"Hermit? That fellow Zack Winslow living up the gulch? I haven't seen him." He bit into his steak. "What's he look like? An old geezer with a beard down to his knees?"

"Oh no," Pfouts shook his head. "He's a slight fellow, not bad looking. Got the lightest blue eyes I ever saw—and the middle finger of his right hand is gone. Only odd thing about him is his hat. He wears pretty ordinary clothes, but a fancy derby— English type." He told them about the Indian woman and Buck.

"He's pretty crowded for a hermit," Bron said.

"He was sorta forced into it, Bron," Parris shrugged. "He's a pretty hard chap. Doesn't trust anyone."

"He can't be too tough," Billy observed, "if he lets himself in for taking care of people."

"That's true," Parris agreed.

Parris and Bron continued the discussion, talking about the church. Their animated conversation made Page feel excluded. Pfouts was not a handsome man, Billy noted, but he was neat and well-off—even more significantly, the most active Christian in town. The latter, Page knew, would be important to Bron Morgan. *Wouldn't be too surprised if Pfouts didn't make her forget the man she lost*, Page mused.

"What are we going to do about the Mize children, Parris?"

"Emmett's kids?" Billy interjected. "What's the matter with them?"

Pfouts shook his head. "The woman left him a month ago— without a word. That was bad, but two weeks ago, Emmett was shot to death."

Billy lifted his eyebrows in surprise. "Who did it, Parris?"

"Nobody knows for sure. Most of us reckon it was Ad Cantrell. Mize had given him a bad beating a while back. Cantrell was running around after the Mize girl, Lillian. But there was no evidence. Dillingham's investigating, but it could have been anybody. Mize was on his way home in the middle of the night, dead drunk as usual. He was found the next morning in an alley with a bullet in his back and his money gone."

"Ad would be up to that, I guess." Billy glanced at Bron. "Little different from Wales, eh?"

"People are murdered in Wales, too, Billy." She turned the topic back to that of the children. "They've got to have some help, Parris. Did you know they've been served notice to move out of their house?"

"I suppose that's some of Ray's doing," Pfouts spewed angrily. "He owns the place."

"He rented it to a man named Parker for storage," Bron said. "The children have to be out in a week."

"That'll be Christmas, won't it?" Page noted. "Not much of a Christmas present for kids."

Parris rose. "Come on over to the store, Bron. I'll get some food to take to them. We'll find some way to help."

"I've had a little luck," Billy said, taking some bills out of his pocket and giving two of them to Bron. "Maybe this will help some."

"Thank you, Billy," Bron said with a smile and left the Rainbow with Pfouts.

"Billy has a good heart, doesn't he?" she commented as the two walked along.

Parris nodded. "Yes, but he's wasting his life. Does nothing but gamble and—and other things."

"Women, I suppose?"

"Why, yes, he's known for that."

"He's a handsome fellow," Bron remarked. The cold bit at her lips and cheeks, and she drew her scarf tighter around her neck. "Women would be drawn to him."

"You seem to have a pretty extensive knowledge of man's sins, Bronwen," he said. "For a young woman who's not been in the world, you see it very clearly."

"Why, people are the same, Parris, as I told Billy. Some cover their sins better—but we're all lost. Men like Boone Helm and whoever it was that shot Emmett Mize are dramatic. Their sins are wicked. But I needed Jesus just as much as they do now."

The cold wind bit into his hands and Pfouts shoved them into his pockets. "You're right, of course. Billy is such a likable chap, sometimes it's hard to remember that he needs saving just as much as Helm."

After buying some food at the store, they walked to the Oriental, where the Mize children lived. Parris knocked on the door and it opened slowly. Aghast at the scene before him, Parris exclaimed, "Why, Paul!" Paul Mize was wrapped in a dirty blanket, his face pinched and lips pale. "It's freezing in here! Why don't you have a fire?"

He didn't answer, and Bron said, "Parris, you make a fire. Where's Alice, Paul?"

He pointed to the broken-down sofa. Bron hurried over to the blanket-shrouded little form. Pulling back the cover, she stared at the disheveled four-year-old peering up with large questioning eyes. "Hullo," the child said faintly, her body shaking from the cold.

"You poor thing," Bron said and gathered her up and carried her over to the stove, where Parris had the beginnings of a fire going. "Where's Lillian, Paul?" Bron asked, holding the girl's hands close to the stove.

"She went out."

"Went out? Where did she go?"

"I don't know."

Bron gave Parris a quick glance. "I'll fix them some supper. And I think I'd better stay here tonight."

"Yes, perhaps so."

The children were huddling around the stove, but lest they hear, Pfouts lowered his voice. "This is horrible! I'll go find the girl."

Bron fixed some eggs for the children, and talked to them as they ate, hungrily shoving the food into their mouths as if they were starved. By the time they had finished, the warmth of the room hit them, and soon both were sound asleep on the couch.

She washed the dishes, then sat and waited. Two hours went by, and finally the door opened and Parris came in with Lillian. The girl's face was seething with anger.

"I found her with Harry Ide," Parris stormed.

"You got no right to boss me around!" the girl yelled, tossing her head back and staring at them defiantly. "You ain't no kin of mine!"

"Lillian," Bron said gently, "Paul and Alice could have frozen to death."

Lillian flushed but said defensively, "I left a fire in the stove."

"You were gone long enough to let it die down," Parris said. He was angry with the girl and showed it. "You can't leave two children alone with a fire, don't you know that?"

"Parris," Bron interjected, "why don't we talk about this in the morning? I'll stay here tonight."

"Nobody needs you!" Lillian cried.

"I think you *do*," Bron countered.

Lillian whirled and ran out of the door leading to the back.

"I'll try to talk to her, but I don't see how they can live alone, Parris."

"I know. I'll see what I can do."

As soon as Parris left, Lillian came out, her face a mixture of resentment and guilt. She had been so glad to get away from the responsibilities thrust at her that she had welcomed Harry's invitation for a meal at the cafe. Time had slipped by and she had forgotten about Paul and Alice until Pfouts had come and almost dragged her out.

"I wasn't doing nothin' wrong," she said defensively to Bron. Her face, though pretty, was worn with the strain of the past few days. She had slept little, wondering what would happen to them. Now it was catching up with her.

"I'm sure you weren't, Lillian," Bron soothed. "Would you like me to fix you something to eat?"

"No." Lillian fully expected the woman to scold her, but when Bron began to talk about the blizzard and how it would make things harder for them, she said, "You're some kind of a preacher, ain't you?"

"Yes. I'm a missionary."

"What's that?"

Bron told her about God's call on her life and the desire to bring the gospel to the Indians.

"Why do you want to go to them?" Lillian demanded. "They're nothin' but a bunch of wild savages."

"But God doesn't see them that way," Bron said gently. "He loves them, just as He loves you, Lillian."

"God don't love me!" Anger flared in the girl's eyes, and she shook her head, adding, "If He did, he wouldn't let bad things happen to all of us."

Bron prayed silently, then began to speak about the love of Jesus. The girl listened, but her face expressed a hard light of doubt. She had been so mistreated by her father that kindness was foreign to her.

Finally Bron said, "My, it's late! Let's go to bed."

"We only got the one bed—in the back room."

"Would you share it with me?"

"I—I guess so."

Bron built up the fire, checked the children to see if they were covered up, and then she and the girl went to bed. The room was so cold that neither one removed her clothes. They snugged the blankets around their faces and bade each other good night.

For a long time Bron lay awake, praying for some answer to the problem. If this had happened in her village, there would have been relatives or friends to help care for the children. But this Montana was a different world, she had discovered. It was a savage place, much like the storm that prowled the country like a hungry wolf. She drifted off to sleep thinking of possibilities for helping the Mize children, but none seemed to fit.

Toward morning Bron awakened with a start. A dream—simple, but vivid.

She lay quietly for a while, then got up and went into the front room. The fire was low so she added more wood and sat nearby, thinking about her dream. When the children awakened, she fixed them a hot breakfast, and left them in Lillian's care, saying, "I'm going to get some more blankets."

Bron stepped out into the frigid air, shivering at the cold assault. The fresh snow crunched under feet as she made her way down the street. By the time she got to the hotel she was numb. She washed her face, changed clothes and went to the Rainbow for coffee. As she sipped the hot liquid, Parris joined her.

"I haven't found anything yet—for the children, I mean," he said. "We may have to send them to Helena or someplace."

"An orphanage?"

"May come to that."

"Let's pray about it first," she said. "I think Lillian is sorry about leaving Paul and Alice."

"She's an emotional wreck. Can't be trusted to raise those children."

"She needs help, Parris, but we must wait on God."

For three days she did just that, praying much. The blizzard subsided, and although it was cold, it was not the killing kind. As the sullen earth warmed itself with a pale white December sun, Bron nourished the dream she'd had. Though she shared it with no one, it was always just beneath the surface of her conscious thought.

Like the Welsh and the Irish, she was sensitive to dreams. Both races have produced more than their share of dreamers, and Bron would often lie awake and think of the tales she had grown up with. Her uncle David had dreamed of his death in great detail two months before he died. Many times her grandmother Margaret, whom she greatly admired, had found an answer to a problem through a dream, despite her strong conservative Christian faith. She never failed to express her fierce faith in the Bible—from "cover to cover."

Bron remembered Margaret telling her once, "God has many ways to speak to people, and if He chooses to speak to someone in a dream, what then, my Bronwen? If the scholars make fun of such, no matter. Hang on to your dreams, for the voice of Jehovah may be in them!"

Three days before Christmas, Bronwen Morgan made up her mind that her dream was a direction from God. But even then she did not speak of it. As good a man as she knew Parris Pfouts to be, he would not understand—nor would any other person in Virginia City.

She prayed that God would show her how to carry out the dream, but nothing presented itself—until the day before Christmas.

When she stepped into Pfouts' store that day, he was talking with an Indian. "This is Fox," Pfouts said. "He's a member of the Arapaho tribe that lives near where the mission was. Some of his people went there."

Bronwen was stunned by the sudden encounter with one of the people for whom she had left her home. She took a deep breath and nodded. "I'm glad to know you, Fox. I've come all the way from across the big water to try to help your people."

Fox fastened his keen eyes on her. "Good. Much hunger now. Need help."

The direct reply took Bron off guard, but with it an idea flashed into her mind concerning the dream. "Your people need food."

"Need food bad!"

"Very well, they shall have it." She turned to Parris. "I've got some money left—about a hundred dollars. Get that much food ready and I'll bring the wagon around."

Astonished, he asked in alarm, "You don't have the notion of delivering it yourself?"

"Why not? Didn't I come here to help? Doesn't the Bible say that if we see our brothers hungry, we are to feed them?"

"I'll go with you," Pfouts offered.

"No, I need to do this alone. Fox, will you take me to your camp?"

He had followed this exchange perfectly and nodded. "I take."

Within an hour Bron was back. Parris argued against her rash decision. "You could get killed, Bronwen!"

"So if they kill me," she laughed, "they could do it only once! And if they did, I'd be in the presence of the Lord—so load the wagon, Parris, and praise the Lord with me for the chance to serve Him in this way."

When the wagon was loaded, she got into the seat and took the lines. "I've only driven a pony cart," she said. "But it's all the same, I guess. Goodbye, Parris."

He was distressed, but there was nothing he could do. "Fox, you rascal!" he said. "You watch Miss Bronwen, you hear me?"

"I watch!" he grinned. He nudged his mount and led the way down the almost deserted street.

Dillingham had gotten wind of the venture and had stopped to watch the departure. "The lady preacher leaving us, Pfouts?" he asked.

"Going to take some stuff to the Indians."

"Why, that's right bold of her!" the deputy exclaimed.

"Too bold," Pfouts grunted. He found it difficult to work the rest of the day, and when Blackie Taylor brought him a note at five o'clock he snapped, "What's this, Blackie?"

"Note from Miss Morgan," he said. "She told me not to give it to you before five." He watched as Pfouts opened and read the message. "Ain't no bad news, is it, Parris?"

Pfouts seemed stunned. "I don't know whether it's good or bad, Blackie." When Taylor left, he read the note again and again.

Dear Parris:

I am sorry to have deceived you, but this is something I must do. You would not agree, I know, so I am taking the responsibility from you for what I plan.

You and I have prayed much about what to do with the Mize children. I believe God gave me direction in a dream the first night I stayed with them.

It was a simple dream, but very vivid. I saw myself and the three children huddled together in fear. We were weeping because of a dark shadow creeping toward us. The closer it came, the more frightened we were, and I began to cry out to God for help.

Just as this huge ugly shadow was about to swallow us, I saw a man standing in the sunshine. When I looked at him, he motioned me to come, saying, "Bring the children." Immediately I jumped up and we began to run. He kept his arms outstretched. Just as we reached him, the shadow vanished, and I awoke.

Parris, the man in the dream was the one you described to Billy Page, the man named Winslow! He was exactly as you related—slight of stature, with bright blue eyes. He wore the English derby you mentioned, and when he lifted his hands, I saw that the right middle finger was missing.

I am taking the children with me to the Indian village. After we have delivered the food, I will ask Fox to take me to Winslow. What he will do, I can't say. That is up to God.

I'm sure you think this is wrong, but I have struggled over the interpretation of the dream for several days. I must do this.

Sincerely,
Bronwen Morgan

CHAPTER TEN

"GOD BROUGHT US HERE!"

★ ★ ★ ★

Black Pigeon stared at the crowd gathered around the wagon, then turned his eyes to Bronwen as she stepped to the ground. She approached him slowly, allowing him to take in her appearance—white skin, red hair, green eyes. Finally he said to Fox, "What is this woman?"

"She Jesus woman," Fox replied. "She say she come long way to help our people."

"It is time white eyes help us," Black Pigeon said abruptly. He was a clear thinker, and though he nourished a bitterness against anyone with white skin, he could see—unlike some of the more explosive chiefs—that the lands of his people were slowly being disposed of.

"Ask her what she want."

When Fox relayed the question, Bron said, "I have heard that the Arapaho are hungry, so I have brought food. Accept it in the name of the Lord Jesus Christ. It is all yours, except for the one box behind the seat."

When Fox translated this, Black Pigeon said, "I thank you for my people." He turned to a squaw standing behind him and gave her orders. To Fox he said, "Who these?" He gestured toward the Mize children in the wagon.

"Some children who have no one," Fox answered.

"Tell them come to my lodge."

At Fox's urging, Bron spoke to the children. "Come along, now," she urged.

"They'll scalp us all!" Lillian whimpered. From the moment she had discovered they were going to the Indian camp, she had been petrified with fear, and now clung to Bron's arm.

"Don't be silly," Bron chided, and the three followed her into the tepee. It was dark, and the acrid smell of smoke curling upward stung their nostrils. A hole in the peak of the tepee was directly over the fire burning in the center of the floor. Bron sat down awkwardly, and the children huddled close.

"Tell the chief I am sorry that I don't speak the language of his people—but say that I will soon learn."

Fox gave Black Pigeon's answer. "The white eyes do not think it important to speak our language."

"I do!" Bron insisted. "As soon as possible the mission will be rebuilt. Then the children can learn to read and write."

Fox repeated this, then gave the chief's answer. "He say it not good for our people to leave old ways. It is better for young men to hunt, not read."

Bron was wise enough not to point out that the old days were no more. "Perhaps there will be other ways I can help."

Fox spoke to the chief, then to Bron. "Black Pigeon say he remember when other Jesus people come. They say Jesus God is better than our gods."

"Jesus is the great God, Chief," Bron replied. "Perhaps when I have proved myself a friend to the Arapaho, you will let me tell you more about Him?"

Her politeness surprised both Fox and Black Pigeon. "This one is wiser than some," Black Pigeon said to Fox in their tongue, a light of approval flickering in his dark eyes. "Say I will listen when that time comes. Now, we will eat."

While the meal was being prepared, Bron and the children walked around the camp, escorted by Fox and followed every-where by members of the tribe. The food was strictly controlled and distributed fairly by Black Pigeon's squaw. All around the camp cooking fires were glowing and the squaws laughing and talking. "It good to hear my people laugh," Fox remarked. Some of the squaws came to examine Bronwen at close range, and the tall Indian smiled at one of the questions.

"What did she ask?" Bron wanted to know.

"She wonder if you white all over like on face," he told her. When her face flushed red, he said, "White woman not like Indian. We one color—you sometime red, sometime white. Maybe something else all over."

Bronwen surmised he was teasing her, so smiled. Some of the smaller children edged in, and soon they had engaged Paul in a game. As they sat down and waited for the meal, Alice ran around pursuing a puppy, but Lillian stuck as close to Bronwen as possible.

"How long do we have to stay here?" she whispered.

"After we eat, we'll go."

The food preparation seemed to take forever, and it was late by the time Fox said, "We eat now." Bron and the children again went inside Black Pigeon's tepee, where they were given clay bowls. Black Pigeon reached out for Bron's bowl, dipped it into the bubbling contents of the black kettle on the fire and handed it back to her. As he served the others, himself last, Bron was faced with the problem of how to eat stew without a spoon. She watched Fox tip the bowl so the stew fell into his mouth. It was very hot, and Bron burned her lips with the first bite. The taste was good but she didn't recognize it—something like beef stew, but stronger. She helped Alice, but the other children seemed to manage, and they all ate hungrily.

The Indians devoured the food and refilled their bowls from the pot so often Bron knew they must have been on low rations for some time.

Bron finished her bowl, and when Fox asked if she wanted more, she shook her head. She was still a little hungry but was reluctant to take any more in light of the tribe's great need.

"Your wife is a good cook, Black Pigeon. What sort of stew is it?"

Fox asked, then when the squaw answered he turned and said, "Puppy stew. Very good."

Bron felt her stomach lurch, thinking of the small puppy Alice had played with, but she kept a smile frozen on her face. Lillian, on the other hand, gasped and dropped her bowl. Bronwen quickly picked it up and spoke to Fox. "Pease tell the chief that we have been honored to eat in his lodge, but we must go."

"You go now?" Fox asked in surprise.

"Yes, but you must help me. We must go to the cabin of the man called Winslow. You know it?"

"I know," he said and told the chief.

"Black Pigeon say too late to go. Be dark when you get there."

"I know, but we must. Will you take us?"

Fox shrugged, but felt a debt to the white woman, so got to his feet. "We go quick."

Bron shook hands with the chief and his wife, who was much surprised. Then they got into the wagon. As Fox came back on his pony, several of the Indians clustered around, chattering.

"They say 'thank you' to Jesus woman," Fox said, then called out, "We go quick," and led the way out of the camp down the trail.

As they passed through the pines, zigzagging to avoid the large boulders pushing their way through the thin soil, Lillian asked, "It's almost dark. How far is it to where we're going?"

Bron had no idea, but she tried to be as cheerful as possible. "Not too far." Her own faith faltered as the darkness closed in. Back in Virginia City she had been certain God wanted her to bring the children to Winslow, but now doubts began to gnaw at her. *What will I do if he refuses to let us in for the night?*

Fox kept up a quick pace, leading them across a narrow trail that overhung the sheer face of a cliff.

Lillian cried out in fear, but Bron had no choice but to follow the Indian. When they reached safety, she murmured, "Thank you, God!"

Fox turned his head. "Not far now."

An hour later, he stopped and pointed. "There is cabin." Yellow lights penetrated the darkness. "I go now, you bet," Fox said, wheeling his pony and disappearing into the thickets.

"Well," Bron said, "let's go meet Mr. Zacharias Winslow!"

★　★　★　★

"There he is—right in front of that old log."

Buck strained his eyes but couldn't see the rabbit Zack pointed at. The two had left at two o'clock to go hunting. The game bag pulled at Buck's shoulder, heavy with the six rabbits they had bagged. It was his first hunt, but he had shot two of them himself, and now stood there anxious for another.

"I can't see nothin', Zack," he whispered.

"Get your rifle up. I'll flush him out and as soon as he takes off, shoot." Zack slowly reached down and picked up a rock, then threw it toward the old log. Before Buck's startled eyes, what he had taken for a bunch of dried grass exploded into action—and a gray jackrabbit streaked across the broken field.

Buck fired, but just as he pulled the trigger, the rabbit cut. There was no time for disappointment because two explosions at the boy's side jolted him, and the rabbit dropped. He whirled just as Zack replaced his pistol in the black holster he wore. Amazed, Buck whispered, "Gosh, Zack! I didn't know you could shoot like that!"

"Lucky shot," Zack said.

But as Zack walked over to pick up the rabbit, Buck was doubtful. He knew Winslow was a first-rate shot with a rifle—but this wasn't luck.

"A man wouldn't have much chance against you in a gun-fight," he said as he took the rabbit and stuffed it into the bag.

"Rabbits don't shoot back," Zack shrugged. "Lots of fellows in my outfit were good marksmen. Could hit the center of the target right smart. But when the Rebs came charging across the field at us and the minie balls started whistling, some of the best shots at a target couldn't even shoot. Anyway, this took two shots—and a real marksman needs only one."

"But he was moving so fast!" Buck cried.

"Well, the trick with a rabbit—or a duck in flight—is that you don't shoot at 'em, Buck. You shoot where they're going to be." Zack asked, "How many we got?"

"Seven."

"That's a lucky number. Guess we better get back and skin these critters."

"We going to fry 'em, Zack?"

"Nope. I got my mouth all set for some rabbit stew."

As they walked back, Zack asked, "You know what tomorrow is?"

"Why, Tuesday, ain't it?"

"It's Wednesday, but it's Christmas."

Buck shrugged. "Reckon it is."

"Don't seem interested. Guess you haven't been too happy at Christmas, Buck."

"Just another day most of the time. Once at the orphanage some people came and gave us candy and a toy apiece." A smile lit up his face. "I got a toy dog. He was all white and fuzzy, so I named him Whitey. Used to sleep with him—" The boy broke off abruptly, shooting a glance at Winslow, but Zack seemed to be paying little attention. "Anyway, somebody stole him the next week."

Zack had picked up bits and pieces of Buck's history, giving him a good idea of the barren life the boy had led. He made no comment, for he knew Buck was as sensitive as a girl. Instead he said, "You know, we ought to go toward Bannack and try to pick up an elk." He began to make plans, being careful to treat the boy as an equal, and by the time they got back to the cabin, Buck was excited about the proposed hunting trip.

When they got to the cabin, Zack showed Buck how to skin, clean and dress the rabbits. "Might as well save the hides. We'll make some stretch boards tomorrow." As they worked, Zack instructed him, "Watch for anything that looks like a big lump. A man can get Rocky Mountain fever from a rabbit that's got a tick under his hide. Bad business!"

When they were finished, he said, "Let's boil these things out here in the big pot, Buck. You gather the sticks for the fire and I'll get some seasoning."

"You had good luck," Choiya said as Zack entered the cabin. She had been watching from the window and seemed angry. She was like that, Zack had discovered—calm one moment, angry and cold the next. In a flash she would turn her back and shut everything out.

He wondered why she was angry but made no comment.

"I cooked supper—but I suppose you don't want it," she said stiffly.

Then he understood. "Oh no! You're wrong about that! Soon as Buck and I get these rabbits in the pot, you'll see." He grabbed the salt and some other seasoning from the shelf and went out to Buck.

"Get a light from the fireplace—but watch out for Choiya,"

he warned. "She's on the warpath."

"What's she mad about now?"

"Who knows?" Zack shrugged. "She's cooked us some supper, so be sure you brag on it a lot. We'll eat it along with this rabbit stew. Bad business having to live with a cantankerous female!"

"I didn't know Indian women were so fussy."

"They *all* are, boy!" Zack said, a martyr's expression on his face. "Touchy as a blamed rattler that's just shed his skin—the whole bunch of 'em!" His voice carried the anger he felt.

Supper that night was strained. Choiya had tried to make biscuits, but they were a failure, tough and flat. Both Buck and Zack choked a couple down. "Need to add a little yeast to your dough next—" Zack began, then stopped when he saw the fury his advice brought. He ate some of the venison she had cooked and the stew he and Buck had prepared.

After they finished the meal, Zack pulled out a copy of Charles Dickens' *Oliver Twist* and sat down to read. He loved to read and thought anyone who couldn't read was cut off from the world. Whenever he and Buck went to town, they'd bring more books back.

The air was heavy with suppressed rage, but Zack continued to read as Choiya moved about the cabin, venting her resentment on the pots and pans.

Buck didn't know how to take the Indian woman, so he just kept quiet and concentrated on cleaning the rifle and Zack's pistol. Buck and Choiya had kept their distance from the beginning, speaking only rarely.

Zack glanced up at them, then shrugged and plunged into the book, soon lost in the misfortunes of the character.

"What's your book about?"

Startled to find Buck watching him, Zack shifted in his chair, looked at Choiya who was rocking Samuel, trying to get him to sleep, and said, "Why, it's about a boy named Oliver."

"Is he rich?"

"Well, no. He's got no father, and when his mother dies, he's put in an orphanage. Later on he goes to London and gets in with the wrong bunch of people. They make a thief out of him."

Buck stared at him. "What do you want to read a book like

that for? If I could read, I bet I could find a story better'n that!"

Zack realized that Buck's life paralleled poor Oliver's, and he didn't know how to answer. Finally he said, "Well, Buck, I don't know why people write books like this. But I've read a few like you're talking about, where everything always come out all right. Nobody gets hurt or dies or has any trouble." He shook his head. "When I read that kind of book, I keep thinking, 'But things just aren't *like* that!' "

"So what if they aren't?" Buck challenged. He leaned forward, his face intent. "It's bad enough to have to go through hard times. I don't see any sense in readin' about other people havin' to go through them."

"Well, I've read a couple of this fellow's books, and in both of them the hero always came out pretty well in the end." He smiled. "I'll let you know as soon as I finish the book."

"Someone is coming." Choiya's voice sounded a warning, and Zack jumped up and plucked the pistol from the peg. "Stay in the house," he ordered, then stepped outside.

He took station beside the cabin and listened. The snow muffled the sounds, but soon he heard a horse blow, and out of the darkness emerged a shape. He waited, holding the cocked gun at his side. *Not Indians,* he thought. *But who else would be way out here this time of night?*

He waited until the shape turned into a team pulling a wagon, which stopped in front of the house. The light from the front window revealed a driver and one other on the seat, but he could not tell anything from the bundled figure. He stepped cautiously out from the side of the cabin and called, "Who are you?"

The driver turned to face him. "I'm looking for Zacharias Winslow."

A *woman*! Shocked, he lowered the gun and peered at her. "I'm Winslow. Who are you—and what in God's name are you doing up in these hills in this weather?"

"May I get down?"

"Come into the house," he said gruffly.

"I'm not alone. I've got three children with me."

"Just what I need," Zack blurted out. "Bring 'em in, lady. This is Winslow's Haven for Strays—we never close!" He knew he was behaving badly, but again he was faced with the unexpected.

"Lillian, if you can take Alice, I'll carry Paul," the driver said as she stepped down.

The young girl moved to the back, reached down, picked up a bundle, and handed it to the woman on the ground. Then she picked up another, climbed out of the wagon, and they walked into the cabin.

The visitors huddled together just inside the door, anxiously eyeing Buck, who was still holding the rifle he had grabbed.

"I'm Bronwen Morgan, Mr. Winslow," the woman said. "These are the Mize children—Lillian, Paul here, and that's Alice."

"Hello, Lillian," Zack said.

The girl gaped at them, dumbfounded. She remembered the man and Buck's visit to the Oriental.

"How'd you get lost?" Zack went on.

"Lost? We're not lost, Mr. Winslow."

"But—what in the name of heaven are you doing here? There's nothing here, Miss Morgan—no town or anything!"

"You're here," the woman said quietly.

Zack glanced at Choiya, who was studying the visitors with an unreadable expression.

"How did you find this place?" Zack asked. "What do you want?"

Bronwen took a deep breath. "God brought us here, Mr. Winslow," she replied, watching the effect of her words. Unbelief flickered in his eyes, but she went on. "And I want you to let these children stay for a time."

Flabbergasted, he eyed her in stony silence. Finally he sighed in resignation. "All right—for now. You're sure there're no more in the wagon?"

"No," Bronwen answered. "This is all."

"Well, maybe you can go back into town for another load tomorrow," Zack said sarcastically. "I'll put the team up." He stalked out, with Buck at his heels.

Bronwen wanted to cry, hurt at his words. She looked at Choiya, who stood mutely watching as she held the baby. "I'm sorry for intruding," Bron said, then turned to Lillian. "I'll get the blankets."

The frigid air seemed to close around her heart as she moved toward the wagon. Her prayer felt dead. What about her dream? Could she have been wrong?

CHAPTER ELEVEN

JUST FOR A FEW DAYS

★ ★ ★ ★

Bronwen entered the cabin with the blankets piled high in her arms, humiliated but determined. She looked at the Indian woman, who had moved to the window, and said, "My name is Bron. What is yours?"

A slight hesitation, then a brief answer. "Choiya."

Bron noted the hard light in the woman's eyes, but did not give any indication of it. "I know we're going to crowd you, Choiya, but we'll try to be as little trouble as possible. Do you think we might have that corner over there to make our beds?"

"It's not my house," Choiya said, every word loaded with resentment.

Bron smiled and nodded her head toward Lillian. "Let's make some beds for the children." When she had finished she called to Paul, "Come, you and Alice can sleep here," pointing to a spot.

Paul shook his head. "Not sleepy." He was standing close to the fire with Alice beside him. Both had slept on the way from Black Pigeon's camp and weren't in the least bit tired. They gazed at Choiya with inquisitive eyes.

Hawk began to kick, and Alice walked across the room. She looked up at Choiya and smiled, "Baby?" She reached out to touch Hawk's face, and laughed when the baby caught her little finger. "Look, Lillian!" she cried. "See the baby?"

Lillian was not fond of Indians, having heard nothing good about them from anyone, and she spoke sharply. "Alice, leave that baby alone." Instantly she felt the weight of Choiya's eyes, but met her gaze defiantly.

The cabin door swung open, and Zack entered, followed closely by Buck. Both of them felt the tension in the room, and Zack nodded with satisfaction. He wasn't going to make it easy. "Well, are you ladies getting acquainted?"

Ignoring his question, Bron said, "Thank you for unhitching the team, Mr. Winslow. I don't think I could have managed that."

Zack grunted and walked over to the fireplace. He poured himself a cup of coffee and gazed into the fire.

The silence grew heavy. Finally Buck said, "I guess maybe you folks are hungry."

Bron smiled at him gratefully. "We ate in the Indian camp— but the children might be hungry."

"I reckon there's plenty of that rabbit stew, ain't there, Zack?" Buck asked. He took Zack's nod, then said, "We're a little shy on plates—but I reckon we can rig something."

He turned to the meager supply of plates and tableware and began setting them on the table. Bron, relieved at the break in silence, said, "Let me help you. What's your name?"

"Buck."

Bron extended her hand. "It's Bronwen, I am."

She was very pretty, and he was rattled by her closeness. To cover his confusion, he said, "You don't talk like folks around here."

"No, I come from Wales."

"Wales?" he asked. "Where's that?"

"Far over the sea, Buck. It's part of Britain." As they set the table, she sensed Zack's cold indifference. *He's built himself a wall and is firmly behind it,* she thought. Fear crept into her throat, but she forced it down, saying a quick prayer, then calling out, "Come, now, let's try some of this fine stew."

Paul dashed to the table, but Alice didn't want to leave the Indian baby, so Lillian had to pick up the four-year-old and put her on the chair. Buck served the stew, spooning out portions into every bowl, plate or cup, then joined them.

Once more an awkward silence filled the cabin, and Bron asked, "Won't you two join us?" When Zack shook his head and Choiya made no response, she said, "Well it's grateful I am for this fine food! Let's thank the good Lord for bringing us safely here."

She bowed her head and began to pray. The rest just gaped as she asked a simple blessing on the food. Lillian glanced at Buck, his surprise equaling hers. Their eyes met. Then he blushed and ducked his head. Zack seemed preoccupied with the fire, his face stony. Choiya glared with icy indifference.

"Amen!" Bron finished, appearing oblivious to their reaction. She took a bite of stew and exclaimed in delight, "This is delicious!" Paul and Alice followed suit, both finally abandoning the spoons and turning the cups up to their lips.

Lillian tasted it hesitantly. "Oh," she said, "it's better than what we had at the Indian camp."

"What was that?" Buck asked.

"I don't think I even want to say it," she answered. She shot a quick glance at Choiya and added, "It was awful! Stew made out of puppies! I don't see how they stand it—but I guess Indians will eat anything."

Zack grinned, noting the flush of anger in Choiya's face, but Buck was embarrassed at the obvious slur and tried to cover it up. "Well, I ate an armadillo once—and I'd rather have puppy anytime."

"What's an armadillo?" Bron asked. She, too, was uncomfortable by Lillian's actions, but hoped she would change in time. After Buck's description, Bron said, "I think I'd rather not try one of those, but I've heard that the French eat snails," and she laughed—full, rich, deep laughter. "I suppose since all things are made by God, we should be willing to eat anything."

Bron ate little, but drank the strong coffee Buck offered her and tried to sort out the situation she had created, wondering if God was really leading her.

After the meal was finished and the table cleared, Zack picked up *Oliver Twist* and sat down at the table. For the next hour, he kept his nose in the book, ignoring the activities around him. The arrival of the last "guests" had shattered the relative peace of his life, and he was resentful. To some degree he had adjusted to the others, and had accepted the fact that Choiya and Hawk were part of the price he had to pay for agreeing to care for Samuel. He had also decided to keep Buck—but to be invaded by a horde of uninvited children and another woman was too much! He was determined to have it out with her, but would wait until they could talk privately.

Oliver Twist was no pleasure to him tonight, and he finally snapped the book shut, replaced it, and jumped up into the loft.

Bron had busied herself with the children, washing off some of the travel grime from their faces while furtively watching Winslow. His stiff back and the stubborn cast of his face told her he'd get rid of them as soon as possible. But she said nothing to Lillian as they put the younger children to bed.

Nervous at finding himself alone with three women, Buck scurried up the ladder he had made. "See you in the morning," he said, pulling the ladder after him.

"Good night, Buck." Bron felt less secure with the only friendly voice gone.

She didn't want to retire yet, and was surprised and happy to see a Bible on top of the mantel. "I left my Bible in the wagon," she said to Choiya. "I'd like to read a bit. Do you think he'd mind?"

Choiya was nursing Samuel and didn't care much what Bron wanted to do. She shrugged, "I told you—it's not my house."

Bron read a chapter and then undressed and slipped in beside Lillian, aware of Choiya's constant watchful eyes.

The physical activity in the cabin ceased—but not the minds of the inhabitants. If their thoughts had taken form, both the lower cabin and the loft would have exploded from the weight.

ZACK: *Tomorrow I'll have it out with her. She planned it pretty well—waiting until after dark to come in—knew I couldn't send those kids on their way at night! She's too bossy, that's what! Good looking, though. I'll give her that. Never saw such red hair and those green eyes are somethin'.*

But she's got to go—all of them do. I wonder if Parris put her up to it? No, he wouldn't do that. He told me she was a preacher . . . never heard of a woman preacher . . . but preacher or not—tomorrow they all go! By heaven, a hermit's got some rights!

BUCK: *Zack sure is mad, by gosh! I don't see why he has to be so* mean. 'Course he's set on bein' a hermit, and it sure does make it hard with a bunch of kids around. Feel sorry for them—they could wind up in an orphanage, and that'd be the ruination of 'em! That gal, Lillian—she sure is a looker! Zack'll send 'em all packin' tomorrow!

LILLIAN: *Why did I ever listen to that lunatic woman preacher? I must be crazier than she is! Eating dog stew! . . . That man Winslow, he's got a mean streak. He ain't very big but he's got a look about him I don't like. . . . I got to get away from here. Harry all but asked me to marry with him, and maybe I can talk him into takin' Paul and Alice. . . . That boy, Buck, he's sort of cute, but too skinny and real bashful! He keeps looking at me when he don't think I know it. I bet he'd help me get away if Bron won't let me go. . . . I'll just make up to him.*

CHOIYA: *Why did they come here? It was her—the red-haired one. She is bold! No good woman of my people would do such a thing. . . . The younger one is not good . . . she won't stay long. But the woman says God sent her here! Fah! She has no man. That is her trouble. She is beautiful, so men would say. Zack acts very angry, but I could see him looking at her. Why did they have to come? I hope he sends them away!*

BRONWEN: *Well, Bronwen Morgan, it's silly you are! What! Did you expect the man to kill a fatted calf for the troop you've brought into his home? He's got "no" written in his eyes. . . . He'll be talking to me soon enough, and I know well what his words will be! The boy, he is kind, but he has no say. He's an intruder himself! And the Indian woman. She'd put a knife in me if she had the chance. . . . She's a pretty thing, and it's jealous she is, though he's not her man. Or, maybe he is? All alone out here. Who knows what they are to each other? Hard it is, Lord, to see your hand in all this! But there it is—out of my hands. If he tells me to go, what's to do but leave? He's a hard man. But I ask you to change him—just enough, Lord, to let us stay for a time! Change his stubborn mind, O God!*

The winter wind crept down out of the hills and brushed against the cabin. It touched the panes of glass, then dropped down and fingered the chinks between the logs, seeking entrance, then finding none, moved away sullenly. The cabin was an intrusion in the wilderness. It was surrounded by trees and snow and furry denizens of the wild, and some of the unrest of the inhabitants inside seemed to communicate itself. A great horned owl swooped down, sinking steely talons into an unsuspecting white-footed mouse, then carrying the tiny victim off on downy wings, as if to get far away from man's invasion of the fowl's territory.

* * * *

Bron awoke with a start when the door closed, not knowing for one frightening instant where she was. Then memory flooded her mind, and she slipped out from under the blankets in the dark cabin and dressed. She could feel Choiya's eyes— watching, watching, watching. *Will she never stop?*

She went to the fireplace, poked the ashes up, then put two logs on. A thought came to her, and she went outside to the wagon, pulled a heavy wood box from under the seat, and staggered inside with it. Placing it beside the fireplace, she opened the box and began putting the items on the table. She was in the middle of fixing breakfast when Buck came down the ladder, his hair disheveled and his eyes at half mast. "Good morning, Buck," she said. He nodded, then plunged out the door.

When Zack came in, he took one look at the supplies, but made no remark.

"I brought some things from Pfouts' store," Bron explained. "Is it all right if I go ahead and cook breakfast?"

"Sure." He looked less harried than he had the night before, but there was still a hard stubbornness in the line of his lips, giving a pugnacious set to his jaw. He picked up *Oliver Twist* again and read. Soon the cabin was filled with the delicious aroma of food, and when Buck reentered with a load of wood, he said to Bron, "Boy, that smells good!"

"It's about ready."

"Go get some of those boxes for seats, Buck," Zack said. Paul and Alice were still asleep, but Lillian came to the table. Choiya didn't move. Even when Zack said "Come and get it," she refused, choosing rather to stare out the window.

Bron tried to eat, but the sinking sensation in her stomach rebelled against the food. The others didn't seem to have any problem and dived in, relishing the eggs, bacon, grits, bread and honey. Finally Zack sat back and sipped his coffee, thinking of the last time he'd seen Lillian; and since Bron had brought them to this place with her startling announcement, he'd wondered about her. "How're your parents, Lillian?"

The girl glanced nervously toward the sleeping children. "Ma run off, and Pa, he got killed."

Zack felt like a fool for bringing the subject up. "I—I hadn't heard that. Sorry."

The problem was getting more complicated all the time. *What will the children do?* He felt trapped again. He got up and said hastily, "I guess I'll go try to shoot something for the pot." He grabbed his rifle, threw on a heavy coat, and left.

In a flash Bron donned her coat and was out the door, racing across the snow, calling out, "Mr. Winslow!"

Zack halted. In the sunlight she was even more beautiful, he thought. Somehow that fact cemented his stubbornness. He resented the creamy white of her cheeks, the brilliant green of her eyes, and the soft red curve of her mouth. *Looks more like a dance-hall entertainer than a preacher.*

"Mr. Winslow," she said, the words tumbling out, "I may have been wrong to bring the children here."

Surprised, he nodded, "I'd say you were. It's dangerous in these hills."

"No more dangerous than in town—for Lillian, I mean."

Her meekness made him feel like a bully turning her down.

"She's going to go bad if something isn't done," she persisted.

"That's not my problem!"

"I suppose not—but it's mine."

"Don't see how that could be. She's no kin of yours—and you don't have any authority over her."

"When we see someone in trouble, that makes us responsible."

"No, it doesn't!"

"Don't you care at all about what will happen to her—and to Paul and Alice?"

He shifted his feet. She was putting him in a bad position. "I used to think it was my job to help when I could—but you can't take care of the whole human race!" He grimaced. "Sure looks like I've got a good start, though!"

"Mr. Winslow—"

"My name is Zacharias or Zack."

"And I'm Bron," she said, glad to be more informal. "If we

don't help each other, it's no better than wild animals we are!"

"You're dead wrong! I've seen men stand up and shoot each other down until the ground was red with blood. And I've had people betray me—so you can't expect me to go galloping to the rescue every time somebody gets in trouble."

"But—"

"Why do you think I chose the backside of nowhere to live?" he demanded. "To get away from people. Haven't you heard? I'm a hermit! Don't people from Wales know what a hermit is?"

"But you can't cut yourself off from people."

He looked back at the house. "Well, it's not real *easy*," he said ironically. "But I aim to do it."

Bron saw that despite his boyish face, he was basically a headstrong man. She tried to think of something else that would change his mind—but nothing came. Her head dropped and she bit her lower lip as it started to tremble. She whispered, "I—I'll go load the wagon." She lifted her eyes to him, the pain evident, and turned.

He hesitated, then grabbed her arm, pulling her around roughly. "Now just a blamed minute! You don't have to go right now."

"I think it would be better."

Her vulnerability melted the chord of stubbornness, and to his horror he heard himself say, "Look, you can stay for a little while—a few days."

Her head shot up, tears of relief in her eyes. "You mean it?"

Actually, he didn't, but it was too late. *Got to be a way to fix it*, he told himself. His brow furrowed in a deep frown. "You come out here and I'm caught like a bear in a trap! You got to give a man a little slack! Can't just point a thing like this at his head like a loaded gun!"

"I know I didn't do it well, Zacharias," she said, and her lips curved upward in a tremulous smile. "God bless you!"

"Now don't drag God into this!" he snorted. "It's just for a few days, you *understand*?" He scowled. "Just for a few days, you got that?"

CHAPTER TWELVE

ZACK'S CHOICE

★ ★ ★ ★

Buck backed away to admire his handiwork. "Looks a little rough, but it beats sleepin' on the floor."

"Oh, Buck. What a great carpenter you are!" Bron put her mixing bowl down to examine the bunks he'd worked on the past two days. He had cut young trees four inches in diameter for the four uprights, and after slipping the bark, had firmly nailed the posts to the floor and to the joists of the ceiling, forming a rectangle two and a half feet wide and six feet long. He used smaller tree trunks for the framework, one a foot off the floor, the second three and a half feet, and the top one about six feet. One-half inch rope drawn tight and nailed into the ends, then woven and fastened to the sides for support completed it.

Bron stepped on the lower frame, sat down on the middle bunk, then lay full length. "This is wonderful, Buck! How did you ever think of such a thing?"

"Oh, it's nothing," he shrugged. "I saw one like it once in a bunkhouse."

"Nothing?" she said. "After sleeping on the floor, it'll be like heaven." She impulsively reached up and pulled his head down, giving him a resounding kiss on the cheek. "You just wait and see if I don't fix you a pie the angels would swoon over!"

His face turned crimson, and she realized she'd embarrassed

him. "This will fit us all," she said quickly. "Paul and Alice on the bottom, me in the middle, and Lillian on the top. Won't hurt her to do a little climbing, will it now?"

"There's some straw in the shed," he offered. "If we had some ticking or canvas, we could make mattresses."

"The very thing!" Bron said. "I'll put that on my list." She hurriedly jotted it down on a slip of paper. "Look," she laughed, "the list is getting almost too long for the paper!"

He nodded. They were standing by the table as she worked a mixture in a bowl. Lifting his eyes to the window, he said, "Sure has turned warm, ain't it, Bron?" He didn't intend to say that, but the sight of Choiya stirring a load of clothes over the large pot caught his eye. Nearby Sam and Hawk in leather carriers were hanging on nails driven into the large walnut tree. *Looks kinda funny. Ain't seen anything like that,* he mused. Choiya had made carriers for both babies. The other children, Paul and Alice, were chasing each other around the tree, stopping often to talk to Sam and Hawk, trying to get them to laugh.

Buck's face grew sober as he watched, and unconsciously a frown drew two vertical lines between his eyes. Bron looked up, saw his expression, and asked, "What's the matter with the Old Man now?" She had started calling him that on the second day of their stay, poking fun at his serious ways, he knew.

He shifted uneasily, reluctant to speak his thoughts. He had never had anyone to share with. Nobody really cared. But Bron, he discovered, would listen intently, stopping what she was doing and looking directly into his eyes. It had silenced him at first, for he had learned to keep away from people, but soon he found himself talking to her more freely.

"Been thinkin' about this last week—sure has been funny, hasn't it, Bron?"

She laughed. "Funny? I don't think Mr. Zacharias Winslow would agree."

"Well—" Buck said quickly, "He was just a little surprised, Bron."

"Right! And what man wouldn't be, with a houseful of women and children dumped in his lap for a Christmas present!" She gave the mix a good swish, and poured it out in a deep iron pan.

Buck watched as she put a lid on it, set it in the ashes, then wiped her hands on her apron. "I didn't mean funny to laugh at," he said. "I mean it's been—sorta peculiar."

Bron lifted the lid on a large pot hanging over the fire, reached in with a spoon and got a sampling. She tasted it, turned and held the spoon out to him. "See if that's salty enough." He tasted it and nodded his approval. "We've been a houseful, right enough," she said. "As different as we all are, it's God's mercy we've lived cooped up this long without pulling hair."

"Lillian don't like it much," he said off-handedly. "She likes it better in town."

Bron nodded, but her eyes were cool. "What she likes and what's good for her may be different."

"She says she's not gonna stay here, Bron."

"I know. She says the same to me." Bron repressed an urge to hug the boy. "We may not have to worry about it. Zacharias said we could stay a few days—and I expect we've been here long enough to fit that."

"He gets short with us sometimes, Bron," Buck said defensively, "but he's a good man."

"I expect he is—but no man is good enough to put up with a houseful of strangers, is he?"

"He didn't mean what he said last night." Zack had become angry when he discovered that Alice had torn several pages out of one of his books, and had muttered, barely under his breath, something about getting rid of the blasted nursery.

"I think he did, Buck," Bron said slowly. "He said last night that when we go to town tomorrow, he is going to make 'other arrangements.' Meaning us, of course."

Buck shook his head. "We're making out all right. I don't see why he has to be so stubborn about it."

"He's been hurt somewhere along the way, Buck—very badly, and he's made up his mind that nobody's ever going to hurt him again. He's like a man who's put a NO TRESPASSING sign over his heart."

"But he's been good to me!"

Bron's eyes widened. "Saying nothing against him, I was. He's just going to get hurt more if he keeps on this way, Buck.

We've all of us got to learn to trust people—even if they hurt us."

She had touched a sensitive nerve, for Buck was just as leery as Zack. "How do you do that, Bron?" he asked, puzzled. "It's easy with you, but most people, if you don't watch out, they'll do you wrong."

"I can't tell you that," she answered. "But I'd rather be hurt once in a while than live in a dark hole and keep people away with a sharp stick!"

Late in the afternoon Zack came in with three fat grouse. He didn't say much, but that night after a delicious meal of roast grouse and corn bread, he said, "The weather's clear. Guess tomorrow would be a good time to go into town."

Bron was cutting a piece of corn bread and her hand faltered. "All of us, Zacharias?"

He stirred under the question. "I expect so," he mumbled. He felt the weight of her gaze, and added, "Look here, this warm weather can't last. Sooner or later we're going to get snowed in, and there's no way we can all survive if that happens."

"I can hunt more, Zack," Buck offered.

"Not in snow four feet deep, you won't. And it's more than a matter of food. Sometimes just *two* people get on each other's nerves so bad they want to kill the other. Cabin fever, they call it." He swung his arm around the cabin and demanded, "How in the name of common sense do you reckon this bunch would make out, stuck here in this one room for weeks?"

No one said anything, and he added with a touch of desperation, "And what if one of the kids gets sick? He'd die, that's what!"

"Zack's right," Lillian broke in. "We can't all stay here in this one room all winter. There's got to be someplace in town where we can stay."

"Maybe we could build another room on the cabin," Buck suggested. "You did this one by yourself, Zack, so with all of us helping, we could do it."

Bron said, "It's not a matter of room, is it, Zacharias? You just can't put up with us any longer. That's the truth, isn't it?"

The color rose in Zack's face and he said angrily, "You always make it out to be my fault, don't you?" He stood up. "All right,

I'll say it straight out. I didn't leave civilization and come out here to start a social club, Bron. I came to be *alone*—and that's about as plain as I can put it."

He walked over and stood staring into the fire defiantly. Alice came over and looked up into his face. "Why is Zack mad?"

Bron rushed over and picked her up. "He's not mad at you, Alice. Just leave him alone for a bit."

The air was tense and both Zack and Buck retreated to the loft.

Bron put the children to bed, praying silently. After a while Lillian whispered to her, "See? I told you it'd never work!" and climbed up into her bunk.

Heavy of heart, Bron searched the Bible for answers, but nothing seemed to make sense. She read a psalm twice, and realized she hadn't the faintest idea what it said. She tried to pray. That, too, seemed futile. Deep in thought, she was startled when Choiya spoke.

"You will be better off somewhere else."

Bron looked at her. The Indian woman had not spoken to her once in the days they'd been there, but now there was a triumphant gleam in her dark eyes.

"Why do you hate us so much, Choiya?"

Something passed across the eyes of the Indian woman, but she only shook her head. "He does not like so many people around," she said finally. "You are pretty. Many men will want you. These children"—she waved at the bunks—"they will not die. Someone will take them in."

Bron shook her head. "I feel that my God has told me I am to take care of them."

"I know about your God. My father was white. He sent me to a mission school for six years—the black robes. They taught me to read, and they taught me about Jesus and Mary."

Bron's eyes widened in surprise. "I wondered why you spoke English so well. But why did you go back to your people?"

Choiya's eyes narrowed. "Because the men of the Cheyenne are more honorable than any white men, that is why! I could tell you things—things about how white men come to a young Indian girl, promising her things—but they are all liars!"

"Not all white men are liars, Choiya. Nor are all Cheyenne

braves truthful. You must have seen that both peoples have their good men as well as their bad."

Choiya shook her head. "It doesn't matter. I can't belong to either world. Many Cheyenne won't have me because I am half white. And I found out very quickly that your people have no use for a half-breed squaw."

Bron got up and faced Choiya. She faulted herself for not trying harder to make a friend of the woman, but now it seemed too late. "I'm sorry you feel hatred toward us." She thought she knew why, and said carefully, "I am no threat to you, Choiya—not in any way."

Choiya's eyes mirrored disbelief and she lifted her chin. "It is better for everyone that you go."

Bron's heart ached, her stomach churned. It was hopeless. She lay on her bunk and for the first time let the tears flow. "Lord, I tried my best. I'm sorry I failed you."

The next morning she prepared breakfast, then hurriedly packed all their belongings in the wagon. When Zack came out, he avoided Bron, but was surprised when Choiya came out of the house and said, "I would like to go with you."

Zack looked at her quizzically. He had not expected this and wondered what was in her mind. *Women! What a bunch of unpredictable creatures!* His face settled like granite. "We'll have to take my wagon, then. Buck, let's hitch up the mules."

Zack took the lead, with Bron directly behind. She turned to look at the cabin as the trail bent around a clump of tall trees. She felt a pang go through her, and once again the despair of failure robbed her face of its customary cheerfulness.

They crossed Dancer Creek, then turned down the narrow trail leading through the thickets. Choiya sat silently beside Zack on the wagon seat. Buck had jumped in the back where the two babies lay on thick blankets.

They pulled into Virginia City in late afternoon and stopped in front of Pfouts' store. Zack got out stiffly, and turned to help Choiya. She stared at him, then took his hand and stepped to the ground. She had put on a soft doeskin skirt and a red cotton blouse under a fringed doeskin jacket. She took Hawk, and Buck picked up Samuel. "I'll take him," he said, stepping to the ground.

Zack looked at Bron, who was sitting beside Lillian in the other wagon. He wanted to say something, but several men had already slowed down to watch. He turned abruptly and walked into the store. As soon as they were inside, he said, "Choiya, get what supplies we'll need. Buck, you better help her." Then he stomped to the back room, angry and uncomfortable.

He threw the door open and Parris jumped up from his desk, his face shining with pleasure. "Zack! It's good to see you!" Then he looked toward the door. "Is Bron outside?"

Before Zack could answer, Pfouts headed for the door.

"Wait a minute, Parris," he called. "I need to talk to you."

One look at Zack's face, and Parris stopped. "Is there trouble?"

"Yes! there's trouble. You've got to help me on this thing!"

"You mean Bron and the children coming to your cabin?"

"Yes—why in the name of heaven did she ever think of such a thing? Couldn't you talk sense to her, Parris?"

"She was gone before I had a chance."

"You've got a chance now!" Zack spat the words out. "Now listen, Parris, I'll help with the kids—anything! I'll pay the bills. Just find a place for them to live. You know it's not right, an unmarried girl staying off in a cabin with a man all winter—and a preacher woman at that!"

"Never gave it a thought, considering you already had one unmarried woman with you," Parris said.

Zack's lips tightened. He gripped Pfouts' shoulder. "Look, it just *won't* work, Parris! We've got to find another way."

"I'll talk to Bron right away," he said and left.

Zack pulled out his handkerchief and mopped his brow, then reluctantly walked back into the store. Around the corner he saw Choiya and Buck examining some yard goods and stopped. "I'll be back in about an hour."

He walked rapidly out and headed for the first saloon, which happened to be the Silver Moon. It was almost empty, and a man behind the bar, wearing a black patch over his eye, called, "What'll it be?"

"Whiskey." Zack hated the stuff, but his nerves were frayed. He downed that one, then another, and by the third one he began to feel the raw tension subside. The man with the patch introduced himself. "I'm Ned Ray. Own this place. Don't believe we've met."

"Name's Zack Winslow."

A light touched the one-eyed Ray. "Oh, sure." He poured another drink for Zack. "On the house."

Zack gulped that one too. He wanted to run—but where to? Ideas to settle the dilemma he'd gotten himself into fluttered through his mind. For an hour, he racked his brain, absent-mindedly drinking one swig after another as Ray kept filling his glass. The last glass he reached for eluded him, missing his hands by several inches. *Why, I'm drunk!* he thought with amazement. The saloon keeper was watching him, and Zack waved him over. "How much do I owe you?" he said, speaking very slowly, and enunciating every syllable, trying to prove he was not drunk.

"Three dollars."

Zack carefully counted out the money and dropped it on the bar. "Got to—go," he said and turned. The floor seemed tilted, but he steadied himself and cleared the door, the laughter of the men following him.

He walked slowly and deliberately down the street, stepping off the sidewalk as if it were two feet high. He shook his head, trying to clear his brain for the journey to the other side. He raised his foot at least six inches too high on the other sidewalk, and fell headlong on the board planks. He stumbled to his feet, pretending he had merely twisted his ankle, and ignored the grins around him.

Finally he got to the store and walked in to find himself the target of every eye. He lurched forward until he stood in front of them.

Weaving from side to side, he mumbled, "Well—have you been—sayin' what a dirty scoundrel ol' Zack Winslow is, huh?"

Parris was distressed, and walked over and grabbed his arm. "Zack, come into the office."

"No—I don't need to go—to no offish—office!" He shook his head and pointed his right hand with the missing finger at Bron. "You can't make no saint out of a sinner like me," he said loudly.

"Look, his finger is gone!" Alice laughed. "What happened to your finger, Mister Zack?"

"A bear bit it off!" he shouted at her, bringing a burst of tears. He stared at her as she ran to Bron, then grinned broadly. "Now, you know what—kinda man—I am, preacher woman! The scum of the earth—and you're lookin' at 'im!"

He ranted and raved and finally yelled at Choiya, "Get the shtuff in the wagon!" Then he turned back to Bron. "Best day's work I ever did—gettin' rid of you and these kids!"

He tottered out of the store, and Parris said, "He's drunk, Bron. He doesn't mean it."

"Yes, I think he does, Parris." Her eyes flooded with tears despite her effort at control.

"Go on back to the office. I'll take care of the children."

"What'll we do, Choiya?" Buck whispered.

"Pick up the supplies and get him out of town," she said crisply.

Pfouts had been impressed with the woman when Buck introduced her, and now he was filled with admiration at the way she handled a tough situation.

"I'll help put everything in the wagon," he offered, grabbing a bag, and with Buck it was all soon loaded. "I don't reckon Zack's used to hard liquor," he said in defense. "It sort of sneaked up on him."

"Thank you," she said, and turned to Buck. "He's probably in one of the saloons."

"The Silver Moon. It's the only one open this early," Pfouts said quietly. "Shall I go get him?"

"I'll do it, Mr. Pfouts," Buck said. "We need to get him out of town. Choiya, get the babies and drive the wagon. I'll go find him."

Buck went straight to the Silver Moon, which was down the street. He reached the door and went inside, feeling strange about his mission.

Zack was at the bar, drinking, and looked up as Buck entered.

"Zack, we're ready to go if you are."

"Whaszat?" He steadied himself, his eyes unfocused. "Oh, Buck, it's you." He put his arm around the boy and whispered, "You don't wanna be seen with me. Not a reshpecktable character. Re-speck-able!" He pronounced the words slowly, then said ponderously, "I think you've had enough to drink, Buck. I gotta get you outta here!"

He put some money on the bar and Buck guided him out and toward the wagon where Choiya was waiting in front of the saloon. Buck gave Zack a gentle push. On the first attempt to climb up, Zack missed the step. He was just trying again when a loud voice jeered nearby, "Well, lookee whut we got here, Boone—a hermit!"

A red-haired man and a huge hulking form laughed as they stopped to watch.

"Blast if you ain't right, Red," Boone said. "And the hermit is drunk as Cooter Brown!"

Zack straightened up, and felt Choiya helping him into the wagon.

"Well, ain't the hermit got him a pretty little helper?" the man called Red taunted. He walked over to Choiya and touched her cheek. "Now, ain't you the purtiest leetle thing!"

Zack socked the man's arm. "Get your hands off that woman!"

"Watch out there, Red!" Boone warned. "The hermit's threatening you with bodily harm, I reckon."

One blow from Red sent Zack sprawling. "Get lost, drunk!" he roared, then caught Choiya as she tried to help Zack. "Come on in, sweetheart," he said. "Me and you got some talkin' to do."

Choiya raked her fingernails across Red's face, but he laughed gleefully. "Come on, Boone, we got us a lady friend."

Boone grinned and took Choiya's other arm. "Why, shore, Red. We gotta be hospitable to our red brothers—and sisters, especially!"

Buck jumped in front of them, yelling, "You let her go!" His heart was beating like a trip hammer, and he wanted to run, but he stood there with trembling legs.

Boone looked at him for a moment, a grin creasing his brutal lips. His fist shot out, and Buck landed in the dust. He rolled over on his hands and knees and struggled to his feet.

The two men were already pulling Choiya through the doors. They marched her up to the bar. "Ned, give this little lady some good liquor."

Billy Page was sitting at a table playing solitaire, and looked up with distaste, but said nothing.

"Take her outta here, Red," Ned Ray ordered.

"What's the matter, Ray? My money no good? I said let's have a drink for the lady."

Ray hesitated. He poured the drink, but gave a slight nod to his swamper, who moved quietly out the door.

"Now, just get this one down, and the next'll be a lot easier," Red said, and as Boone pinned her arms, Yeager held her head with one hand and put the glass to her lips. Choiya shook her head violently and spit in his face, spilling the whiskey.

"Now look at that," Yeager said, swiping his jaw. He poured another glass and was just about to force her to drink when Zack burst through the doors. His head was wet from dunking it into the horse trough. Not quite sober, his youthful face was pale, but his voice was clear and menacing. "Let that woman go!"

Red smiled as he faced him. "I told you to get lost, drunk." He threw the liquor in Zack's face and smashed him in the mouth. Zack fell backward, and Boone yelled, "Break him up, Red!"

Yeager waited until Zack got to his feet. He was a cruel and rough fighter of repute and let Zack take his time. Cocky and sure of himself Red said, "I'm going to bust you up, boy. I'm going to break your nose so that you whistle when you breathe. And you ain't gonna have nothin' but stubs left for teeth."

Zack desperately wished he were sober—for he knew his reactions were gone. But he said, "You're a dog—a yellow dog!" and threw a punch at Yeager. Red side-stepped and caught Zack around the waist, spinning him around and sending him crashing into the wall. Zack fell to the floor with a thousand lights flashing before his eyes.

Yeager roared with laughter. "I won't even soil my hands with you, drunk," he sneered. "Boots will be good enough."

He walked forward and drew back his foot to kick. "Now, hermit—"

"Don't do it, Red!"

Yeager turned to see Billy Page. He knew Page slightly, but thought of him only as a fancy tin-horn gambler. His lip curled. "After I kick his teeth in, I'll see what *your* insides are made of."

He turned back toward Zack, but stopped at the deadly click of a revolver.

"It'll be the last mistake you ever make." Page held the gun steady as Red faced him.

Yeager had a gun on his hip, and he knew Boone was armed, but the bore of Page's revolver was unwavering, and the brown eyes dared him to go for it.

"There's two of us, Red," Boone interrupted, shoving the woman aside, his hand over his gun. "What're we waitin' for?"

Yeager stood motionless, looking into the mouth of Page's gun.

"Why, Red's trying to figure out if it's a good day to die, Boone," Page jibed.

Yeager nearly went for his gun, but he saw Billy's finger flicker on the trigger, and he threw up his hands, yelling, "I'm not drawing!"

At the same instant, J.W. Dillingham entered. He took in the scene and commanded, "Put up your gun, Billy." Then he turned to Choiya. "Ma'am, you can go now."

"Thank you," she whispered, and after a look at Zack, left the room.

Red Yeager knew that he'd have to have it out with Page to keep his reputation. "Page, I'll see you later."

"Any time, Red. Now that I see what a fancy gunman you are, I'll hire a couple of bodyguards." He walked back and took his seat, picking up his solitaire game as if nothing had happened.

Yeager said, "We don't need your help, J.W." He glared at Zack. "The hermit there, he threw the first punch."

"And you and Boone were just a couple of innocent bystanders?" Dillingham asked softly.

Boone said loudly, "Why, you know about him, Dillingham. He's the one who keeps a harem up in the hills. Got that Indian gal, and from what I hear, he's got that good-lookin' preacher lady, too!"

"That's right," Red added. "We can't have a thing like that goin' on round here. It's a shame on our community."

"Didn't know you took such an interest in the morals of our town," Dillingham said. He was a soft-spoken man, but Yeager knew J.W. was a fearful man in a fight. Now his soft gray eyes were hard as he said, "I think I'll put you in the slammer, Red."

"What! You can't do that!"

"Let's just see if I can, Red. Now you can go with or without trouble. Make up your mind."

Yeager was careful not to move his hands. "All right, J.W., I'll go." He pulled his gun out slowly, and as he handed it to the deputy, he threw a hard look at Zack. "You get rid of them women, Winslow," he said. "Soon as I get out of jail, I'll be lookin' for you. And if you've still got them up at that cabin, I'll finish what I started!"

Zack stared at him, then asked curiously, "You mean that, Red?"

"I reckon he does, Winslow," Ned Ray spoke up. "If I was you, I don't think I'd stick around here."

Dillingham nodded as he herded Red out of the door. "None of my business, Winslow, but Yeager here will try for you. He's got his reputation to think about." He shoved Yeager out the door. "He'll be looking for you, so better keep out of town."

Zack nodded, and walked back to Page. "I'm obliged to you."

"I don't like to see a thing like that. If you'd been sober, I'd have let him do it." He frowned. "I don't think much of you, Winslow. Bronwen Morgan is a friend of mine. I reckon now you'll do like Red says."

"Like Red says?" Zack's eyes bored into Billy's. "You mean kick them out just because a cheap gunhand like Red Yeager says so?"

"He's a killer, Zack. He runs on his reputation, and he'll carry out his threat if you don't get rid of them." Billy shrugged. "Be a lot easier on everyone—including Bronwen—if you pulled out."

"Saving me from a stomping may not have meant much to you, Page, but it means a lot to me. Maybe I can make it right with you someday."

He walked out of the saloon. Choiya was waiting in the wagon, talking to Buck.

"I'm going back to Pfouts' store," Zack said. He was weak from the beating and he had a splitting headache, but his mind was no longer cloudy with alcohol. He turned into the store and saw only the clerk.

"They're in the office."

Zack pushed the door open. Bronwen, her face streaked with tears, whirled to face him.

"Bronwen, I want you to come back," he said flatly.

Shocked, she studied him. "Why, Zacharias?"

"Because no cheap gunman is going to tell me what I can or can't do." He told them what had happened, and said stubbornly, "That's why I'm asking you to come back. I'm no more noble than I ever was, and I still think you're crazy. I don't believe it'll ever work, but if you want to come, I'll keep you till it snows ink!"

"Don't, Bron!" Parris warned, his face agitated. "Zack's right. It won't work."

"I won't go back up there!" Lillian cried defiantly. "I'll run away!"

Bron looked at Zack, a strange smile on her lips. "I will go with you, Zacharias. I'm ready now."

He swallowed. "Let's get going. We've got to build another room on the cabin before the snow gets here."

Choiya had a murderous look on her face as they came back. Zack tossed a screaming Lillian into the wagon after prying her from the hitching post. Buck looked stunned, and the rest of the children, frightened out of their wits by all of this, started a chorus of screaming as the wagons moved down the street.

Parris raised his eyes and whispered, "God help them all!"

CHAPTER THIRTEEN

A CRY FOR HELP

★　★　★　★

·Bron had expected things to go better after they returned to the cabin, but they worsened. No matter how she tried to ferret out the source of friction, nothing made sense.

Everyone was touchy and agitated at the slightest provocation. Choiya drew into a shell, a sullen anger shrouding her every move. At times she would flare out, her eyes reflecting the smoldering anger, especially when the close confines of the cabin produced the inevitable problems from crowded conditions.

Lillian became unbearable, finding ingenious ways to irrritate everyone, doing her chores only when threatened with a switch. She ignored or insulted Buck, and though they were the same age she saw him as an overgrown boy. Buck, on the other hand, did his best to be friendly. Obviously smitten with her, and very sensitive, he became more introverted and withdrawn at her mistreatment.

Zack was worst of all. Bron had expected him to be more communicative, now that he had openly asked them to stay, but he, too, seemed to live in a world of his own. Unknown to her, he was horrified and ashamed at his behavior in town. He despised men who drank themselves into a stupor, and had long ago vowed that he'd never be one of them. Now in full view of Virginia City, he had staggered along the streets, fallen flat on his face in the dirt, and been roundly whipped by a man he knew he could have beaten had he been sober.

He lived that scene over and over again, seeing Yeager's leering face and feeling the blows that fell uncontested. Drunks usually don't remember fights—but this one was carved into Zack's brain with stark clarity. He remembered every detail—the splinters in the boards his face pressed against, the sharp splat of Yeager's fist.

Though he didn't realize it, above his humiliation at being kicked around by Red was Zack's deep shame at his inability to defend Choiya. She had been at the mercy of the two men, and it was his responsibility to protect her—but he had failed. Had Billy Page and Dillingham not come to Zack's aid, Yeager would probably have killed him and done as he pleased with Choiya.

Though Winslow didn't reason any of this out, it ate at him; and perversely he began to resent not only himself but those who had seen him humiliated—which included everyone in his tiny cosmos. He was short with everyone and stayed outside as much as possible, coming in only when forced to.

The weather made it more difficult because three days after their return, the winter cold came roaring over the peaks, snowing and dropping temperatures to sub-zero levels almost overnight.

They had enjoyed the relatively mild temperatures and the recent chinook. The weather had been deceptively moderate until now, keeping even some of the slower mountain streams ice-free.

Zack spent long days cutting firewood, hauling it back to the cabin on the wagon and adding it to the wood he and Buck had already stockpiled. Buck became exhausted and when he protested, Zack sent him back to the cabin with a curt word. Zack himself continued to work until darkness closed in, coming in so spent he could hardly eat or crawl up to the loft.

The snow began to fall again, lightly at first, then in large flakes that fell heavily instead of drifting down. Zack decided it was time to take the wheels off the wagon and convert it into a sledge. He guessed right, as it snowed hard for two days, making it difficult to get outside for more wood or to care for the animals. Doing anything else became impossible.

Zack prowled the cabin like a caged beast, sitting down to read, but unable to concentrate for over thirty minutes before throwing the book down and finding some pretext for going outside.

Once when everyone except Bron had gone to bed, he came in from one of his trips outside, his head covered with snow. He stood over the fire, steam rising from his clothes as the heat penetrated. He had not shaved for a week, and the snow melted on his whiskers, dripping down onto his shirt. Bron was reading the Bible, as usual, by the light of the kerosene lamp, and put it down. "Are the horses all right?"

"They won't freeze, I guess."

"I made some fresh coffee." She took the pot and poured a cup of the hot brew and handed it to him. He sipped the coffee, silently staring into the flames.

Bron looked across the cabin at the sleeping figures in the bunks. "It's harder than I thought it would be. You were right."

He shook his head. "I don't take confinement too well." He raised his cup to his lips and looked at her. "I've been pretty terrible, Bron."

"Not your fault, it is," she said quietly. "Are you sorry you brought us back?"

He shifted his feet. The set of his jaw and the bleakness in his eyes reflected a despair within. The turmoil in the cabin had caused a lot of other feelings to surface—bitter anger that he had thought long buried. The faces of George Orr and Emma kept coming to him, bringing a discord into his spirit. He would think of Emma for hours, usually of those close, tender moments when she had lavished her love on him, assuring him that he alone would have her heart. Yet how easily she had moved from him to George. At the memory, an implacable rage would rise in him.

"I know you think God works good out of everything, Bron, but that doesn't make me feel any better," he said bitterly. As he faced her, the unhappiness that had fed on him spilled over. "How can you believe in anything? I had a girl once, almost as beautiful as you. And I had a friend." His face was etched with pain, making lines she'd never seen before, and she longed to reach out and smooth them, but dared not.

"And they betrayed you?" she asked, knowing the answer before he spoke.

"Yes! They said all the right things to me—how they loved me and trusted me. Then when I was out of sight, they practically fell into each other's arms."

"Not everyone is like that, Zacharias," she said.

"How do you know?" he challenged, and he saw in her beauty the same soft trap that had led him to trust Emma. For that one moment in some strange way, she seemed to be Emma. He seized her arms and said harshly, "You had a man, but he's gone! Now you'd take another one."

"That's not the same, and it's not true!"

"Isn't it?" He pulled her roughly to him and pressed his lips to hers. Shocked, she tried to push him away, but he held her tightly, pressing harder against her, roughing her lips with his. Then he dropped her so quickly she staggered backward.

The logs shifted in the fireplace with a soft movement that sent sparks flying, and he looked at her with self-loathing. "Well, Bron, that proves you're good and I'm a rotter."

"No, it proves nothing of the kind, Zacharias," she said, stepping forward to look at him closely. "It proves you're a man, that's all."

"How do you figure that?" he snapped.

"How dull you are!" Bron put her hand out and touched his shoulder. Her eyes were filled with compassion. "This woman hurt you—and you kissed me to show your contempt for her—and to prove that I'm as little to be trusted as she was."

He stared into her eyes, then said glumly, "I can't straighten it all out now. Good night."

Without another word, he moved to the ladder and disappeared into the loft. Bron gazed blindly across the room, then blew out the lamp. She undressed and was just ready to slip into her bunk when Choiya's voice came softly to her.

"Was it a good kiss?"

Bron glanced quickly toward Choiya's bed. "It was an angry kiss, Choiya." She waited for a reply, but none came, so she climbed into her bunk and wrapped the blankets around her. Closing her eyes, she tried to sleep, but she thought of his kiss. Finally, she shook her head angrily, rolled over, and willed herself to sleep.

The next morning after breakfast, Zack announced, "Snow

stopped last night. I'm going over to Seven Point and see if I can bring down some meat."

"Can I go with you?" Buck asked.

"You'd better stay here," he replied; then seeing the boy's disappointment, added, "I don't like to leave the women here with no man. Keep your rifle loaded and your eyes open."

Buck brightened. "Sure. I'll take care of things."

When Zack was ready to leave, Bron handed him a lunch she'd made, asking, "Will you be gone long?"

"Don't expect so. Be back by dark," he said tartly, avoiding her eyes.

She watched as he rode Ornery out of the yard. *We don't need any meat. He's just getting away from me—from all of us*, she thought. More than ever she doubted the wisdom of what she'd done, wishing she'd never come to him.

Zack did not push Ornery, but let him choose his own speed. The silence of the world fell on him, washing away the noise and tension of the cabin, and he felt his muscles loosen as he moved into the wilderness.

He stopped at nine and ate one of the sandwiches. He was surprised to find that he could still break the ice for a drink for himself and the horse. By eleven he reached the bank of Seven Point, a small stream called a river, but really no more than a creek. He grained Ornery, watered him again, then tied him to a sapling. Pulling his rifle from the boot, he made his way with difficulty through the deep snow; but once he entered the fir forest, the snow was not deep.

It was like a cathedral, with the high arching branches far overhead, letting a few bars of pale sunlight lay their touch on the snow. The crunching of the snow crust under his feet sounded like pistol shots in the quiet.

He followed the creek to a wide spot, an old beaver dam, and made his way carefully across the logs that lay in all positions. They creaked and gave under his weight, but he moved carefully. When he reached the other side, he turned to his left, walking five hundred yards down the river until he came to the spot the deer used for a crossing all year long.

He checked the loads in his rifle, cocked it, and sat down to wait. The silence was heavy, almost palpable, and he thought only of the woods and the deer he waited for. A peace settled on his mind, and the tormenting thoughts of the past few days slipped away.

A wolverine came sniffing out of the woods, maneuvering within ten feet of Zack. He sat there motionless, admiring the wildness of the animal, one of the most ferocious pound-for-pound in the world, then said, "Hello!" Instantly, the wolverine bared her teeth and scrambled into the brush.

Game was scarce, and it was hours later when a buck with a large rack stepped out of the shadows not thirty feet away. He sniffed the air, then lowered his head to drink. Zack raised the rifle slowly and pulled the trigger. The animal dropped, and by the time Zack got to him, he lay still.

Zack removed his knife from his boot and dressed the carcass. When he was finished, he shouldered it and began his trip back. By the time he got to the dam he was worn out. It was too far to carry the buck back to where he'd tied Ornery, so he decided to carry the deer across, then go get the horse. He stepped onto the dam, balancing the heavy load carefully and holding on to his rifle with his left hand. The logs were coated with several inches of snow, and he tried to step in the places where he'd crossed earlier. Several times he had to stop to shift the load.

He was within ten feet of the bank when the log he stepped on gave way as he shifted his weight. He was caught in mid-stride, completely off balance, and plunged into the freezing water up to his waist. In his attempt to keep his balance, he dropped both the carcass and the rifle, swinging his arms wildly, and in the process disturbed more than the one log, for a larger one suddenly rolled over and struck him in the small of the back. He was driven forward, his entire torso going under, and came up sputtering. The larger log moved relentlessly down, crushing against his legs. He lunged frantically trying to escape, but was caught.

He rolled over to push the log off with his hands, and as he did, another one slipped behind him, trapping him in a sitting position. He pushed against the log, but his hands slipped off the slick surface. He pulled with all his strength to free his legs, but he had nothing to hold to gain leverage.

He sank back, trying to think. He knew he was in a dangerous situation. Though his head and shoulders were out of the water, the freezing temperature would pull his vitality down in no time. He had his knife, but no way to use it. His rifle was gone, so he couldn't fire a shot to attract attention—and there was nobody to hear it if he did.

He thought about those at the cabin. They would begin to worry several hours after nightfall if he didn't return. Maybe by morning Buck would follow his trail and come looking, but he would find only a frozen corpse, for he could not survive even an hour submerged in the icy river.

Before long the sunlight would disappear, and already his legs were numb. More than once during the war he'd faced death, but that was different. The blasting of muskets, the yelling of men, and the screaming of shells overhead enabled a man to lose himself in the fury of battle.

But to die this way! He had to fight to choke down the fear rising in his throat. He knew how it would be. The entire process flashed before him, and the paralyzing horror of it gripped him.

And as the terror rushed over him again and again, he began to pray. . . .

★　★　★　★

For most of the morning Bron sat beside the fire, reading stories to Paul and Alice, but they grew tired and after lunch went to sleep. She was restless, and paced the floor, going outside to see that the horses were watered and fed. Each time she would look east to the spot where Zack had disappeared, feeling vaguely upset and troubled.

Finally at twelve-thirty she tried to take a nap, but could only toss and turn. She got up and went to look out the window, but saw nothing, and went to read her Bible. Her mind was not on the Scriptures, however, and the restlessness increased. At one-thirty she shut the Bible with an impatient gesture, closed her eyes and leaned back in her chair. The heat from the fire made her drowsy, and she began to pray silently. For a long time she sat there with her head back, and most of her prayers were for Zack.

She drifted off into a fitful half-sleep in which she was only vaguely conscious of things around her. Thoughts flitted across her mind—strange thoughts that seemed to make no sense. She swept her hand across her face to brush them away.

Then her eyes flew open and she cried out, jumping up with a frightful start.

"Bron! Wake up!" Lillian urged, grabbing her shoulders. "You've had a bad dream!"

Bron looked at her without seeing her for a moment; then she began to tremble, her hands shook, and her lips twisted with fear.

"What's wrong, Bron?" Buck cried, dropping the leather he was braiding.

She gave her shoulders a shake and said slowly as if her lips were frozen: "I have a premonition that something has or will happen to Zacharias!"

Choiya sprang lightly off the bed and moved close. "What is it? A dream?"

"I don't know—but he is in trouble, terrible trouble!" She bracketed her head with her hands, then dropped them. "We've got to go help him."

"Bron! It was only a dream!" Lillian cried. "We can't go out in this weather."

"If you feel so, we must go," Choiya said. She had lived with both the Cheyenne and the Arapaho for many years. Dreams to them were much more real—and much more meaningful—than to white people. She knew of many instances when dreams turned out to be reality.

Buck said, "No, I'm the one to go. You can't leave the babies here, Choiya. I'll saddle up and follow his trail."

"Buck—wait!" Bron was thinking fast. "We'll have to take the sledge. If he's hurt, we'll need it to bring him home."

"Right! I never thought of that."

Buck raced out the door, and Bron grabbed the blankets off her bed, saying, "Get the blankets from the loft, Lillian." When the girl hesitated, Bron yelled, "*Get them,* I said! Now!"

Lillian whirled and scrambled up the ladder like a squirrel. Bron began throwing warm clothing, some food, and a lantern into a gunny sack.

"What did you see in your dream?" Choiya asked as she moved to help her.

"Only his face. He may be hurt. He called my name—that's all."

"I wish I could go to him," Choiya said.

"You must stay with the babies."

"Do you think your God will lead you to him?"

Bron looked intently at Choiya's face, now no longer stolid and still. She saw the fear lurking behind the dark eyes, and she said gently, "Yes, sister, I believe that."

"Then I will pray to Jesus," Choiya replied quietly. She brought her doeskin coat and half moccasins to Bron. "These are better for cold than yours."

Bron nodded, "Thank you, Choiya."

The team pulled up and Buck called, "Let's go!"

The two women ran out, threw the things inside the sledge, and Bron jumped in. Buck gave the mules a touch of his whip, and they leaped forward, plowing rigorously through the snow. The cabin was soon lost as they rounded the edge of the trees, and Buck asked, "What time is it?"

"It was five after two when I—when I woke up."

"It'll be dark by five," Buck said. "If we don't find him by then, we won't be able to follow the trail." He hit the team again, and they increased their pace. "Not hard to follow his trail," he shouted. "That's good!"

They raced across the snow steadily, stopping to rest the mules. They were breathing hard as Buck pulled them up at a creek. "Look, the ice is broken," he said as the mules drank. "He got this far."

"How far is it to Seven Point?" she asked.

"About five miles, but we've come a long way." He whipped the mules up, and they struggled through the snow until finally they came to a clearing, and Buck shouted, "Look, Bron! There's his horse!"

He drove the team up to where Ornery was tied, and fell out of the sledge. "His trail goes this way, Bron—come on!"

"Wait! We'll need the lantern." She got it out of the sack, checked the oil, then joined him as he plunged along beside the river. They both feared they wouldn't find him in time, so they ran until their breath rasped and their lungs burned like fire.

"He crossed here—at the old dam," Buck gasped. "Come on!"

"Wait!" Buck stopped and saw that Bron was standing very still, holding her hand up.

"What is it?"

"Shhhh!" she said. Both of them listened. Then they heard a very faint cry.

"Where are you, Zack?" Buck yelled.

"Over here—in the water . . ." came the reply.

"There he is!" Buck pointed.

Bron rushed ahead, stepping carefully over the logs. When she reached him, she cried, "Oh, Zack!" She leaned down and touched his face—by now ashen, with a bluish cast. He tried to smile but his lips wouldn't move easily, and he mumbled, "Bron . . ."

"What should we do?" she asked, the hot tears running down her cheeks, so relieved she was to see him.

"Legs are stuck."

Buck came up and looked over her shoulder. He had lit the lantern, for darkness was descending fast. Swinging the light back and forth, he studied the situation. "Don't want to shift the logs—"

"We've got to get him out!" Bron cried.

"Wait a minute," Buck said. "Hold the lantern, Bron." He had spotted a small log on the bank. He scooted over and picked it up—just three inches in diameter, gnawed to a point at one end. He walked the log back like a tightrope walker, then paused and put the larger end in the water, probing for the bottom. "It seems real solid here, mostly gravel, I think."

"What can we do?" Bron asked.

"Put the lantern down," Buck said. "I'm going to pry that log up just enough for his legs to slide out, but he's probably too numb to move them."

"You're right there," Zack whispered.

Buck braced himself, then plunged into the freezing water. The icy temperature nearly drove him into shock, but he only gasped, then picked up the pole. He shoved it under the large log, felt around for a purchase, and said, "All right, Bron—when I holler, pull for all you're worth."

Bron bent over on her knees and said, "Lean back—let me hold you." Zack did as she directed, and she put her arms around his chest. "Hold to my arms!"

Buck moved up under the pole until he had to bend his knees. He took a deep breath, then suddenly straightened up. The log cut into his shoulder, bending as he pushed, and he thought with despair that it was too flexible; but he took a half step forward and with the last ounce of strength in his slender frame, gave a mighty heave—and he saw the log rise several inches.

"Now, Bron!" he gasped, and she flung herself backward, her fingers clawing at Zack's jacket. He didn't move, and she strained until the blood pulsated in her head—then she fell backward as he slid free.

"He's loose, Buck!" Bron cried, holding Zack tightly until Buck came splashing to them. "Let's get him to shore." Together they pulled him across the logs until he lay on the bank. "I'll get the sledge, Bron. We've got to have a fire!"

He stumbled off, carrying the lantern, while Bron sat holding Zack. He looked up at her, awed by everything. She opened the deerskin coat, pulled him within as if he were a child, then closed it around him. The heat of her body soaked into him, and he whispered, "Thanks."

"I'm just glad we found you!"

"How—what made you come?"

She shook her head, holding the coat tightly to keep the chill wind from him. "Are your legs broken?"

"No. The log just pushed me down and held me." He was quiet, and soon they heard Buck shouting at the mules as he drove them beside the river. He looked up at her and asked again, "Why'd you come, Bron? I was a dead man."

She looked down at him. "I heard you calling me."

Puzzled, he asked, "When?"

"About two o'clock."

Trying to comprehend, he said, "Now that's a strange thing. A very strange thing. Maybe He *does* hear before we speak and answer before we call!"

Buck pulled the team up and came racing over with the lantern. In short order he had a fire going so they'd have some heat while changing into warm clothing. They got Zack into dry clothes, wrapped him in blankets, and put him in the back of the sledge. Buck changed his own clothes, and they made the long trip back to the cabin by midnight, stopping to get Ornery.

Choiya met them and Zack smiled at her as Buck pulled him out of the sledge. His legs folded, and Choiya rushed forward. "Legs don't seem to work," he complained.

"You must soak in water, and it will hurt very much," she said.

"Won't complain," he said. "Guess I'm pretty lucky to be feeling anything at all tonight."

Soon as the water was heated, Zack was immersed in a tub of warm water. He had demanded that the women make some sort of curtain, and they hung a blanket over a rope. Though he sat with his back to the opening, he still had little privacy. They kept sending Buck in with something to eat or drink. The women, concerned that he was doing all right, poked their heads around the curtain at frequent intervals. The children, too, not to be left out, came to stare at the big man in the small tub who almost "got drownded."

The pain came, too, with frightening force, and by dawn he grumbled, "I felt a lot better than this under that blasted log!"

"I know it hurts, but Choiya says it's what we have to do," Bron said. She and Choiya had stayed up with Buck in case he needed help.

Finally Zack felt he was ready to get out and begged for his clothes. But when he tried to stand he discovered that his legs were like rubber, so Buck wrapped a blanket around him, then with Choiya's help, half carried him to her bed.

Zack flopped down with a sigh and looked up. They were circled around him—Bron, Choiya, Buck. "You remind me of buzzards looking down at a dying calf!" he groaned. Then he closed his eyes, fatigue hitting him like a fist.

"Got something to say," he mumbled. He struggled to a sitting position, wincing with pain. "I had a few close calls in the war—but this thing was different. I was dead in that creek—but somehow I'm here. So—I think God must be giving me a second chance." He saw Bron's eyes glisten, and added, "I'm not in real good shape with God—but He sure did get my attention while I was in the water with that log in my lap!"

He nodded and said with some satisfaction, "I came to be a hermit—" He looked around at the faces surrounding him and smiled. "Well, I've not quite made that—but I'm not sure I'm satisfied with it anymore." He shifted around to get more comfortable. "I think I could learn to live with all of you—and we've got the whole outdoors to spread out. No crowding here at Alder Gulch! We'll build some more space, and go to town when we want to—and there'll be nobody to bother us, no sir!"

CHAPTER FOURTEEN

NEW DEVELOPMENT

★ ★ ★ ★

The snows of January melted in a sudden February thaw, and when the mud of March appeared, Zack attached the wheels, hitched up the wagon and drove to Virginia City. The others clamored to go, but he was adamant. "Nope, I've got something on my mind. You can all go next trip." He drove off that morning whistling happily, as he had often done since his brush with death.

He had been a different man since then, gentler with the children and talking with a freedom he'd never had. But Bron was still worried about his trip to town. She spoke to Buck about it while she was washing clothes in front of the cabin.

"I wish Zack would come back," she said. The water in the pot boiled, and she shaved some lye soap into it, then stirred it with a stick until it dissolved into a froth. She picked up a dress and put it in the pot, then looked across the meadow where the trail bent obliquely. She had watched that road all afternoon, hoping to see the wagon appear.

"You worried about him meetin' up with Red Yeager?" Buck asked. He himself had been watching the trail but said nothing. He had asked to go with Zack when he left for Virginia City, but Zack had refused.

"It hurt his pride—getting knocked down by that bully," Bron said. "We didn't have to have anything from town." She put a pair of pants into the pot, and looked again toward the trail. "I wish he'd come back."

"He's been real quiet since that time, Bron." Buck stood up, stretched, and said, "But I'm glad you and the kids are here."

"Choiya's not happy with it," she said, looking troubled. She hesitated. "I shouldn't have said that, Buck."

"Neither is Lillian. She plans to run off first chance she gets."

"I know. She thinks she's missing out on life." Bron added more soap, then stirred the clothes slowly, her eyes thoughtful. "She's anxious to grow up, Buck. Right now, she's neither one thing nor the other—too young to be a woman, and too old to be a child. It's not a good time of life for most people. Sad it is, and full of all kinds of fears."

"Were you like that, Bron, when you were growing up?"

"Oh yes!? Why, I was so skinny and plain and full of freckles, and the other girls so pretty, I knew I'd never get a man! Every night I cried myself to sleep, and the mornings I hated to get out of bed!"

"Aw, Bron, you were never ugly," Buck protested in unbelief.

She laughed and shook her flaming red hair that cascaded down her back in soft waves. "Nothing to buy a stamp for, I was then, Old Man! It was a hard time for me."

To Buck, Bron was not only beautiful, as he admired her creamy skin and sparkling eyes, but she was understanding. He had learned to trust and confide in her, something he'd never been able to do with any woman. She was the closest thing to a mother he'd known, yet young enough for him to talk to as a friend.

"I feel that way, Bron," he said. "I don't see how I can ever amount to anything. Skinny as a bean pole and ugly as a pan of worms. Zack's the only man who ever done me a good turn in my whole life."

Bron stretched to put her hand on his shoulder, he was that much taller than she, and tilted her head back. "You know what I see when I look at you, Buck? A fine, strong tall man. That's what you're becoming. Right now you're like a young fawn, all legs and a little clumsy, but in a short time—very short now!—you'll be filled out, and you'll be like that great stag we saw this morning at the spring! You mind how handsome he was? All strong and clean and proud!" She smiled up at him. "And you'll be a man of God, too, Buck, for there's a hunger in you to be good."

He felt that flush of warmth that always came when she touched him or when she talked to him, not really believing what she said, but hungry for approval. A movement caught his eye, and he turned and said with excitement, "There he comes!"

Bron wheeled and shaded her eyes with her hand. "Yes—I see him." Her face changed, and he knew she had been worried about him. "But," she said, "it looks like two wagons!"

Buck looked again. "You're right. Wonder who's in the other one?"

Choiya came from across the yard where she'd been scraping rabbit skins, but kept her distance, standing alone with her eyes on the two wagons. The children rushed out to join Buck and Bron.

As the wagons drew near, they saw that the second one was filled with men, talking and laughing.

Zack pulled up in front of the cabin, with the second wagon creaking to a stop directly behind. Zack threw the reins down, jumped to the ground, and smiled broadly. "Well, there's the new cabin." He waved his hand toward the men who were piling out of the wagon. Bron counted seven—a bearded rough-looking bunch, dressed in blue pants, colored flannel shirts, and knitted caps.

"They're our logging crew," Zack explained. "Found them between jobs, and hired them to cut the logs and build the new cabin." He turned to the men. "Raoul, you want to cut a few logs before supper?"

"By gar, we do it!" The speaker, the largest of the loggers, a dark man with teeth that gleamed when he smiled, stepped forward. "You show us the trees, Zack, and we show you how to cut trees!"

Zack grinned. "Buck, you want to take them up to the stand of timber I showed you?"

"Sure." Buck grabbed his hat. "It's up this way." He waited until the men gathered their tools, jabbering in a language the boy couldn't understand. "What are they talking?" he asked.

"French, down from Canada," Zack said. "Raoul, we'll have supper ready when you get back. Buck, you can take the team and start snaking the logs back as they're cut."

As the loggers hurried up the hill, Zack turned to Bron. "We got to cook a big supper," he said. "Those fellows can do a lot of work, but they eat a lot, too. I brought back extra food, though."

He was more excited than she had ever seen him, his eyes alive with life. She asked carefully, "Did you have any trouble?"

"With Yeager?" He shook his head. "He wasn't in town. I saw Billy Page, by the way. He's coming out to see you." He gave her a questioning look, adding, "He's quite a fellow."

"Yes. I don't see how I could have gotten here without him."

Zack shifted his feet as he thought of that, then turned and walked toward Choiya. She watched him approach, her face changing slightly as he neared. "I got you a present." He smiled and reached into the side pocket of his coat. Her eyes followed his every move.

She took the package and unwrapped it slowly. It was a beautifully wrought gold medallion with a polished blue stone in the center, and a chain of tiny links of gold. She stared at it so long Zack grew anxious.

"Don't you like it?"

She lifted her head and there was a peculiar expression in her eyes, one he'd not seen. "Do you know what it means?" she asked. Her lips were soft and her face had an expectant air as she waited.

"Means?" Zack looked at the necklace. "Why, I guess not. An Indian was selling it, and I thought it was pretty and would look good on you. What does it mean, Choiya?"

She dropped her eyes. "Oh, nothing really." Then she smiled. "Thank you, Zack. It's beautiful." She turned and walked away.

Zack felt he'd hurt her, and shook his head. *Try to please them and they act like you bashed them in the head!* he thought.

He walked back to Bron. "I got you a present too, but it won't be ready for a week."

"What is it?"

"A cow and a calf," he grinned. "You can't wear that around

your neck, but it sure would be good to have some fresh milk, wouldn't it?"

"Oh, Zacharias—how wonderful!" she exclaimed. "Wait you," she said, "until I get her! Then it's cooking you'll see, with fresh milk!" She was so excited that she did just what she'd do with Buck. She threw her arms around him and gave him a hug. "Oh, see how kind you are!" The touch of her firm rounded body sent a shock through Zack, and he was speechless. Her hair was fresh and clean, and smelled like soap, and when she drew back, her eyes were laughing into his. "What color is she?" she asked, unaware of the volcano her embrace had released.

"Why, red, I think," he stammered, and then covered his confusion with, "You better think of supper for that crew. I got some boards from the mill to make a table and some benches."

Bron rushed into the cabin and began the preparations— Choiya cut steaks from the elk Zack had shot earlier, while Bron and Lillian baked bread and pies. Zack made a long rectangular table with two benches for the loggers. Time flew by and before he knew it, Zack saw Buck come out of the woods snaking a log.

After unfastening the log, Buck said, "Gosh, Zack, I thought you were pretty good with an axe, but them loggers, why, they just seem to fly!"

"Every man to his trade," Zack grinned. "Bet they can't shoot as good as you, but right now we need loggers more than shooters."

By the time Raoul led his crew out of the woods, there was a tidy stack of logs on the ground, and supper was ready. The men fell on the steaks and bread with a ferocity such as Bron had never seen. They laughed and made jokes, and Zack whispered to Buck, "I'll bet those jokes are pretty raw. Good thing they speak French!"

After supper, Raoul and his crew set up the tents they had brought, while Zack and Buck made a bonfire. Then to everyone's delight the men got out an accordion and a fiddle. Soon the clearing was filled with lively strains.

The loggers began to dance—evidently one of the joys of their lives, for they danced well. Raoul approached Bron. "Mees Morgan—maybe you dance for us, eh?"

"Oh, she's a preacher, Raoul," Zack interrupted. "Preachers don't believe in dancing."

"'Tis wrong you are again, Zacharias!" Bron cried. "None of your sinful dances, but the old Welsh, I can do." She stood up and began to twirl gracefully around the fire. The musicians hesitated only a moment, then picked up the quick rhythm of her feet. She raised her hands and performed the Welsh dances enjoyed before America was discovered. Her face lit up with a smile, and her feet moved in the intricate patterns she had learned as a young child.

It brought back memories of the last time she had danced—with Owen before he left for America—and that thought brought a wave of sadness. But she finished the dance and fell into a chair, protesting "No more!" when the others applauded and asked for another.

Finally the musicians played a waltz, and some of the loggers began to dance around the fire, laughing and singing. Zack saw Choiya away from the fire, and on impulse walked over to her. "Not much like the dance of the Cheyenne, is it, Choiya?"

She said, "No—but my father taught me this when I was a little girl."

He said, "All right, let's have a sample," and held out his arms.

She stood motionless. "No, it would not be good."

"Oh, come on," he laughed. "Do you good." He pulled her forward and she followed his steps. They had not moved more than a dozen steps before he exclaimed, "Say, you're a lot better at this than I am!"

She smiled, and the two spun around the fire as smoothly as if they were on a polished dance floor. The music floated on the air, and she was very conscious of his hand around her waist, and the movement of the thick muscles of his shoulder where her arm rested. Her feet matched his every move, like a feather, and somehow she forgot everything else. The night was dark, but the fire sent waves of yellow light over the clearing, and the golden sparks flew upward to mingle with the silver stars, it seemed.

She was wearing the medallion he had given her, and the gold reflected the light of the fire. He admired it, and grinned, "Been a long time since I went to a party."

"A long time for me too," Choiya said softly.

"I feel like a fool. Here I come a thousand miles to be a hermit—and now look at me." He sobered. "I've never thanked you for what you've done—taking care of Sam." He tightened his grip on her hand. "Couldn't have made it without you, Choiya. Thanks."

She felt her face grow warm with the praise and said, "It is nothing."

The waltz ended, and Raoul asked Choiya, "You dance with me?" And without waiting for an answer, he took her hands and swept her around the campfire.

Buck and Lillian were on the sidelines, watching, and she whispered, "Aren't you going to ask me to dance?"

He was astonished, for she had paid little attention to him since their return, except to ridicule. "Why—why, I can't dance."

"Oh, it's easy. Here, let me show you." She moved in front of him. "Put that arm around my waist, and hold my hand like this." She put his arms in position. "Now, we'll go very slowly—watch my feet. One—two—*three*. One—two—*three!*"

Buck found himself moving around, conscious of her nearness. He felt as clumsy as a bear, but as she kept on coaching him, he began to get the hang of it.

"That's very good!" Lillian said with a smile, the first he'd seen for days. "Now, a little faster."

He went around the campfire, feeling self-conscious but concentrating on his feet.

After a few minutes, she said, "Now, that wasn't so hard, was it?"

"It is for me," he muttered.

"Oh, you're doing fine," she countered, smiling up at him. "I didn't realize you were so tall. I like tall men."

He missed a step when she said that, and said, "Sorry, Lillian."

"You're doing fine." She was happy, and it made her look pretty. "I love dancing!" she said joyously. "When I get old enough, I'm going to dance every night."

He was acutely aware of holding her, and felt embarrassed. He had never been around a young woman, not like this, and he was both sorry and relieved when the music finally stopped and Raoul called, "All right. To bed!"

The loggers groaned, but he was adamant, and soon the yard was silent. Up in the loft, as Zack and Buck lay down to sleep, he asked, "Zack, how long you think it'll take to put up the new cabin?"

"Be pretty quick the way those fellows work. Why?"

"Oh, I was just wonderin'." He lay there thinking of dancing with Lillian. "Maybe we can have some music every night."

"Wouldn't be surprised." Zack lay thinking of the night, not quite sure about himself. The merriment had released something within, and he wondered what had changed him, but he fell asleep without any answers.

The new cabin seemed to fly into place. When the stack of logs grew large enough, Raoul sent a man down to notch them. He did the job so quickly with his razor-sharp axe that Zack was amazed. It took only two days for them to cut enough logs, and by the time the crew came out of the woods, there were enough logs notched to begin raising the walls.

He had decided to make the new cabin face the original cabin, with a ten-foot space in between. The roofs would join so that there would be a covered section for a porch between the two sections. The men began raising the logs early on Friday morning, and by late Saturday, the walls were in place.

"We get him finished by Tuesday, roof and all!" Raoul promised.

On Sunday morning, Bron announced there would be a service, and Raoul brought his crew. They gathered in the new cabin, and Bron began by singing hymns. The loggers were Catholic, and didn't know them, so there was little support from anyone except Buck, who had learned a few. She read from the Bible, and Raoul translated each verse into French.

Then she spoke briefly about Jesus Christ and His death on the cross. It was very quiet, and her words carried over the walls. The sky above was clear, and the sun shone on their heads. Again, Raoul interpreted for her, and the loggers sat on the floor with bare heads, studying Bron's face with curiosity. They were a rugged breed, but the sight of the small woman with the peculiar green eyes and red hair stirred something in them.

Not a person moved as Bron finished. "God has such a great love for each one! None of us could ever find our way to Him, but He has sent one who can show us the Father—and that one is the Lord Jesus Christ!"

Her fervent voice and joyful eyes held them spellbound, including Zack. There was no faith in him, only doubt. But he had a wistful look on his face, and deep in his heart he wished he could believe as Bronwen did.

After she had prayed, they filed out quietly. During the service Bron had noticed Choiya standing to one side, holding Hawk in her arms. Later that day, she asked, "Choiya, when I go to preach to the Arapaho people, would you interpret for me?"

Choiya showed surprise. "I do not believe in your Jesus."

"I know—but you can tell them what I say."

"How do you know I will tell them your words truly?"

Bron smiled. "I know. Will you do it?"

"We will see." She hesitated, then asked, "Would you like to learn to speak the language of the Arapaho?"

"Oh yes! Would you teach me?"

"If you like."

By Tuesday the cabin was finished, shakes in place and door hung, and Raoul and his crew left. Almost at once, Zack was besieged on all sides to go to town, and he laughed. "You folks sure do make sorry hermits—but I guess we better go get your cow, Bron."

They all climbed into the wagon, and as they drove along, both Bron and Choiya were hoping that Red Yeager would still be gone, but Zack didn't seem to be perturbed about anything. He was happier than any of them had seen him. When they neared town, he said to Choiya, "Well, there's civilization."

"It seems very busy."

Zack looked closer. "Sure does. Must be some kind of celebration."

As they drove down the street, which was lined with wagons, mules, and horses, Zack scanned the crowd. The sidewalks were jammed, and everyone seemed to be shouting.

They pulled up in front of Pfouts'. store, and spotted Parris in the doorway. "Hey, Parris!" Zack yelled.

Pfouts looked up and came running over. "Well, guess you heard the news?"

"News? No, we just came to buy supplies. What's going on?"

"Why, it's gold, Zack! Right here in Virginia City. Mostly out toward the Gulch." He laughed. "Your place is pretty much in that direction. You're probably sitting on a million dollars worth of gold!"

Bron and Buck had come to stand beside Parris. "You look unhappy, Zack. What's wrong?" Buck asked. "It's great! You're maybe a millionaire!"

Zack slumped in his seat, and pulled the English derby over his brow firmly. "No, sir, I'm not in this thing. And when you see this place in about a month, you'll wish you'd never heard of gold!"

"Why, Zacharias?" Bron asked.

"Because every mining camp on earth is a slice right out of hell!" he grunted. He waved at the street. "Every other building there will be a saloon or a dance hall. Every tough and every crook in the territory will head straight for Alder Gulch, and in two months killings will be as common as flies!"

"It won't be that bad," Parris protested. "We'll have law here."

"You'll have what law you make, Parris," Zack said. "But not me. We're sitting the whole thing out." He nodded firmly, adding, "You can have your gold rush, but it's not for us."

"You won't be able to avoid it, will you?" Choiya asked. "Those gold seekers will be all over the place."

"They can do what they please, but we're holing up at our place." Zack looked around with distaste, and then said firmly, "I came here to be a hermit—and a hermit is what I'll be!"

PART THREE

THE INNOCENTS

★ ★ ★ ★

CHAPTER FIFTEEN

HOLDUP

★ ★ ★ ★

By April of 1863 Virginia City had swollen from a town of six hundred to a burgeoning mining camp of over four thousand prospectors along Alder Creek. Under the shadow of the Ruby Mountains and the Tobacco Roots, they gutted the hillside with sluices and pans and long toms, where once an old river's channel had dropped its gold treasure.

Billy Page sat in the Fair Lady, one of the dozens of saloons thrown together from logs and mud, looking at the losing hand he'd just tossed on the table. Fay Nettleton scraped the money together, apologizing. "Sorry. Never saw such a streak of bad luck, Billy. Makes me feel guilty to take your money."

"Enjoy it, Fay. When my luck turns, you can bet I'll take yours." Page leaned back in his chair, his face unruffled. Across the room a bar skirted the edge of a dance floor, and heavy-footed miners whirled the brightly gowned women around for a dollar a dance. On a raised platform at the far end of the room the fiddles and guitars pitched into a quadrille as the announcer twanged out the routine.

Billy stretched and yawned. "Guess I'll get something to eat." As he made his way across the floor, the music halted, and the women led their partners toward the bar where they paid fifty cents for two drinks—straight whiskey for the men and ginger beer for the women. Nell Seymore seized Page's arm, smiling up at him. "Let's have a dance, Billy." He only grinned, "Later, Nell," and left.

The relative quiet of the street was a relief, and he leaned against the building to smoke a cigar, savoring its fragrance. It was the last one he had, and little cash in his pocket. His scanty earnings these days were depressing, and he strode down Holland Street, driven by a gust of impatience.

He had six dollars—all that was left of the killing he'd made in Helena. His hotel bill was overdue and he wondered if he should move on. But he had no way of making a fresh start. *Why not stake a claim?* Every week some lucky miner hit a pocket and became rich overnight. But Billy's luck wasn't running. He was an indolent man, averse to physical labor.

He stopped at the Rainbow for a late supper, which reduced his scanty funds still more. When he was half finished, Colonel Wilbur Simpson joined him. Simpson—tall, thin, with a shock of white hair and steady gray eyes—was a lawyer by profession. "Place is getting rotten, Billy," he said, sipping his coffee.

"Ought to be good for a lawyer," Page smiled.

"Only law here to speak of is what the miners make for themselves," Simpson grunted. "Always that way in these mining camps. Civilization is a thousand miles away, and the only thing a man can look to is a gun in his pocket." He shifted his position. "And it's going to get worse," he added. "Did you hear about Dan Dempsey?"

"No. What happened to Dan?"

"He was killed by a gunman yesterday in broad daylight. Del Regan and Phil Overton were behind him, on the road to Bannack, and saw the whole thing. Phil said the gunman jumped out from behind a gully, shot Dan without a warning, then took his poke, and galloped off."

"I hadn't heard of it. I'm sorry. Dan was a good man."

"Stage has been robbed twice in the last month," Simpson said bitterly. "Somehow the reprobates seem to know when it's carrying gold." He got up and dropped a coin on the table. "Good night, Billy."

Billy finished his meal, then paid for it and walked back to the hotel. He went to bed, but lay awake for a long time, trying to figure out a way to get some cash. He knew nobody in the camp to borrow from, for although he was a cheerful man, he made no fast friends.

A thought nudged at him, and he shook it off, but as he lay there, he began to consider it. The stage would carry money, but a holdup was a risky business. It was the outgoing stage that carried the gold shipments from the camp. But that one, he thought slowly, always had at least one armed guard on the box, and often a rider with a drawn shotgun who would shoot first and ask questions later. It would take a gang to do a job like that.

Billy let his mind drift to other possibilities. The incoming stage from Bannack never carried a guard. The mail came on it, but no gold shipments to tempt a robber. There were passengers, however, and they would have money and jewelry. The more Page thought about it, the more convinced he became that it was his only option. The question of morality didn't enter his mind, for he was not a man who concerned himself with right or wrong. He had stolen before and believed a man should look out for himself. If he permitted himself to be robbed, he ought to be more careful.

Page fell asleep with his mind made up, and rose at six. He picked up a brown suit he'd never worn in Virginia City, a rough garb used for camping or grubby work, and stuffed it into a sack, along with a soft cloth hat. The stable was nearby where he rented a horse, then went to the Rainbow and spent his last three dollars for breakfast and a tip for the waitress—this last in a gesture of defiance. Now he was completely broke and would have to carry out his plan. He rode out of town in the opposite direction from Bannack, circled around, and returned to the road leading to Bannack. About five miles out of town, he dismounted and changed into the brown suit.

The spot he'd chosen was where the road bent around a sweeping grove of fir trees on a steep slope. He could sit on his horse on the rise, giving him a clear view of the road. When the stage rounded that curve, he'd race down the slope and put a gun in the driver's face so fast there'd be no room or time for him to resist. Drivers, he thought, were cautious about putting up a fight. After all, it wasn't their money, and unless there was a heavy guard, they'd stop the stage instantly.

Forty-five minutes later he sighted his prey rolling toward the curve. He tied a handkerchief over his face, pulled the soft hat down till the brim covered his hair and shaded his eyes. His heart began to race as he galloped down the steep hill, pulled his gun and waited. The stage rumbled around the curve, and he spurred forward, shouting, "Hold it!" sending a shot close to the driver's head. The man jerked the lines back, bringing the stage to an abrupt stop. Page moved alongside and yelled, "Outside—one move and I'll shoot!"

Three men stepped out. Billy had hoped for more, but he leveled his gun, commanding, "Drop your guns and toss the money on the ground!"

Two of them, obviously miners, obeyed. The third passenger didn't move. The well-dressed man, average height, with fresh, light skin, eyed him watchfully, the small wrinkles in the corners converging. *He's a dandy!* Billy thought as he aimed the gun at him and drew the hammer back. "Hurry it up—and I'll take that watch, too."

The man said nothing, but slowly reached into his pocket, took out a fat expensive-looking wallet, and tossed it on the ground. Keeping his eyes fixed on Billy, he unfastened his watch and laid it next to the other items, then stood up.

"All right, get back inside. Driver, throw down the mail sack."

He waited until the sack hit the ground; then as the door shut, he cried out, "Get going!" and fired a shot into the air that startled the horses. The driver whipped them into action, and the stage rolled down the dusty road. Billy dismounted, stuffed the wallet, cash, and watch into his coat pockets, grabbed the mail bag, then leaped to the saddle and left at a dead run.

He rode toward Bannack for less than a quarter of a mile, then stopped in a thick grove to change clothes. He stuffed the brown suit and the cap under a rock, then checked his loot. The cash from the two miners amounted to less than a hundred dollars, but the fancy wallet belonging to the dandy had over five hundred in cash! He transferred it to his own wallet, then searched the mail pouch. There were only two bulging envelopes—one, filled with legal papers; the other, fifty dollars in greenbacks, which he pocketed. He stuffed the empty wallets and the mail sack under the rock with the clothes, then mounted and rode away.

Instead of returning to Virginia City, Billy circled around and headed toward where the Ruby River led toward the foothills. It wouldn't do to appear back in town so soon after the stage rolled in, and he'd already planned what he would do. Although he had never been to see Bronwen Morgan, he'd heard Parris Pfouts speak of Winslow's place, giving some general directions. Billy headed for the hills, and after a false start, found the landmarks Pfouts had mentioned, and a little after one that afternoon spotted a slow spiral of smoke rising ahead. He made his way along, and as he rounded a curve in the timber, saw the cabin up on a rise.

As he rode up the slope, the door of the cabin opened, and Bron came to meet him. "Well, now, look who's come to visit!" she said. Her happy greeting made him feel good.

"Got tired of my own company," he said, dismounting. "Quite a place," he smiled, nodding at the cabin.

"Tie your horse, Billy, and we'll visit," she said, coming to stand beside him. "How good to see you. I've thought about you often."

She was fresh and clean in the afternoon sun, and he had forgotten how green her eyes were as they sparkled. "I've been fine," he said, adding, "I've wondered about you, though. Parris keeps me posted, but you're cut off out here. Don't you get bored?"

She laughed and took his arm. "No. Come, see my cow."

They walked around to the back of the cabin where a red cow and a yearling stood looking over a fence as the two approached. Bron put her arms around the cow's neck. "This is Penelope." She was obviously very proud of the animal, and of the chickens that scurried toward her as she clucked for them. "We get two dozen eggs a week now, and plenty of milk and fresh butter," she said. "Come now, and you'll have a glass of it."

She led the way to one wing of the cabin, seated him at the table and poured a glass of milk. "That's good milk, Bron," he said as he drank. "But, where is everyone? I thought you had a mob out here."

"Oh, Choiya and the babies are in the other wing," she said. "Buck took Alice and Paul fishing."

"What about Winslow?"

"Why, he's gone to town, Billy. I'm surprised you didn't meet him."

Page faltered slightly, then said quickly, "Guess you didn't think you'd be doing this when you got to Montana, did you, Bron? I mean, you haven't been able to missionary much."

She smiled and leaned forward. "Why, that's going to happen, Billy. Choiya's teaching me to speak Arapaho, and Zacharias has taken me over to Black Pigeon's camp twice."

"You preach to them?"

"Well, not so much." Bron smiled and there was a trace of self-mockery in her eyes. "I try to use what little I know of their language—and they think it's funny." She laughed ruefully. "Last time I was trying to say 'God made everything—from snakes to babies'—and they all laughed at me!"

"What did you actually say?" Billy asked.

" 'The snake fell out of the tree and ate the baby!' Wasn't that awful? But they've accepted me now. I know that God's going to do a great work with them."

Her easy references to God disturbed Page, and he changed the subject. "Winslow find any gold yet?"

"Why, no, Billy. He's not prospecting."

Page shook his head. "That's a shame. I don't know anything about mining myself, but I heard the assayer say the creek that runs through this land could be rich."

"Some men have taken up claims on both sides of Zacharias's land," Bron nodded. "I guess they must have found some gold, because they work at it steady. But Zacharias will never do it."

They visited for an hour; then she insisted on fixing supper for him. He protested at first, but realized it would be a good alibi if he stayed the night. Besides, it was a nice diversion.

By suppertime the place was busy as an anthill. Winslow came driving in just before dark, and greeted him warmly. "Billy, I'm glad to see you. You're staying the night, of course?"

Page had seen Winslow only once, and then he was drunk. Now there was a steadiness in his eyes and an air of competence that discounted Billy's first estimate of him. This man could be trusted. That realization brought relief, for Page had not liked the idea of Bron being allied to a weakling.

The supper was fish, squirrel and dumplings, slices of tender deer steak, fresh bread, and peach pie, all washed down with fresh milk and scalding black coffee. Billy rather enjoyed the constant refrain of talk and laughter throughout the meal. It was a refreshing change.

He did his share of the talking, too, for they all were eager to hear fresh news—especially Lillian. "I wish I could live in town," she blurted out. Page caught the touch of bitterness and recognized the subject was a source of contention.

"You're better off out here," he said. "The town is filled with toughs, and getting worse all the time. It wouldn't be safe for a woman to go out alone. Matter of fact, it's not safe for a man." He spoke of the holdups, the shootings, and how the saloons and dance halls were rich pickings for the owners. "The miners work like dogs for their gold," Billy continued. "Then come in and throw it away gambling and drinking."

Zack nodded. "I knew that'd happen. But one day the gold will play out. Then the town will dry up. All the rough characters will move on to the next place—and the Gulch'll be like it was before."

Billy grinned at him. "You're just going to sit out here and be a hermit till that happens, huh?"

Zack scanned the group around the table. "Well," he said ruefully, "I'm not sure I'd qualify for the office of hermit anymore, Billy, but I sure won't leave this place and go fight just to stay alive in a town like Virginia City."

A tinge of jealousy hit Page, and he smiled wryly. "We can't all have your luck, Zack," he said. "I mean, I don't know any other man who winds up with all the benefits of marriage without any of the responsibilities. You've got a bunch of women to wait on you and do all the cooking and cleaning, but they can't even nag you if you decide to go into town and party with a pretty girl."

Bron's face flushed, and Choiya's eyes flared with anger. Billy knew he'd overstepped his bounds and hastened to say, "But I don't know of another man who'd take on all this."

His careless remark had created an underlying tension, and despite the apparent warm atmosphere, the remainder of the meal was subdued, though outwardly pleasant. During the rest of the evening Billy didn't miss anything. He could tell that

Choiya still chafed from his rude comment, but he also noted the way her eyes followed Zack constantly.

The women and children slept in the one cabin, and the men in the other. For about an hour Zack and Buck discussed the war with Billy. Since none of them were directly involved, the conflict seemed very far away. Page said it looked as if England would recognize the Southern Confederacy. "We'll have two countries then. Guess it'll be better that way."

Zack disagreed. "I'm out of it—but if the North loses, two bad things will happen. First, there'll still be slaves in the South, and that's just plain wrong. Second, if we're sliced into two small countries, either France or England will keep picking away until one or the other gets us under her flag. They've never really given up that idea."

Page exclaimed, "Why, that can't happen to the United States!"

"Why not, Billy?" Zack said, a trace of sadness in his voice. "It's the strong against the weak. You know that. As soon as some country feels strong enough to take us, they'll try. We won't be able to stand up to them if we're divided."

Neither one wanted to yield on his position, so they retired for the night, and the next morning Billy rode off, promising to return soon.

As he rode toward Virginia City, Page mused over the events the evening before. He was puzzled by what he had seen. He cared primarily for Bron, and though she looked happy, there was, he perceived, a potential for disaster in the situation. He liked Winslow, but thought him a strange man, the way he chose to live.

When he arrived in town, Billy stabled his horse and went to the Rainbow for dinner. He joined Pfouts and Simpson, and covered his whereabouts immediately. "I've been out to see Winslow," he said. "You know, that's a funny situation—but Zack's done more than most of us would, taking all those people in."

"I never thought it would work for Bron, but she seems happy enough," Pfouts said.

Soon the conversation turned to the stage robbery, as Page had known it would. "You didn't know about Barney being held up yesterday?" Parris asked.

"Why, no," Billy said. "Anybody get hurt?"

"No. Barney said it was just one man—not a gang."

Simpson shook his head. "Nobody thought the incoming stage would be hit. Now they'll have to carry a guard both ways. Plummer sent two more deputies over, but they won't be able to do much. Names are Forbes and Lyons."

"Dillingham needs help," Pfouts agreed. "The toughs are getting out of hand."

Billy listened to the conversation for a while, then went to his room and later to the Silver Moon and played blackjack for an hour. This time he won over a hundred dollars. *My luck's changed*, he thought with a streak of pleasure. He got up and walked around the saloon, listening to the talk of strikes and big nuggets. One man held up a huge chunk. "Worth maybe two—three hundred." But as Page watched, he saw the miner lose it in a poker game and then write an IOU for another hundred.

It was dark when he left the Silver Moon, his mind on the huge nugget he'd seen. *I'd like that chunk but not—*

"All right, stick 'em up!"

Billy whirled, a spasm of fear shooting through him as he recognized the man. "I've not got much with me . . ." he said, slowly reaching for his wallet.

The gun held on him was as steady as his voice. "I'll take the cash and the watch you stole from me yesterday."

Page knew he was a dead man, but he assumed an air of nonchalance. "You found me quick enough."

"Not hard. Let's have your gun, carefully! Now, the watch."

"Up in my room—so's most of the money."

"Let's get it, Page." He motioned with his revolver.

Billy stepped out into the street with the man right behind. "Is your gun out?" Page asked.

"It's in the holster. But it'll be out if you make a break. Let's go."

Page walked into the hotel, past the sleepy clerk and up the stairs. His mind raced as he climbed, and by the time he unlocked the door and stepped in, he'd made up his mind.

"Get the cash and the watch. I've got you covered."

"All right." Billy stepped to the dresser, his back to the man. As he opened the drawer he reached in, picked up his spare gun, and whirled. "It's one against one now. What do you want?"

"You're pretty sharp." The man didn't seem too concerned. "My name's George Ives." He waited as though the name might remind Page of something. "You've heard of me?"

"Yes. You've made a name along the way." Ives was not posted as an outlaw, but in the Grasshopper strike he had come close. He was an expert gunman and always in the midst of trouble. Now he smiled fearlessly at Page.

"Neither of us wants to die, but one will for sure. Let's make a deal. I like the way you handle yourself. I like smart people, and you're smart."

"How'd you find me, Ives?"

"I'm not so dumb myself! You covered yourself pretty well, but not many men wear a ring like that. Next time you hold up somebody, you better take it off."

Billy wore a massive gold ring with a blue stone and a heavy letter P in the center. He was chagrined, but showed nothing to Ives. "What makes you think I'll hold up another stage?"

Ives laughed softly. He had strange eyes, gray-green and bright even as he stood facing the other gun. "Why, you'll be doing that—or something like it, Billy. Here's the deal. I'm in the same line myself."

"What makes you think I won't shoot?"

"I'm not alone, Billy," Ives shrugged. "We're organized, and the boys know about you." He laughed shortly. "I'll admit I was stupid coming alone. I thought I could take you. But if you get me, you're finished. You'll never get out of Virginia City alive. That's the way we work."

"Who's we?"

Ives said, "There's about thirty of us. We're here to fleece this town. It's ripe for the picking. Right now there's over fifty thousand in the safe at Jackson's office. He'll have to ship it—and when he does, we'll know about it. How'd you like to have part of that piece of cake?"

"Join you?"

"Why not? Like I said, you're smart, and we need smart people."

Billy stared at him. "What if I double-cross you?"

"You won't do that, Billy Boy," Ives said. His agate eyes suddenly turned hard. "You think it's funny I'd trust you? I don't trust you. But there's a fortune to be made here—and I see in you a man who likes easy money."

"Always liked to play a lone hand."

"Won't do this time," Ives shook his head. "If you're not in with us, we'll do you in."

Ives said no more, but stood there confidently. He was a sharp student of the human race.

"You're the boss?" Billy asked.

"I'm the boss in this place. Well, Billy, are you in or out?"

"I don't mind."

"Fine! You'll do well for yourself."

"It's a deal." Billy lowered his gun, aware of the risk.

"Don't worry. You're with us now." He touched the knot in his neck piece. "See that? All of us wear a knot like that."

"What do you call yourselves?"

Ives smiled. "If you ever get in a jam, just holler 'I'm innocent!' and we'll be right with you." He turned to leave, a sly humor in his eyes as he said, "That's what we call ourselves—the Innocents."

After the door closed, Billy stood there, thinking it over. He had a quick inclination to leave, to get away from the whole thing, but his natural carelessness made him confident. He began to whistle as he washed his face.

CHAPTER SIXTEEN

A VISIT FROM YEAGER

★ ★ ★ ★

As summer wore on, Alder Gulch continued to grow. Though it lay in one small fold of the obscure Montana hills, the fever generated by the yellow metal floated across the boundaries, reached across the country. It was a restless America, torn by the war, and many of the disillusioned, the misfits, and the seekers of quick wealth flowed daily into the Gulch's confines. They came up the Missouri to Benton and across the Rocky passes, or over the Oregon Trail to Fort Hall or from Lewiston through the Bitterroots.

To accommodate the travelers, a stage line was started by A. J. Oliver, running through Bannack and on to Salt Lake. The population in Alder Gulch swelled to twelve thousand—men of all sorts: frontiersmen from the Platte, trappers out of Ogden's Hole, Maine men and Ohio men and Tennessee men, dance-hall girls, and gunmen. Even professionals—doctors and lawyers—turned to mining.

The gulch around Virginia City was staked out solidly, and the newcomers pushed into adjoining gulches and deeper into the Rocky Chain. Whereas the previous fall Zack had seen only a roving trapper or a solitary Indian hunter on his way to town, now the country was busy with prospectors all the way to the hills, digging into the earth and panning the small streams for yellow gold.

Two of these were John Crenna and Nolan Stone. They had come from the east to find the early comers elbow-to-elbow along Alder Creek, and had gone to the hills looking for new territory. The two staked claims on Dancer Creek, just south of where it ran across Zack's land.

Zack had known that would happen, and dreaded to see it, for he knew if they struck pay dirt, others would follow. But he had no choice, so he carefully staked off the section of the Dancer he held title to.

Late one afternoon, Crenna and Stone showed up at Zack's cabin asking if they could buy some food. "Sure could use some fresh grub," Crenna said. He was the younger of the pair, not over twenty-five, with an easy manner. He was strongly built, thick in the chest, with over-sized hands. The slow soft echoes of the South were in his talk, and he took off his hat at once when Choiya emerged from the cabin. He nodded, "Howdy, ma'am," which made Zack relax.

"Why, you'd have to ask this lady about that," he said indolently. "She's got a fine vegetable garden over there."

"I saw it," Crenna said. He smiled at Choiya, adding, "Makes me think of home, back in Tennessee. I get so hungry for a fresh tomato I'm likely to head out one day just to get one."

"I think we can spare a few tomatoes—and some other things too," Choiya said.

"Be real kind of you, ma'am," he said. "My name's John Crenna, and this is Nolan Stone."

Stone was a slight man with black eyes and sharp features. "We'll be glad to pay whatever you ask," he said. He had none of the rough speech of most miners, and there was a trace of culture in his voice that Zack identified as eastern.

"I'm Zack Winslow and this is Choiya." He hesitated, and added, "She and another lady, Bronwen Morgan, take care of all of us." It was a poor way to phrase it, but he could not put their delicate arrangement any better.

Nolan Stone seemed to sense his awkwardness, for he smiled. "I've heard of Miss Morgan from Parris Pfouts. My own parents were missionaries, so I'm anxious to meet her."

"Is that so? Well, right now she's milking in the shed around back. Maybe you can talk her out of some milk and butter while Crenna wheedles Choiya out of vegetables. If you need any fresh meat, I can let you have half a doe I shot two days ago."

"John, you check it out with Choiya," Stone urged. "I'll see if Miss Morgan can spare a drop of milk for a fellow missionary—or at least the son of one."

"I'll introduce you," Zack said, and led Stone to the milking shed.

Choiya picked a bucket off the table beside the cabin. "I'll get you a few things. What do you like besides tomatoes, Mr. Crenna?"

"Just John will do, ma'am." He hesitated, then asked cautiously, "Do you have a last name I can call you by? Like Miss Smith or something?"

She smiled. "My father's name was Lafayette. He named me after his own mother—Jeanne."

"Why do they call you Choiya, then?"

"That's what the Arapaho named me after I was captured. It means cactus. They said I was as hard to get close to as a cactus—all sharp needles."

Crenna stole a glance at the young woman, admiring the smooth oval face and clear eyes. He was a shy young man, having little experience with women. "Why," he remarked, "that don't seem likely, Miss Jeanne. Maybe they meant that pretty little bloom that's right in the middle of some of the cactus. You know, with those fine pink centers and the tiny little yellow edges."

Her lips tightened with suspicion, but he had such an open, honest face that she relaxed. "They didn't mean that."

They walked to the garden, and she picked a big red tomato. "How does this look?"

He reached out, took it almost reverently, and whispered, "Glory to God! That's the most beautiful thing I've seen since I left Tennessee." Then he flushed. "I—I mean except—" He stopped and his face grew even redder. "Didn't mean to offend you, Miss Jeanne."

Her eyes opened wide at the sound of her name. "It's all right. Why don't you sample that one."

He nibbled at the tomato, tilting his head back, and as the juice touched his tongue, his eyes half closed with pleasure. He ate the entire thing, not allowing a drop to escape, then sighed. "That's better than any nugget in the creek! Lord, I've missed my vegetables."

She was very proud of her garden, having watered it by hand and fought the bugs constantly. "Do you like carrots?" She began filling his bucket.

"Now, don't cut yourself short, Miss Jeanne!" And he got down on his knees as they moved along the rows, admiring the neat lines. Soon they were deep into a conversation about the best way to fertilize the soil and to kill bugs.

Meanwhile, Bron had been sitting on a stool, her head leaning against Penelope's flank when she heard Zack say, "Bron, you've got a customer." She straightened up and looked quizzically across. "This is Nolan Stone, Bron. He's got a claim south of us. This is Bronwen Morgan."

"I can't shake hands just now," Bron smiled, "but if you'll wait until I get through, it's glad I'll be to talk with you."

"His folks were missionaries," Zack informed her. Turning to Nolan he said, "I'll cut you off a quarter of that doe while Bron's finishing."

"Where were your people from, Mr. Stone?"

"From England originally. A little village called Boughton."

"Oh, I've been there!" Bron exclaimed. "My own home isn't too far away."

"Are you serious?" Stone exclaimed with surprise. "I've never been there myself, but my parents told me about it so many times sometimes I get to thinking I've seen it. They came to America before I was born and worked with the Indians in New York before moving onto China."

"It's a lovely little village. My fiance and I went there in May three years ago. We held services in a little Methodist church."

"Unless there were two Methodist churches, it must have been the same one my parents were married in."

"There was just the one. It sat in a little valley facing a small stream—I've forgotten the name of it."

"The Cooley River?"

"Why, there it is! The Cooley, and a lovely stream it is!"

She paused in her milking motions, and her eyes half closed. "We stayed there a week, with a lovely family. And the sermons Owen preached—!" She broke off, and the light faded from her face. She began milking again, silenced by memories of Owen welling up in her, and she blinked her eyes to free them of the tears that surfaced.

Stone noticed the change, something about that time that had brought sorrow, and with great tact, said, "My parents left shortly after they were married. They moved to London where they studied before going to the mission field."

"Where did they go?"

"To China. With a minister, Robert Morrison."

"Reverend Morrison! I've known all about him! Owen and I read stories of all the missionaries, and the dear Reverend Morrison, why he was a prince among them!" She got up and set the frothy bucket of milk down, then came to stand near him. "Is it home they are now?"

He dropped his head. "They would say so. They died in China. I was only sixteen years old." He managed a smile. "But they wrote me just before they died, and Father said, 'We'll be going home soon, Nolan—not to America, but to a house not built with hands.' "

Tears rose again in Bron's eyes, and she whispered, "How beautiful!"

"I didn't think so, Miss Morgan," he shrugged. "As a matter of fact, I got so angry with God that I've pretty well kept out of His way ever since."

She shook her head and her soft red hair swung freely. "Wait you—I will have a word or two on that subject!" Then she said, "Will you carry the milk for me?"

"Certainly."

As they rounded the corner of the cabin, Bron spied Choiya and Crenna on their knees examining the small shoots that pierced the ground. "Well, devil fly off!" she exclaimed. "She won't let the rest of us into that precious garden of hers."

"She's a very beautiful young woman," Stone said. "Her story is well known in town—as is yours."

"I suppose we're pretty well discussed then?" Bron asked. "Well, no matter. Zacharias Winslow may not be a Christian, but how kind he is—taking in this whole menagerie."

The men were invited to stay for supper, which they accepted with only a slight protest. John Crenna said little, but Stone made up for it. Once he started there was no stopping him. He had traveled widely and made the places come alive as he told story after story. Obviously, he was well-educated and aroused curiosity as to why he would be in a mining camp, working with his hands. He divulged nothing, however, but he did make one disturbing comment.

"We had a visit the other day. Two men rode up and made us an offer for our claims."

"Offer!" Crenna scoffed in disgust. "They wanted our claims for nothing, that's what it amounted to! It was Red Yeager and Long John Frank—part of the Ives' crowd."

"Who's Ives?" Buck asked.

"George Ives," Crenna replied. "He's the kingpin of the toughs. Nothing's been proved on him, but everybody knows he's up to his ears in all the robbing and killing that's been going on."

"Better not say that too loudly, John," Stone warned. "Everybody knows what Ives and his crowd do—but nobody's tried to stop them." He frowned. "Frank and Yeager put it pretty strong to us. Oh, nothing you could pin down, just vague warnings about how 'dangerous' it was way out like we are."

"They made it worse when they went to see Nick Tybalt," Crenna said. "He's got a claim downstream from us. He gave Yeager a tongue lashing, and the two men beat him to a pulp. If they come around again, I'll let them have it with my shotgun."

"No, they're gunmen, John," Stone said. "We'll just have to hang on until the law gets a better footing."

After the meal, the pair rose and Stone spotted Zack's little library. "Who's the reader?" he asked, going over to look at the titles. He read a few titles and said, "I like Dickens—especially *Great Expectations*."

"Don't know that one," Zack said. "Take any of these if you need something to read."

Stone took a copy of a book of essays. "See you got some of Emerson's stuff. You like him?"

"Can't read it," Zack confessed. "He's over my head."

"He's over his own head," Stone snorted. "Once in a while he blunders into saying a really fine thing—but most of the time he's full of hot air. I've got a copy of *Great Expectations*. Stop by and pick it up."

When they walked to the door, John Crenna said, "I sure do thank you for the vegetables, Miss Jeanne."

Zack and the others looked blank, and then they realized he was speaking to Choiya. Her cheeks flushed, and she said quietly, "You're welcome, John."

After they left, Buck asked, "What did he call you?"

"My real name is Jeanne Lafayette."

Zack stared at her. "You never told me that."

"You never asked."

"Lafayette?" Bron mused aloud. "I wonder if he was related to the Marquis de Lafayette who fought with Washington in the Revolution?"

"That was his uncle," Choiya said. "My father had a silver presentation sword that belonged to him."

They all looked at her in amazement. Zack said in awe, "Well, I'll be . . ."

"I studied all about him in school," Bron said.

Choiya was embarrassed at the attention.

Zack hastened to ask, "Well, what do we call you?"

"It doesn't matter."

Bron put an arm around her. "See how soft you are! Are you having a name or not?" Morgan fixed her eyes on the others. "You can do what you please, but I'm calling her Jeanne from now on."

"Good enough," Zack grinned. "Jeanne Lafayette—sure does sound important." It was a game at first, confusing Paul and Alice, but by the time a week had gone by, she was Jeanne to all of them.

★　★　★　★

"Be at the top of Highland Ridge at seven tonight . . ."

Ives had stopped by to drop that single sentence in Billy's ear on Tuesday morning, and after supper, he got his horse and made his way out of town. The stores and saloons were open, and the solid procession of gold seekers made a continuous line, heading for town, all the way to the ridge where Billy found George Ives waiting. The lights of camp and tent and hillside fires burned endlessly.

"Let's go," Ives said, and led the way for ten miles, coming at last to what appeared to be an abandoned house—except there were at least fifteen horses tied to saplings around the place. "Come on in," Ives said, and stepped into a single large room. Some of the men Page recognized at once. Ned Ray, the saloon owner, Boone Helm, and Steve Marshland. Others he knew only by sight, but was most surprised to see Jack Gallagher, Henry Plummer's deputy sheriff in Virginia City, as well as the other two deputies, Hayes Lyons and Buck Stinson.

Ives introduced Page. When he pointed to Red Yeager, Billy could feel the vibes. Yeager squared himself and muttered, "I ain't forgot you laid a gun on me, Page!"

Ives broke in brusquely, "Forget it, Red. Page's one of us now." When Yeager immediately changed his stance, Billy had no doubt as to who wielded the power. Yeager would not forget the incident, Billy understood, but the man would not go against Ives. George Ives was a rough customer, but he was also unmistakably the chief. He had quick eyes, a fertile brain, and nerves like steel.

Billy swung around as a back door opened, surprised to see Sheriff Henry Plummer walk in.

Ives wasted no time. "Henry, this is Billy Page. He's all right."

Plummer nodded after sizing Page up. "Listen to me, now, I can't stay long." He began to spew out information on gold shipments, who had money in their vaults, and which claims should be snapped up. Page was shocked at the man's knowledge, not only about Virginia City but every camp in the country. The gang was far more powerful than he had thought, and it was evident that Henry Plummer was the brains behind the whole operation.

"Keep your ears open," Plummer directed. He called out a series of names and assigned them a spot. "Ives, Marshland, Wagner, Carter, Long John—and you, Page, will be at Alder Gulch." He paused and said emphatically, "We're going to make enough money to retire in a few months! The gold is rolling out of the ground, but we've got a stranglehold on the whole country. Not a stage can leave without our knowledge of what's on it. We've got our men spotted, and they can't get out without our knowing."

He took a few minutes to speak to each group, then motioned to Ives' group. "You can put the pressure on the fellows who've moved out of town. Rough them up, shoot into their cabins at night. You know what to do."

"Tybalt's scared now," Ives said. "And I think with a little persuasion, Crenna and Stone will fold."

"Take care of it, George." Plummer nodded at them, and paused to say to Billy, "We all work together, Page. Glad to have you with us. You're onto a good thing."

Plummer left, and as the party rode back to the Gulch, Ives talked confidentially with Yeager and Long John Frank. The men veered off, and Ives rode up to Page. "You're going to be a rich man, Billy." He laughed and slapped his saddle horn. "These miners are like sheep—all we have to do is fleece them when the wool is right!"

★ ★ ★ ★

Zack and Buck were outside cleaning the weapons when Zack said, "Somebody's really in a hurry."

Buck lifted his head and saw a horseman racing toward them at top speed.

"That's Stone," Zack said. "Must be something wrong. Get these guns together."

By the time Stone pulled up, his horse lathered, Bronwen and Lillian had come out of the cabin. "What's the matter, Stone?" Zack asked.

"Crenna is bad hurt, Winslow!" Stone fell off his horse. "It was Yeager and Long John Frank," he said hoarsely, his face pale and damp. He forced himself to slow down. "They'd come to make trouble, force us to sign our claims over to them. While they were harassing us, the Indian woman drove up. She had some food for us, and Yeager started in at once—you know what a foul mouth he's got. He pulled her out of the wagon and started mussing her up, and John went for him. He didn't have a chance! Yeager pulled his gun and bashed him over the head, then started kicking him!"

"What about Jeanne?" Bron broke in angrily.

"They—they roughed her up—kissed her and tore her clothes," Stone said. "But she's all right. They told me they'd be back with the papers for us to sign. We've got to get a doctor for John—quick!"

"Buck, hitch up the wagon. We'll take him to town."

"I don't think he can make the trip over the trail," Stone said.

"All right. Buck, go help Stone. I'll bring Doc Steele as soon as I can get him." He saddled the horse, mounted, and spurred the startled Ornery, who shot out of the yard at a full gallop.

As Buck hitched up the wagon, Bron turned to Nolan. "Do you think he'll make it?"

"I don't know. I thought Yeager was going to kill him. I tried to help him, but it was no use." He kicked the dirt in disgust. "That's how much good I am. Stand around and do nothing while two hoodlums kill my best friend!"

"We will have them for it!" Bron declared. "Now we need to make a good bed in the wagon to bring him here. Come now, help with the blankets!"

They made a fast trip down the trail. When they got to the shack, Buck drove up to where Jeanne was sitting in the dust, holding Crenna's head in her lap. She looked up and Stone asked, "Is he alive?"

"Yes—but he's hurt bad."

They put him in the wagon on the pile of blankets, and she jumped in. "I'll hold his head in my lap so he won't feel the bouncing so much. Hurry, but be as careful as you can."

Bron met them in the yard. "Bring him inside. The bed's ready," she said. They carried Crenna into the new cabin and carefully put him down. Bron looked at his face, took a deep breath, then said, "We'll have to cut his clothes off. He may have broken bones."

They did the best they could, but time dragged on. Stone and Buck sat outside on the walkway between the two cabins. The women moved silently from one section to the other, and from time to time, the men heard a groan. The sound of it went through Stone, and Buck said, "He's still alive—that's good."

Finally they heard the sound of horses, and hurried to the front. Zack and Doc Steele rode up, and Steele slipped from his horse and unlaced his bag from the cantle of his saddle. "Where is he?" he asked gruffly, then followed Bron into the cabin.

"How's he doing, Nolan?" Zack asked.

"Bad."

"Buck," Zack said, "walk these horses, will you? I don't want them to catch cold."

Zack moved around the yard, stretching his muscles, then stopped. "How's Jeanne?" His mind had been taken up solely with the need to get the doctor.

"All right, I guess. She's stayed with John most of the time." They waited nervously for the doctor to come out with good news—they hoped. Buck joined them after taking care of the horses.

Finally Steele appeared, his coat off and his shirtsleeves rolled up. He was frowning. "I can't tell you much," he blurted out. "He's got some busted ribs, a broken collarbone—but I'm not sure about his head. He was really hit hard, gave him a bad concussion."

"But he'll live, won't he, Doc?" Stone asked.

"Maybe—but he may never be the same." Steele shook his head, and they could see he was furious. "Yeager kicked him in the head, you say?" He cursed and they could see he was angry enough to kill. "And he'll get by with it, the scum!"

"No, he will not!" They turned to see Jeanne, her eyes stormy. "I will kill him myself if no one else will!" she declared.

Stone looked at Zack. "I forgot to tell you. After he got through kicking John, Yeager gave me a message for you."

"For me?"

"Yes. He said to tell you that he's taken a liking to your women and your place. And the next time he sees you, he's going to do the same thing to you he did to John."

A stillness fell over the group, and Zack knew they were all expecting him to accept the challenge. Buck spoke up. "I'll go with you, Zack. I can shoot."

Bron had come out on the porch just in time to hear what Stone said. She watched Zack's face. He looked tired, but there was an emotion in his eyes she couldn't read. He said nothing.

Jeanne couldn't stand it any longer. "I am under your roof. Will you let this man do this to me and to your friend?"

Zack felt the pressure, but he was strongly bound by forces

of the past. Once, he thought, he would have rushed across the world to have it out with Yeager—but that was before he had given up on people. Before he'd been deceived, and before he'd learned that a man can't right all the wrongs in the world.

He said, "I'll ride in and report Yeager to Dillingham tomorrow."

Even Buck saw that futility. "Why, he's got no authority out here, Zack!"

Bitterness like bile rose in his mouth. They did not understand. "What should I do? Go in and put a bullet in Yeager? He's just one man. I can't kill every man in the Gulch who's vicious— and I don't propose to try." He saw the stark disbelief in their faces.

He added, "I'll do all I can for John. If Yeager comes on this place, that's different. But I won't go looking him up, and that's final!"

Jeanne's Cheyenne heritage boiled over. "You are *no* man!" She spun around and disappeared into the cabin, leaving an awkward silence.

"Think what you want," Zack said wearily. "I'm looking out for myself. That's what I came here to do, and it's all I'm going to do."

Steele's shoulders drooped. "Well, I guess it's asking too much at that, Zack. The man's a killer." The anger seemed to have drained out of him. "I'm going to sit with John. Get me some hot coffee."

Relieved to get away from the scene, Zack offered, "I'll do it," and left.

Stone knew this affected Buck, and gripped his shoulder. "Don't be too disappointed, young fellow. There's really nothing your friend can do."

Buck was speechless. His world had fallen apart. If the earth had swallowed him, he could not have been more shocked than when Zack had refused to fight. To Buck, that meant his friend was afraid. Now the security that had been built up since Winslow had taken him in crumbled.

CHAPTER SEVENTEEN

A MONUMENT TO INJUSTICE

★ ★ ★ ★

"John Crenna, if you get out of that bed one more time, I'm going to tie you in!"

Jeanne had left the injured man alone an hour earlier, but now coming into the cabin unexpectedly, she saw him hastily take the last few steps to his bed and fall into it. She angrily strode over, her hands on her hips. "You're worse than Hawk or Sam! I leave you alone for ten minutes and you're into something!"

Crenna squirmed, looking guilty. "Aw, Jeanne, don't carry on like that. I've been in this bed for weeks now. Getting sick of being treated like a baby."

"You've been there only twelve days, and you'll be there another twelve, Dr. Steele says." She reached over and touched his face, her hand gentle. "You're going to have scars, John." Dr. Steele had taken out the stitches, but the wounds were not healed. "We've got to keep those clean or you'll get an infection."

She filled the basin with fresh water and began washing his face. Her eyes were on the wounds, and she did not see the look on Crenna's face. He remembered when he'd first awakened after a two-day coma to find her at his bedside. She'd scarcely left him during the first week, it seemed; for every time he awoke, she was there. Steele had pronounced him out of danger after a week, but his broken ribs tied him to the bed—or should have. "Don't be shifting around, or it'll just take longer," he'd warned Crenna. "Only God's mercy that you made it—God and this young woman," he had added, smiling at Jeanne.

For days she had given him the intimate nursing care necessary when a man is immobile—feeding, bathing, changing his dressings. But he still reddened with embarrassment when she put her hands on him. She knew it, and found it amusing, as she did now. "Stop squirming," she commanded. "You're worse than Hawk!"

Her face was very close, and he was forced to hold his head still while she worked on the wounds. She had the smoothest skin he had ever seen, olive-toned with red cheeks and even redder lips. When she was not with him he was sure she could not be as beautiful as he thought—but now as he smelled the sweet fragrance she always carried, he saw no fault.

She looked down and caught him watching her. She smiled as he blushed. He was a puzzle to her, for although she knew he admired her, not once had he ever indicated by word or motion such a thing. He was a rough man, very strong, but sensitive and shy. Once he had asked to hold Hawk, and the black-eyed baby had looked very small in his massive hands. She had watched while he examined the tiny ears, marveling at them, and at the fingernails, then the smooth black hair. He had looked up and said, "I was the oldest of twelve. Seems like I was always either working in a cotton field or taking care of a baby. Ma always said I was better at it than my sisters." She'd said impulsively, "But this is an Indian baby." He'd stared at her in amazement. "A baby isn't Indian or white, Jeanne—it's just a baby."

Now she saw him flush at the intimacy of her touch, and smiled. "You're the shyest man I ever met," she commented as she took a last stroke. Then she paused. "I've never thanked you for what you did, John."

"Well," he protested, "I didn't do anything."

She put the basin down, turned, and said with the intensity that marked everything she did, "You tried. Not many white men would have stood up to Red Yeager for an Indian woman."

"Why, Jeanne!" His voice rang with surprise. "I never think of that—you're being Indian."

She gave him a look that he couldn't interpret. It was a mixture of doubt and pleasure. She burst into laughter and put her hand on his as it lay outside the sheet. "You are something, John Crenna! Here the whole white world is at war with the Indians—and you say you never even think of my being Indian."

"Well, I *don't!*" he said, and was so intent on making himself clear that he blurted out everything he'd felt for days but never would have said under normal conditions: "Jeanne, when I look at you, I see the prettiest and kindest woman I've ever known, not the color of your skin!" His face colored as she laid her dark eyes on him, but he daringly put his free hand over hers and added, "I—I never have had much to do with women, so I don't know how to talk to you."

She let his hand rest on hers as she studied his blunt, scarred face, finding in his honest blue eyes something that held her. She smiled. "You're doing very well, John."

He was groping for words when Hawk broke out in a cry, interrupting the little interlude.

Jeanne turned to attend the baby, saying wistfully, "When I leave here, I'll think of you."

"Leave?" Alarmed, he said, "You're leaving?"

"Oh, not right away. But Zack hired me to take care of Sam. When he's old enough, I'll be going."

Crenna tried to digest that bit of news, but said only, "You'll marry, I expect."

"No. I don't think so." She got up, the baby in her arms. "I'll fix you something to eat. You be still, you hear me?"

"Put Hawk up here."

"He might hurt your ribs!"

"I'll be careful." She laid the baby on the bed, and as she left the room, she looked back. Already he had the baby smiling and chortling at the amusing faces he was making.

Jeanne was putting John's food together when Bron entered the kitchen.

"How is he today?" she asked.

"He was out of bed when I got back," Jeanne said, adding, "He can have solid food now, I think. He moves much easier. Tomorrow he can begin taking short walks."

Bron nodded, "That's good, Jeanne. He was in terrible shape.

I think it was the good Lord who healed him—" Then she laughed, "But as Dr. Steele said, good nursing helps the Lord along."

"He's a strange man," Jeanne commented. She paused in her preparation, stared into space, then shrugged. "Just when I decide men are worthless, one comes along who risks his life for me." She turned to Bron with a sharp glance, asking, "You think I was too hard on Zack when he wouldn't go after Yeager, don't you, Bron?"

"Are you thinking that?" Bron asked. "You were very angry, that was all."

"No, I would still kill Red Yeager." Jeanne looked defiantly at Bron. "That is the Cheyenne way, the Indian way. Your way is to forgive—but I cannot do that!"

Bron tried to think of a way to answer, for she knew it was, in some sense, the key to presenting the gospel to the Indians. She nodded slowly. "Yeager hurt you, and you want to hurt him. All of us are like that, Jeanne. It's part of what we are—because we've all done wrong. But Jesus said that we are to forgive our enemies."

"Then they will hurt you again!"

"If they do, no matter, Jesus said. He let men nail Him to a cross when all He had to do was call down the angels. And He said, 'Father, forgive them, for they know not what they do.' But that's hard—when someone is hurting you, to not strike back."

Jeanne eyed her with a puzzled expression. "I could *never* be a Christian!" she exclaimed. "I have to fight when someone hurts me or mine."

"But what does hate do to you?" Bron gave her a steady look, saying, "It makes you hard, Jeanne. No matter that you get back at them, hate does something to you. I found that out long ago, when I was a little girl. A cousin of mine had done something to me, and I hated her! Oh, how I longed to pull her apart. I used to lie awake in bed thinking of awful things to do to her! You wouldn't believe! She moved away from our little town— but something had happened to me. My mother knew it, and when I told her, she said, 'Bron, you've set out to destroy a little girl—and you did—but not the one you think. You've made yourself into a nasty little creature!' "

Jeanne had finished dishing up the food, and picked up the plate. She paused long enough to say, "It may be so—but it's not the Indian way."

Her rejection depressed Bron, and she went about her work that day with less than her usual cheer. She was also worried about Lillian, who had developed a fever the previous day and seemed to be getting worse. When Zack and Buck came in at noon, she said, "I'm worried about Lillian."

"She's no better?"

"No. I think Dr. Steele ought to take a look at her."

Zack nodded. "Maybe I ought to take her in."

"I'd like to see Parris, anyway," Bron said.

When they were ready to leave, Bron told Crenna, "I'll tell Dr. Steele what a good job he did on you, John." She walked outside and heard Zack say, "I'll send Stone up to stay until we get back, Jeanne."

"No, I have your rifle," Jeanne replied, her gaze fixed on him.

He shrugged and they left in the wagon, taking Paul and Alice along. Buck sat in the back with Lillian, who lay on a pallet, her face flushed and her eyes cloudy.

As they passed into the gulches, Zack said, "Something's wrong, Bron."

"What is it?"

"Look around." He waved his hand toward the creek. "Where is everybody? Something's going on."

They found out when Nick Tybalt greeted them. He was hurrying toward town and pulled up long enough to ask, "You hear about Dillingham?"

"What about him?" Zack asked.

"He's dead, Zack! They caught Hayes Lyons, Buck Stinson and Charley Forbes!" He kicked his horse into a gallop, shouting, "They're going to be tried soon—better hurry!"

The streets were packed with miners, and talk filled the air as Zack worked his team along to Steele's office. He pulled up and said, "We better get off the street." He leaped to the ground and saw that Lillian was almost unable to sit up. Buck helped her to the edge of the wagon, and Zack picked her up. "You're too sick to walk." He carried her up the stairs that led to the office.

"What's this?" Steele asked with a look of surprise.

"Lillian's got a bad fever," Bron explained.

Zack headed for the door. "I'll be downstairs when you're ready."

Outside he spotted a small group, Pfouts among them. "What's going on, Parris?" he asked.

"Dillingham was in the recorder's tent with Doc Steele. He's president of this district. Forbes, Stinson and Hayes Lyons rode up and yelled for Dillingham to come out. Just as he pushed the tent flap back, they shot him!"

"Why? They were all deputies, weren't they?"

"Nobody knows. Dillingham was straight, but those three are crooked as corkscrews!" Pfouts went on. "Jack Gallagher popped up and arrested them—but he's another bad one!"

Dutch Beidler, carrying his shotgun as usual, broke in. "Dillingham was the only square lawman in the Gulch. He probably wrecked their plans in some way. "We'll hang 'em for it. Trial starts tomorrow. Doc Steele and Doc Bissell and Sam Rutgar are judges." His eyes probed Zack's. "We need every square man we can get. *You* be there in the morning, Winslow."

Everyone stared at him with a "don't you dare back out" look, and he nodded. "I'll be there."

He listened to the angry swirl of talk until Bron came down. "Doc. Steele's worried about Lillian. He wants us to keep her in town overnight."

"I'll see about a room," he said.

"No, he's found a place for her. A new family in town named Rogers. Steele says they have room and we can check in tonight."

"All right. Buck and I will make out."

The next morning Virginia City was filled with throngs of men from other towns along the Gulch—Summit and Virginia and Nevada and Central. They filled Main Street, where the three judges—Steele, Bissell and Rutgar—were seated on a platform mounted on a wagon. As Zack and Buck arrived, the attorney for Stinson and Hayes Lyons was making his plea.

When he finished, Ed Cutler, the prosecutor for the court, made an extremely brief speech, declaring the men were guilty of murder beyond any doubt. They ought to be hanged. Even as he spoke the friends of the pair began to shout.

"They're going to fight this thing," Pfouts predicted to Zack. "These toughs are organized!"

The vote was informal, Steele saying, "What's your verdict?"

The crowd roared, "Hang 'em!"

Steele shouted over the noise, "Beidler, see that a gallows is built and dig some graves!"

Charlie Forbes was tried next, and the crowd grew more lenient—in addition, the toughs began to protest any hanging. Forbes made his own appeal. He was different from the other two—younger and with an air of honesty about him. He made a good speech, admitting he had been with the other two, but claiming he had not fired on Dillingham. When Steele called for a verdict, the crowd shouted out for acquittal. Gleeful, Forbes raised his arms in triumph and jumped to the ground.

The court was adjourned for two hours. The judges returned after conferring about the three defendants; then Dutch Beidler reported that the graves and the gallows were ready. The crowd grew silent when Steele stood up. "I sentence you both, Hayes Lyons and Buck Stinson, to be hanged."

At once the sympathizers in the mob began to shout. One man pulled a gun and shot into the air, shouting, "They won't hang them while I've got a gun!" Several fights broke out and Zack turned to Pfouts. "That ought to be stopped."

The two sentenced men were hoisted into the wagon, and Beidler ordered, "Move this thing along!" Several men picked up the tongue and began to trundle the wagon along toward the gallows at the next corner.

Up to this time, Hayes and Lyons had been cocky, but now both grabbed the side of the wagon, faces white as the death they faced. Lyons cried out, "I am innocent!"

Instantly a group of dance-hall girls began screaming, "Let them go! Let those poor boys live!"

At the sound of the women's cries, Jack Gallagher ran forward and stopped the wagon. He waved a piece of paper in his hand. "I've got a letter Lyons wrote to his mother!"

"Let's hear it!" the toughs shouted.

Gallagher jumped on the wagon and read a letter of such grief from a wayward boy that it brought murmurs of sympathy from the crowd. As soon as he finished, the women cried, "Let them go!"

Shouts began to grow louder.

"Let's have another trial!"

"We want another vote!"

Beidler contested, "You've already voted!" But he was drowned out as Gallagher called for a new vote. "Everyone who wants them hanged, go up the hill—everyone who doesn't, go down!"

It was obvious the mob had changed its mind, and as the mass moved downhill, Lyons and Stinson jumped from the wagon, grabbed the arms of the girls, and headed for the saloons.

As they moved, Red Yeager came face-to-face with Zack and laughed rashly. "Well, if it ain't the hermit!" The crowd formed a small circle, enclosing the two men. The gunman grinned. "J.W. won't be around to fight your battles for you, will he now?"

"No."

The curt answer amused Yeager and he winked at George Ives nearby. "This here is the squaw man, George—the one I told you about. She got to loving on me over at Crenna's place— couldn't keep her hands off me!"

"I heard you had a little trouble with Crenna about that, Red," Ives said. His eyes gleamed as he looked at Zack, adding, "I thought this was the fellow who should have stood up to you."

"How about that, Hermit?" Yeager asked. "You got anything to say?"

The pressure was mounting. Zack knew that every man listening expected him to accept Yeager's challenge. Yeager was braced for trouble, eager to fight; and the crowd stepped back, half expecting Zack to go for his gun.

"I'm not looking for trouble, Red," Zack replied quietly. A gasp swept through the crowd, and he saw Beidler, who had come closer to hear, shake his head angrily.

Yeager taunted, "You've got a yellow streak a mile wide. I've a good mind to open you up and let it run out."

Zack stood stoically, waiting, but before Yeager could strike, Hayes Lyons interrupted.

"Beidler," Lyons said as he rushed forward, cursing, "you're the one who dug a grave for me!"

"Yes," Beidler replied, "and you'll get there yet—you and all your kind," casting a meaningful look at Ives.

George Ives shifted uncomfortably. He hated to take anything from anyone, but Beidler held the shotgun loosely, and was known to be a man who would pull a trigger. Ives had nerve, but he saw half a dozen men around them who would support Beidler, and grinned. "Go fill your graves in, Beidler," he said, and stalked away, his cohorts following him to the Silver Moon.

Zack, too, left.

"What's the matter with that fellow, Parris?" Beidler asked, puzzled.

"He's got problems, Dutch," Parris shrugged. He looked down the street at the gallows and sighed, "There's a monument to defeated justice."

"It'll be a lot worse now." Beidler nodded at the miners, adding, "They cried for Lyons and Stinson—but they'll be crying for themselves soon enough. Lyons and his kind will let a pack of wolves loose on the Gulch!"

Meanwhile, Zack ran into Steele and got the scoop on Lillian and how to find her.

Buck had been trailing along, and now Zack said, "Let's go see about Lillian." When Zack pulled up, Bron came out.

Zack spoke up. "Doc says Lillian has to stay. What do you want to do, Bron?"

"I'd better stay with her. Besides, I need to see Parris. Can you come back in about three days to pick me up?"

"Sure." He lifted the lines and drove off.

Wonder if there'll ever come a time when I'll get to the real Zacharias Winslow? Bron pondered.

CHAPTER EIGHTEEN

AT DANCER CREEK

★ ★ ★ ★

Billy Page intercepted Bron walking down Ballard Street and doffed his hat, saying, "Carry your packages, lady?"

"You'd be bored stiff, Billy," she smiled. "Men hate shopping."

He ignored that, took the basket out of her hand, and the two strolled along together. The sun was hot and the dust raised by the horses rose in the air to form a fine screen, but Billy looked immaculate.

"You always look so cool and comfortable, Billy. How in the world do you stay that way?"

"Never hurry, never take anything seriously."

"Why, that sounds like a definition of a corpse!"

He burst out laughing. "You say the dangedest things, Bron! But tell me, how's everything in the back country?"

"Oh, I've been in town for almost a week," she said. "Lillian got sick and she's staying with a family called Rogers until Dr. Steele says she can to go back, but—"

"But what?" he prompted.

"Oh, like an old mule she is!" Bron's eyes flashed. "She hates the country, Billy. She's been nagging me to let her stay with the Rogerses. They have a daughter two years older than she, and they seem to get along."

"Might be a good thing," Billy suggested. "Must get pretty boring for all of you out there. I'd go loco in a month."

Bron walked along, her head down, and he saw she was troubled. When they reached the Rainbow, he suggested lemonade. As they sipped their drinks, she began to talk, mostly about Lillian. She told him of the girl's background and her attraction for men. "But I can't keep her cooped up forever, Billy. She's fifteen years old, and that's a woman for many."

"You can't change people, Bron," he offered.

"What a funny old boy you are!" she exclaimed. "Of course, you can change people—or you can help them to change themselves!"

"Don't really believe that," he returned. "We come into this crazy world with something in us. Some have honesty, some are crooked. You can take a crook, send him to the finest schools and put him inside a mansion—and he steals the first chance he gets. Or, you can take a girl who's born straight, and no matter how tough it gets, or how many try to get her off track, she'll keep clean."

"Oh no! If there ever comes a time when I start thinking like that, look for me on the floor!" she countered. "You mean you've never seen a man or a woman on the bottom who has come out of it? I have! Not a few times, either, Billy!" She leaned forward. "In the revival in Wales, I saw prostitutes saved! They became pure women! David McCollum was a drunk and a womanizer, but he gave his heart to Jesus Christ—and he's one of the finest ministers in Wales to this day!"

"But, Bron, those people were born with the will to lift themselves up. Some have it—most don't."

"You're wrong. None of us can lift ourselves up. No matter what we are when we come into this world, we've all got a chance. The Captains and the Kings, the Tinkers and the Tailors—all of us are what Jesus came to change!"

"I'm glad you believe that way, Bron," he said soberly. "I hope you never change—but I think it's all written out for me."

Beneath his jolly ways, Billy Page showed a sadness. Bron suspected she was one of the few he'd ever permitted to see it. "I'll pray that you see how much Jesus Christ loves you, Billy," she said simply, then added, "You and Zacharias Winslow are the two sheep I long most to come into the family of God."

He laughed, "You picked a sorry pair, Bron. A gambler and a coward."

"He's no coward!" she defended, her cheeks coloring when he smiled at her reaction. "Well, he's not! And you're no gambler."

"Not a very good one," he admitted. "But I hate to see you put such confidence in Winslow. He's pretty well proved to be afraid of Yeager. The whole camp's nailed him as yellow."

"You're wasting your life, Billy," she said, "but I can see something in you that's fine. Zacharias refused to fight Red Yeager, but he has all kinds of courage. Sometimes it takes more courage to refuse to fight than to roll in the dust like an animal."

"You don't think a man ought to fight—ever?"

"A boy should learn to fight, or let him put skirts about his knees!" she snapped. "But fight for what? A dog will fight, but it doesn't mean anything. Let a man or a woman fight for something that's *real*, Billy, not for some silly pride!" Then she realized she was lecturing him, and laughed, "Oh, Billy Page! You just like to keep me all stirred up." She rose to her feet. "Come to church tomorrow morning, and I'll give you a really good currying down!"

He paid for the drinks and walked her to the Rogers' house. At the gate he removed his hat and smiled, "I'll see you in church."

She blinked in surprise. "Right, you. In church."

She went into the house and Lillian met her. "Who was that, Bron?"

"Billy Page. He helped me get here from Lewiston."

"He's so handsome! What does he do?"

"Nothing, if he can manage it," Bron shrugged. She put her basket down. "How do you feel this morning? Any fever?"

"No, not a bit." Lillian hesitated, then begged, "Bron, Ann wants me to stay with her—*please* let me!"

Bron knew she had little choice. Better to give in while she had the power than to have the girl run away for good. "I'll talk to Mrs. Rogers. If she says it's all right, you can stay for a week."

"Oh, Bron! Thank you!" she cried, her face glowing. "Ann

wants me to help her pick out some clothes, and there's a social next week at the hall."

Bron reached into her purse for some cash. "Here's a bit for you. Not much, I've got, but maybe enough for a dress and a ribbon." Lillian hugged her, and Bron thought, *I should have done this before! I'll bring her to town more often after she comes back.*

The next morning was Sunday, and Parris stopped by to pick her up. The Rogers were warm-hearted people, though not church-goers, and she said as much to Parris as they walked along the streets. "Someday we'll have lots of families like them in church, Parris," she said confidently.

"Of course. Just a matter of time." He looked at her and asked, "Are you going back, Bron? To stay with Winslow?"

"Why, yes," she answered, then saw that he was disappointed. "I always intended to, Parris. I just stayed with Lillian while she was sick."

"I see. Are you still determined to begin a work with the Indians?"

"As soon as possible! It's what God brought me here to do!"

"Well," he smiled, "I've talked to a few folk, and we feel it's time to begin mission work. We've started a fund, but we need you to give us direction."

"Oh, Parris!" She stopped stock-still. "See how proud I am of you!" She reached out to touch him, but drew back with a giggle. "I'd kiss you if we weren't in the middle of the street!"

Pfouts had little humor, but he said, "Well, later, perhaps, when we're in private."

She burst into laughter. "Have you got some romance in you, then?"

He smiled. "I'll hope to let you see that side of me."

She took his arm and chuckled. "And I'll bet all the people watching us think we're talking about sermons. Wouldn't they be shocked if they knew it was kissing you were saying?"

Her comments gave him courage and he waved his hand with a flourish. "To every time there is a purpose—a time to embrace and a time to keep from embracing."

"Oh, ho! Now it's careful I'll have to be around you, Mr. Pfouts! When you start using scripture to get a girl soft on you, I know it's old Slewfoot who's been at you."

They interchanged lightly until they entered the church. "Looks like a fair crowd this morning," Parris said with pleasure.

It was a typical service. The forty-five people who gathered were a good sample of the population of the camp—mostly roughly dressed miners, a few storekeepers, and a few families with children. Tod Cramer, the sawmill owner, was the song leader. He had a clear tenor voice, and knew the verses to every song written insofar as Bron could tell. The others followed him.

Pfouts led in prayer and made several announcements, including the one about the mission work for the Indians, then said, "Next week Reverend Simms from Bannack will be here to preach for us. This week our own missionary, Sister Bronwen Morgan, will speak."

Bron smiled to herself at the word "speak." In public she was never said to "preach" but to "speak." It was not acceptable among Methodists for women to preach, but she had noticed that the churches usually found a way to do what they wanted.

Her messages were more like a friendly talk than a sermon. Most of the Methodists in the West were rough fellows, many with little education. Their congregations were prone to judge the quality of a sermon by its volume rather than its content. "Lots of thunder—no lightning!" was the criticism thrown at them by the more educated Presbyterians.

Bron always began with some sort of homely truth, usually embodied in a story from the Bible or her own experience. Then she would move through the Bible, reading texts that added or expanded her thoughts.

Today she began with a personal account. "When I was a little girl of nine years, my parents took me to London. That was a long journey for me—at the time it seemed as far off as China!" She told briefly of the wonderful things she'd seen. As she spoke, the back door opened and Billy Page walked in and took a seat on the back row. She did not acknowledge his entrance, but continued. "The one place I remember best was the Tower of London. Like all little girls, I loved jewelry—though I had very little, you can be sure! But I remember going through a long passage with guards everywhere staring at us. Then we came to some cases with heavy glass in front—and there behind the glass were wonderful jewels! Diamonds, blazing their reflections;

sparkling red rubies, big as pigeon eggs; and sapphires bluer than any sky you ever saw—all of them so bright and dazzling. I tell you! Case after case, and all containing gems worth a kingdom!"

She looked out over the rough building, built of alder logs and filled with people dressed in the simplest attire. Their eyes were riveted on her. She lowered her voice. "And in the last case, the crown of England with the biggest diamond in the world right in the top of it shone like the sun under the lights. And I knew, even as a child, how that one diamond was worth more money than many states and nations!"

Then Bron raised her voice and motioned toward her hearers, saying, "How many of you would like to have a chance to go through that treasure and fill your pockets with those diamonds and rubies and precious stones? All of you, I see," she smiled. Then she opened her Bible and said, "In Matthew, chapter six, and verse 19, we have a description of the *real* value of those jewels: 'Lay not up for yourselves treasures upon earth, where moth and rust doth corrupt and where thieves break through and steal—' "

She raised her eyes. "What will happen to the gold that men in this camp—and women, as well!—are scraping out of the ground? You all know well—most of it will be stolen in some way. The gamblers and the prostitutes and the thieves are gathered around this camp like vultures! We have a growing graveyard filled with the bodies of men who were killed for their gold—and what good does it do them now?"

Her cheeks were flushed, oblivious to her beauty, Page thought—and every other man in the building. He wondered how many came to hear her sermon, or if, like himself, they came to feast their eyes. Bron herself, he knew, sought no praise or admiration; but these men, far away from good women for the most part, could not be blamed for exulting in her beauty.

"Gold is only yellow gravel," she said, then smiled. "Ah, but the color makes a difference! you tell me. Well, in this world, yes—but go to the pharaoh who stood against Moses. Ask him, 'Do you still run your hands over your golden crown?' Ask the kings of this world who are in their gorgeous tombs, 'Do you still fondle the jewels you loved when you were alive?' No, they do not, for verse twenty gives us the truth: 'Lay up for yourselves treasures in heaven, where neither moth nor rust doth corrupt, and where thieves do not break through and steal.' "

Then she looked up and said, "For where your treasure is, there will your heart be also." She spoke for twenty minutes on the nature of true riches, and how that when death came, the hands would open and all prizes would fall to earth. Billy found himself swayed by her words, and leaned forward as she came to the end.

"And what are these true riches that God tells us will never rust, will never be stolen?" she asked, "Why, the one who spoke these words—Jesus Christ, the Son of God. He is the only one we can have forever. He is the gold and the diamonds, the pearl of great price—and since I came to possess Him—all else is ashes!"

She pleaded with them to come to the cross. "We sang a few moments ago of the blood of Jesus. It can wash away our sin, we sang. And nothing else will do that work! As God told Moses to speak to the children of Israel on the night of the Passover, telling them to put the blood of a lamb on the doorposts, saying, 'When I see the blood, I will pass over you.' So now the true Lamb of God is come, and when you stand before God, He won't ask you for your gold or your diamonds, nor if you are educated. He will look for one thing only—the blood of Jesus Christ."

As Billy sensed the service drawing to a close, he slipped out. But for many days afterward, her words rang in his mind: *He will look for one thing only—the blood of Jesus Christ.*

The rest of the people stayed to express their appreciation to Bron, and she was truly grateful for the work God had done in hearts—even bringing Billy to church. She expressed this to Parris as he walked her home.

"I'm glad Billy Page was there. I long to see him converted!"

"He's an engaging young man, Bron, but don't get your hopes too high. He's hanging out with the Ives crowd. Then again, I guess God is able, isn't He?" He turned to leave, hesitated, and said, "By the way, my clerk Jenkins broke his arm. I've got to hire someone to help with the work. Do you think Buck Smith wants a job?"

"He's coming to take me back tomorrow. I'll ask him."

When Buck arrived she told him about Pfouts' offer.

"I don't know anything about clerking," he responded.

"Well, he thought you could use the money, but it's up to you, Buck." She picked up her bag. "I'm ready to go. Could we go by Pfouts' store? I forgot to get the needles Jeanne asked me to bring."

"What about Lillian?" he asked as he assisted her into the wagon.

"She's going to stay with the Rogers girl for a week."

He frowned his displeasure but didn't say anything.

Pfouts saw them enter and asked Buck, "Miss Bron tell you I needed a man?"

"Yes—but I've never worked in a store."

"Oh, Jenkins can do the bookwork; he just can't lift anything heavy. This won't be permanent, you understand, but I thought you might need to pick up a little extra money."

"I guess it'll be all right. I'll have to drive Bron back, though."

"I'll drive her back," Parris said. "Jenkins can show you where to put the goods; some are piled pretty high. I think by the time I come back, you should have most of it done."

Bron had listened to the exchange and broke in, "I can drive back by myself."

"No. I'd like to get away for a few hours." He explained the work to Buck and said, "Jenkins will be here, and he'll show you around." He turned to Bron. "I'm ready if you are."

He tied his horse to the back of the wagon, and they drove out of town. As they passed the gallows, Bron shivered. "Ugly thing, isn't it, Parris?"

"Yes. So are the two graves Beidler dug for Stinson and Lyons. But sooner or later it'll come to that. The evil in this place is rampant!"

It was a relief to drive into the countryside, passing onto the road leading along the creek. Along the way men crouched with their pans, slowly dipping and rocking. Back from the creek other men had staked dry bars, shoveling up the soil in buckets and carrying it to the water; farther up the hill, men scraped away topsoil to reach gold-bearing gravel.

Eventually the road wound away from the creek and began to rise as they passed out of the valley. The air seemed cooler, but that may have been an illusion created by the sight of the blue line of hills in front of them. The crispness in the air brought some relief from the hot July sun, and they talked amicably as the wagon wheels lifted the dry earth and sifted it back in a steady flow.

When they came to Dancer Creek, he halted the team and let them drink. A large oak spread its branches over the creek, and he said, "Let's cool off, Bron." They got out of the wagon and walked, following the creek around a bend shaded by a line of alders. They stopped at a spot where a large pool had been formed. Parris reached down and picked up a stone and tossed it in.

"This is nice," Bron said. She sat down and leaned back against the trunk of a large tree and closed her eyes. "It's so quiet, isn't it, Parris?"

"Yes." He inched closer to her. She opened her eyes and smiled. Flustered, he moved his feet nervously, took a deep breath, and blurted out, "Bron—" and stopped, swallowing hard. He was a straightforward and direct man, though not eloquent.

Bron was puzzled. She had been in his company a great deal, and one of the things she admired him for was his decisiveness. He always seemed to know what to do. Now there was an uncertainty in his manner that aroused her curiosity.

"Is something wrong, Parris?" she asked quietly.

He forced a smile, paused, and turned to face her. His jaw was set as if he had a difficult job to do and was determined to carry it through.

"Bron—I'm wondering if you have ever thought of me as a man you might marry?"

His words caught her off guard, and a quietness settled over them. Then her eyes opened wide and her lips parted, and she said evenly, "Yes, I've thought of that."

Her honesty was a marvel to him. "I'm not a dashing sort of man, Bron, as you know. Not much to look at. Most young women find me a little dull."

It was typical of him to be so forthright, and she admired him more. "Are you a rat with green teeth, then?" she asked. "You tell me all the things you think are wrong with you. But I'll expect a little more than that, Parris Pfouts!" She stood up suddenly and waited to see what he would do.

He choked with alarm, then obeyed the impulse he had had the first time they met—he wrapped her in his arms and kissed her, gently, yet demanding; and as she responded to the pressure of his lips, she knew this man was much stronger than he appeared. She waited until he stepped back, then said, "Well, you've taken quite a while to come to that!"

The kiss had shaken *him* more than her. He stood before her—frank, honest, guileless. "I love you, Bron," he said simply. It was typical of him: direct and matter-of-fact. But the rapture in his heart radiated from his eyes.

"We will think on it, yes?" she asked.

CHAPTER NINETEEN

BUCK AND LILLIAN

★ ★ ★ ★

After the leisurely pace and quiet at the cabin, Buck was confused by the noise and almost frantic tempo engulfing him in Virginia City. The first two nights he tossed and turned, for he slept in the office of the supply store, and the constant noise of the saloons and gunfire filtered through the thin walls of the building.

During his waking hours, Buck thought of the past months, which had been the happiest of his life. Before that he had known only cuffs and blows, unkindness and abuse. Indifference from others used to be a welcome reprieve—it kept him free from physical harm. But that had changed after Zack Winslow caught him trying to steal. Thoughts of the following days were warm and pleasant. That had been only eight months ago, but it seemed as if he had known Zack forever. They had spent much time together, hunting, fishing, working. At first Buck had been shy and stand-offish, but Winslow had never forced his way into Buck's private life, letting him slowly learn to trust—and that trust had become the strength of Buck's life.

Now something had entered their lives to spoil those good days. Buck had absorbed enough of life to understand that in the world a man had to fight—and Zack's refusal to fight was an enigma to him. Zack had become a branded man in the Gulch.

Even on his first day at the store, Buck became acutely aware of the stigma. He was working in the back of the store when he overheard a fragment of conversation: "Yeah, that's the kid who stays up in the hills with Winslow—you know, the hermit that runs like a whipped dog every time Red Yeager shows up!"

Even today as he ate his breakfast at the Rainbow, he was sure one of the miners sitting across the room with two others pointed him out. He finished hurriedly and returned to the store just as Pfouts arrived.

"Morning, Buck," he said as he took off his coat. "You've got this place in good shape. Not much more to do except carry supplies out for customers. I've a lot of bookwork in the office, though. Why don't you help Jenkins wait on customers? If you run into problems, just give me a call, all right?"

"Sure, Mr. Pfouts. I'll probably be calling a lot." Buck picked up a broom and went out to sweep off the front walk, then came inside as customers appeared. He was slow, but as the day wore on he could handle nearly all the sales. Most of the customers were miners, wanting hardware of various sorts, but a few housewives came in as well, looking at the rather small selection of ladies' wear and accessories. To Buck's relief, Jenkins took care of these.

At ten he took a break and had coffee with Pfouts. Twenty minutes later, Pfouts took a canvas sack from his desk and said, "Take this down to the stage office, Buck." He smiled briefly, adding, "Try not to get held up—that's the cash from the last two days."

Buck took the heavy bag filled with a mixture of greenbacks, gold dust, and coins, and gave Pfouts a peculiar look. "You trust me with all this money?"

Pfouts gave him a steady nod. "Of course." He leaned back in his chair. "There're mostly two kinds of men—the good and the bad. Sometimes the distinction gets a little blurred, but any man in business has to learn to tell which is which—or he'll get trimmed. There're the Ives, the Yeagers and the toughs—and there're Simpson and Doc Steele and Zack Winslow, men who'll stand by what they say. Honest men, and you're one of those, Buck."

The boy ducked his head at the praise, then lifted his eyes

and said, "Everybody says Zack's a coward, Mr. Pfouts. Do you think so?"

Pfouts studied Buck for a moment. "It's hard to figure, Buck. Before all this business came up with Yeager, I'd have said no. But most of us have a weakness, and I guess Zack's no exception. I knew a marshal in Bismarck. I saw him go out once single-handed and face three hard men who were armed and had sworn to kill him—but that same man was so afraid of high places he'd get physically sick if he got on a cliff no more than thirty feet high."

Buck thought of that, and sighed, "I guess you must be right." He turned and left.

An hour before closing time Buck looked up as George Ives entered the store and approached the counter. Since Jenkins was waiting on another customer, Buck stepped forward. "Yes, sir? Something for you?"

"Haven't seen you here before. Must be new, huh?" Ives said.

"Just started a short while ago. My name's Buck Smith."

Ives nodded and gave him the once over, as if filing the name. "I need this list filled, Buck. While you're getting the things, let me see what you have in the way of razors."

"Yes, sir." Buck turned and pulled a walnut case from the shelf behind him, put it on the counter and opened it. "Here's what we have, Mr. Ives. The price is right beside them."

Ives seemed pleased to be recognized, and said, "I'll look them over." Buck moved away and began collecting the items on the list—bath soap, shaving soap, a few other toiletry items and several kinds of food.

He was putting three ripe apples in a sack when the door opened and Lillian stepped inside with another girl he'd never seen.

"Why, Buck!" she said in surprise. "I didn't know you were working here."

"Just started, Lillian." She was wearing a dress he'd never seen, an expensive one it seemed to him. He guessed that it probably belonged to the other girl. It was lightweight, not like the heavy ones she usually wore, ice blue and trimmed with a dark blue ribbon. It clung to her figure, and he was startled to see how much older she seemed.

"This is Ann Rogers, Buck. I'm visiting with her for a while."

Buck nodded, "Happy to know you, Miss Ann." She smiled and spoke, a girl of seventeen, with straight brown hair and dark skin. "Hello, Buck," she said. "We want to see the prettiest dresses you've got."

"Sure. Let me finish with this gentleman—"

Ives had turned to look at the girls and broke in smoothly, "Why, Buck, I'm in no hurry." He took off his hat and smiled, adding, "And even if I were, it wouldn't be courteous to let a pair of beautiful ladies wait, would it now?"

He made an impressive picture, his eyes dancing as he gave a slight bow. He wore a well-cut suit and a large diamond ring, which he flashed as he lifted his hand to adjust the flowing black tie. When Buck said, "All right, Mr. Ives," both girls gaped in wonder. He smiled more broadly. "Perhaps you'll allow me to give you my impression on which dress is the prettiest?"

Both of them had heard of Ives, for he was well known, but neither had ever seen the man. Ann Rogers spoke up with a sudden daring, "Why, you wouldn't know that much about women's fashions, would you, Mr. Ives?"

He smiled and shrugged. "You may as well know—my weakness is for pretty girls in beautiful dresses. I was in New York a few months ago on business, and I confess that I may have paid more attention to the ladies promenading in their newest fashions than I did to business."

His boldness intrigued both girls, but Ann Rogers was quick to respond. "Well, you won't find any of the latest fashions from the East here in Virginia City, Mr. Ives."

"That may be true," Ives replied easily. "But the woman makes the dress, I've noticed. Why don't we take a look and see what Pfouts has in stock?"

He moved away with the two girls who were flattered by his attention. He was no more than thirty, and his reputation somehow made him more attractive. If either of them had been alone, it would have been improper to carry on such a conversation or to allow him to comment on the dresses they examined—but it didn't seem wrong with two of them. They looked at the few dresses in stock, then gave up and began to examine the bolts of material. Lillian was drawn by Ives' raw masculine power.

Even though she knew he was probably an unsavory character, it was like being close to a wild animal—exciting and . . . a little frightening!

He seemed to know something about cloth, for he touched a bolt of light blue material and commented, "This would bring out the blue of your eyes, Miss Rogers—and that dark green over there," he said to Lillian, "why it's made for you!"

Buck watched as the three talked and laughed, and he didn't like it. Ives was an easy man with the ladies, he saw, but he had seen the ruthless streak in the man at the trial of Lyons and Stinson. Nor did he like the way Lillian looked up at Ives, smiling with obvious admiration.

Eventually both girls decided on material, and Ann said, "Miss Denton, the dressmaker, will come by to get as much of this as she needs, probably this afternoon."

"I suppose you ladies will wear the new dresses at the social next Tuesday?" Ives asked.

"Oh, we'll have to see," Ann said coyly.

"Both of you must save me as many dances as you can spare," Ives insisted. "There'll probably be a line of young fellows, but I'm asking well in advance."

They turned to leave, and when they were outside, Ann whispered hoarsely, "My father would *kill* me if he knew I'd been talking to George Ives!"

"I know," Lillian replied. "But isn't he the best-looking thing you ever saw?"

"He's a ladies' man," Ann agreed. "Though I'm sure he won't have the nerve to ask us for a dance at the social."

"I'll bet he will, Ann! He looks as if he'd do anything! What would you do if he *did* ask you for a dance?"

"Why, I—I'd do it if you would!" The two hurried off to the dressmaker, excited by the encounter.

Inside the store, Ives came back to the counter and chose a razor. "This one looks good. By the way, do you know those young ladies, Buck?"

Buck had no choice. "Well, the one called Lillian, I do."

"Who is she?"

"Her last name is Mize. That'll be fourteen dollars for these things."

"Mize," Ives said slowly. "Somebody told me there was a man by that name who was shot to death a few months ago?"

"That was her father."

"She stays with her mother, I suppose," he asked casually as he counted out the money for the purchase.

Buck took the cash and said reluctantly, "No, sir. Her mother left some time before the murder."

Ives sensed the boy's reluctance, and pursued no more. "See you later, Buck," he said as he left the store. He went back to his room, then later as he talked to Ned Ray at the Silver Moon, he mentioned the incident.

"Why, that's the kid who stays with Winslow up in the hills, George," Ray nodded. "The Mize girl and her little sister and brother too, I hear."

"She's a cute kid, Ray."

"That's what got her old man killed."

Ives gave him a shrewd glance. "How's that?"

"Why, the girl was chasing around with the fellows, and Mize gave one of them a beating. Ad Cantrell."

"Sure, I know Ad."

Ray lowered his voice. "Never been any proof about who shot Mize, but it had to be Ad. He carries a gun all the time, and he was plenty sore."

Ives took another drink, then asked, "How come Winslow took all that crew in, Ned?"

"It was that lady preacher, I hear." He repeated the common talk about Winslow, and Ives listened.

"Well, the old man's not around to take care of his little girl anymore, is he, Ned?" He got to his feet and added with a laugh, "And I hear that Winslow wouldn't have the guts to say anything."

"You thinking of that girl? She's pretty young."

"Sure, Ned. I'll be her teacher. Wouldn't want some of these wild young fellows leading her astray." Ives' lips creased in a feline smile as he moved away, thinking of the freshness of the girl called Lillian. The other one had a father and maybe brothers who could cause trouble, but Lillian was prettier anyway—and no one was likely to come gunning for the man who took her.

* * * *

Zack missed Buck. The boy had entrenched himself into Zack's life much deeper than he realized, and as one week ran into two, he found himself spending more time with Crenna. Though the Southerner was no reader, he was a wily checker player, and the two men carried on a continual warfare as they matched wits over the board. Bron was amused but Jeanne was puzzled by the seriousness of the rivalry. "How can two grown men get so serious over a simple game?" she asked.

Bron herself played with them, but was no match for either. She often watched, and was surprised to see that the style was the man—the way each played revealed something about his personality.

Zack, she noted, relied more on strategy. He planned far ahead, giving up several men in order to lay a trap that would allow him to sweep the board. It surprised her at first, for she had not perceived him as one who would play like that. The more she watched, the more complicated he seemed. Perhaps he had learned not to be impulsive, but to be astute, holding himself back from the game, letting Crenna plunge recklessly ahead, while he waited for a wiser move. As she watched this pattern unfold in one hard-fought game, she thought, *That's really what he's like. He's not going to be reckless anymore. He'd like to be—but he's afraid to. He won't risk himself again. That's his way of keeping from losing.*

Crenna was a violent player, slamming the board when he jumped, and taking bold chances that sometimes won the game, but just as often led him into disaster. He liked quick games, fought hard and openly—win or lose, and get on with it! It was like the man, Bron thought—straightforward and direct.

Apart from checkers, Crenna seemed to have a growing interest in Jeanne, and Bron wondered what would come of it. Crenna's eyes followed the Indian woman almost furtively, for he was not a bold man with her. Bron watched Jeanne to see if the attraction was mutual, but could not tell, for she kept herself apart from the rest of them.

By now Crenna was able to get about, though he moved carefully. One night after supper he said, "I've got to get back to my claim. Nolan can't do all the work."

"You'll spring those ribs again, John," Zack warned. "Wait another week."

"Zack is right," Jeanne nodded. "You're not ready yet."

"I feel like a bum, sitting around here all day doing nothing—getting waited on."

"Better enjoy it," Zack grinned. "How about another checker game?"

"Let me help with the dishes; then I'll whip you again."

"Again? You haven't won a game in three days!" Zack laughed. Turning to Bron he offered, "I'll milk your Penelope for you."

"No you won't. You make her nervous," Bron replied. "But," she added, picking up the bucket, "you can come and get another lesson."

He followed her out to the open shed, and watched her milk. "That cow hates me," he remarked. "Every time I put a hand on her, she tries to kick my brains out."

"It's too rough with her, you are," Bron nodded.

He leaned back against the supporting pole, listening to the rhythmic beat of the milk as it drummed into the pail. "I didn't mean to hurt her," he remarked. "Guess I *am* too rough."

She smiled. "You're rough with Sam and Hawk. With Paul and Alice—but they love it." She referred to his habit of tossing the children high in the air until they squealed.

"I guess I'm better with kids than with grown-ups."

She looked at him questioningly, but he didn't appear to refer to anything in particular. He had stayed away from town, going only if necessary. She wondered if he was brooding over the affair with Yeager.

He didn't elaborate on his remark, but said, "I was surprised when you let Lillian stay another week with the Rogers girl."

"It wasn't what I wanted. But she begged so hard I just couldn't say no."

"Have to come home sometime."

"Next week. I told her that."

"Buck seen much of her?"

"He said no." She hesitated, adding, "He's worried about her. Says that Ives came into the store and had quite a time flirting with Lillian and Ann."

Startled, Zack asked, "Was that all? I mean, she's not been seeing Ives, has she?"

"Buck didn't know. She was having supper once with a man called Harry, he said."

"Lillian's a lonely girl, Bron. Hungry for attention."

"Why, that's right!"

"You didn't think I knew that, Bron?"

She finished the milking, stood up, and slapped Penelope on the flank. "I thought you were too busy with your own problems to notice."

"I'll take the milk," he offered and took the bucket. "What about Lillian? She'll fight against coming back here."

"We'll have to take her to town more. See that she goes to functions nice young people attend." Then she laughed and he lifted an eyebrow. "I was thinking, Zacharias, we sound like an old married couple trying to handle the lives of our children."

The idea amused him, and he jerked his head toward the cabin. "Have you noticed John mooning over Jeanne?"

"Do I have eyes? Sure, he's headed for a bad bump."

"Maybe they'll make a match of it."

"No. She'll not have him."

"Is that your mystic Welsh blood speaking? Has she told you something?"

She stood there in the dim twilight, and almost told him that Jeanne was watching *him* in the same manner Crenna was doing with Jeanne. But she said only, "No, I just think that way."

Suddenly he asked what had been on his mind for a long time. "What about you, Bron?"

"Me?"

"You've seen Crenna staring at Jeanne. I guess you haven't missed the looks Parris has been giving you."

She flushed, caught off guard. "Why—I don't know that he does."

"The first bit of feminine wiles I've heard out of you," he laughed. "If you don't want to talk to me about it, it's all right. Can't think of a better husband for you."

They continued on to the cabin. *Why didn't I tell him that Parris wants to marry me?* she wondered with a streak of irritation.

CHAPTER TWENTY

A BITTER HARVEST

★　★　★　★

"Lillian!" Ann exclaimed. "You look beautiful!"

They were in Ann's room, and Lillian had just tried on her new dress. It was a light green with a water-marked design, broken by dull gold insertions and lacework. Her figure had been emphasized by the tightness of the dress. Her waist was pinched in, and the curves above and below were accentuated by the cut of the fashion.

Mesmerized by her reflection in the full-length mirror, she whispered, "Ann, it's so beautiful!"

Ann was a rare girl, for she had contributed to Lillian's meager funds, enabling her to have the dress made. Now she smiled. "No point in my going to the social—or any other girls, for that matter. The men will be so busy looking at you, they'll never have time for us."

"It's the first new dress I ever had, Ann," she said, then threw her arms around her friend, murmuring, "You've been so good to me!"

"Well," she laughed, "let me try on this old rag Mrs. Denton made me. We've only got an hour."

Ann's dress proved to be quite lovely, and Lillian lied gallantly, insisting that of the two Ann's was *much* prettier. "You won't go to heaven telling lies like that," Ann said with a smile as they drove down the street in her father's carriage. The Rogers family would be along later, and it added a bit of spice to the outing by going alone.

"Does your mother know you use rouge?" Lillian asked. She touched her cheek lightly, for it was the first time she'd ever used cosmetics.

"Sure," Ann said, then sobered. "I guess Harry will be here tonight. I saw him walk you home a couple days ago."

Lillian blinked in surprise, for she was unaware that Ann had seen young Barstow. "Oh, I just ran into him on the way home from the store with those things for your mother."

"I noticed it took you over an hour and a half to run that errand." Seeing the hurt look in Lillian's face, Ann put her arm around her. "I wasn't spying on you, Lillian, but if my mother or father had seen you, they'd have told Miss Morgan—and you'd have been back on the farm in a hurry!"

"We weren't doing anything wrong!"

"I didn't say you were, but I think if that preacher lady ever knew of it, she'd say it was wrong enough—just to *walk* with him. Harry's got a bad reputation."

Ann's words burst Lillian's bubble of joy, and she set her lips angrily. "I'll be glad when I can do what I like!" she spewed.

Ann laughed, "Nobody does that."

"*I* will—as soon as I get away from here."

"Why, Lillian, that's silly. You'll either marry and do what your husband wants—at least some of the time—or you'll work and do what your employer wants."

Lillian was in no mood to listen to common sense. The last few days had been close to heaven for her. "I'll be sixteen soon. Lots of girls are on their own when they're sixteen."

Ann did not argue, for she saw the stubbornness on Lillian's pretty face. She tried another tact. "You remember what George Ives said the day we saw him at the store?"

"He's going to ask us to dance with him."

"That's what he said, but don't be a fool, Lillian."

Lillian stared at her. "It wouldn't hurt to dance with him. He couldn't do anything on the dance floor."

Ann sighed. "Honey, you have to understand, if I danced with him, my daddy would give me a taste of the strap. He spoils me rotten, but there are some boundaries—and George Ives and men like him are off limits."

The carriage drew up to the large tent erected for the celebration. As they got out of the carriage, Ann instructed the driver, "Wilson, Daddy said we could stay until 10:30, so please pick us up then."

The girls walked toward the tent with excitement and exhilaration, handing their tickets to the attendant.

"Oh, look at all the decorations!" Ann cried.

It was a dazzling sight. Red, white, and blue streamers hung from the ceiling with numerous lanterns interspersed throughout the tent, spreading a golden light over the crowd milling around on the sawdust floor. On a platform at one end a band was hammering out music.

Almost at once, Ann and Lillian were surrounded by a group of young men, all insisting on the first dance. Ann calmly selected Nathan Potter, a lawyer, and they moved out across a large section of planked floor built for the occasion.

Lillian knew none of the men but chose one at random. Though she had danced little, she had a natural grace and was able to match his steps. He spoke rapidly, but the dance was soon over as another man cut in. Soon she lost track of all her partners.

The dance was open to anyone with a ticket, so it was no surprise to see Lyons and Stinson in the crowd, which Dutch Beidler pointed out as he and James Miller and Colonel Simpson watched from in front of the refreshment stands. But it made Beidler stew with anger. "I wasted my labor digging their graves. Grates on me the way they rub shoulders with honest men."

Simpson nodded. "Yes, and there's Ives and Yeager. They've all gotten bolder since they got by with killing Dillingham."

James Miller, a quiet and respected man, spoke up. "It's getting worse. The stage was held up twice last week, and three miners have been killed in holdups this month." The others listened intently. "Ives just laughs at us—and Gallagher is as crooked as a snake."

The three discussed ways to clean out the gangs. "It'll have to get even worse before it gets better. The miners will have to forget to cry for the likes of Lyons and Stinson," Miller said.

"We may have to organize a vigilante group—like they did in San Francisco," Simpson decided.

"No, Simpson," Beidler said. "It'll take a man the miners will follow. Right now they're like a herd of sheep and—"

"Who's that girl Ives is talking to?" Simpson interrupted. "I've never seen her."

Miller looked across the tent and said, "That's the Mize girl—the one Zack's been keeping up in the hills."

"He'd better keep her away from Ives," Beidler grunted. "He's not fit to be around a decent woman!" He gave Miller a curious look. "You reckon he knows about this?" Then he shrugged, "Don't matter. If he won't stand up to Red Yeager, he sure won't buck Ives!"

Ives had come up behind Lillian as she was taking a break at the refreshment table. "Well," he said, "I'm here to claim that dance you promised."

Lillian wheeled. "I never promised you a dance!"

"Guess that's right, though you can't fault a man for trying, can you?" He looked very dashing as he stood there, quite aware they were being watched. Ever since he had seen Lillian, he'd planned this, but the sight of her took him off guard. He remembered her as an immature girl, shy and withdrawn, but what he saw was a beautiful woman. She was still afraid of him, he perceived, and played on that.

"I knew you'd be afraid to dance with me," he said easily. "But I thought I'd ask anyway. I never saw anything as pretty as you in that dress."

"I—I'm not afraid of you."

"That's good," he said. "I know people say I'm a pretty hard character, but I've never hurt a woman in my life." The music started up again, and he put on his charm. "I don't like to beg for anything, Lillian—but *please* dance with me."

Lillian was thrilled that the famous Ives would make such a request, but she was still hesitant.

"What can happen on a dance floor?" he urged. "Just one dance, and then I can tell the fellows I danced with the prettiest girl at the social."

He seemed so harmless, and Lillian wavered. She thought of what Bron would say, but Ive's suddenly reached out his arms and without thought she stepped closer and then found herself dancing. It was a waltz, and he did it very well. His hand was warm on her back, and as she looked up into his face she saw the approval on his face. "I knew that material was right for you," he nodded. "Never saw a finer dress, not even in New York or Frisco."

"You're just saying that," she protested.

"Why, Lillian, I'll admit I've been known to exaggerate a bit when I'm with a young lady—but there's no need for that sort of thing with you. And where'd you learn to dance like you do?"

He glided around the floor with strength and ease, and she was surprised to discover the music had stopped. "See?" he smiled. "You danced with the terrible George Ives—and you're still as sweet and beautiful as ever! Now, one more—all right?"

She nodded, and that was the beginning, for as the evening wore on, she danced with him several times; and when he took her to the refreshment table, he was so amusing she found herself laughing with him.

Ann caught up with her once, her brow cloudy. "Lillian, have you lost your mind?"

"Don't worry about me, Ann," she said quickly. "George is all right."

"All right? George Ives?" Ann stared at her angrily. "You realize, don't you, that he's monopolized you? The other men are so afraid of him they won't ask you to dance."

"He didn't do that!"

"Of course he did." Ann forced herself to calm down. "Now, you stay beside me, and I'll cut him when he comes to ask for another dance."

"No—I'll do it! I'll tell him I can't dance with him anymore."

The music began and as expected, Lillian saw Ives coming her way. "I can't dance with you anymore, George," she told him.

He knew what had happened. "I understand. It's part of the price I have to pay for refusing to go the way of the crowd. Every time I find a nice girl, her parents lock her in a room before the terrible Ives with the long sharp teeth gets her."

He knew the cunning words would arouse her, and it did. "I

have to do what they say," she lashed out. "If I had my way, I'd dance with you all night!"

"Would you, Lillian?" he whispered, pulling her close. "I wonder if you would."

"I would!" she protested.

"Well, then meet me tomorrow for a ride. There's a little spot beside a river I go to—just to relax. I could bring a lunch and we could have a picnic."

"Oh, I couldn't!"

He let her words roll over him, saying, "See, you *are* afraid of me."

She lifted her face. "I am not!"

"Good!" he cried. "I'll get a carriage, and you be at the old stable at the end of Holland Street at one o'clock. Tell your friend you're going to run an errand," then added, "I get lonesome for someone to talk to, don't you, Lillian?"

Again his clever ploy seduced her.

She nodded and whispered, "Yes! I-I'll try to come!" The music stopped, and he left.

"I'm glad you got rid of him," Ann said with relief. "Now, you dance with that handsome Dick Summers—he's been dying to meet you!"

★　★　★　★

Buck was awakened out of a sound sleep by the sound of a door slamming. He bolted off his cot and grabbed the loaded .44 Pfouts had given him in case someone tried to break in.

"It's me, Buck—Pfouts."

Buck looked up as the merchant entered. "What's the matter, Mr. Pfouts?" he asked, seeing his alarm.

"It's Lillian." His voice was unsteady. "She's been hurt."

Buck couldn't believe he heard right. "What—what happened?"

Pfouts licked his lips, reluctant to go on, but forced himself. "She sneaked away with a man, Buck. The Rogerses had no idea anything was happening—not even Ann! And this man—he hurt her . . . real bad!"

"She's not going to die?"

"No, no! Doc Steele's taking care of her—but she's been severely beaten. I think you'd better get Bron."

Buck nodded. "Sure, I'll go right off. Can I see Lillian first?"

"Not now, Buck," Pfouts said quietly. "Steele had to do some stitching, and he put her out with laudanum."

Buck began to dress, and Pfouts said, "I'll stay with her while you go for Bron."

"Mr. Pfouts?"

"Yes?"

"Who was the man?"

Pfouts' lips grew thin. "She wouldn't say, Buck. But one witness—who said he'd never testify in court—told me he saw her get into a buggy this afternoon over by the old stable on Holland Street. It'll never come to court—the man's afraid for his life if he tells who it was."

"Who'd he say it was?"

"George Ives." He looked at the boy with compassion and said gently, "There will be a reckoning," and turned on his heels.

Buck's hands seemed numb as he fumbled with the buttons on his shirt. He pulled on his boots, put on his coat, then paused and looked at the loaded .44 on the table for a long time. Slowly he picked up the gun and stuck it in his belt, adjusting his coat to conceal the weapon. He left the store, locked the door behind him, and made his way down the walk.

Cold with fear, but without hesitation, he strode on, unaware of those who spoke to him. It was only ten o'clock and the saloons were wide open. In his mind he was rehearsing what he had to do, knowing fully the risk involved, but didn't sway from his determination.

He came to the Silver Moon, paused one moment to listen to the tinny music and the shouts of the dancers and the girls as they whirled around, then squared his shoulders and pushed his way through the door.

Ned Ray was sitting at a table, and spotted him instantly. He took in the boy's pale face and tight lips, and a warning went off. He had been a saloon keeper too long not to know the signs of trouble, and he said to a houseman, "Lou, watch that kid. He's got something on his mind."

"Sure, Ned."

"I think I saw a gun under that coat, so be careful."

Lou, a burly swamper, nodded and melted into the crowd. Ray watched as Lou came up to the boy's left and stood waiting.

Buck had been looking for Ives, and at first didn't see him. He walked farther into the room, and there, in an alcove half hidden by the huge bar that ran the length of the room, he saw him seated with his back to the wall, playing cards with three other men.

Taking a deep breath, he walked closer, not noticing the large man following him. When he came to the end of the bar, he swung around and called, "Ives!"

At the shrill voice, Ives' head jerked up, and he saw Buck. A deathly silence spread over the room. Ives jumped to his feet, a wild awareness on his face. "Boy, what do you want?"

Buck drew back his coat and put his hand on the gun. "I'm going to kill you, Ives," he said, his voice like steel; and before Lou could make a move, Buck drew the gun and shot.

It creased Ives' shoulder. Ives grabbed his own gun and fired. The slug knocked Buck backward, and Ives shouted nervously, "You all saw it! He drew first!"

Jack Gallagher came forward from the bar. "He sure did. Wonder what got into the kid?" He bent over and pulled at Buck's shirt, then said, "Somebody get him up to Doc Steele's. He's got to sign the death certificate."

"Is he dead, Jack?" Ives asked.

"Not yet, but I figure he will be by the time he gets to Steele. He's bleeding like a stuck pig."

The owner of the Rainbow Cafe examined Buck and pressed a handkerchief over the boy's bleeding wound. "Okay, two of you guys help me with him."

As the three men left, Ned asked Ives, "What was that all about, George? He exploded before Lou could grab him."

Ives holstered his gun and said, his face pale, "I took the kid for his bankroll, Ned. He's a sore loser."

CHAPTER TWENTY-ONE

A CERTAIN NOTICE

★ ★ ★ ★

Bron got up from the table to get the coffeepot, and glanced out the window. "Someone's coming."

"Probably Nolan," Zack said. "He wants to go hunting with me." He reached out and caught Paul by the shirttail as he headed for the door. "You sit here and eat," he commanded.

Bron filled the cups, then replaced the pot, again looking out the window. "Why, it's Parris!" she exclaimed. She ran to the door and threw it open. "Come in, Parris—plenty of breakfast left."

She was smiling as he stepped down from the buggy, but as he hurried toward the cabin, her smile faded at the tense look on his face.

"What's wrong, Parris?" Bron asked quickly. "Is somebody sick?"

"Paul, will you take Alice outside for a little while, please?" Parris asked.

At this the pair begged to stay, but Bron said, "Go or you will have a couple swats!" As soon as they were outside, she asked, "Now, Parris, what is it?"

He took a deep breath and began. "Yesterday noon, Lillian got into a wagon and went for a ride with a man. Last night about eight she was found where he'd dumped her."

"Dead?" Bron cried, and her eyes begged for denial.

"No. He attacked her, but she won't die. Doc Steele says she'll have some scars—and they won't all be on her face, I would think."

"Who did it?"

"Well . . . there's more—and it's worse," Pfouts said, looking at Winslow, who had not spoken but sat at the table, his eyes fixed. "I went to Buck, told him to come out here and get you, Bron. Then I went back to Steele's office. But Buck took things into his own hands."

Bron whispered, "Parris—he went for the man who hurt Lillian!"

"Yes!" His voice was filled with self-reproach. "I never even *thought* of such a thing! Who would?"

"Let's have it all," Zack said tonelessly, his face rigid. He had not moved since Pfouts' first announcement about Lillian.

"He took a gun and went to the Silver Moon. Called out a warning, shot, but missed—and was shot himself."

"Is he dead?" Zack asked.

"Not when I left. But Doc says it'll be a miracle if he makes it."

A stricken cry escaped Bron's lips.

"Who was the man, Parris?" Zack asked, unemotional, as though inquiring about the weather.

"George Ives—he can't be touched, Zack. Only one witness saw Lillian leave with Ives—and that man won't ever testify. Too scared. And everybody in the saloon saw Buck pull his gun and shoot first. Gallagher's already called it self-defense."

"I'll get my things, Parris." Bron ran out the door into the other cabin.

"It may not be so bad," Parris said quietly. He looked at Zack, still sitting motionless, his head bent.

Zack slowly straightened and got to his feet. He looked at Pfouts with a stony expression, then without a word turned and walked out. Jeanne ran to the window and saw him head toward the woods behind the cabin, and disappear into the dense undergrowth.

Crenna's face contorted in hatred. "Parris, why don't we all get our guns and go clean out that nest of vipers? There're two thousand honest men—maybe a hundred crooks. What's stopping us?"

"Those two thousand men are a mob, John. There'll have to be a leader they'll follow before they can do anything."

Just then Bron came in carrying a bag. "I hate to leave you, Jeanne. Do you mind?"

"No. You take care of Lillian and Buck. Don't worry about us."

Crenna joined Jeanne at the window as they watched them drive off. "Why do we stay in a hellhole like this, Jeanne? Why don't we go where people are decent human beings?"

Jeanne turned, her back against the wall. "You think there's such a place?" she asked mildly. "All my life it's been one fight after another. I don't think one place is any better than another, John."

"I don't believe it. There's got to be something better!" He stretched his arms over his head, grimacing with pain, and exploded, "Blast it all! I'm sick of being an invalid!"

"Be careful of your ribs, John," she warned as she left to care for Hawk, who had just awakened. For over an hour she stayed with the babies, feeding and bathing them. She put the little ones on a pallet and went outside—just in time to see Zack emerge from the woods.

He walked toward the corral, saddled his horse and led him across the yard, tying him to a post. He stepped up on the porch, and without a word passed inside the cabin. Crenna looked up with surprise. Jeanne, too, had seen something in Zack's face that startled her, and followed him in, watching carefully as he lifted his holster off the peg. He pulled the revolver free, tossed the holster on the table and checked the loads in the cylinders. He replaced the Colt, looped the belt over his shoulder, and for the first time looked up.

"I've got an errand, Jeanne," he said evenly. "Crenna will be here."

She tried to read his face, but apart from the tight creased mouth, he looked the same. He walked out without another word. She stood there uncertainly, then ran lightly outside. He had gathered his reins and was about to swing into the saddle when she caught his arm and turned him around. Her eyes were wide and imploring, her lips soft and vulnerable. He waited, and finally she said, "I called you a hard name—because you would not punish Yeager for what he did to me. I said you were no man."

"Don't blame you."

Her hand tightened, she searched his face, and whispered, "You're going after them, aren't you? But there are too many of them, Zack! They'll shoot you in the back!"

The muscles in his arm contracted, matching the thin line of his lips. He stood there, a compact body concealing a rage that would explode into action when it met its victim. His eyes glinted, and he asked, "What would you have me do, Jeanne?"

"Wait awhile," she begged, and her eyes grew soft. "Soon there will be others to help. Nobody will stand against Ives and his outlaws—everybody knows that!"

"Nobody ever tried, I guess." He shook his head and his face was filled with grief. "If I'd stood up to Yeager when I should have, maybe this wouldn't have happened."

"You can't fight them all!" she whispered, and shook his arm gently. "I am a Cheyenne, and you know what fighters they are—but they never throw their lives away in a hopeless case." Then she paused and added, "Look how we all depend on you. What will happen to Sam if you die? He'll have nobody!"

He took off his hat and the slight breeze stirred his hair. "I've sat on this mountain for a year, trying to hide from life, Jeanne. But now it's time for me to come down. Some things are worth fighting for. You for one, and Hawk."

"If you care for us, don't go!" She realized that it was the white blood in her speaking, for the Indian in her would never have tried to hold him back.

"I guess that's why I've got to do this thing, Jeanne," he said.

At his words, she reached up and pulled his head down and kissed him. "Be careful!" she begged. "Oh, be careful, Zack!"

He stepped back, swung into the saddle and, wheeling his horse in a tight circle, left the yard at a fast gallop.

She stood watching him intently until he was lost around the bend. Then a sound behind her wrested her eyes back and she saw Crenna with his coat and hat on. "Why, John, you can't go!"

He said, "I'm taking one of Zack's horses to town."

There was hurt in his honest eyes, and she thought, *He saw me kiss Zack.* "You can't ride a horse, and I can't stay out here. I'll hitch up the team and we can go to town together."

"He may go down, Jeanne." A touch of bitterness shaded his eyes and he said, "He's got what I'd give my right arm for—and doesn't even seem to care."

"If you mean me," she shot back, "you're wrong. He cares for me as he cares for Buck and the rest of them. That's all."

He hesitated. "And what about you, Jeanne?"

She looked directly into his eyes. "You are one of the lucky ones, John. You never have to wonder what you are or what you want. If you were a half-breed as I am, it would not be so simple."

"All right," Crenna said, "I'm going into town to try to give Winslow a hand, Jeanne. Then if I come out of it, you're going to have to give me a straight answer. Now, go hitch up the wagon. We'll stop by and pick up my gun on the way."

★　★　★　★

Zack rode into Virginia City as the shadows were beginning to lengthen. It was twilight. Businesses had closed, citizens were home eating supper, and the saloons waited for patrons. As Zack rode down the street, James Miller came out of the Rainbow Cafe and stopped so abruptly that Nick Tybalt bumped into him. "What's up?" he asked, then spotted the solitary figure. "Oh, it's Zack." They watched as Zack reined in beside the assayer's office, dismounted, and walked inside.

"Didn't know Zack was doing any panning," Nick commented. "Never saw him on the creek." Then he straightened up and said, "Look, Harold's putting some kind of notice on the board." Harold Reiner's office was one of the most important spots in Virginia City. It was here that the samples were brought and analyzed. He also kept a board inside the glass window, posting announcements for all to see, and he was posting one for Zack now. Zack came to the door, and Miller and Tybalt could see Reiner follow him outside, arguing with him. Zack shook his head, got on his horse and continued down the street. "Harold posted something he didn't want to post. Let's see," Nick said.

"Well, that puts the icing on the cake, don't it, James!" Nick exclaimed as he read the notice.

"Yep, the Gulch always likes a show, Nick. Reckon this ought to draw a crowd. Come on, let's get the word out."

Down the street Zack reined in his horse at Doc Steele's office. When he walked in, Steele looked up in surprise. "Winslow!"

"How's the boy?" Zack asked.

"Better than I expected," Steele grunted. "Bullet hit a rib—saved his life. Smashed the rib and sent the slug up over the heart."

"Get a lung?"

"That was what I was afraid of—but it missed by a hair. Tore him up pretty bad, but if he doesn't get an infection, I guess he'll pull out of it."

Zack took a deep breath, and Steele could see some of the tension leave the man's face. "How about Lillian?"

The old physician frowned. "You know, Zack, in a way I'm more worried about her than the boy." He paused, then went on. "It's one thing to see these fool miners putting bullets in each other—but another to have to patch up a young girl who's been torn by one of the beasts in this stinking town!"

Zack studied the doctor's face. "How is she?" he asked again.

"Oh, physically, she's not too bad. Had to take a couple of stitches on an eyebrow and another on her lower lip." Steele glared at the ceiling. "She must have put up some fight for him to bust her up that way."

"If she's not hurt worse, why are you more worried about her than Buck?"

"Because she's going to carry the memory of this assault around as long as she lives, Zack!" Steele shook his head. "I've seen it before. Somehow when a young woman—or any woman, I guess—is attacked like that, she feels she's guilty. Don't know why, but it happens. And most of 'em will hate men forever."

"Can I see them?"

"Both asleep," Steele shrugged. "Buck's in there." He pointed to the door that led to the other room where he did most of his work. "Bronwen's with Lillian in room 204 of the Palace Hotel, but I gave her enough laudanum to keep her out all night."

"I'll see them in the morning."

Zack turned to go and Steele said, "Some of us are getting

together tomorrow to talk about this. Like to have you come. Be in Sander's office at noon."

Zack had reached the door, but he turned and gave Steele a strange smile. "At noon?" he mused softly. "Sorry, Doc. I've got something else to do at noon." He waited long enough to see outrage creep into Steele's faded eyes, then left the office.

Zack steered Ornery toward the stable, where he unsaddled him, grained him, and put him in the corral. Picking up his saddlebags, he headed for the Palace Hotel.

The clerk was half asleep, and pulled himself out of his chair long enough to ask, "Need a room?"

"Just for tonight."

"Take 210."

Zack nodded and walked down the hall, pausing at room 204 for a long moment, then went to 210. He took off his coat and gun, placing them on the bed, then filled the basin with water from the pitcher and washed his face. Instead of flopping on the bed, he moved the chair to the window.

Two hours later he was still there when the street below was lit up, and the raucous sounds of the saloons filled the air. He had a good view of the Silver Moon, and for an hour he watched men enter and leave. The streets were active as the miners, weary and bored with man-killing labor, came to let off steam.

At ten o'clock, he jerked off his boots, drank some water, and opened the saddlebags. He pulled out a book, plumped up the pillow and lay down to read. He glanced at the title and a wry smile touched his lips as he read aloud, "Great Expectations." He glanced toward the street. "Guess that's what I've got."

After reading for two hours, he put the book down and lay flat on the bed. He thought of those nights in the army, before a battle, when he and the others had been keyed up tight. He felt no such pressure now and wondered why. He fell asleep, and slept through the night, awakening only when the first rays of the sun touched his face.

He got up, washed his face, and went to look out the window. He had a clear view of the assayer's office down the street, and saw a crowd gathering. Every once in a while a man would pull away and scurry down the street, sometimes stopping others and pointing toward Reiner's office.

He smiled, picked up his book and sat down beside the window. At ten he read the last page and closed the book. "Well, now, that's a good book," he said aloud. He shoved the novel into the saddlebags, buckled on his gun, shrugged into his coat, then stepped into the hall. There was nobody in sight as he made his way to room 204 and knocked on the door.

"Who is it?" Bron asked.

"Me. Zack."

When she opened the door and he stepped inside, the first thing Zack noticed were the dark circles under her eyes.

Lillian was asleep in the single bed. Her face was puffy and the stitches in her mouth and eyebrow looked frightful. He stood near the bed for a few minutes.

"She's going to be all right," Bron assured.

Zack went to the window to survey the situation. The people were still coming, milling excitedly in the street. She came and put her hand on his shoulder. "You and I . . . both of us feel responsible."

He faced her, the pain in his eyes openly displayed. "Not you, Bron," he said heavily. "I was so busy posturing up in the hills—playing hermit—that I let it happen."

She whispered, "It's hard to forgive others, Zacharias, but much harder to forgive yourself."

He shook his head, and she looked down on the street. "What's happening? That crowd's getting bigger every minute! Is it a hanging?"

"Well, something like that," he said. "I've got to go, but I'll come back when she's awake."

"Zack—when you come, don't be surprised if she's afraid of you. She was frightened of Dr. Steele—because he's a man, you know?" Then she drew her shoulders back and said, "But I will pray for her. God can heal wounds inside as well as those on the outside."

He could sense her deep faith in God and the love for Lillian expressed with such devotion. Her eyes were weary from the long vigil, her mouth soft with pity for the helpless girl. "I'll be back," he said.

Zack slipped down the back stairs and made his way through the alley to Pfouts' store. The back door was locked, but he rapped hard until he heard a bolt slide. The door opened slowly and Pfouts peered up at him.

"Zack—come in!" he cried, pulling him inside and slamming the door. Pfouts' eyes were a mixture of fear and agitation, very unlike the calm, collected businessman the world saw. "Are you insane?" he whispered.

"Probably," Zack replied. The sight of Pfouts amused him. "I was depending on you for a little help, Parris, but you've got to calm down before you can do me any good."

"What do you mean, Zack?" Parris asked waving his hands. "That notice you put in Reiner's window, every miner in the Gulch has seen it!"

"That's why I put it there. Now listen, here's what I need . . ."

★ ★ ★ ★

George Ives came downstairs from his room over the Silver Moon and sat down to a breakfast brought in by Lou, the swamper. Lou gave Ives an odd look as he set the tray on the table, but said nothing. He moved away, and as he expected, three men rushed into the saloon before Ives had finished.

"You haven't heard about it?" Hayes Lyons half shouted. Buck Stinson and Long John Frank crowded around Ives, stark surprise in his face.

"Heard about what?" he asked, "Stop talking so loud—nobody's deaf!"

Long John spoke up. "There's a notice in Reiner's window on the board. I made a copy of it for you." He handed a slip of paper to Ives and the three watched him as he read it aloud:

> There are two yellow curs living in this town. One is Red Yeager; the other a dirty coward named George Ives.
>
> At noon tomorrow, I'll be in the street in front of the Silver Moon. If these two dogs don't come out to meet me, I'll go drag them out.
>
> I'll use my fists on Yeager till he is pulp. Then I'll give the other cur a chance to pull his gun, and I'll put a bullet between his eyes.
>
> All invited. Bring your friends.
>
> Zacharias Winslow

The blood rose in Ives' face as he read. He crumpled the notice in his hand and threw it on the floor, asking, "What kind of a *joke* is this?"

Stinson snorted, and waved a hand toward the street. "George, you hear that crowd? Every miner in the Gulch is comin' in. They don't think it's a joke!"

Ives rushed over to the door. Sure enough, the street was filled, and when one of the miners spotted him, he hollered, "Hey, Ives, you and Yeager ready for the party?"

Ives cursed and wheeled around, his eyes bright with anger. "Where's Red, Lou?" he called out to the swamper.

"Still asleep."

"Go get him!"

As the swamper scurried upstairs, Ives stared at the three men. "It's probably someone's idea of a joke," he muttered. "Winslow probably didn't even put the notice up."

"Yeah, he did," Long John nodded. "I talked to Harold Reiner. He said that Winslow came in last night and asked him to post it."

Ives went back to the window, his mind working at lightning speed. He stayed there until Yeager came stomping into the bar, yelling, "Whut you get me up for? I got one great big hangover, George."

Ives gave him a quick run-down, and Yeager picked up the note, spread it out and read. With a curse, he threw it down and said, "You don't take this serious, George?"

Ives was smarter than Yeager, and replied, "I don't think it's what it looks like, Red." He paced the floor and said finally, "I think it's a trap. What they'll do is draw us out on the street using Winslow for bait. They'll have some men ready, and somehow they'll find an excuse to open up on us."

"Why, we better not go then!" Yeager said.

"Wake up, you idiot!" Ives yelled. "If we don't go out there, we're admitting we're what he calls us in that note. We don't have any choice—but we can handle it." He thought again and began to speak rapidly. "Get as many of our boys as you can. There's going to be a thousand men out there, but there's just a few we need to worry about. You know them—Miller, Pfouts,

Simpson, and Beidler. If there's any shooting, drop them and the rest won't matter."

"I'll get the boys," Stinson said and scooted out the door.

"Wait a minute," Yeager said. "He's going to tackle me first, George. When I get through with him, he'll be dead meat. I'll get him down and kick his brains out."

Ives considered Yeager's bulk and nodded. "Do it then. It'd be better. When lead starts flying any of us can get it."

"I been waiting to get my hands on that punk!" Red grinned. "Now he's serving himself to me like a Christmas turkey. Let's have a drink."

"Better wait till later," Ives warned, but Yeager cockily went to the bar and poured himself a large whiskey.

"That clown don't weigh over a hundred forty, if that much," he scowled. "I'll have a little fun with him before I put his lights out, George. Be a lesson for the next pup who sets himself up against us!"

CHAPTER TWENTY-TWO

THE FIGHT

★ ★ ★ ★

At five minutes before noon, Zack stepped out of the front door of Pfouts' store. Immediately a shout went up: "There he is!" The street was packed, but a way opened up for him as he walked slowly toward the Silver Moon with Pfouts beside him.

The crowd pushed and shoved, trying to catch a glimpse of him, and when he looked up, he saw that every window was occupied. He smiled at Parris. "I bet you wish it was this easy to get people to come to church, don't you?"

Pfouts was pale, his forehead clammy. He groaned, "You're a fool, Zack! They'll have to kill you now! They can't afford to let you live!" But Zack had told him earlier that it had to be done in public. "Ives has got to be humiliated, and I want every man in this camp to see it!" he'd said.

Then it had made sense, but now in the midst of this mob, Parris wished he'd tried harder to dissuade Zack. But it was too late.

Zack stepped into the clearing in front of the Silver Moon, and as he did he saw Yeager and Ives postured in front of the door. Zack called, "Well, it's noon. Come on out here, Yeager!"

Yeager lunged forward with a curse and came to a stop ten feet away from Winslow. His eyes were red-rimmed and he looked huge in the strong sunlight. He surveyed the solid ranks of men, then looked up at the windows and flat roofs, also packed, and laughed derisively.

"You must be drinking bad whiskey, Hermit. I been aching to get at you, and now you come crawlin' down outta the hills spouting garbage." He began to work himself into a rage, cursing and striking his hands together.

"You think you can whip me, Red?" Zack challenged, loud enough for all to hear.

"I'm gonna stomp you!"

"I got a little cash," Zack said. "You want to make some easy money, I'll give you a bet. Last man on his feet takes the purse."

Yeager gaped in disbelief, then grinned. "How much—a hundred?"

"Two hundred," Zack said with a grin. "Let the boys see the coin, Pfouts." Pfouts held up a heavy pouch, and Zack said, "Even money, Red."

Yeager looked confused. "I'll take it. My money's in the vault at the Station."

"Write out a release, and Colonel Simpson there will hold the stakes," Zack said. He stood there while pencil and paper were shoved into Simpson's hand. "Last man on his feet takes the pot, right?"

"Right," Simpson said. "Now get ready—"

"One more thing, Red," Zack broke in. "My hands are tender. I don't want to cut them up when I'm knocking your teeth down your throat, so I've asked Pfouts to put some bandages on. Come and have a look."

Yeager came forward, and Pfouts showed him the strips of cotton cloth. Yeager felt one of them, then laughed. "Go ahead, put them bandages on so I can get started."

As Zack had showed him earlier, Pfouts quickly wrapped the cotton strips around the outstretched hands, first one, then the other. Zack said, "Take a feel, Red. Just bandages—no horseshoes inside." He held his hands out, and Yeager gave them a casual touch.

"One more thing." Zack unbuckled his gun belt and handed it to William Clark, saying, "Will you hold these for me just for a few minutes, Bill?"

"All right, let's go," Zack said.

"Back off!" Yeager shouted. "Gimme some room while I work on this stupid clown!"

A heavy silence blanketed the crowd as Yeager lifted his hands and moved toward Winslow, a confident smile on his thick lips. He looked like a huge bear as he planted his feet solidly with each step. When he drew near, the difference in the sizes of the two men spelled doom for Winslow. Yeager was six feet two or three and weighed over two hundred thirty. Though his middle seemed encased in fat, great balls of muscle bulged under his shirt as he drew nearer. Winslow was about five ten and weighed a hundred seventy-five—all well hidden, for it was perfectly distributed over his frame. His chest was deep rather than wide, and his muscles strong and supple.

He waited for Yeager's move. Zack kept his right fist cocked and close to his chin, his left extended. He stood on the balls of his feet watching Yeager's feet, not his hands.

He saw the feet come together, brace; then he looked up in time to see Yeager's long looping right hand. The man was even clumsier than Zack had hoped, and he deftly moved to the left, allowing the blow to slip by harmlessly. The force of it threw Yeager off balance, and Zack delivered a punch. It traveled no more than six inches, but it started from his left foot, surged up his leg and torso, and then down his arm, exploding in Yeager's face like a pile driver.

Yeager's head snapped back, and blood gushed from his broken nose. He staggered back two steps, and stood transfixed, his eyes unfocused. He lifted a hand to his face, and stared at the bloody evidence.

A shocked silence fell over the crowd. But Yeager's supporters came to the fore and began to shout, "Get him, Red! Use your muscles on the cur!"

Zack waited, baiting his enemy. Then Yeager roared in, his arms windmilling, certain to catch Winslow in their trap. But Zack was too good. With an ease that surprised everyone, Winslow ducked under the huge arms and smashed a wicked blow over Yeager's belt buckle. Zack felt his fist sink in and a gust of air explode from Yeager's lips. He whirled and clutched his hands over his stomach, his mouth open as he gasped for breath. Zack lunged forward, pummeling unmercifully. His lightning moves caught Yeager in the mouth with a straight right, then as he was driven back, hit him over the left eye with a piston-like left, then a swift right uppercut to the nose as he was falling.

A wild, volcanic yell erupted from the crowd as Yeager flew over backward. He lay rolling from side to side, his hands over his face. From the sidelines, a pale, unbelieving Ives watched, aghast at the demise of his crony.

"I'm coming, George!" Zack yelled. "Soon as I get this tub of guts opened up, I'll be right with you!"

Pfouts turned to stare at Simpson. "I never saw anything like it, Wilbur!"

Simpson nodded. "The man's a professional, Parris. He'll kill Yeager." He looked at the big man as he rolled over and struggled to his knees. "If he'd been smart he'd have stayed down," Simpson added. "But he's not—and I'm glad. He's ruined too many good men with those fists and boots!"

Yeager stood up slowly, his face a bloody mask. In addition to his broken nose, the violent blows had split his eyebrow and his lower lip. Yet the animal force in his huge bulk refused to give up, and he glared out of his good eye, rasping hoarsely, "Stand still and fight like a man!"

Zack wasted no time and began peppering Yeager with short crisp punches he could not see, much less block. A few blows rocked Yeager's head back. He raised his arms in defense, but Zack delivered four more to the stomach—so fast that even the spectators couldn't separate the sounds. Yeager dropped his arms and the next punch caught him flush in the mouth, knocking him to the ground.

"Stop the fight!" one of his henchmen shouted.

"You shut your face!" Miller snapped, jabbing an elbow into the man's ribs. "Nobody stopped Yeager when he stomped John Crenna!"

Yeager crawled to his knees, his mouth hanging open, revealing a large gap where his upper front teeth had been. He choked and gagged.

"Time to put out the lights, Red," Zack said, and waited. Yeager struggled to his feet and made a blind attempt to strike. Zack pivoted and caught him under the jaw, driving his head upward. He fell loosely—and lay limp.

Without another look, Zack walked across to Pfouts and stuck out his hands. "Get these things off!"

Pfouts stripped the bandages off, and Zack flexed his fingers. He took the gun belt from Clark and strapped it on. Then he stepped back into the street. Ives had not moved, though his eyes were searching the crowd.

"Your turn, George," Zack challenged. He walked slowly across the dusty street, his chest rising and falling from the exertion. He halted ten feet away, and paused. His hands were held loosely at his sides, and when he said, "Start blazing away, George," men behind him scrambled to get out of the line of fire.

Ives stood motionless, shaken by the brutal beating Yeager had taken. "I've got no quarrel with you, Winslow."

Zack smiled, and said loudly, "I'll give you one then. You're a cheap two-bit card sharp, Ives. Your mother slept with every man in town." He paused. "That make you mad enough to fight, Ives?"

Jack Gallagher suddenly caught a sign from Ives and shoved his way through the crowd up to Zack and said, "I've got to take your gun, Winslow."

Zack shifted to face him. "Why, take it then, Jack. Lots of other honest guns here today."

Gallagher realized he was facing a situation he hadn't bargained for. "You can't buck the law, Winslow!"

"Why can't I? That sorry bunch who call themselves the Innocents do." He raised his voice and shouted, "Any of you big bad Innocents here? Step out and let's have a look at you!"

He looked around and spotted Boone Helm. "Boone, you one of those yellow curs?"

Boone tried to shrink back, and a jeer went up from the crowd.

"Get out of my sight, Jack!" Zack said evenly.

Gallagher flushed, then slunk away. Seeing this, other toughs followed—even Ives saw it.

Zack said, "I'm trying to think of an insult that'll make you pull that gun of yours, George—but you're too yellow. Why don't you go put on a nightgown with the rest of the girls?"

Ives was caught and knew he had to do something. He was a tough man, but the scheme had backfired. He sprang into action. "I am Innocent!" he cried.

Instantly Miller shouted, "Look out, Zack!"

But Winslow had already seen Long John Frank pull his gun, and he downed the man with one shot. At the same time Billy Page shoved his revolver against Buck Stinson's upraised hand. Stinson's gun exploded, and Beidler followed by driving two bullets into Stinson's body.

The rest of the Innocents were frozen in place by this show of resistance.

Zack whirled and sprinted across to face Ives. "Ives, you're a dog!" he said, slamming his fist into the man's jaw. He fell as though struck by a log.

Zack glared at the crumpled mess, then turned and raised his eyes to the second story of the Palace Hotel. Bron's horror-stricken eyes met his and held—for an instant. Then she whirled and disappeared.

The crowd milled around the street, talking animatedly; Yeager was out cold; Stinson lay inert; Long John Frank screamed with pair:.

Beidler walked over to Zack. "I dug one grave for Stinson already. Now I'll dig another—and this time he'll be in it." Simpson and Clark joined him.

"It was rough justice, Winslow. And high time," Clark said.

All at once Zack felt tired. He nodded and as he pushed his way through the crowd, he heard Pfouts say, "They'll all want him to help them clean up the Gulch. Hope he realizes that."

Zack headed for Steele's office, and found the physician waiting for him. "Buck's awake, Winslow. Wants to see you. I . . . ah . . . told him what you just did."

Buck looked up as Zack came in. "Doc was just in. Sure wish I could've seen it!" he whispered.

"I'm glad you didn't, Buck. The thing is, they didn't know I could fight." He pulled up a chair and for the next twenty minutes they talked.

"You see," Zack began, "I always was a fighter, first in the streets as a boy, then as a young man. I almost turned professional. I was good enough, but I soon discovered that the professional side was a degrading business. Still, I loved the sport, boxing for the fun of it whenever I could during the time I was a soldier. I had a good trainer who taught me well, and I soon learned that being left-handed was to my advantage, because most fighters got so used to a right hand in their face that they were confused when it was the other way around. That's what happened to Yeager."

"Gosh!" Buck said. "And here we all thought you were afraid to fight! Why didn't you?"

"I got sick of fighting in the war. I came out here to find peace and quiet—just leave me alone, the hermit, you know. I don't like to fight, but when this happened to you and Lillian, I realized some things are worth fighting for—even if you don't always win."

"Gosh!" Buck's voice was filled with awe.

At that moment Doc Steele entered the room. "Time's up. No more company for a while, Buck."

"I guess that's my cue to leave," Zack said. "I'll be around tomorrow. Glad you're better. Don't want to lose you."

He walked straight to the Palace, conscious of stares from every man he passed. He hated it.

"Billy!" he said as he almost bumped into him. "How many more times are you going to save my life?"

Page shook his head. "Never mind that, Zack. You've got to get out of town. The toughs have already decided you'll go down."

"How do you know?"

"Why, everybody knows," he replied. "It won't do you any good to try to hide at your ranch. They'll pot you through the window. It better be quick!"

"Come on, Billy. Let's go eat," Zack said, shrugging it off.

"You're not leaving?"

"I came two thousand miles to get away from trouble, Billy. Now it's caught up with me. I guess there's no getting away from what's in store for me."

"They'll kill you, Zack," Billy said evenly, then added, "Get out, Zack!" Then he was gone.

He entered the hotel, ignoring the open-mouthed stare of the clerk and climbed to the second floor. He tapped on room 204. Bron opened the door and stepped outside, closing the door behind her. "Lillian woke up, and all the noise scared her."

"She see any of that on the street?"

"No, thank God! Dr. Steele left some laudanum, and when I saw what was happening, I gave her enough to put her out."

An awkward silence fell between them. Things had changed, and she was staring at him in a way that disturbed him.

"What's wrong, Bron?"

She fingered a button on her blouse, and shook her head. "Nothing's wrong." Then she said, "That's not so, Zacharias. I'm afraid. Everything is going to pieces!"

"It'll all straighten up."

"I didn't know you down there," she whispered. "You were so—so deadly."

"You can't stop men like Ives and Yeager with a hymnbook, Bron. What do you want?" His face burned with anger as he lashed out. "You don't want things like what happened to Lillian and Buck to go on, but when I do something about it, you look at me as if I were some sort of monster!"

She began to tremble. "I don't know—I don't know!" she whispered, as she leaned against him, her face on his chest. He held her as she wept. Finally she drew back and looked up at him. "Let's leave the Gulch! This place is too far gone!"

He shook his head. "Now you sound like *you're* the one who wants to run off and be a hermit, Bron." He motioned toward the door, saying, "We've got Lillian to look out for. And Buck. What about the kids? And what about this town? You came here to preach to the Indians, Bron. Isn't your God big enough for Alder Gulch?"

She blinked as though he had slapped her, and her hand went to her cheek. "Yes, He is that!" she whispered. "He is!" Her eyes met his with a glimmer of the old courage he'd always admired.

"We'll not be hermits, then, Zacharias!" She smiled, adding, "See what a strange man you are! Come to be a hermit, and now you've got to save the whole town!"

PART FOUR

THE VIGILANTES

★ ★ ★ ★

CHAPTER TWENTY-THREE

WHAT LOVE MEANS

★ ★ ★ ★

As soon as Henry Plummer heard of the incident in front of the Silver Moon, he sent for Ives and Yeager. When they walked in he lit into them. "You two managed to ruin *everything* I've been trying to do in the Gulch!"

Ives' anger matched Plummer's and he yelled back in defense, "We'll take care of Winslow!"

"You *had* your chance, George. What stopped you?"

"It would have been suicide!" Ives swore. "Beidler was right in front of me, waiting for me to draw—and so were Miller and Clark. They'd set it all up, and as soon as I saw it, I backed off."

"You backed off all right," Plummer growled. "You looked like scum right in front of the whole town." He glared at Yeager, noting the swollen eyes and missing teeth. "And *you* let him make a sucker out of you, too."

"He's a pug," Yeager mumbled through thick lips. "Nobody in camp could stand up to fists like that—but all it takes is one bullet!"

Plummer's displeasure creased his smooth face. "All right," he growled, "it's done. Red, you go out and help Sam Bunton. George, you'll have to go back to Virginia City or else leave the country. "

"I'm not leaving, Henry!" Ives snapped back bitterly. "The

only reason I came here was because you sent for me. We'll put the squeeze on the Gulch tighter than ever—and don't worry about Winslow."

"You're the man to worry, George. Get him or you're not worth a dime to us."

Ives had gone back primed to face Winslow, but found that he was staying close to his ranch. The outlaw bided his time, but pushed even harder against the town and the miners. Hold-ups became even more common than they'd been before the encounter with Winslow as Ives drove the Innocents hard. All through August there was scarcely a day when some miner didn't get held up, and no matter how Simpson and other leaders tried to ship gold, the Innocents were always ready with an ambush.

"We'll have to wait for a break," Simpson told a small group that met in his office. "I wrote to Washington and asked them to put the town under martial law, but they haven't got the men. All of them are fighting Lee in Virginia."

"When the time comes," Miller nodded, "we'll organize a vigilante troop—but it wouldn't work now." He shook his head, "If Winslow had only said one word about organizing a group after he faced Ives down, it might have happened."

"What's he waiting for?" Simpson asked.

"I think he feels outside of it, Colonel," Pfouts shrugged. "He's in the backwoods and doesn't have to see what we do every day. Besides, he's had his hands full taking care of Buck—and those children."

"Well," Clark said, "I don't wish him any bad luck, but I hope something'll stir him up! We need him and every man we can get—or we're going to be eaten alive by the toughs!"

"Zack caught the hearts of the people in the Gulch when he pounded Yeager and humiliated Ives," Simpson said. "They're all watching him. If he made a move, the whole camp would follow—but he's a loner and won't do a thing about it."

"I think you're right," Beidler nodded. "When Yeager and Ives hurt those kids, Zack blew off like gunpowder. Wish he'd do the same when the rest of the world gets hurt—but that's why he wanted to be a hermit, I guess."

The violence increased. One man was killed for a two-dollar

nugget on his watch chain. Two others vanished when they tried to ride at night with their money. Three thugs murdered a man in broad daylight between the stable and the gunsmith's shop in full view of twenty witnesses, then rode away. Most people stayed inside after dark behind locked doors with loaded guns handy. The gold kept coming out of the ground, but large portions went to the toughs.

★ ★ ★ ★

Zack had noticed that Bron no longer smiled at him as much as before the fight. Why, he wasn't sure. He knew she had been shocked by the violence that boiled out of him, but she was also preoccupied with starting a work among the Indians. He'd given her the money he won from Yeager, explaining, "I don't know where this money came from, Bron. Probably stolen. I don't want it. Think you might use it to help the Arapaho?"

She had taken it without any compunctions. "Old Slewfoot's had this money long enough. We'll see what the Lord will do with it!" She and Pfouts had immediately begun rebuilding the mission, often spending whole days on the site overseeing. She had also worked hard on learning the language, and seemed pleased with the way things were going.

Buck had healed quickly, but Lillian was not herself. She never mentioned going to town anymore; indeed, she refused to go when asked. She became introverted, going for long walks alone and speaking only when addressed. They all were patient with her, but Zack wondered if her mind was affected.

As for Jeanne, she was almost as quiet as Lillian. Crenna had moved back to his claim, and came by the cabin several times a week, ostensibly to get vegetables, but managed to spend as much time with Jeanne and Hawk as he could.

Zack had no inclination to go into town either—unless to get supplies, and then never lingered. Yeager had left the area. As for Ives, Zack didn't go looking for him. Pfouts and Simpson tried to persuade Winslow to attend the special meetings to discuss the problems of the town, but he always refused. The truth was, he had cut Virginia City out of his mind, thinking now of how to help those close to him.

In the middle of September he came home with two letters,

and after supper pored over them until bedtime. Bron wondered what they were as she sat sewing. She and Zack were alone since everyone else had retired early.

Finally he said, "Bron, I got two letters this morning." He handed her a sheet of paper. "That's from Sam's grandmother back East."

Bron read the letter and handed it back. It was filled with thanks to Zack for taking care of Samuel, but she was living with distant relatives, and in very poor health. "Please take care of Sam, be a father to him."

"That's very sad, Zacharias. Poor woman! I know you were hoping there'd be a relative to take him in."

"It'd be better for him. A person needs a family."

"What will you do?"

He shrugged. "Don't know. Just keep on as we have been." He put the letter aside and picked up a fat envelope. "I guess I'm thinking he needs a family because of this."

"What is it?"

He pulled several sheets out and laid them on the table. "Come and look at this, Bron." When she stood beside him, he said, "The letter's from a relative of mine—an old man named Whitfield Winslow. He's trying to get in touch with all the living members of the Winslow family."

"What a lovely idea!" she exclaimed. "And what are all these names with the lines to them?"

"A family tree. Sorta looks like a tree, doesn't it? All start with one couple, then their children—and so on down to me." He pointed. "Look—there's my name. And right over it, my mother's and father's."

She read the names out loud: "Silas Winslow and Martha Howard." She studied the others. "And George Winslow was your grandfather."

"Yes. He's dead, but I remember him very well."

She was fascinated by the novelty of the chart. "I never knew there was anything like this! Do you know any of these people?"

"Well, some of them. Father used to talk about them, and I was quite impressed. Look here, Christmas Winslow—he was my grandfather's brother. He was born on Christmas Day in Valley Forge. His father was in Washington's army."

"Christmas Winslow," she smiled. "What a nice name!"

"He was a rough character—at least when he was young. Went to prison. Another Winslow who was sort of famous got him out. Captain Paul Winslow. He was a naval hero in the War of 1812."

"What happened to Christmas?"

"He went west, Father said. Married an Indian girl—see here's her name—White Dove." Zack stared at the chart, then shook his head. "It's odd, Bron. Their son was named Sky Winslow, and the letter says he's Jefferson Davis's right-hand man—and has several sons in the Confederate Army."

An odd look crossed his face. "You know what I thought as soon as I read that? I may have killed one of my own family! This man, Captain Whitfield Winslow, was in the U.S. Navy and he says he has a grandson named Lowell who's in the Union Army. Winslows fighting against Winslows," he murmured. "That's sad—this world makes no sense, Bron. None at all."

"It will one day—when Jesus comes back and makes a new heaven and a new earth!"

"A new world," he mused. "Look at the name at the very top—Gilbert Winslow. He came over on the Mayflower. He was looking for a new world—and I guess it was, for him. But it's sure gotten spoiled!"

"This country of yours isn't like other countries," Bron said. "It was founded by men and women who came to make a place where God could be worshiped freely. I think after this war, He'll make it a better place, and people will come from all over the world to find a land where they can worship God."

He was standing so close to her that he could smell the fragrance of her hair. It was the first time in weeks that she had allowed the warmth of her smile when she looked at him. He remembered how he'd kissed her in anger. Now he had the impulse to kiss her again, but in a different way. Yet even as he watched, she discerned what was in his mind, and the guarded expression returned. "I'd like to hear more about your family sometime," she said, and moved away. "It's late. Good night, Zacharias."

He stared at the door as it clicked shut, feeling the wall she had put between them. *Nothing I can do about it, I guess.* He picked up the chart to put it away, and sighed, *Strange. I'm one member of a family that's spread out all over the country.* He had not thought of it a great deal since he was an only child, and there was little family close by. He wondered what his relatives were like, and if he'd ever meet any of them. Even after he went to bed, he kept thinking about the chart. *Family is important. We need people. Got to do something for the kids.* Soon he drifted off to sleep, but the next morning he awoke with an idea.

When breakfast was over, he looked across the table. "You've been loafing around here long enough, Buck," Zack said as he drank his last cup of coffee. He leaned back in his chair and a smile touched the corners of his mouth at the surprise on Buck's face. "I figure on starting a new career. Thought you might like to join me and get rich."

Buck nodded, "Sure, Zack. What you got in mind?"

"Stone and Crenna are taking some pretty fair dust out of their claims. We own a long stretch of Dancer Creek, so I guess we might as well make a little money."

Buck's face lit up. He had often wondered why Zack let the gold stay in the ground. Now he asked, "How come you decided that, Zack?"

"Oh, guess I'm getting miserly in my old age." Zack looked around the table and noted Bron and Jeanne watching him closely. Paul and Alice were across the room, playing a game, moving Hawk and Sam against one another as if they were punching puppets, much to their enjoyment. Zack sipped at his coffee, then added, "All these kids need shoes, don't they? How about if we all go down to the creek today and dig enough for a set of new winter clothes for the whole tribe? Take some grub and maybe fish a little."

"That sounds like fun." Bron's eyes sparkled. "We won't be having many picnics in a few weeks, I'm thinking." She looked at Buck. "But you're not going to do much work, you hear me?"

It was six weeks since he had been injured, and he had healed remarkably fast, so he said, "Aw, Bron, I'm as good as new. Let's go. I'll hitch up the horses."

Zack laughed, "Well, now, I don't see as how we can dig a wagon load of gold the first day. It'd make us all sinful if we did, I guess." He pushed his chair back. "We'll be ready by the time you get us some grub thrown together."

"I don't think I'll go," Lillian said. "Maybe I'll just clean up around here."

"None of that," Zack warned. "We'll need all the miners we can get, girl!" He passed by her chair and let his hand drop on her shoulder, adding with a smile, "Besides, you can fry fish over a campfire better than these other women—so I can't spare you."

"All right," she said quickly, and pulled away from his touch. His eyes caught Bron's, and he knew she had seen Lillian's reaction, but said only, "Let's get moving."

As he joined Buck outside, he knew the boy had seen Lillian's look of fear at Zack's touch. After they had hitched up the mules and gathered tools and fishing poles, Buck voiced his fears. "Zack, do you think Lillian's ever gonna get over bein' scared?"

"Sure she will. Just takes time."

"But she never smiles anymore," Buck protested. His face reflected the worry he felt. "She don't even fuss about bein' stuck out here in the backwoods. It's like she's half asleep all the time, ain't it?"

"You'll have to be patient with her, Buck," Zack advised, picking up another shovel and tossing it into the wagon. "She's had about the worst that life can give to a young woman." He said no more, but drove the team to the front door, and soon they were all loaded and on their way.

When they arrived at the creek, Buck suggested, "Let's start panning right now, Zack!"

Zack looked around and saw the same enthusiasm in the others. Even Lillian seemed interested. "All right," he conceded, picking up a pan as he leaped to the ground. The others followed him as he led the way to the creek. There they crowded around as he squatted down and scooped up a panful of sand and small gravel. Then he swung and spilled the gravel from the edges of his pan, working the residue down to black sand.

"Where's the gold?" Buck asked eagerly.

"Isn't any," Zack said. He laughed at their faces and asked, "Did you think all you had to do was just scoop it out like sand?"

"But where is it?" Bron asked too.

"May not be any," Zack shrugged. "More creeks without any

gold than with it." He stood up and studied the creek. "Let's try over where the creek makes a bend. Maybe the water's banged up against the rocks and laid down some color."

He moved to the spot, tried twice with no luck; but as he surveyed the immediate area, an idea struck him and he stepped back from the water. "Let's have the pick," he said. He dug down about a foot, then filled his pan with the gravel from that level. He carefully worked it, and held it out for them to see. "We've struck gold, Buck," he grinned.

Buck nearly fell over, and the others crowded in. "Where?" he asked in a puzzled tone.

Zack touched a pea-sized stone. "That's a gold nugget—and see the glittering specks in the sand? That's gold, too."

Open-mouthed, Buck asked, "How much is it worth, Zack?"

"About a dollar."

"Gosh—that's not much!"

"No. You can break your back digging for gold and not make wages," Zack said. "It's not going to pop out of the ground. But sometimes a man will hit a spot that's yellow as the bottom side of a hound. Every shovelful worth a hundred dollars or even more." He stood up and handed the pan to Buck. "Go to it, Partner. You've got a strong back, and that's about all it takes to be a miner."

Buck wasted no time and began panning.

"I'm going fishing while you make us rich, Buck." Zack took Alice and Paul to the wagon, rigged some lines and soon they were laughing with joy as they pulled small panfish out of the creek.

Bron and Jeanne walked along the stream, helping Hawk and Sam to walk along. They stopped from time to time, and Bron said, "It's nice out here. Good for the children."

"Yes." Jeanne took a stick from Hawk that he'd picked up and was trying to poke into his eye. Jeanne had said little for days, and now there was an uneasiness about her that Bron had seen coming. Jeanne went on. "Soon the snows will come. I have thought of going back to the Cheyenne."

"Why, I didn't know—"

She gave her a quick look and asked, "Why are you surprised? They are my people."

Bron was embarrassed and said quickly, "I guess I've almost forgotten that, Jeanne. I always think of you as being here."

"I will soon have to leave. Sam could do without me now—and that is all Zack sees in me."

"No, that's not so," Bron protested. "He needs you."

"He does not need me as a man needs a woman," Jeanne said.

"Are you sure?"

"Don't you know when a man wants you?"

The elementary meaning of the question brought a red touch to Bron's cheeks. She thought of Owen and nodded. "Yes, I think any woman knows that, Jeanne. But it may come."

"No, the time is past. I hated him when I came. I told myself I would kill him if he ever tried to touch me." She faltered, and her eyes dropped. Then she lifted her head and said, "Then I began to want his touch—but it never came. He has no eyes for me in that way."

"He came here to get away from people," Bron said. "I don't know if he ever will want a woman to share his life." She had turned to watch Zack as he fished with the children, and did not see the quick look she got from Jeanne. "He's a strange man, Jeanne. I thought I knew him, but since I saw him butcher Yeager and try to kill Ives, I'm afraid of him a little."

★ ★ ★ ★

Lillian had left the group to walk alone, but when she came back she saw that Buck was still doggedly scooping gravel. He had dug a dozen holes and when he looked up to see her approach, his face brightened. "Look, Lillian!"

"What is it?"

"A big nugget—look at it!" He held it up, and she took it in her hand. "It looks like a four-leaf clover, don't it?"

She examined it. "Yes, I guess it does."

She gave it back, but he shook his head. "You keep it. I thought if we could get a gold chain—it'd make a nice necklace."

"I won't be wearing a necklace," she said wearily. "Did you find lots of gold?"

"Oh, not so much—except for this nugget. But I'll bet we do." He gave her a covert glance. "You know why Zack is doing this, don't you? He don't care nothin' about money for himself. He's doing it for all of us—so we'll be able to do what we want."

Lillian was surprised but said only, "I guess so, Buck. What'll you do with the money if you get a lot of it?"

He shrugged. "Dunno what I'd do. But I bet you'd like some nice things—dresses and stuff like that."

A shadow crossed her face. She had healed, except for two scars, which Doc Steele assured her would fade even more. "I don't think so," she said, and walked away.

"Lillian!" Buck sped to her side. She seemed so small and vulnerable. How could he say what was on his heart? He had never been able to speak freely with her; now it was even worse. He took a deep breath and plunged in. "I hate to see you so— so sad. You've got such a nice smile, and you're so pretty." He swallowed hard, forcing himself to go on. "Lillian—you got to forget what—what happened to you. It was real bad, but it's over."

Her mouth trembled, and she shook her head vigorously. "No, it's not over. It'll *never* be over!" Tears welled up in her eyes, and she dashed them away with a shaky hand.

He wanted to touch her, to put his hand on her shoulder, but some deep wisdom cautioned him. "You got to let it go," he said quietly, yet with urgency.

"If I could forget it, Buck, do you think everybody else would?"

"Sure! Those that matter!"

"You're wrong! A man would never forget. He'd always be thinking about what happened."

"Not if he loved you."

She looked up at him as if seeing him for the first time. He had been so young when they'd first met, she thought, but he seemed older now. His face had matured and his tall frame was beginning to fill out. Her eyes opened wide. "What about you, Buck? Could *you* forget about it?"

He paused for a long moment, thinking before he answered. "I don't know that we ever really forget anything, Lillian. I still remember the beatings I got when I was eight years old from an old man who hated me. But it's over. All I do now is thank God I'm not still going through that. I guess that's the way it is with a hurt. While it's going on, we think it'll go on forever—and that we can't stand it. But the hurt passes. And then as time goes on, the pain of it somehow fades away."

She listened to him, wanting to believe his words. Finally she shook her head. "So, you *would* remember."

"Maybe I would, Lillian," Buck replied gently. "But not like you think. I'd remember anything that hurt you—but it'd only make me try harder to love you more."

She gave him a startled look, and he bit his lip. "Didn't mean to say that." Then he lifted his head defiantly. "It's true—but I didn't ever think I'd say it out loud."

Lillian felt numb. A silence fell over them, and he expected her to laugh at him. But she only whispered, "That was nice of you to say, Buck." She turned and quickly walked away. He watched her go, his hands at his sides, wanting desperately to help her.

★　★　★　★

Bron had left Jeanne cleaning the fish while she had gone to where Zack was fishing. They had watched the fish nibble at the bait, then dart away. Bron finally broke the silence. "Buck and Lillian have been talking a long time. That's a good sign, but she's such a hurting girl!"

The word *hurt* prodded him to ask as he pulled in the line, "Bron, why are you so cold toward me?"

She blinked with surprise, then shook her head. "Sorry you think that, Zacharias. I—I've been thinking about a lot of things."

A fish broke the surface of the water downstream, but he never noticed. Bron had come to fill some sort of void in his life that he never knew existed until she pulled back. A restlessness seized him, and he took her arm. "What's wrong with you? You look at me, Bron, and it's like you've put up a sign: No Trespassing. Keep Out!" His grip tightened, and he said roughly, "I used to see something in you when you looked at me. What changed it?"

She winced at the power of his grip. "You're hurting me!" she said. Then she nodded. "I used to think you were wrong not to feel things about people. Oh, you were always doing something for us—but it was just a charity. Something you had to do, until we were gone. Then I thought I saw something change. Maybe it was when you nearly died in the creek and called on God. You seemed—gentler, more loving."

"I guess that's right," he nodded.

"But later—when I saw you punish those men—" She wrapped her arms around herself and shut her eyes. "I never saw such anger! You would have killed them!"

A roughness ran through him. "What do you want, Bron? A monk? You didn't like me when I showed no concern—and when I do wake up and start taking care of people, you slam the door and hide behind it. What in God's name do you want from me? Maybe you wish I'd be more like Parris!"

She opened her eyes at his anger. "Yes! You need some of his gentleness."

"Gentleness won't work with Ives and Yeager," he shot back.

She hung her head. "I know that—and I know there must be law, and those who keep men from harming others must use hard ways."

"What then, Bron?" he asked raggedly, shocked at the depth of feeling she had aroused in him. "What do you want a man to be?"

"I can't say, Zacharias," she replied unsteadily, for she had been torn by that scene. "But a man must have compassion—no matter how hard he has to be. And I don't think you have it. You're hard—very hard. And until something breaks you, you'll not have what a real man must have—love for others . . . and trust."

He stared at her, an emptiness deep within him. "You want a man to be a saint—but the Gulch is no place for saints," he said evenly. "That's what happened when the crowd let Stinson and Lyons kill Dillingham. It cried for them, got soft and let them go. But tears won't stop the toughs from killing."

"You'll have to be broken, I think, before you can know what love means," she said wearily, and walked back down the creek, not looking back.

CHAPTER TWENTY-FOUR

TWO VISITS FOR BILLY

★ ★ ★ ★

Billy Page slouched in his chair at the Silver Moon. He took little interest in the poker game, and after losing three hands in a row, he threw his cards down. "Can't beat your luck, gentlemen." He strode toward the door but stopped when he heard someone say, "Billy."

Ives came down the stairs and jerked his head to the left. Billy followed him to an empty corner of the saloon.

"What's up?"

"Be out by Clay Singer's old place at five this afternoon," Ives said, lowering his voice. "Got a job on hand."

"Don't want to leave town, George."

Ives gave Page his full attention, his eyes brittle. "I'm not *asking* you—I'm *telling* you to be there, Billy." He cocked his head. "You've not been worth a dime to us the last few weeks. What's wrong with you?"

Page shrugged. "Nothing. Just don't feel like going. I'm thinking of pulling out of here."

Ives shook his head. "You'd be crazy to leave now, Billy. You've taken in a bundle—and there's a lot more." He glanced furtively around. "In two weeks they're going to ship over fifty thousand in dust. Not on the regular stage—that'll just be a decoy. But we know how they're going to send the real gold. I want just three more men, and you're one of 'em, Billy. Fifty thousand, cut five ways! You can pull out with your pockets lined."

Billy hesitated, then nodded. "All right, George—but I'm leaving after that job."

"All right with me—but you be out at Singer's old place at five today—and keep it quiet. Boone and Red will be there. Red will give you the dope." Ives smiled. "It'll be worth your while. A nice bit of cash to add to your traveling money." He clapped Billy on the shoulder.

Billy left the saloon and went to his room to change clothes, then walked toward the stable. The December wind was sharp, holding a promise of snow, and he decided the coat he wore wasn't warm enough. He made his way to Pfouts' store and found the owner alone. "Got to have a warmer coat, Parris," he said.

"Snow brewing, Billy," Parris nodded. "You going on a trip?"

Page said casually, "Thought I'd run out to see Bron. Had a little run of luck at the tables and wanted to take some Christmas cheer to the kids. You pick out some candy and stuff they might like, will you?"

Pfouts searched Page's face. He was worried about the young man, for he never worked and he was constantly seen with shady characters. Bron had shared her concern with Parris, and the two had often spoken of his easy ways. "That's a real kind thought, Billy. I've got a few things to send them myself if you can take them."

"Sure," Billy nodded. "But I got to have a warmer coat. Never could stand cold weather!" He followed Pfouts over to a selection of men's winter coats and picked out a thick wool coat with wide lapels and big pockets. It was dyed a bright green, and had a hood lined with rabbit fur. He put it on, pulled the hood up, and nodded. "This will do fine." He paid for the coat, then helped Parris fill a sack with candy for the children and some gifts for the adults. He took the package, saying, "See you later."

Parris struggled with an impulse, then called, "Billy—" He walked over to Page. "Billy . . ." he began again.

"Yes. What's on your mind, Parris?"

"This camp is no good for you, Billy," Parris blurted out. "You ought to get out of this place."

Billy stared at him. "With a blizzard brewing up? It'd be a rough trip."

"I can think of a worse one," Parris said. "You've got a lot to live for, my boy. Go somewhere else, make a new start."

Page searched Pfouts' eyes for the real reason, then saw something that made him nod. "You may be right, Parris. I've been thinking on it. I'll be leaving in a few weeks."

"Be best for you." Pfouts smiled with relief. "Why don't you tell Bron that, Billy? She's been worried about you."

"Sure." Page left the store and went straight to the stable. As he rode out of town, he passed Pfouts' store. *Parris knows I'm with the wrong bunch*, he thought bitterly. *I guess Bron knows too— maybe Zack.* He had been only half serious when he told Ives he was leaving, but now he knew he had to get out. Just this job today—then the gold shipment. That'd be the end of it!

The new coat felt snug and warm against the cold air. Page looked up at the sky and decided the snow would hold off for a day or two. *Just two jobs*, he mused to himself. He rode steadily on, and a little before noon pulled up in front of Zack's cabin and slid from his horse. The door opened as he tied his horse to a post, and there stood Bron with Paul and Alice on either side.

"Christmas is a little bit early," he said as they came out to meet him. He untied the sack, and they all hurried in, the children jabbering and pulling at him for attention.

"Well, Billy," Bron smiled. "Come to the fire and thaw you out."

Handing her the sack, he said, "Thanks, Bron." He added, "Got to thinking that you might be snowed in by Christmas— so I thought I'd have it early. Hello, Zack—Buck." He turned and gave Jeanne and Lillian a smile. "How are you, ladies?"

"Have some coffee, Billy," Zack said. He got up and went to the fireplace. As he poured Page a cup of steaming coffee, he asked, "How's things in Virginia City?"

Page swallowed a mouthful of the coffee, then replied, "The same, Zack. Getting ready for the winter."

He thawed out, and for the next two hours entertained them all. He played a game with Paul and Alice, then told Lillian about a drama troupe that had put on a performance two weeks earlier. Bron noticed how the girl's face relaxed as he spun the story out, and thought, *Billy's at ease with anybody he meets. What a wonderful gift!* He talked with Jeanne and with Buck, both of them smiling at his humor. Finally he said, "Well, I've got to get back to town. Let's have Christmas!"

He stood up and began pulling presents out of the sack. The next thirty minutes were filled with an enjoyment he had rarely had. Alice and Paul stuffed their mouths with hard candy, and all the others laughed and exclaimed over their gifts. He had gotten a set of silver brushes and a comb to match for Jeanne, which caused her eyes to shine with warmth. For Lillian, Parris had chosen a pair of soft doeskin gloves and half boots to match. Bron stood there looking pleased with the sewing kit enclosed in a finely wrought leather case, and Buck could not believe his eyes when Billy handed him a Navy Colt with a tan leather holster.

Overcome with the coveted gift, he swallowed and said, "I never saw anything so nice." He looked up in awe and whispered, "Thanks, Mr. Page!"

"You're welcome, Buck." Billy next plucked a bulky package out of the bottom of the sack and handed it to Zack. "I knew you liked books, so I asked Parris to pick you out a good one. Haven't seen it, though."

Zack opened the package, hesitated, then held up a beautifully bound volume. "The Bible," he smiled. He ruffled through the pages and looked up. "Thanks, Billy—and I'll tell Parris he made a good choice." He handed the Bible to Page. "Sign it for me, Billy, with the date."

Page took the Bible, and Bron scurried around to get the ink and a quill. He paused, and gave a rueful grin at them. "This has been a fine Christmas. Best I ever had, I reckon. I'm no scholar, but I know one verse." He squared away and wrote slowly on the first page of the Bible, then handed it to Zack.

Zack read it aloud; "There is a friend that sticketh closer than a brother—and I'm glad to have a few friends in this dark world. Merry Christmas to you, Zack."

"Don't know where that verse is," Billy confessed, somewhat embarrassed by the sentiment he'd expressed. "But you people have been the best friends I've ever had." He jumped up suddenly and said, "I've got to get out of here. Next thing you know I'll be bawling."

"Stay for the night, Billy," Bron urged, and the others tried to prevail on him, but he shook his head.

"Got to get back to town. Don't want to get snowed in for the winter out here in the woods!"

He walked to the door, but Bron said, "Wait you now, Billy Page!" She threw her arms around his neck and gave him a loud kiss on the cheek. "Merry Christmas!" Then the others came, Lillian giving him her hand, shyly, and Jeanne smiling and doing the same. Alice and Paul hugging him, and Buck nearly breaking his hand with a bone-crushing shake.

He pulled away, and Zack walked with him as he left the cabin and mounted his horse. "That meant a lot, Billy," Zack said. He put his hand out and smiled. "Thanks for the Bible. I need it."

Page gave him a quick glance. "Do you? Well, now, I reckon Mrs. Page's oldest son could use a little of it himself." He took up the reins, then paused, "Zack, I may not see you again."

Winslow looked at him sharply. "You pulling out, Billy?"

"In a couple of weeks." His horse fidgeted, and Billy said, "Got to go. Tell Bron, will you?"

"Sure." Zack studied the young man's face. "Maybe I won't see you again, Billy. So you've got to hear me say something. You pulled me out of the fire twice, Billy—once with Yeager and then when you kept Stinson from putting a hole in me. I won't ever forget that. Thanks."

"Sure. Makes me feel a little better, Zack, knowing I gave you a hand." He glanced at the cabin. "Take care of Bron. She's special." Then he grinned and pulled his horse around. "Merry Christmas, Zack!"

He kicked his horse into motion and rode away from the cabin, turning around to wave at Zack, then disappearing around the flank of alders that skirted the road. A mile away, he slowed his horse to a walk and thought with pleasure of the visit. He had formed few ties in his life, staying at no one place long enough to make fast friends. Regret came to him at the prospect of leaving Zack and Bron.

The dark streak of pessimism that ran underneath his cheerful manner rose to the surface; and as he turned off the road to take a shortcut to the Singer place, the dull winter sky seemed ominous and foreboding.

He emerged from the woods two miles south, and followed an old game trail that tilted downward across the land. When he got to the small barn—all that was left of Singer's abortive attempt to farm—he saw two horses tied to saplings. He dismounted and went inside.

He stood by the fire where Yeager and Boone were cooking a supper of beans and bacon. "You want some grub?" Yeager asked.

"No. Just coffee." He poured himself a cup and sat back on his heels while the pair ate. Yeager, he noticed, had trouble eating with his upper front teeth missing, and Page knew that a bitter hatred raged against Zack.

The trio scarcely talked while they ate; then when they finished and had thrown their cooking gear into saddlebags, Helm asked, "Did George tell you what we come to do?"

"Plummer says we been too easy on these miners strung out here away from town. Told George we got to get tough."

Yeager said, "Clubfoot heard Stone tell Harold Reiner he'd took five thousand out of that claim of his over on Dancer Creek." He grinned and said through the toothless gap, "We'll pick that up, Page. That's the job."

"Might put up a fight," Billy said. He wished he hadn't come, but it was too late to back out now. "Him and that fellow Crenna could be pretty tough."

"Crenna went over to Bannack," Helm said. "We won't have no trouble with Stone all by hisself. Let's go."

They mounted and Yeager led the way across the ridge to Dancer Creek. The sun was falling behind the mountains, throwing a dull reddish glow across the creek as the three came out of the woods and looked down on the small cabin built back against a line of fir trees. The cabin windows showed orange, and Boone said, "We'll get a little closer, then sneak up on him. Don't make no noise, and when we get there, I'll go through the door first. You two follow."

They moved down the trail, then left their horses tied to saplings as they crept closer. No sound came from the cabin. When they were alongside, Helm pulled his neckerchief over his face, and the other two did the same. Boone drew his gun and motioned with it toward the front of the cabin. There was no window on that side, and they all ducked under the one in the front. When they were all in front of the door, Helm nodded, then threw his shoulder against the door.

Nolan Stone jumped out of his chair as the door burst open, but halted when he saw a gun trained on him. "Hold it right there!"

Stone grew pale, but nodded. "Looks like you're calling the shots."

"You just behave and you won't get hurt," Boone growled.

Yeager moved forward to stand beside Boone Helm, while Billy closed the door and waited.

"Let's have your cash," Helm demanded.

"Haven't got much, boys," Stone shrugged. He pointed with his pipe to the shelf nailed to the wall. "It's right there."

Yeager whirled and pulled the pouch off the wall. He gave it scarcely a look and cursed. "You've got your dust cached here, Stone!"

"Took it into town last Friday," Stone said. "I dug that out since then, but the rest of it's in the safe at the Station."

"We know better!" Helm said. "Think we don't know who puts his dust in that safe? Now, just give us the dust, Stone, and we'll be on our way."

Stone said steadily, "I thought somebody might be by, just like you fellows. Crenna and I talked it over, and we took the dust in last week."

Yeager lunged forward and brought his gun down hard over Stone's head, driving him to the floor. Red yelled, "Lying ain't gonna help you none. Now, get that gold—or we'll have to burn it outta you!"

Stone was dazed, and made two attempts to stand before he got to his feet. He wiped the blood off his face and said, "All you have to do is ask Tyler. He took the gold and put it in his vault."

"Where's the receipt?" Helm demanded.

Stone blinked, "Crenna has it."

Yeager cursed. "We gotta work on him! Come on—let's tie him to that chair."

He stepped forward, and at the same time Stone reached out and pulled Yeager's bandanna down. "I thought it was you," he said. Then his eyes opened wide and he cried, "Don't—!"

But it was too late. Yeager drove two shots into Stone's chest, killing him before he crumpled to the floor.

Helm leaped forward, crying, "You fool! Now he can't tell us nothin'!"

Yeager sheathed his gun, turning from the body of Stone. "Got to be in this cabin. Let's find it."

For over an hour the three plundered the cabin, tearing out shelves, digging in the floor, but the gold was not to be found. "Let's get out of here," Helm swore in disgust. "We'll have to work on Crenna when he gets back from Bannack."

Yeager walked over and bent over the body of Stone, taking a ring off his finger and the watch out of his pocket. He rose and followed Helm out into the night where Page had already gone. They groped their way back to their horses, and rode back to town. Yeager and Helm talked as they rode along, but Page said nothing. The night was dark, and the thought of Nolan Stone lying dead in his own blood made Billy ill. He had opened his mouth to protest just as Yeager's gun had lifted, but the shots had drowned out his voice.

He was sick to his stomach, and when he left the pair, he gripped the reins until his fingers cramped. He had known Stone, had played cards with him a few times. He'd liked the man, and now he was dead. It did Billy no good to think he'd not been the one to pull the trigger. Bile rose bitterly in his throat as he put his horse up in the stable. He went straight to his room and lay down on the bed fully clothed, staring at the ceiling. When morning came, he had not slept, but the cold light of the winter sun struck his eyes, and he rolled over on his face, wishing he'd never left town. But no matter what he wished, he kept seeing the body of Nolan Stone crumpled and still in the cabin on Dancer Creek.

CHAPTER TWENTY-FIVE

SHOOT OUT

★ ★ ★ ★

Stone had been well liked in the Gulch, so his death brought sorrow to the community. His funeral was held in the church, which was filled to overflowing. Reverend Phineas Wiley, the Methodist pastor from Bannack, gave the sermon, and afterward read the scripture at the graveside, quoting "I am the resurrection and the life. . . ."

The biting wind that swept down out of the Bitterroots numbed Bron's face as she stood between Buck and Lillian. She had shed her tears in private over Stone, for he had not been open to the gospel. As the minister read the words, she looked around the circle of roughly dressed men, noticing that John Crenna's face was scored with grief. He was not a man to show his feelings, but even as Bron watched, the man's eyes glistened with unshed tears as he stared down on the rough pine box. Jeanne stood beside him, and Bron's heart warmed as she saw the woman put a hand on Crenna's arm. He turned to look at her dark face with some surprise, and she said something to him in a low voice that seemed to give him some support. He nodded and reached out and touched her hand before turning to face the preacher again.

Zack stood between James Miller and Dutch Beidler in the open field that had become the burial ground of the Gulch. The three men had been friends of Nolan Stone, and their faces mirrored the bitterness they felt. The gusty wind swept across the field, blowing Zack's hair over his forehead. He lifted his eyes and met Bron's gaze. Gone was the humor she'd seen in him during happier times. Instead, his face was frozen with the same fury—his jaw set, his eyes like steel—as when he challenged Yeager and Ives. Again, the intensity of it shocked Bron, and she dropped her head and tried to concentrate on Reverend Wiley's words: "Ashes to ashes and dust to dust. . . ."

After the service, Zack and his "family" dispersed for a short while. Bron met with Parris and Tod Cramer at the church. Buck and Lillian took Alice and Paul to the cafe for dinner. Zack needed to see the gunsmith, and as he turned to go he saw Jeanne and Crenna walk away, carrying Sam and Hawk. Zack continued on to go to the gunsmith shop. He found Will Porter at work, and handed him his Navy Colt. "See if you can do something about the trigger action, Will. It's hanging for some reason."

"Sure, Zack."

Zack sat down to wait, and picked up a month-old Helena newspaper. Though the news wasn't current, it gave him some perspective of the war, which was far from being resolved. Grant was forging steadily on, losing more men than anyone had thought possible, while Lee still managed to regroup his ragged Army of Northern Virginia after every battle in time for the next one.

"All finished, Zack," Porter said thirty minutes later. "Had a burr on the heel of the tension bar."

Zack tested the action of the Navy Colt, then holstered it. "Seems good. How much?"

"Two dollars, I guess." As he took the money from Zack, Porter gave him a searching glance. "Miller and Clark talk to you yet—about organizing to stop this kind of thing?"

Zack put on his coat and shrugged. "They're always talking, Will."

"This time we got to do it!" Porter's face was stiff with outrage, and he hit the workbench with his fist. "Nolan was too good a man to die like that!"

Zack nodded, but said only, "I guess we'll never know who

did it. But if I knew, I wouldn't wait for any committee." He left the shop and made his way down the street to Pfouts' store. Bron was already there, sitting in front of the stove drinking coffee with Parris. *They look like husband and wife,* Zack thought. *Don't think I like that.*

"Have some coffee, Zack," Parris said, getting up to pour a cup of the brew. The three talked about mundane happenings, but didn't broach the subject of Nolan's death. They all felt the weight of the tragedy, though.

After fifteen minutes, Zack wanted to get away from the oppression and rose to leave. "Guess I'll go down and see if I can find—"

"Parris!" The door opened and A. J. Oliver, manager of the stage station, burst in, his countenance agitated.

"What's wrong, Oliver?" Pfouts asked.

"You know how I keep gold coins on hand? Sometimes people like to change their dust for hard coin." It was a common practice, for most of the miners found it easier to carry coins than pokes of dust. "Well, a fellow came in a few minutes ago, wanted some coins, so I took his dust." He held up a leather poke, pulled the drawstring, and removed something. "See that nugget?"

Zack took it. "Looks like a little skull," he said, handing it to Parris. "What about it, Oliver?"

"That nugget belonged to Nolan. He and Crenna came in last week. They wanted to put their dust in my safe, and they did— all but this nugget. Nolan said he was going to have it made into a charm for his watch chain."

"Who brought the poke in?" Zack asked quickly.

"Boone Helm."

"I'll get Miller," Pfouts said to Zack, then called to his clerk, "Watch the store."

Winslow shook his head. "You won't get him—or if you do, he won't hang."

"We can't just let this ride, Zack!" Parris protested. "Let's go." He waited but saw Winslow had no intention of going, so he said, "Come along, Oliver."

After they left, Bron turned to Zack. "You're going to kill him—Boone Helm."

"Nolan was my friend."

"Then go with Parris—help the others!"

"They won't touch Helm. If they arrest him, the crowd'll yell for his release, and they'll turn him loose just like they did Stinson and Lyons." He gave her a look she couldn't read. "What's the difference whether I kill him, or a bunch of men hang him? He'll be just as dead."

"Oh, Zacharias," Bron urged, "don't you see? God made men to live together—and that means we *have* to have law! Otherwise we're just animals!"

"That's what Helm and the others like him are," Zack countered. "They'll kill with no more mercy than a lobo wolf."

"And are you different if *you* kill them?" she responded. "You'll hunt him down and kill him; then they'll try to kill you—and there'll be no end to it!"

He knew she was trying to tell him something, but the rage that had settled in him from the moment he'd seen Nolan's body at the cabin would not leave. "What do you want me to do? Let him get away with it? No! Let the people have their committees and organizations—I'm going to make sure Nolan's killer pays the price!"

He saw her fright and clamped his lips, trying to curb his emotions. "Bron," he said, "don't you understand? I've *got* to do it. Why, if it was you that had been killed, do you think I'd let them get by with it? I love you more than—" He stopped abruptly. He hadn't meant to say that.

Startled, her lips opened as his words hung in the air. "You love *me*?" she whispered. Even as she spoke, she was faced with her own true feelings. For months she'd refused the little nudgings that wanted to surface, afraid to think of such a possibility. He'd been so distant. Furthermore, she thought he was in love with Jeanne.

Now she realized that her feelings for him were as deep, though different in many ways, than the love she'd felt for Owen. Even as she stood there, she knew that many things separated them—most important, he didn't know God.

"Do you really love me, Zacharias?" she asked again.

"Yes, I love you," he said slowly, even reluctantly. Then a wry smile touched his lips. "It'll never come to anything, Bron—but I want you to know you've done something I never thought could happen: made me trust another woman. You've shown me how wrong I was. You're the finest girl I've ever known."

"Zack," she pleaded, "don't go after Helm. If you love me, do this one thing for me—and it's not Boone Helm I'm asking it for, but you. You don't know how hatred makes you hard—but I saw it when you went after Yeager and Ives. You'll destroy yourself unless you learn to show mercy. It'll be Helm now, then the next time somebody crosses you, it'll be easier. Finally you'll wind up just like them—hard, cruel, merciless!"

Zack admired the softness in her—but he wouldn't budge. "Bron, I'm going after him. I couldn't live with myself if I didn't."

He waited for her to speak; instead, she threw her arms around his neck, pulled his head down, and pressed her lips to his. The action was instinctive, propelled by the fear that he would be destroyed. Her body trembled, and when she drew back, her eyes were filled with tears.

"Zacharias, I can't love a man who won't join with others. You came out here to hide from the world—but you took us all in. That's what made me first begin to favor you—because you showed love and compassion to me, and Jeanne, and Buck." She shook her head and said fiercely, "You've got such a heart for love—but it's all tied up! This—this may be your last chance! Please—go find the others. Help them! They'll follow you!"

Her kiss had surged through him, and he knew he'd never find another woman like Bronwen Morgan. But the stubbornness that had entrenched itself would not allow him to do the one thing he yearned for: to give in, to love her, to do as she asked.

"Bron, I've *got* to do it!"

Her lips firmed, and she said slowly, "If you kill Helm, I can't think of you as—as a man I might love, Zacharias."

He stared at her, then said briefly, "Wait here for me."

"I won't be here if you go. I can't love a man who thinks he's bigger than the law."

Zack dropped his head, letting her words hang in the silence. Then he said quietly, "I'm sorry," and wheeled, striding out the door.

Unaware of the cutting wind, he headed straight for Helm's livery stable, but the hostler said, "He ain't here." Zack turned and half ran back down the street into the first saloon—Del Timrod's place. He was told Boone was not there, but Zack lifted his voice and called out, "I'm looking for a skunk named Boone Helm!"

"Well, he ain't here, Winslow," Timrod replied, his words guarded.

"If you see him, tell him I'm lookin' for him. Tell him to bring his gun."

"If I see him, I'll tell him."

Zack made the same statement in three more saloons, and noticed as he emerged from the last one that a man was scurrying up the street. "Gone to warn Helm, I bet," he muttered, touching his gun as his coat whipped back in the wind.

Word of trouble traveled fast in Virginia City, and in house after house doors were flung open. Faces pressed against windowpanes. Men emerged to follow Winslow's progress along the cold street. Up ahead, Zack saw a figure step out of the Silver Moon—Boone Helm! His mind raced ahead, and as he approached the spot, he saw Hayes Lyons far over to the left of Helm, and Snake Walker, a tough half-breed, to the right. Both men turned to face Zack as he stopped thirty feet from Helm, who called out, "Hear you're lookin' for me, Winslow."

Zack's eyes caught a flash on the roof of the Silver Moon, like the sun striking a shiny object. *Man with a rifle up there*, he thought. "Boone, we buried a good man today."

Another man slithered out from an alley to Helm's left. Helm looked quickly, reassured, and flexed his shoulders cockily. "Too bad, but it's got nothin' to do with me."

The man in the alley had disappeared, but Zack threw caution aside and challenged, "You're a liar, Helm!—a yellow dog!"

Helm's jaw tightened and he yelled, "Nobody calls me *that!*"

He clapped his hand on the butt of his gun, threw one quick glance toward Hayes Lyons to give a signal, then stopped. James Miller was standing face-to-face with Lyons, forcing him out of the play. Beidler had followed suit with Snake Walker, and A. J. Oliver and several other merchants stood like cocked guns, watching Helm carefully.

Helm made a half turn, his bravado fading fast, and lifted his hand from the gun. "You got nothin' on me, Winslow! I never—"

A movement to his left shattered his nerves and he uttered a cry, thinking Miller was gunning him down. He yanked his gun out and shot. The figure dropped.

Zack shot simultaneously, sending a bullet into Helm's temple, killing him instantly. Winslow wheeled and ran to the person Helm had downed. "Bron!" he cried as he gathered the bleeding woman into his arms. At the same moment, the man on the roof aimed his gun at Zack's back. Suddenly the gunman flew backward as Beidler's shotgun pellets tore into him. He plunged to his death below.

Oblivious to Pfouts, who had come with Bron, and the gunfire around him, Zack raced toward Doc Steele's office—praying as he ran, his shirt stained with Bron's blood.

CHAPTER TWENTY-SIX

THE TRIAL OF GEORGE IVES

★ ★ ★ ★

Jeanne waited in Doc Steele's office for his report. Worry creased her wan face as she fidgeted. She had been there off and on the past few days, hoping for good news as the wounded woman fought for her life. She and the children had found a place to stay for the time being.

"She's better today," he said as he came out of Bron's room. "Fever stayed down all night, and her breathing is less ragged." He scratched his head and sighed. "If she'd just wake up and eat something, she'd get some strength."

"I will try to feed her a little."

"You might try to get Winslow to eat, too," Steele suggested. "I don't think he's eaten enough to keep a cat alive since he brought her here."

"I will try—but he feels that it is his fault."

"I know—and I guess it was, in a way. But most men don't just stop living like he's done—even if what's happened is their fault." He moved to the door, saying, "I'll be back this afternoon."

After he left, Jeanne went into Bron's room and stood beside the bed. She grasped Bron's hand, willing her to respond, to wake up. But she only moaned. Zack sat nearby, watching. His unshaven face and grief-stricken red-rimmed eyes showed the agony of the past three days. Not only did he refuse to sleep, he couldn't even *think* of food because of the weight of his guilty conscience. Jeanne turned to him. "She is better," she said. "You go down and get something to eat. Rest awhile."

He got up and stretched his aching muscles. Coming over to the bedside, he looked down at Bron, studying her. "I can't see she's any different." With all his heart he wanted to believe Jeanne, but there had not been even a minute change that he could see.

"But the fever's gone and she's sleeping normally." Jeanne hesitated, then said, "You're not to blame, Zack. There was no way you could have known Bron was going to be there." She saw the words meant nothing to him, and gave an angry snort. "If you want to blame someone, blame Parris! He was the one who let her drag him down there!" The words fell on deaf ears, so she shrugged. "Well, I've got to give her a bath. Go get some sleep, Zack."

"Jeanne," he said, "I don't know what's wrong with me." His eyes were filled with confusion, and he rubbed his hand over his face, then looked down at Bron. "I can't do anything—that's what makes it so bad. If I could just—just—!"

"Just what?" Jeanne interrupted, grabbing his arm. "Maybe it's the first time you ever got caught up in a thing you can't handle, Zack. You've been strong enough to stand against any situation because you could *do* something—even if that something was only running away from the problem. Now you *can't* run away—because you love her. Isn't that what it is?"

He nodded. "I guess so, Jeanne. It'll never amount to anything—but you're right. I've been here for three days, and it's like being in a deep, dark hole with no way out. I'm not a doctor, and I'm not a praying man—and I can't . . . don't want to . . . run off and leave her," he said, his eyes dropping to the still form. Her fiery hair garlanded the pillow, her long dark lashes lay against her velvety cheeks. *Oh, God! Oh, God!* his heart cried. Aloud he said, "What does a man do at a time like this?"

Pity touched Jeanne's dark eyes. "Every one of us comes to that, Zack, sooner or later. Death reaches its fingers out to one we love, or what we want most is wrenched from us. And we cry or we curse—and we blame God, or ourselves. But it's always the same, I think. We all bump up against something that we can't handle."

His eyes opened wider. "Why, that's the way it is, Jeanne! How did you know?"

Turning away from him, she replied quietly, "Because I've been there."

With a nod, he stumbled from the room and down the stairs. The snow had begun to fall, dusting the muddy street with a white coat. Exhausted, Zack shuffled his way to the cafe. There were only three miners at a table across the room from where he sat down. One of them asked respectfully, "How's Miss Morgan, Winslow?"

"Doc says she had a good night. Fever's gone."

"Good. She's going to make it! We can't lose our Alder Gulch Angel, can we, fellows?"

Zack ate a little, forcing each mouthful. He was interrupted several times by men who inquired about Bron. Their concern was genuine, for to these rough miners, the woman they called the Alder Gulch Angel was a symbol of something they missed. In the lawlessness and infamy of the camp, she stood for the purity and virtue they longed to see in something.

He got a room at the hotel, fell into bed, and slept all day, getting up just as darkness was beginning to fall. The snow was almost two inches deep as he made his way back to the cafe. Beidler waved a hand at him as he entered, so he made his way through the packed room, joining the stocky Dutchman who shared a table with Colonel Simpson and Tod Cramer. "I just left Steele's office," Simpson informed him. "Miss Morgan woke up this afternoon and sipped a little broth. Doc's very optimistic about her."

Relief washed over Zack and he bowed his head, staring at the tablecloth. His action silenced the others. Finally Dutch cleared his throat. "Well, one thing came out right, anyway."

Zack pulled his shoulders back and said, "Got any pie, Blackie?"

"Apple and peach."

"I'll have the peach—and some coffee."

He ate the pie, listening as the three men talked, taking no part. He felt Simpson's disapproval, and knew it was because he had not been willing to join the common effort to clean up the Gulch. He regretted Simpson's reaction, for Zack admired the man.

He finished his pie, and sat watching the snow fall. Just as Simpson said "I've got to get home—" James Miller pushed through the door. His eyes swept the saloon until he spotted the four men. He rushed over, his eyes blazing. "Mike Ameche just brought Nick Tybalt in with a bullet in his head. Mike found him in the brush."

"Nick?" Dutch asked, getting to his feet. "Where'd Mike find him?"

"Out near the shack where Charley Hildebrand and Long John Frank live."

Everybody in the cafe had heard Miller's words, and the angry sound of voices rose. Nick was one of the best young men in the camp, well liked by everyone. Somebody shouted, "It's time we stopped this thing!"

The miners were angry, but they had no leader. Simpson knew he didn't have what it took to make men follow. He got to his feet wearily, saying, "I guess we'll have to bury him tomorrow."

Miller looked at Zack, a question in his eyes, but seemed to have little hope, so he headed for the door.

"Wait a minute, James," Zack called.

Every eye was riveted on Zack as he rose to his feet. He hadn't shaved, and looked rough, but the vehemence they had seen the day he shot Yeager, or when he had gone after Ives, was gone. Now there was a set, determined look as he said, "There's enough of us to do the job." Immediately a yell split the air as the men leaped to their feet, anxious to hear what he would say.

Zack looked at the miners and knew that Bron had been right—that Pfouts and Simpson and Miller had been right. "I'm ready to go—but we all go together. Simpson," he turned to the older man and asked, "what's the best plan?"

Simpson was astonished, but delighted. "A posse, first, to catch the men who did this. Then we organize into the Alder Gulch Vigilantes. Zack, you and Miller go bring the men in, and by the time you get back, we'll be ready to hang them!"

"You're the boss," Zack said. "Come on, Miller." Loud cheers bounced against the walls as the men hurried out.

Simpson searched the faces of the others and said, "Remember, if we start this thing, there's no turning back. Some of us may not make it—we might even have to lay our hands on men we've never dreamed were in with the toughs. Don't start if you're not going to finish!" Simpson's silhouette against the falling snow made him look even taller and stronger as he waited for their response. The voices diminished for a minute as each man thought about the consequences, then raised as one cry of assent.

Simpson searched their faces again, grateful for the support. "All right, get your horses and be sure you have plenty of ammunition. We'll head out in thirty minutes."

At the time appointed, eight of them left Virginia City, riding steadily until two o'clock in the freezing darkness. They had set out with vigor and enthusiasm, but the bitter cold seeped into the very marrow of their bones, slowing their reactions and chilling their ardor. One man started to complain, and Miller said bluntly, "Shut your mouth, Whitey! We're going to finish this job if we freeze our ears off doing it!"

At three o'clock, Miller called a halt. "I'm going to see what's at Frank's cabin. Wait till I get back." The men piled off their horses and stomped their feet to get the circulation going. Zack's hands were stiff, and he beat them together, saying to Dutch Beidler, "They may have skipped by now."

But when Miller returned a half hour later, he was excited. "There's a pack of horses outside the cabin. Must be a meeting. Let's close in."

"Better wait for a little light, James," Zack murmured. "We could start shooting each other in the dark."

"Sure," Miller nodded. "We'll wait awhile."

They stood there in the snow waiting until just before dawn. Finally Zack said, "Let's take 'em, James."

"All right." Miller motioned them forward, and they crept stealthily up to the cabin, taking strategic positions. When they were all in place, Miller moved around the front corner, raised his gun and yelled, "Frank! Come out here!"

There was a momentary silence; then somebody inside cursed. "Who's out there?"

"Get out here—all of you!"

The door opened and Zack recognized Long John Frank. "What's goin' on?" Frank asked.

"You come with me," Miller told him, holding his gun on him. "Winslow, you and Beidler come too. The rest of you get the others—be sure and take their guns," he said as he prodded Frank around the corner of the shack.

Seventy feet away, he stopped and said, "Nick Tybalt was found out here with a bullet in his brain."

"Don't know nothin' about it," Frank said nervously.

"He was laid out in plain sight, but you didn't bring his body in," Miller charged. Something in his face frightened Frank.

"I didn't kill him, Miller!"

"I think you did. You'll hang for it, Frank!"

"No! It wasn't me!" Sweat popped out on Long John's brow despite the cold, and he began to tremble.

Zack saw the fear and said, "I guess we can do the job here, Miller. No sense taking him back to town. It's his cabin, and he had to be in on it."

Frank held up his trembling hands. "Wait! I swear it wasn't me." He sighted the rope ahead, and threw all caution to the wind. "It was George Ives who killed him! He shot Tybalt for his money and his mules."

"Who else is here?" Miller asked.

"Just some drifters that came in last night."

"You'd better be telling the truth—get going!" He herded Frank back toward the front of the cabin. Zack had spotted George Ives standing in the doorway, his hands raised, the other men from the shack in like position, with guns aimed at them.

"What's all this, Miller?" he asked.

"We're taking you in, Ives."

"For what?"

"You shot Nick Tybalt."

Unimpressed, Ives smirked, "You'll have a hard time proving it."

One of the posse called out, "Let's do the job here."

Miller shook his head. "No, we're taking them back to town. They'll have lawyers and a legal trial."

Ives glared at him, then at Winslow. "You two are on top

now—but that won't last long," he warned.

When they hit Virginia City, they found the town alive with excitement. The miners had heard about the posse and had filled the saloons to overflowing as they waited. Miller, Zack and Beidler locked the prisoners up; then they left.

"The word is out that the toughs won't let them be hanged," Pfouts said as he and Simpson met Miller. "They've got a lawyer, but Simpson will prosecute for us. Tomorrow we'll do it. The right time has come."

"The miners may cry for them again, like they did before," Zack offered.

"Makes no difference," Miller said. "We've got to do it this time."

Zack nodded. "I'll be here." He left the group and went to Steele's office. The physician looked up from his chair and smiled. "I hear you got Ives."

"Yes, and a few others. How is she?"

"She's out of the woods, Winslow," Steele replied. "The Indian woman and Lillian have taken good care of her. You know, I think this has helped Lillian. She's done something for somebody else—and that's always better than sitting around studying your own hurts."

"Can I see Bron?"

"She may be asleep, but go on in."

As Zack headed for Bron's room, Steele asked, "You think Ives will be convicted?"

"He better be, Doc," Zack said slowly. "If he's not, every member of the posse and every man who has a hand in this trial will be shot sooner or later."

Steele nodded. "I guess that's so. But it'll break the back of the toughs if we can do it. Go on in, Zack."

When he opened the door he saw Lillian and Buck sitting near Bron.

"You get 'em, Zack?" Buck asked.

"Sure." He glanced at Bron, then said to Lillian, "You look plumb wore out."

"I'm all right," she said, and smiled at him. "She's so much better, Zack! She's going to be all right." Then she did something he'd not expected—ever. She came and put her hand on his arm, saying, "Don't worry. I—" She stopped. Whatever she wanted to say, he could see that she was struggling. Finally she gave Buck a quick look, then said, "I want to thank you, Zack. I never have—for all you've done for me and the kids."

He blinked in surprise as he realized the haunted look in her eyes was gone. Lillian smiled again. "Buck and I've had a lot of time to talk. He's a pretty good talker, believe it or not." She nodded toward Buck, then added, "I've given you a terrible time, Zack—and I probably will again—but, I feel much better now."

"I'm mighty glad of that, Lillian—!"

"Come on, Lil," Buck broke in. "Let's go get something to eat. You'll sit with her, won't you, Zack?"

"Sure." He looked after them with a puzzled expression, and then he heard Bron say, "Zack—?"

He swiveled around to find her eyes open, and rushed to her bedside.

She licked her lips. "They say—you've been here ever since I was shot."

"I guess so."

She was sleepy, but he could see that she had gained color. "I wish you hadn't gone to fight with Helm. They told me how you killed him."

He stood there, making no defense, and she shook her head. "I wish you hadn't done it," she repeated and dropped off to sleep.

He sat down heavily. *She'll never forget it. She begged me not to go—but I went anyway.* The thought tormented him, and when Jeanne came into the room a short time later, he got up and left without a word. Jeanne was taken aback, and when Bron woke up, she said, "Did you and Zack have a quarrel?"

"Zacharias—was he here? I don't remember," Bron said with surprise.

★ ★ ★ ★

Morning saw the crowds moving into town exactly as they had done for the trial of Stinson and Lyons. Simpson met with Pfouts, Miller, Beidler and Winslow to plan the trial.

Pfouts was doubtful of the outcome. "The toughs will want an open jury—and they'll sway the crowd."

"That was last time," Miller said. "The miners were afraid, but now they'll have to cooperate with the law."

"I dug two graves for nothing then," Beidler said. "We'll have to fill 'em this time."

"It all depends on the miners," Zack commented. "I need to find Billy. I'll be back."

He searched for Billy Page, but couldn't find him. When he stopped in at the Silver Moon, Ned Ray looked at him queerly, but gave no information. By midmorning Zack joined the others, who had adjourned to Pfouts' store.

"We had a bad time getting a jury," Miller said. "But we got it. Simpson, do you think we'll get a conviction?"

"Ordinarily, I'd say yes," Simpson replied. "But I'm afraid every tough in the territory is here. They may stampede the miners as they did at Stinson and Lyons' trial."

"Not this time," Miller said roughly. "We've got to organize. San Francisco was cleaned up by a few vigilantes; we can do the same. Pfouts, you'll serve as president."

Pfouts looked surprised and tried to protest, but was overruled by the others. "All right, James, but you'll have to be the executive officer." They worked quickly, Simpson writing out an oath of secrecy; then several men were brought into the meeting. They had planned the strategy well, Zack saw. Now it was put into effect immediately. There were to be several companies, each with complete judgment and authority to pass sentence—death or banishment.

"We don't know all the Innocents," Miller said. "So we've got to move fast. As soon as the trial is over, we'll hit hard. Now, here's what we've got to watch—if the jury convicts Ives, the toughs will make a play. We can't let them sway the miners."

From their meeting they went directly down the Gulch to where a big Shuttler wagon had been set up in front of a two-story building as it had been for the previous trial. A semicircle of benches from an adjacent hurdy-gurdy house had been placed around a fire built in the street, and the clerk sat at a table near the fire. Behind the semicircle a place was reserved for a cordon of guards with their shotguns and rifles. Behind them, round on their flank, stood about fifteen hundred miners, teamsters, mechanics, merchants, and gamblers. It was a noisy crowd—shouting advice or insults at one another and at those in charge of the trial.

Zack took a place by Miller, who whispered, "We've got men stationed by the rope. If the toughs make a rush to set Ives free, we'll have to make a stand."

The trial began, and Simpson rose to present the case. He put Long John Frank on the stand first. Frank made a full and elaborate confession of how Ives had murdered Tybalt. Two others, Jen Romaine and Steve Marshland, also testified to the guilt of Ives. Immediately the toughs raised a riot, crying the witnesses down, shouting, "Those liars won't be alive by morning!"

Simpson roared back, and began naming men who had been killed in their camp. His rhetoric had a visible effect on the crowd, and they quieted down. He continued calling witnesses, until finally he came to make his conclusion.

"George Ives is a murderer," he said to the jury. "You've heard testimony enough to convict a dozen men. He should be found guilty, and he should be hanged."

The defense lawyer had been drinking heavily, and could only ramble for thirty minutes, saying that Ives was a fine fellow, that they shouldn't jump to conclusions. He asked for mercy, then sat down.

"The jury will retire to Pfouts' store to consider their verdict."

In less than half an hour the jury returned, and when asked if they had reached a verdict, the foreman said, "Guilty."

"No! We want a new trial! A new trial!" The toughs wouldn't give up, but Simpson's voice rose above the opposition: "I now move that the verdict of the jury be approved by the miners here assembled!"

A roar erupted through the crowd, and Simpson waved his arm for silence. "I further move that George Ives be hanged!"

Once again the roar of approval drowned out the cries of the toughs, and Judge Byam instructed two men to make the arrangements. When they were gone, single voices began to be heard. "Let's have another trial!"

"Let's hear from that jury!"

"Ives won't hang!"

The voices came from different parts of the crowd, and were beginning to sway some of the miners. Ives saw his chance and jumped up. "Colonel Simpson, I would like to have some time to write to my mother and sisters."

Simpson wavered.

"Wait!" All eyes turned to the voice on the roof of a nearby cabin: Dutch Beidler. "Simpson," he called, "ask Ives how much time he gave Tybalt!"

Simpson's voice carried over the noise. "You've heard the verdict and the response. The decision stands. We'll give you more time than your victim got. Write your letter. Then we'll carry out the sentence."

As Ives got down the men assigned to find a proper spot for the hanging came back. "Can't find a place."

"This will do!" Beidler yelled. He climbed up on a cabin under construction and tossed one end of a top log down. The log's high end made a projection over the street, and a rope was tossed over it. A man laid nine turns around the end, forming the hangman's knot.

Judge Byam said, "Bring him up."

A box was found for Ives to stand on, his hands were tied and the rope slipped around his neck.

A last desperate effort was made to save Ives when Jack Gallagher pushed through the miners, cursing and waving his gun. "You can't railroad a man like that!" he yelled.

Zack pulled his gun as he and others made a cordon around Ives. Winslow's eyes bored into Ives'.

Ives, his eyes wild, cursed, "I wish I'd killed you!" Then he lifted his voice, crying out, "*I am Innocent!*"

"That's the signal!" Miller yelled. "Watch out!"

The toughs rushed forward, but Simpson called out, "Men, do your duty!"

Instantly the toughs were faced with a row of leaded guns. Someone knocked the box out from under George Ives' feet. He gasped and his body went limp.

CHAPTER TWENTY-SEVEN

THE POSSE

★ ★ ★ ★

The hanging of George Ives took something out of Zack. It had broken the resistance of the toughs, at least temporarily; but as much as Zack had hated the man, there was no sense of satisfaction. On the contrary, he felt empty, squeezed out, and for three days he rode with the vigilantes, saying little.

On the fourth day, he told Miller, "I've got stock up at my place, James, and it looks like a bad snowstorm coming over those mountains."

"Go take care of them, Zack," Miller said. "Looks like we've scared the Innocents to cover. If something comes up, I'll send for you."

He found Pfouts and asked, "Do you think we could find a house for my bunch for a while, Parris? I've got to go take care of my stock, but it's too rough to take children to the hills right now."

"Let's see what we can find," Parris nodded.

Zack made his way to the hotel where Steele had moved Bron. When he knocked on the door, Lillian swung it open, wide enough for him to see a happy-faced Buck as well as Bron.

"Hello, Zacharias," Bron smiled. She was wearing a white gown and sitting up in bed, her left arm in a sling. The bullet had caught her in the chest, but had gone upward and to the side, ending in the shoulder muscle. Though her head had not been injured, the shock had put her in a coma.

"You look fine . . . real good," he said, standing by her side. There was a delicate air about her, her skin almost translucent, her eyes clear. He added, "I've got to go back to the place, but Parris is finding you a house for a while."

"Are you all right?" she asked, touching his hand.

The touch made him feel odd, and he said, "Me? Why, sure." He stood there, somehow speechless—

"Zack," Lillian broke in, much to his relief, "I need a few clothes. Is it all right if I get some things from the store before you leave?"

"Get what you need, Lillian—and you too, Buck."

"Let's go, Buck!" When she reached the door, Lillian turned and looked at Zack. "Thanks. I appreciate everything you've done."

After the door closed, Bron raised her eyes to Zack. "Sit down, please."

"Thanks, but I've got to go soon." He searched for words, and asked, "Has Billy been up to see you?"

"No, he hasn't."

"I think he must have gone on to Helena, like he said." A silence fell between them, and he said awkwardly, "You gave me a big scare, Bron."

"They told me you stayed for three days. It was kind of you." She felt the strain, and added, "Zacharias, I'll not be coming back to the cabin."

He dropped his head. "I figured you wouldn't." He thought of a few things he might say that would perhaps make her think better of him, but they all seemed trivial. The barrier between them seemed higher and more formidable than ever, and he knew no way to tell her how empty he felt. Finally he said heavily, "I'll see that you and the kids have a good place. Don't worry about that."

"What'll you do with Sam?"

"Why, Jeanne will take care of him." He stared at her, perplexed.

With a touch of pity she said evenly, "She and John are getting married. You didn't know?"

Everything is falling apart, he thought. He shook his head. "No. I've been gone with Miller for a few days."

"She told me last night. I think she dreads telling you, Zacharias. She's afraid you'll think she's doing you a bad turn."

He got up slowly. "He's been in love with her since he laid eyes on her."

"Yes, I think he has."

He thought about it, then asked, "Does she love him? I never saw that in her—but I'm pretty slow."

Bron gave him a strange look, started to say something, then changed her mind. Finally she said gently, "She sees he loves her—and that's enough for now. In time, she'll love him in another way."

He was confused, and ran his hand over his face. "I'll have to find someone to help with Sam. I can't handle him by myself."

"Jeanne said to tell you she'll be moving to John's claim. She said she's taken Sam with her and will be glad to care for him as long as you want."

"Well—" He released a deep sigh of relief.

He turned to leave. "Parris will help you find a place."

"Wait," she said. "Do you know why I'm not going back with you?" Excitement rose in her green eyes.

"Why, I guess I do, Bron," he answered slowly. "And I don't blame you. I wish you all the best, though." He turned and left.

As soon as the door closed, tears leaped to her eyes. She clenched her fist and began to beat the bed with short rhythmic blows, whispering, "You *fool*! See how *dull* you are!"

Parris came in two hours later, so absorbed in his good news that he didn't notice the dullness in her eyes. "I've found a house, Bron," he said as he sat down. "It's got to be fixed up, but it's big enough for you and the youngsters." He began to describe it to her, but soon saw that her mind was someplace else. "You worried about something, Bron?"

"Oh, no, Parris. I'm just down a little."

He thought of Winslow, and noted that he, too, had seemed depressed. Putting the two together, he asked quietly, "Are you sad about leaving the cabin?"

"No. It had to come to an end. I've always known that." She shook her head and then looked out the window. She could not see the mountains, but she thought of the cabin and all it had meant—some grief and sadness, of course, but also joy . . . the long winter nights around the fire and the full table with laughter and fun. She turned to him, saying, "That part of my life is over, Parris." Something leaped in his eyes, but before he could speak, she added, "Not feeling too well, I am. I'll sleep a bit."

He swallowed the words he wanted to say, and left the room, shutting the door softly behind him.

She closed her eyes, her heart heavy—not from the pain of her wound, but the pain of having loved and lost something precious.

★ ★ ★ ★

Miller wasted no time, for he soon received word that some of the gang were holed up at Deer Lodge. He rounded up five men, and thought of sending a man after Zack, but was afraid the gang would get wind of the posse and split up.

The posse made their way down the Gulch, passing the makeshift miners' cabins. After riding awhile, the weather got worse, something less than a blizzard, but impossible to travel in. They stopped at a friend's cabin, and as soon as the weather cleared, they hit the trail again. The bad weather may have helped them, for when they arrived at the Lodge, they crept in silently, and caught Red Yeager and Jed Moore.

Yeager began to curse. "I know what you've come for, Miller," he spat bitterly. He glared at them while they took the vote, which was unanimous.

Moore began crying for mercy as the posse tied their hands. Yeager snarled, "Shut up, Jed!" They were led outside to a tree. Yeager took one look at the ropes and said, "Get on with it."

Miller said slowly, "Red, I admire your nerve. It won't help you any, but you'd be doing a good thing if you'd say who the others are."

Yeager eyed him for a moment, then said, the shadow of death on him, "Well, write 'em down, Miller. I can use a little credit where I'm goin'." He took a deep breath. "Henry Plummer, he's the boss."

"Come on, Red!"

"Think I'd lie about it at a time like this?" Yeager said bitterly.

"He set the whole thing up." Then as the freezing wind whipped across the yard, Miller wrote the names Yeager gave: Plummer and Bunton and Ives. Cy Skinner and Steve Marshland, Dutch John Wagner, Alec Carter and Whiskey Bill Graves. Stinson, Hunter, Gallagher and Ned Ray. George Shears and Johnny Cooper and Mex Grant and Bob Zachary. Boone Helm, Hayes Lyons." He named many others, and ended with a final name. "Billy Page. He was in on the Stone killing."

"That all, Red?"

"That's it."

With that the men were hanged and their bodies taken down.

"We goin' home now?" one of the men asked.

"Not yet," Miller replied. "We've got one more job. You fellows get some sleep. I'll be back tomorrow." He left the spot, turned his horse's head to the west and rode through the cold, dreading the task ahead.

★   ★   ★   ★

Zack was asleep when he heard the horse stop outside. He grabbed his gun and came off the bed like a cat.

"Zack? It's Miller."

Zack lowered the gun and opened the door. "Come in, James."

Miller entered and said, "Let's eat, Zack. Then we've got a chore to do."

"All right." Zack saw the troubled look and knew pretty well what was coming. He fixed a quick breakfast, and an hour later they were on their way, moving through foot-deep snow.

"We hung Yeager and Moore," Miller said. "Yeager gave us some names. Henry Plummer was on the list. He's the boss."

Zack thought on it, then nodded. "Guess that makes sense. He's got the power to handle the toughs. I never liked his way."

They went through Virginia City and picked up John Lott and Parris Pfouts. Miller read most of the names, and said, "There're a few others."

They stopped at the Lodge, picked up the other men and then proceeded.

"Where we headed?" Lott asked.

"Up to Sullins' ranch. Got a report that a man was holed up

there. We'll look." They made their way over the Stinkingwater into the barren land lying between the river and the mountains, and at full dark they pulled up in a shallow coulee.

"There's his light," Miller said, indicating a yellow gleam. "The rest of you circle around. Zack, you and me will take the door."

They slipped off their horses, and as soon as the others were in place, Miller said, "Let's go." They made their way to the shack, and when Miller gave a sign, Zack lifted the latch and stepped into the cabin.

Only one man was inside, and he made a grab for his revolver; but when he saw who it was, he relaxed. "Hello, Zack."

"Billy, what are you doing here?" Zack asked. He put his gun away and turned to Miller, who had entered. "Wasted trip, James."

"No, not wasted," Miller said. He walked over and picked up Page's gun, then turned to go to the door. "Come in, you fellows."

Billy's face turned a sickly green and asked, "What's up?"

"We came for you, Page," Miller replied. "You're one of the Innocents."

"Don't be a fool!" Zack snapped.

"Billy, you were in on the killing of Nolan Stone."

Zack's head jerked back, and he stared at Miller, but said nothing.

"I was in town when he was killed," Page protested.

"No, you rode out that day. Burke Prine says he saddled your horse. You left early and brought the horse back late."

A fine sheen touched Billy's brow, but he shook his head. "No, I wasn't there."

"Red Yeager says you were. He gave us the whole story before we hung him."

"You were in on the holdup when Deke Masters was killed," Darrel Jones said. "I was in that coach myself and—"

"You couldn't be sure it was Billy, Darrel," Zack broke in.

"He was wearing that bright green coat of his—the only one like it in camp—and he was ridin' that big bay with the white stockings, Zack. I couldn't be wrong about both them things, could I?"

A deathly silence fell, and Billy's face changed.

"Red named you on the list, Billy," Beidler put in. And then Zack saw the light go out of Page's face as he stepped backward, his breathing shallow.

Zack searched for a defense. "It's not enough to hang a man on. Say something, Billy!"

Page shook his head and said weakly, "I'm not the man." But there was no force in him.

Zack was not satisfied and pressed, "Billy, did you do it?"

Page gave him an agonizing look, then nodded.

The sense of hopelessness that had plagued Zack for weeks rushed in upon him. He had to do something! He looked at the faces of the posse. "Billy knocked up Stinson's arm when he was about to kill me, you'll remember."

"It's not enough, Zack," Miller said. He turned the full force of his gaze on Winslow, saying quietly, "I saw this coming, Zack. You're Page's friend, and I didn't want you to hear about this from somebody else. I wanted you to get it firsthand. He's one of them, Zack, just like Helm and Yeager and Ives."

An idea popped into Zack's mind and he stepped back and dropped his hand to his gun. Instantly Beidler flung up his shotgun and the others drew their handguns. "You can't do it, Zack," Miller said gently. "You want to talk to him while we go vote?"

"Yes."

"Give me your gun." Miller took the gun; then the party left, closing the door.

"Guess it won't take long to get a vote on me," Billy said wryly. He licked his dry lips slowly, giving Winslow an agonizing look. "That's the way it goes sometimes, Zack," he whispered.

"Billy—" Zack began. He wanted to cry. "Why? Why did you do it?"

Page shrugged, his eyes shifting to the door. "Don't know the answer to that. Nobody does."

"What can I do, Billy?"

"Nothing. There's nothing any human being can do for another, is there? Tell Bron that—that she was one bright light for me in a pretty dark world." The talk in the front yard died down, and he said hurriedly, "Zack, I helped you a couple of times against Ives that you don't know about."

"I appreciate it, Billy."

The door opened and Miller came in. He said nothing, but stood waiting.

Billy blinked rapidly as fear ran along his nerves. He said, "I'd like to put on my coat. It's cold."

"Sure, Billy," Miller said.

Page moved to the wall, pulled down the coat and put it on. He buttoned it up very slowly, then turned and with a terrified look in his eyes, whispered, "Goodbye, Zack. I thought I was tough enough to play it alone—but I wasn't." He swallowed, and forcing himself to turn and walk toward the door, he added just before he left, "No man's tough enough to make it on his own, Zack!"

He passed through the door, and it closed. Zack walked over to the bed and sat down, his legs too weak to hold him. He put his hands over his ears, muting the sounds that might come. Finally he heard the door close again.

He looked up as Miller stood there, his face red with the cold. "All over," he said.

Zack got to his feet and paused, feeling as empty and dead as the man outside dangling from the rope. "Miller," he said, "I'm going to bury him on my place."

"Sure, Zack." Miller gave an order, and turned back to Zack. "Will you be coming in when you get him buried?" he asked.

"Can't say." He raised a pair of eyes so empty that Miller was shocked. "To tell the truth—I don't know what to do anymore, James. Seems like everything I touch goes bad."

Miller walked over and put his hand on Zack's shoulder. "Might be good if you did stay up at your place for a spell, Zack. Think things out. Then you come into town and we'll get drunk together. We've both lost good friends. I'll tell your folks you'll be gone a few days."

Zack nodded. "Thanks, James." He moved outside the cabin, mounted his horse and took the reins of Page's horse, not looking at the body strapped in place.

As he rode out, Beidler said, "I guess he's hit pretty hard, Miller."

"Yes. About as hard as a man can get hit. I didn't know he thought so much of Page." He took a deep breath. "Well, we've got some more names on that list, Dutch. Let's move along."

★　★　★　★

Zack dug a grave in frozen earth, under an oak that over-
looked Dancer Creek. It was a view Billy had admired once, Zack
remembered. The earth was like rock, and by the time he was
finished, the wind was howling in earnest. He made a coffin out
of boards left over from building the cabin, then put the body of
Page in it. He lowered the box with a rope, and filled the grave
in, snow mixing with the frozen clods of earth. When he finished, he stood looking at the mound, thinking of the good
things about Billy. Bron had often told how Billy had helped her.
He remembered how Page had stopped Yeager from kicking him
half to death, then again of how he'd saved Zack's life by knocking Stinson's gun up.

The emptiness that had fallen on Zack deepened as the wind
howled like a demented timber wolf. "Sure wish there was a
preacher here, Billy," he said through half-frozen lips. "I guess
you never held with preaching much—but I'd like it mighty
well." He lifted his eyes to the rounded sweep of snowy earth
that stretched out and thought of how Billy had hated the cold.
"It'll be spring soon, and then this spot will get warm; and the
grass and the trees, they'll turn green. Warm breezes instead of
this freezing wind! It'll be better come spring, Billy!"

But the wind whipped around his feet, and he tried to pray.
"God, there's nothing I can tell you about Billy. He was my
friend, faithful and just to me. God, I've got to ask you, be easy
on Billy, will you?" He stopped. He could say no more. He
turned and walked away, and as he made his way to the cabin,
Zack thought of Billy's bone-white face and the last words he'd
spoken: "No man's tough enough to make it on his own, Zack!"

He entered the cabin, washed his hands in some melted snow
water, then built up the fire and sat watching the flames. The
fire crackled, making the logs weep drops of pitch. The warmth
around soaked into him, but he knew that just outside the door
winter lurked, waiting for him to venture one step too far.

For hours he remained by the fire, staring into the leaping
flames, thinking of Emma and George Orr. How little he felt of
the pain and anger that had driven him to the woods then. He

thought of the battles in the war that had raged around him. The war, too, seemed but a dream. Events of the past year streamed before him. In the beginning, he'd been a man filled with resentment with no faith in anyone. Then Sam, Jeanne, Hawk, and Buck had come into his life. The cabin seemed empty without the cries of Paul and Alice, or Lillian's pugnacious ranting. He thought of Sam's dying mother and the frail hand she'd held up to Zack. Most of all, he thought of Bron, and the longing for her grew so intense, he got up and lit the lamp.

He went to the bookshelf to get a novel—but his eye fell on the Bible, the Christmas gift from Billy Page. He picked it up, his eyes falling on the inscription: "There is a friend that sticketh closer than a brother . . ." and his eyes blurred. He took the Bible back to the chair in front of the fireplace and sat holding it for a long time. With a sigh he opened it, and read the first thing his eyes fell on.

> Except a corn of wheat fall into the ground and die, it abideth alone, but if it die, it bringeth forth much fruit.
> He that loveth his life shall lose it; and he that hateth his life in this world, shall keep it unto life eternal.

The words reminded him of something Bron had said once: "You'll never know what it means to be strong until you've been broken, Zacharias!" He read the verses again. He read them many times that day. And for days afterward, as the winds blew outside, he read and read.

He ate and slept, but the cabin was a little cosmos, sealed off from the world, and he had no sense of place or time. Hour after hour, he soaked up the words, reading the Gospels over and over. The character of Jesus had been only a vague figure, but now as he read, it seemed he could see the carpenter of Galilee as He moved among men. As he read of Jesus healing the eyes of the blind man, it was thrilling and Zack could almost feel the excitement of the man who could finally see. The story of the woman at the well fascinated him. He had not known of that story, and he marveled at the way Jesus won the woman's confidence before telling her who He was.

Days passed, then the snow stopped falling and the sun came out. He went out to care for the stock, to break the ice in the creek; but even as he moved, his mind was still on the stories of the Bible. The hard snow turned to mush, and he was surprised to see by the calendar that he'd been there three weeks.

That night he decided he would have to go to town the next day, but he stayed up late. He read in the Gospel of John, the third chapter, and the words of the young Rabbi to Nicodemus seemed rich and strong, though mysterious. "Ye must be born again." He put the Bible aside and laid his head against the back of the chair, thinking of Jesus.

Time passed, and he shook his head, muttering, "I don't know how to find God!" He thumbed through the Bible and discovered that several verses had been underlined. *He* had not done it! Who had? Bron? Parris? He read it carefully: "If thou shalt confess with thy mouth the Lord Jesus, and believe in thine heart that God hath raised him from the dead, thou shalt be saved." Lower down another verse read: "For whosoever shall call on the name of the Lord shall be saved."

Many times he had heard Bron speak of being "saved," but had always felt uncomfortable with the term. Now, however, he read over and over that Jesus said He came to *save* men.

Hours flew, and when the morning light fired the tops of the eastern hills, he slipped out of the chair to his knees. He had no idea how to pray, nor what to expect; and for a long time he made no attempt to form words. The longer he knelt there, the more aware he became of his need for more than life had given him. Finally, he began to speak to God.

CHAPTER TWENTY-EIGHT

"I THOUGHT I'D LOST YOU!"

★ ★ ★ ★

The warmth of the sun's rays touched Winslow's face as he took one last look at the cabin. Loneliness gripped him as he surveyed the countryside he'd come to love, but against the pain of leaving and the memories that floated before him, he turned away. "Let's go, Ornery!"

Behind him a loaded pack horse, Penelope, and the calf followed, all tethered on long ropes, the cow lowing in protest. The snow had begun melting two days earlier, but he knew winter was not over. Crossing Dancer Creek, he turned right and soon sighted Crenna's shack, a spiral of smoke rising to the sky.

"John—hello!" he called as he pulled up in the yard.

The door swung open, and Crenna rushed out, pulling his shirt on. "Zack! Get down, man, and come in the house!" He pulled Zack through the door and said, "Jeanne, look what the New Year brought in!"

Jeanne came across the room, smiling. "Hello, Zack. I wondered if you'd ever come our way."

She seemed content, and he gave her a handshake. "Guess I've not been very neighborly. You're looking well, Jeanne. Hawk all right?"

Crenna reached down and picked up the black-eyed boy, tossed him in the air and said fondly, "He's fine. Got me for a playmate all day long." He put the boy down. "Jeanne, could we round up some breakfast for this stranger?"

"No thanks, John," Zack broke in, but gave in, deciding he should spend a few minutes with them.

They drank coffee as they sat around the table. "How's Sam doing?" Zack asked.

"Just fine. I brought him to Bron and the other children as soon as she was well. Parris found a house for them. Sam needs lots of loving."

Crenna, anxious to get into man-talk, interrupted. "Don't guess you've heard about the way Miller and the vigilantes hit the Innocents?"

"No."

"Well, they got Plummer over at Bannack. He turned yellow when they hung him. Fell on his knees and started squalling. They hung Lyons and Ray at the same time. The next day they came to Virginia City and tried Gallagher, Skinner, Lane, and Frank Parish. All found guilty, of course." He shook his head, adding, "Gallagher went out cussing and raving, Zack. The rest of 'em were in bad shape. I guess they've rounded up some more by now. We ain't been to town for weeks, and Miller was sure pressing it!"

"It'll be a different place from now on," Zack said.

As the men talked, Jeanne felt a wall between her and Zack and wanted to explain her actions, so broke in. "I feel badly, leaving you as I did without speaking to you, Zack."

"Why, bless you, girl!" Zack said and smiled at her and Crenna. "Nothing could have made me happier. Caught me off guard—but I'm a pretty dense fellow!" He looked at Crenna. "You're a lucky fellow, John!"

"I know it," Crenna nodded. "Been lonesome all my life— and now I get up in the morning and look at my wife and Hawk, and I think, 'Lord, I feel sorry for every other man in the world!' "

Jeanne smiled and put her hand on his arm. "You'll spoil me, John—like you do Hawk." Then she said, "Will you be in town long, Zack?"

He put his cup down, pausing for a moment. "Not too long, I guess." He got to his feet and asked, "Can you take Bron's cow and the yearling? I've brought enough feed to carry them through until spring."

"But—what about Bron?" Jeanne asked, puzzled. "She *loves* that cow!"

"Be hard for her to keep a cow in town."

A swift glance passed between Crenna and Jeanne, and he said cautiously, "You and her talked it all out, Zack?"

He shrugged, forcing a smile. "I guess it's past talking. I'm pulling out of the Gulch."

"You're leaving?" The regret in Jeanne's voice was unmistakable.

"Got to see about Sam. Guess I'll go back East and find his grandmother. Would you kinda look in on him until I find his relatives? You've been good to the boy. Goodness knows, I haven't been very helpful. Don't know how long I'll be, though, but I'd sure be grateful." He got to his feet, saying in an off-handed fashion as he turned to go, "You might ask Bron about the cow—maybe she and Parris would like to find a place for her in town. You can keep the yearling for yourselves."

His words came easily, but there was something in the tone that made Jeanne ask, "Why would Parris want to know about Bron's cow?"

"Why, I guess they'll be making a match of it one day," Zack said. He didn't see the look of surprise passing between the couple, and he went on. "I'll put the feed inside for you, John."

"No, I'll get it, Zack." Crenna stepped outside to take the feed off the horse, and as Zack turned to follow, Jeanne caught his arm.

"Zack," she said, her eyes somber, "you've been good to me. If you hadn't taken me, I don't like to think about what I'd be— Hawk and I would have been lost."

"I'm the one to thank *you*, Jeanne. What would Sam have done without you?"

Warmth flowed into her face. "You're not meant to be a hermit, Zack. You tried it once—and it didn't work. Don't do it again."

She was trying to tell him something, but it escaped him. "I'll think of you often, Jeanne. Of you and John and Hawk—I'll let you all know about Sam. God bless you!"

He walked out and swung into the saddle, shook John's hand, and waved to Jeanne, who was standing in the doorway, then rode out.

Crenna went over and picked up Hawk, who was trying to get out the door, and put his arm around Jeanne. He stared after Zack and said softly, "He's got a big hurting in him." Then he smiled fondly at her. "I'll never understand why you turned down a good-looking fellow like that for an ugly bird like me."

Jeanne reached out and pulled his head down and kissed him. A light of mischief touched her eyes and she said, "Maybe I was afraid that if I had a handsome husband, some girl would run off with him." When he laughed, she looked toward the trail where Winslow was just disappearing into the trees. "He's a good man, John—but he's not my man." She smiled at him, and they went back inside the cabin.

★ ★ ★ ★

The breaking of the iron cold by the warm winds had brought the miners out of their cabins. As Zack passed along the Gulch, man after man greeted him, and he realized they had come to admire him. He shook hands as he went, and by the time he got to Virginia City, he was feeling an unexpected shock of pleasant recognition.

Riding down Ballard Street, he was met by even more friends, some whose names he didn't know. Ray Potter came off the sidewalk, a star pinned to his vest. "Glad to see you, Zack." He saw Zack's glance at the star, and grinned ruefully, "Yeah, I'm the new law around here. Ain't that a kick in the head?"

"They couldn't have found a better man, Ray," Zack replied, and meant it, for Potter was honest through and through and tough enough to handle the town.

"Miller wants to see you before you get away. It's just about over. The vigilantes caught up with a whole bunch of the toughs over at Cougar Bend two days ago. They hung Johnny Cooper and Snake Walker. Last week they caught Whiskey Bill Graves, Shears, and Hunter. Miller gave them two hours to either get out of town or hang. They lit out like their tails were on fire. Most of the rest of the gang have left as well." Potter shook his head. "Miller has got just about all the names crossed off his list."

"Sounds like the breakup of the Innocents, Ray." Zack nodded and rode on down the street, thinking of the suddenness of the arrests and executions. He stopped at Pfouts' store, but rode on when Parris wasn't there. Steele, too, was out. Zack made his way to the Rainbow Cafe.

Blackie Taylor greeted him with a slap on the shoulder, and once again, Zack was greeted by almost every man who came into the cafe, among them Dutch Beidler, who headed straight for Winslow's table. "Zack, for a hermit you're sure a popular fellow!" Then he sobered. "It's been tough—but it's over now."

"Hate to think about all the money that crowd got away with," Zack remarked.

"Won't do 'em any good in hell," Beidler said practically. "Anyway, whiskey took it—and women and gambling. All any of them got out of it was a hole in the ground."

After finishing his meal, Zack returned to Pfouts' store. The dapper merchant got up from his desk with a startled expression. "Zack! I was about ready to send a posse after you!"

"Hello, Parris. I hear you and Miller have cleaned up the Gulch."

"Well, it sure took all of us—and you played a big part, Zack."

"I should have jumped in a long time ago. If I had, a few good men might still be alive."

"Can't live on that kind of regret," Pfouts told him. "It's going to be all right now. Yesterday Oliver shipped forty thousand in gold, and it got through fine. Things have changed. It's like a malignant thing has been cut out!"

"Glad to hear that. How's Buck been doing? And Lillian?"

"Why, you wouldn't believe it!" Parris said. "Buck's been working for me steady since my clerk left, and that girl's gotten over her trouble. Always smiling. She's been mostly taking care of Sam. He's fine as silk, by the way." He scratched his head, and grinned. "They're both young, but I wouldn't be surprised if they didn't make a match of it in a couple of years, Zack."

"Wouldn't that be something?" Zack murmured. Then he cleared his throat and said, "Parris, got a favor to ask."

"Name it!"

"Well, I'm pulling out." He saw Pfouts' surprise, but said quickly, "I'm going back East to see Sam's grandmother, to find a place for him. Jeanne told me she'd brought the boy to Bron. Thanks for finding a house for them all. What I'd like for you to do is sell my place. Use the money to see that Buck and Lillian and the kids are taken care of."

"Why, Zack," Parris objected, "you don't want to do that. You've made a name for yourself in this country. Don't know of a man more highly respected." He peered at Zack sharply. "What's wrong?"

"Nothing. Guess I'm just a wandering man. Will you do it?"

"Of course. If you ask it, yes." Something was bothering Pfouts and he said, "Zack, you came here to be a hermit. You're not cut out for that kind of life. No man is, I think. Stay and make your life here. Watch Sam grow up here—and maybe see Buck and Lillian get married."

"I'd like to see you in about twenty years, Parris," Zack smiled. "Richest man in the state, wife and family around you—"

Parris shrugged. "Not certain about that."

"Hey, you were born for it!" he said. "Now, I'll see Simpson and have him draw up some sort of paper to take care of selling the place when I'm gone."

"Have you seen Bron?" Pfouts asked, giving Zack a sharp glance.

"Not yet. Figured I'd go by. How's she feeling?"

"Oh, she's fine. Been busy with the church. Making big plans for the Indian work."

"Guess you two are able to handle that." Zack tried a smile on, and then put out his hand. "I know you'll take care of her, Parris. You two are a lot alike."

"In some ways, yes," Pfouts replied, and there was a shadow in his eyes that made Winslow wonder. "In other ways—we are not." Then he said bruskly, "Go see Bron first—then maybe Simpson. The house is the two-story white one on the road out of town, just down from Sloan's smithy."

Zack nodded and left the store, puzzled by Pfouts' attitude. "He ought to be on top of the world," he murmured as he mounted Ornery and turned toward the south end of town.

He saw the house as he passed the blacksmith's shop, and

got down with some apprehension. He tied his horse to the rack on the street, then walked up and knocked.

Before he could collect his thoughts, Bron stood before him. She was wearing a dress he'd never seen, a dark green that picked up the color of her eyes. He had forgotten how her hair shone—now smooth waves flowing down her back, almost to her waist.

He had caught her by surprise, for her eyes grew larger and she put one hand over her heart in a gesture that somehow seemed more feminine than anything in the world. He had forgotten how beautiful she was, and was speechless for a moment.

"Why . . . Zack!" she murmured. "Come in." She stepped aside and he entered, removing his hat. "The children are both asleep—and Sam too." She smiled, adding, "I think it's the first time since we've been here that they've all napped at the same time."

"I should have come down sooner—to see about them." He could not get over how lovely she was, the captivating curve of her lips. "It was good of you to take care of Sam."

"Oh, he's a joy!" she said quickly. Then a thought came to her, and she asked quickly, "You've come to take him, then?"

He was surprised by the sudden alarm in her eyes. "Well, not quite." He felt awkward, and the words came slowly. "I've let you take care of my problems too long, Bron." She said nothing, so he blundered on, "I've got to do things different. Can't live out in the woods with a little one and no one to take care of him."

"And what will you do, then?" she asked quietly. "Find you a wife, I suppose?"

He laughed shortly. "Who'd go live in the woods with a hermit like me and a kid? No, I'm going to sell out, Bron. Time to move on."

She stared at him, her lips pressed together. She seemed angry, and he could not figure out why, so he said, "I talked to Parris. Asked him sell the place and use the money to take care of Buck and Lillian and the kids."

"I see." Bron's eyes narrowed. "And what will you do with Sam?"

"Guess I'll take him to his grandmother back East as soon as I can—if she can help."

There was a stubbornness in the set of Bron's lips, and she drew her eyebrows together in an expression he'd seen before when she was angry. "And after you make that visit, what will you do with him for the next twenty years?" she asked sharply.

He grew frustrated and said rashly, "Bron—I don't have a blueprint! I'm just trying to do the right thing. I guess you and Parris don't want a kid not your own, and it's all I can think of."

Her lips parted in surprise. "If there ever comes a time when I don't want a boy like Sam, look for me in the grave!" she snapped. "But what's Parris got to do with Sam?"

"Why—I thought. . . !" Zack was on shaky ground, and he finished lamely, "Well . . . I took it for granted that you two would get married, Bron."

"Well, devil fly off!" she cried, striking him a sharp blow on the chest. "Like an old mule you are, Zacharias Winslow!"

He saw the tears rim her eyes, and said, "Why, Bron—what did I say?"

"Nothing!" she retorted, and bit her lips. "Well, go on and do it then! You've run away from life once—so I know you can do it again!"

He was bewildered by her anger, and shifted his feet helplessly. She glared at him, her eyes damp, her fists clenched.

He sighed, "I don't understand you, Bron."

"You never have!" she shot back.

Zack watched her face, and gave up. "I'm just not a discerning man, I guess. I've been a fool, trying to run away from life. I know that. But one good thing's come out of all this." He smiled. "I've been running from God a long time, Bron, but He finally caught up with me!"

She stood transfixed as he told her of his desperate search for God. "Then," he said with wonder in his bright blue eyes, "I knelt down and called on Jesus—and He came in! It wasn't what I expected," he admitted. "I thought I'd fall on the floor or shout, maybe. But it wasn't like that at all."

"What was it like, Zacharias?" she whispered.

"Why, it's hard to say," he answered. "Ever since that moment, Bron, there's been a peace that's like nothing else. Jesus Christ somehow came in—and He'll never leave me. Is that the way it is?"

"That's the way, Zack!"

He drew his shoulders back and forced a smile. "Well, I thought you'd like to know," adding, "I'll come back later when Sam's awake."

She reached out and grasped the front of his coat. "And you think I'll let you do it?"

He looked down at the hand fastened to his coat, then into eyes that had changed from anger to soft pleading. "Let me do what, Bron?" he asked, confused.

She threw her arms around his neck and held him tightly.

"Like an old eel you are!" she whispered. "But you'll not wiggle out this time, hermit or no!" She pulled his head down and kissed him with such ardor that his arms automatically enveloped her. She was firm and yet soft in his arms, and when she finally let him go, she said tremulously, "Do I have to do it all?"

"I—I don't know what you mean, Bron," he stuttered, then clasped her firmly. "I'm just a dumb hermit—but you shouldn't have kissed me like that!"

"Why not?" she asked demurely, lying in the circle of his arms.

"Because I'm just mean enough to take you up on it!" he said rashly. "I'm a tough bird, Bron, and mean, too. I've never tried to fool you about that!"

"That's been your boast," she smiled. "I can't say it's been something I've noticed."

He held her away from him, his eyes blazing with joy. She was his! "Well," he cried, "I can see that it's going to take forty years or so to teach you just how ornery I am!"

She laughed shakily and put her hand on his cheek. "How will you do it?"

"Why, first I'll marry you—then I'll carry you off on a honeymoon. And when I bring you back, I'll make you live with me the rest of your life!"

"Oh, Zack!" she cried, cuddling into his arms, her eyes radiant, "I thought I'd lost you!"

He held her tightly and said with a note of fierce possession, "No, we're *never* going to lose each other!"

Before their lips met she whispered, "See how soft you are, Zacharias Winslow!"